AFTERSHOCKS

ELUDING DESTINY

BOOK THREE

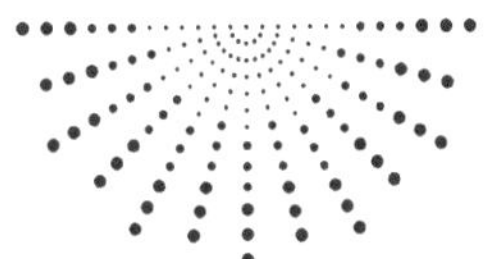

CHARLIE NOTTINGHAM

LIQUID MIND PUBLISHING

THE ELUDING DESTINEY SERIES

Eluding Destiny

The Horrors That Created Us

Aftershocks

The Precipice

Land of Light

The Quiet Army

Sacred Sins

Flash Back

The Shift

Lost to Time

Gods Among Us

The Cover Up

Blank Slate

Sign up for Charlie's newsletter and receive a free copy of the Eluding Destiny prequel, Blood Bar:

https://liquidmind.media/eluding-destiny-prequel/

CONTENT WARNING

This story is intended only for mature audiences.
It contains adult language, drug and alcohol abuse,
violence, gore, mentions of sexual assault,
suicide, self-harm, and other sensitive material.
Please read at your own discretion.
If you're a survivor and need someone to talk to,
call 1-800-654-4673
If you're struggling with addiction and need someone to talk to,
call 844-534-1996
You aren't alone.

This book is for everyone whose heart has ever hurt so bad that they couldn't get out of bed.

For everyone who has contemplated ending it all. I'm not going to tell you that every story has a happy ending.

I'm not going to say that one day you'll wake up and it will all be better. Every day is a battle sometimes. But if you're reading this, you're winning. Keep fighting. Keep winning.

*Even if it feels like you're losing, just remember, every breath you take is a victory. Don't let depression win. Keep **fucking** fighting. I'm rooting for you.*

PROLOGUE

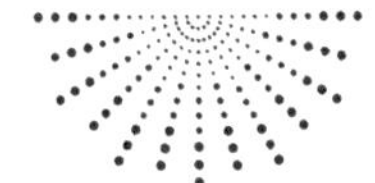

JUNE 26, 2019 - CHRIS

Slow breaths rose and fell from the little chest beneath my palm. He hadn't cried since that bitch put him in my arms, and that seemed odd. Babies cry. A lot, from what I remembered of Hannah as an infant. But I felt his chest moving. The warmth of his skin radiated into mine. The moisture of his hot breath slid against my hand. He was okay. He was alive.

It'd been so long since I touched another person, I didn't even mind how much my back ached throughout the ride. Of course, with each turbulent bounce, my heart skipped. I kept thinking, *Great. Lived through eight years of torture, finally have a piece of my family back, and we're gonna plummet to the ground.*

But we didn't.

"Who's that?" An elbow bumped mine.

I reflexively glanced that way and felt him jump back. A typical response, one that didn't bother me anymore. But I wasn't sure why my head still turned when people talked to me. I knew I couldn't see them. They obviously did. The whole empty eye sockets thing made that pretty clear.

"My nephew," I said.

"Really?" he asked.

I gave a nod. His little fingers wrapped around my thumb and I smiled. That might have been my first smile since this all started. But it really was something to be happy about.

"He's so little though," he muttered. "What is he? Like, a week?"

"Something like that," I said.

"How'd he end up in here?"

My jaw clenched. I didn't want to get into Laila's story. Not only was it not my place, but it didn't matter now. She was gone. He was here, but she wasn't.

She'd done a great thing on her way down though. Said from day one that she'd get us out of that place. And sure enough, she had. We were out. Still in captivity, but out of *that* prison.

I had to give her an A for effort.

Either way. Micah was alive and he was with me. And they'd have to kill me before they did to him what they'd done to us.

"His mom was taken when she was pregnant." I cleared my throat. "She's the one that blew the roof off."

He huffed. "No shit." I nodded. He paused. Then he said, "But they got her kid."

A knot stiffened in my throat.

That didn't matter. Only for now. Someone would find it. Leah, or Adam, or Brody. Hell, maybe even Hannah. They'd find it. Then they'd find us. I knew they would.

We'd get out. Micah and I wouldn't die in here. We'd make it home.

I had to believe that.

"What's his name?" the guy asked.

"Micah." I ran my thumb against the smooth skin of his knuckles. "Micah Christopher Skoulda."

He got quiet for a second. Then he laughed. "Like, *the* Skouldas? Raphael and Adele Skoulda, those Skouldas?"

Didn't surprise me that he knew my family name. We weren't exactly unimportant in the supernatural world.

"Heard of us?" I asked.

Another laugh. "Uh, yeah. Everyone has. Shit, which one are you?"

"Chris," I said. "Raphael and Adele are my grandparents. And you?"

"Noah. Noah Jackson."

Didn't ring any bells. But it wasn't like I took tabs of every name in our world. I was only eighteen when I was taken, I hadn't worked that many cases.

"But I'm no one. Just a Witch. I can barely cast a conjuring spell." His voice lowered. "Don't know why they want me when they have a La Fay sitting in the front row."

I was right then. The infamous Nastya La Fay. She was the Witch working with Peterson. It didn't come as a shock; the bitch was crazy from what I'd heard. But her dad was on the Chambers. What the fuck was she doing working with a human that kidnapped, held captive, and tortured our people? What could she possibly gain from this?

"Who knows what the fuck they're doing with any of us," I muttered.

"Yeah, true," he said. "You don't think—"

"Alright, shut the fuck up," the voice I'd heard earlier, the one that sounded familiar, said just above my shoulder. "Not a peep or I take him away. Got it?"

I clutched Micah closer to my chest. Not like that would do much good. Clearly the guy had the upper hand. Probably a gun at his hip. A voice that roared like thunder. And more than likely, vision.

A big, firm hand grasped my shoulder. His fingertips dug into the pressure point at my clavicle. My neck curled but I tried not to shift. I couldn't drop the baby. "Did you hear me?"

I nodded.

"Good."

The scent of mildew slithered into my nose. The air around me was cool, but not windy. Just cool. Dirty water sloshed between my toes, then damp, dusty concrete. I heard the sound of feet peddling and keys jingling but dripping too. Like water from the ceiling of a tunnel.

Maybe that's where we were. In a tunnel. It was warm when we got off the plane, ridiculously warm. Humid, too. But it wasn't a place I'd been before. Which was saying a lot because, prior to the implants, I was a teleporter. I'd been just about everywhere.

"Drop that kid, and I'm breaking your neck." Cold metal pressed against the back of my shaved head. "I already took your eyes, don't think I won't."

I considered saying the last thing I planned to do was put this baby in anyone else's arms, let alone let him hit the chilled concrete beneath my bare feet. But I'd learned over the last eight years to keep my mouth shut if I didn't want to pay for it. Sometimes, I'd make a quip back, but not now. Now, I had a reason to stay alive.

Micah needed me.

And I knew we'd make it out. Not today, clearly, but we would. We'd get out of here. Wherever the fuck here was.

"Did you hear me?" Peterson repeated, pushing me forward with a fist wrapped around the back of my scrubs.

"Yes," I said. "I won't drop him."

"Good. Keep moving."

"Take the gun off him, dumbass," that familiar man's voice said. "What do you think he's gonna do—run? Just help him down the damn steps."

A tunnel. Now going down steps.

I was right. Thank god, I was right. I thought I heard the pilot say we were going underground. Good thing I was paying attention. I hoped I didn't miss one of the numbers though. That would've fucking sucked.

The gun lowered. Peterson grasped my elbow beneath Micah's head. "Eighteen, about a foot each."

I didn't respond, just carefully lifted my foot forward. It would have been easier if I had a hand to grasp the wall or a handrail. But no way was I handing Micah to the bastard that got him in here. I made do.

Carefully, I moved one foot in front of the other. Hate to admit it, but I braced myself against Peterson as I counted. One to eighteen down the cold metal stairs.

Then my feet touched something different. Something I hadn't felt in years.

Vinyl. Fake hardwoods, or something of the sort. Clean, textured.

My brows fell in confusion.

"This way." Peterson pulled me forward. "Low door frame, duck."

I lowered my head and took another step forward.

Warm air. Circulated and crisp, but warm. Warmer than I'd felt indoors in almost a decade. And the smell. It still had a hint of mildew but something else too.

Paint. Fresh paint.

"I got him," the other man's voice said. Peterson released my elbow, and another hand took its place. A chill stretched up my spine. Peterson tortured me for all these years, yet his touch didn't make me shiver like that man's.

He edged me another ten or fifteen steps forward. Then he said, "Alright, put him down."

I clenched Micah closer.

He scoffed. Then he yanked my hand from his chest and lowered it to something soft. Fluffy. It rocked beneath my touch.

His voice hardened. "It's a basinet. Put him down before I make you."

My heart picked up speed in my chest. I didn't want to, but what choice did I have? Clearly, he had the high ground.

I gently lowered the little ball of warmth onto the rocker.

The man grabbed my arm and hauled me across the room. I nearly fell but caught myself. My shoulder banged against a doorframe, but he kept pulling. Then he grabbed my hand and set it on something cold. Metal.

He released my hand. "Pull it."

Had no idea what I was pulling, but again, not like I had a choice. I pulled.

Warm water splashed against my head. I jolted back.

A shower. Not a spigot in the wall, but a real shower with a handle and warm water. I'd almost forgotten what that felt like.

"You're taking care of a kid, you need to stay clean. Amy will bathe him. I don't want you to risk drowning him. But you, you clean up in here." He grabbed my hand and lifted it upward. Then my fingers touched something soft. Not as soft as the baby blanket, but softer than the scratchy scrubs against my shoulders. "Towels. And rags in case you need to clean up any spit-up. There's a toothbrush and toothpaste on the counter. Use them. Your clothes will be cleaned daily. We'll set them inside the door. Leave the ones you're wearing in their place."

What the fuck?

Why was I being treated like celebrity inmate in a state prison?

He grabbed my elbow and yanked me again. My shoulder banged against the doorframe once more. At least I could take a warm shower to relax the sore muscle now.

After about ten steps, he grasped my shoulders and pushed me downward. And my ass molded into something remotely comfortable. It wasn't a bed, but—

"This is your cot. The crib's a few feet to your left. The basinet's" — he grasped my hand and lifted it to Micah's chest— "right here. Probably best he sleeps in here 'til he's a little bigger. They used to co-sleep with him, but since you can't see, that might not be a good idea. So put him in here when you sleep. There's a rocker in the corner. We'll drop off bottles every other hour. If he shits, knock on the door. Someone will come to clean him. And your meals will be delivered twice a day. Eat them. You're no good to him dead."

What the fuck was going on? Why did I matter all of a sudden? And what did he mean? Micah was only a few days old, *who* used to co-sleep with him?

"This isn't about you, dipshit." His tone lessened in seriousness and grew slightly annoyed. "This is about him. We need him. And most of all, we need him to trust you. So be a good uncle."

CHAPTER ONE

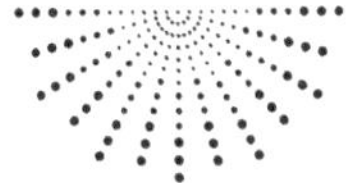

JUNE 27, 2019 - JEREMY

The sickly scent of cleaning agents wafted up my nose. Cold air blew from the humming register behind me. My head rested against Laila's thigh. I slid my thumb along the back of hers, trying to warm its cool feel.

For the first time in well over twenty-four hours, I started to fall asleep. My eyes were so heavy, I wasn't sure how I'd kept them open as long as I had. But the moment they started to fall, I forced them back open.

I couldn't fall asleep because what if I woke to the sound of those beeps again? What if the next time I opened my eyes, she was dead?

She looked it already.

Her long black hair was a mess of knots and matts. Hannah had tried to comb through them but only made it worse. The once plump, mauve-colored lips I'd spent the last three months dreaming of were a pale, nearly white color. Telling where they began against her paper skin was nearly impossible.

Her cheeks hollowed deep into the cave of her mouth. The collar bone beneath her flesh struggled not to rip the skin above it. The dark circles beneath her eyes were nearly black, almost as if she were punched or maybe even bludgeoned.

She looked dead.

She looked like she had no will left to live. Truthfully, I wasn't sure why she would. I wasn't sure that I did. I kept praying to whatever god was listening that she'd wake up, but if she didn't, I didn't want to keep going.

The only thing that kept me alive over the last few months was my hope for this moment, and the hope of being able to hold my son.

My stomach ached when that thought ran through my mind.

What happened to him? Why wasn't he here? What'd they do to him?

But I couldn't think about that.

I had to have hope. Her heart was beating. I felt it beneath my hand. I saw the little mountains climbing up and down on the machine. Her chest was rising and falling with breath—I had to hold myself together.

For the first time in three months, I had her back. She wasn't here, not really, but she was back. She was right in front of me. And I wasn't gonna let her go.

Hannah was the only other one who held onto hope that she was going to make it. Brody cried nonstop from the time he walked into the room until the time that he left. He couldn't even bring himself to tell me what happened back there.

Adam already gave his regards with teary eyes as he pressured me to drink water or take a nap. It wasn't something that I could do willingly at that point. My body was trying to, but my mind wouldn't let me.

Mary hadn't shown so that gave me hope. If Laila was going to die, she would've made an appearance to say her goodbyes. She must have felt the same way I did. That she was still there. Maybe locked away somewhere, but she was coming back. I knew she was coming back.

A doctor mentioned organ donation. It took everything in me not to punch him in the face, but I just turned back to her and squeezed her hand a little tighter.

As her fiancé, I had no legal right to make that call. But I was terrified that when her mom arrived, she would. Laila was an organ donor, she wanted to donate them if she died. Always said that it was the second to last way she could give back with her life upon her death. The last would be by giving a tree new life after I, and I quote, "dump her body in a hole, throw some dirt over her, and put a little maple sapling on top."

I could've seen her mom doing it. Not because she would've ever wanted Laila to die, but because she didn't look like Laila anymore. The scars alone made her look like a different person but the lack of pigment in her skin made it seem like she was already gone.

"I heard about this once." I ran my fingers along her thumb. "It was in one of those books at the library in our other hospital. The underground one, ya know?"

"Yeah." Hannah stifled a yawn. "I think I did too. Eighteenth century, right? It was a Demon though, wasn't it?"

"No, I think it was a Witch. She cast some really powerful spell. It was something to do with a war. I think she killed a bunch of people at once," I murmured. "Then she got stabbed and a Fae healed her just before she died. But her soul just didn't want to stay. Then she died of dehydration before she woke up."

Hannah fell quiet. Then she said, "She used a lot of energy. That Witch, I mean. Passing that much power through your body is physically straining. So did Laila, but she has us. And twenty-first century medical technology. She just needs some time. Leah gets really tired after she heals. Maybe this is like that. Maybe she just needs to recoup."

"Or maybe she just doesn't want to come back." I gazed up at her nearly lifeless body. "What she did back there, all the people she killed that I witnessed alone... That's not something I can see her forgiving herself for. Even if they weren't good people."

"She's not going to die," Hannah said. "She held on when her heart stopped beating. She's coming back, Jeremy."

"I hope." I squeezed her unusually cool hand a bit tighter. "I really hope."

"Why don't you sing to her?" she asked quietly. "Laila loves your voice."

I was sure that if I attempted to sing, I'd end up sobbing. "I don't know."

"What if I tell Adam to bring your guitar?" Hannah said. "She loves music. I bet she'd like to hear that, even if she doesn't realize she's hearing it."

"Maybe."

Honestly, I wasn't sure I could do that either. I didn't want to let go of her hand. I didn't want to move. I just wanted to hold her.

Then, I heard those beeps again. The slowdown of the moving mountains before they turned to another flat plane.

My heart hammered against my chest. Not again.

Please god, not again.

"No." I stood. Hannah jumped to her feet and started toward the bed.

I screamed for help. I'm not even sure what I said. My vision blurred around the edges. Hannah gripped Laila's other hand.

Nurses rushed in a few seconds later. I stepped away, heart falling, stomach aching. A nurse touched my shoulders and began to usher me from the room.

"No, please." I struggled to see through my watery eyes. "I'll stay back, I'll let you work. Just don't make me leave. Please."

She glanced me over to make sure I was serious, then nodded. As they ripped her gown open, Hannah released her hand and joined me in the corner of the room. She placed her arms around my waist, and I put mine around her shoulders. I winced as I watched the metal touch Laila's skin before her body jolted upwards toward them.

I didn't feel it.

A shiver stretched down my spine. My lips curled down, head shaking.

Then the long beep turned back to steady, rhythmic blips on the monitor.

Relief. The mountains were climbing and falling again.

But just as I was about to let my shoulders relax with respite, an almost impossible to describe heave left Laila's lips. Her heart began to pick up speed. Her eyes remained closed, but her chest bucked forward in trying attempts to breathe air into her lungs.

My shaking hand moved to my mouth.

She couldn't breathe.

I heard someone say something about intubation. Then I watched a nurse yank her mouth open, put a long metal tool down her throat, and carefully push a tube into her writhing body.

Tears streamed past my fingers. I struggled not to scream. Once the tube was inside, they attached a large blue bag to the end and squeezed it every few seconds. Between each squeeze, the racing peaks on the monitor began to slow into small, gentle moving hills.

"She's okay." Hannah soothed her hand along my back. "She's gonna be okay."

CHAPTER TWO

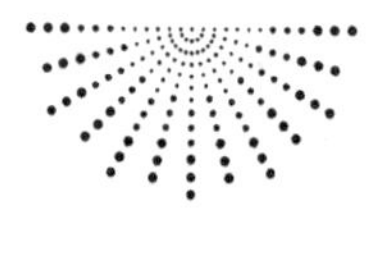

LAILA

I stared down at the beautiful baby in my arms, and my lips slid into a smile. The pearly white of his skin was practically luminous in the rays of the sun outside the window. I breathed in that sweet baby scent, watching the blue binky before his lips bob with each suckle. The heat of his warm body, radiated into mine as I rocked back and forth in the old rocking chair Jeremy found in the attic at his old house and refinished.

The beautiful hues of the green walls brought me this immense sense of peace and tranquility. I gazed out the cherry wood lined window. The warm yellow sun shined in from the Winnie the Pooh curtains. Hues of pink and purple illuminating through the white clouds. The nursery had a warm, yellowish glow to it like the sun on a morning beach. My stomach danced with joyous butterflies.

Love. It felt like falling in love for the first time. A type of love I'd never experienced, yet the purest I'd ever felt. Truly unconditional. That little life could've grown up to be Hitler and I wouldn't love him any less than I did in that moment.

He was perfect.

This was what it meant to be happy.

My baby in my arms. Jeremy sleeping in the next room. The sun coming up over the trees and letting light into the room. My son had just closed his big, bright blue eyes with his favorite blue binky behind his little lips. I would lay him back in his crib and go help with the morning rush downstairs in a moment.

But in a moment.

I had to gaze at him a while longer.

His cute little white onesie, his tiny little fingers, his long, pretty eyelashes.

I held his hand around my finger, feeling them slowly release and drop back to the crease of my arm. My clean, scar-less arm.

"This isn't real," a voice said from the doorway. "But you know that."

I didn't look up. I just continued to stare lovingly at my son with a simple smile.

"I know you remember. You can't forget. That's why you created this little escape." Her footsteps treaded toward me, but I just kept staring at the little ball of warmth in my arms. "This is what you wish your life was. But this is a dream. You know this is a dream."

The baby began to fuss in my arms and I said, "*Shhhh*," and rocked quicker.

"Laila, you need to wake up." She grasped my chin and pulled it up to face hers.

I jolted back and gripped my baby tighter.

It was me. *She* was me.

But a healthier me. Maybe a bit older. Clearly more put together.

She had a few lines at the edges of her eyes, but she was still young. She couldn't have been more than twenty-five. Her dark hair was pulled back in a neat bun at the back of her skull. A neat, black blouse rested over a pair of faded blue jeans.

The scar at her neck stared back at me like a symbol of strength, covered in tattoos of vines. The bite mark—the one I hated more than anything—was almost invisible under the purple and butterfly drawn over top. Her green eyes nearly glared down at me with a look of control and power I didn't realize my soft features could pull off. If a look could kill, hers would.

"You're allowed to feel whatever it is you need to feel to deal with this. I know this is hard, but you can't just die." Her tone was gentle while somehow still firm. "You can never just *die*, Laila. You stand up and fight. You drown yourself in booze and drugs for a while if that's what you have to do to make it through what's happened to you, but you get the fuck up. You go to therapy. You become a workaholic. But one way or another, you don't give up. You get the fuck up and fight. You can't just lay down and die."

The baby in my arms began to glow, casting light upon her face. My breath shortened. My heart sped up, then seemed to stop entirely.

I lifted him out in front of me. The light grew so wide that it engulfed the room.

Then it flicked out.

The swaddled child turned to ash and fell between the gaps of my fingertips.

"No!" I cried.

And just like that, he silently disappeared from my life the same way he'd come in. A wave of love. A bright light. Then nothing.

It all came back in flashes. Getting in the van. Watching them kill Daniel. Each slash against my spine. Peterson on top of me. The pain of each contraction.

Then that white light.

And all that blood.

"My baby." I sobbed, falling off the chair to the wood floor in a dramatic, nearly embarrassing shriek. "He's gone. He's gone."

She lowered herself beside me. "He's been gone, Laila. You know this."

"You don't understand. You don't understand how bad it hurts."

"I do." She put her hand on my shoulder. Her bright green eyes met mine. "I know how bad it hurts because I'm you. I've felt what you feel. I've seen what you saw. I've lived your life. And this is not where your story ends, Laila. This is only the beginning."

"I just want my son back. I want to see his face. I never even saw his face."

"I know. But he's gone, Laila. You aren't. You have to live. You have to find the will to live."

"No." I hung my head between my hands. "Fuck this life. Fuck this! I don't want to live. I don't, I don't want to live. My baby's dead. My baby's dead and it's all my fault," I sobbed. "I want to die. I don't want this life. I don't fucking want it!"

She grasped my shoulders and aggressively ripped me to my feet. The world shifted around us as if we'd teleported.

Then we stood in a tidy, elegantly designed hospital room. It was small, featuring the usual amenities; heart monitoring machines, IV drips, and a small sink with what seemed like a hundred cabinets around it.

She gripped my shoulders and spun me in a one eighty. I wiped my blurry eyes. Then I looked down at my fragile, dying body on the hospital bed.

Covered in scars. A needle poking out of my arm. A breathing tube protruding from my lips. My eyes had no life, my face was so pale. I looked so feeble beneath that thin hospital gown. If that wasn't Death's door, I didn't know what was.

I wanted to throw that body away and get a new one. I wanted to reincarnate and start all over. I wanted it to end.

But there he was.

Jeremy had a chair pulled up against the bottom of the bed. His head lay in my lap. His bloodshot blue eyes stared up at me. The corners of his eyes were red with crusted tears. His hand around mine clenched so tight, his knuckles were white.

"Please wake up, baby," he whispered. Tears welled in his eyes, spilling to the thin white hospital blanket. "Please, Lai. Please come back to me."

He was dying too.

"Micah is gone, and I know that hurts. I know nothing will ever replace him," she said quietly behind me. "I know you think that you've failed, but this isn't close to being over, Laila. Micah may have been your first child, but he won't be your last. You are *going* to have the life that you want. You're going to have the sweet little family and the little white picket fence. You're going have everything you're so desperate for. But not if you give up."

She moved beside me, resting her hand carefully on Jeremy's. "You still have people counting on you. You still have a future. But only if you wake up. Otherwise, none of the amazing things you accomplish will ever happen. Your beautiful children will never be born. You'll never get to plan that wedding. You'll never get to hold your child in your arms. You'll never get to *live*." She paused. "I know it hurts, but you have to live, Laila."

I looked back at Jeremy's sorrow filled face at the end of the bed, and tears overwhelmed my vision.

My gaze turned to Hannah. She sat in a chair on the opposite side of the bed, silently staring at my body. She chewed her fingernail. Deep, purple bags hung beneath her eyes.

Whether I wanted to die or not, she wasn't going to let me.

"And she'll never forgive herself if you do," Laila said. "She already blames herself for what happened to you. And for what happened to Micah. You and I both know she'll never be the same if you don't make it out of this."

At that moment, I realized I had two options. Stay here in limbo, make them miserable, and truly live a pointless life.

Or get the fuck up.

I met her gaze. "How do I go back?"

"Just wake up." She pushed my shoulders. "Wake up, Laila." She pushed me again and I fell backwards. "Just wake up."

CHAPTER THREE

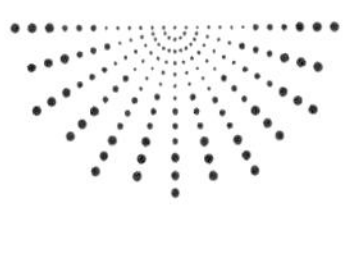

LAILA

My sandpaper eyelids fluttered. They were so dry, I could barely make out anything. My chest hurt like I'd been punched, or... or like I couldn't breathe. I tried to bring a full breath into my lungs, then felt something stiff in my throat. I tried to sit up but my body felt like it was full of weights.

"Hannah," Jeremy said. "Go get a doctor."

There was this scratching ache in my throat like it'd been torn open. I tried to cough, tried to bring in a deep breath, but felt like I was choking. Without thought, my arm flailed, searching for my neck, trying to fix whatever impeded my breathing.

"Hey, hey, it's okay. It's okay, baby, you're okay." Jeremy's hand soothed my hair down to the side of my neck. His bright blue eyes locked with mine. He didn't smile, but his eyes were full of joy. "You weren't breathing on your own so they put this tube in. Hannah's going to get the doctor right now, okay? Just relax, you're okay. I'm right here."

I moved my hand around, striving to touch his. The moment our skin met, when he interlocked his fingers with mine, a wave of comfort coursed through me.

"It's okay." He gave a sweet smile. "You're okay. You're going to be okay."

I tried to take a deep breath but I couldn't. That racing in my chest came back.

Everything felt surreal. The dream felt more legitimate. My head spun, my vision was disoriented, it felt like I couldn't breathe.

I squeezed his hand tight beside my face, unsure if it was a dream come true or another nightmare in the making. Wouldn't be the first time one of those bastards was in my head.

He gently thumbed my cheek. *This is real. It's okay, baby. You're okay.*

I stayed silent, unsure of what to think or say, even if I could speak.

It all slid back again, just as it had in the dream.

The reality of what I'd done in the past three months. What I'd done to him. What happened to our baby because of me. What he'd felt because of my mistake.

All I kept thinking was how sorry I was.

"You didn't do anything wrong." His voice lowered, growing as soft and gentle as the breeze on a quiet spring day. "It's okay, you're home. You're home."

My racing heart slowed at his touch.

I'm sorry. Both eyes watered. *I'm so sorry.*

"Baby." He forced a smile, shaking his head as he thumbed my tears away. "It's okay. Everything's okay."

I desperately reached up for his other hand, nearly flailing before he caught it. His warm palm squeezed mine tighter than it ever had. Then he pulled my knuckles to his lips.

Relief washed over me, heart slowing once more. When my eyes were on his, I felt okay. I felt safe. I just had to keep my eyes on his.

"There you go," he whispered, holding my gaze, caressing the backs of my thumbs with his. "There you go, you're alright. Everything's alright."

With each word he spoke, the overwhelming sense of terror dissipated. Once I'd calmed down enough, I spoke into his mind, *What's wrong with me?*

"Kai healed you, but you wouldn't wake up. Your body was fine, but it's like your soul had already crossed over or something. You flat lined twice, and you stopped breathing on your own the second time about" —he glanced up at the clock— "six hours ago. They didn't think you were going to wake up, but I knew you would." A smile brightened his face. "I knew you would."

I wanted to smile back, but I couldn't. His hand against mine felt like pure ecstasy. I'd missed physical contact on the deepest level. And it felt so good. But it almost hurt too. I could've felt this weeks ago, and I chose not to because I was naïve enough to believe that I could save everyone.

I'm so sorry I didn't let you come sooner. I'm so sorry. I just didn't think there was any way you could do it without getting hurt or killed and—And you, you needed me for this. I knew where everything was and—

"Baby," he said softly, pressing his thumb gently to the water leaving my eye. "It's okay. I'm not mad at you."

It looked like he meant it, and that provided a touch of relief.

Despite that, I wasn't sure if I believed it. If he'd lost our baby, I wouldn't forgive him. Even if it were to save my sister, I would've hated him.

But it felt so good to be with him again. So safe and familiar.

I missed you so much.

"I missed you too. I missed you like I've never missed anything." He smiled, hand gently moving through my greasy hair. "I'm so glad you're okay."

"Excuse me," a voice said behind Jeremy. He leaned away from my face. I got my first glance at the doctor.

For a second, and only a second, I saw Peterson's face on that man's body. I jumped, but Jeremy grabbed my hand. He met my gaze with a soft smile, gently thumbing my knuckles. "It's okay."

The doctor's face turned to mine. He smiled kindly, but it still made my heart skip a beat. Rationally, I knew he wasn't like Peterson. Anyone working in one of our facilities meant the oath they took. But I supposed that rationality was irrelevant where trauma was involved.

"Well, I'm glad to see you awake, Miss Callidy."

I tried to swallow as I often did when I was nervous. But that only irritated my throat more.

Ask him to take this out.

"She wants to know if you can extubate," Jeremy said.

"I can't be sure just yet, we'll have to see if you can breathe without the ventilator for a few hours first." He steadily held my gaze, looking at me instead of my translator. I did appreciate that.

No, I need this out of me. He doesn't understand. I have to get it out.

"She says that she really needs it out. You can understand, given the circumstances." Jeremy cupped his other hand gently around mine.

"If we end up having to reinsert it, we run the risk of having to do a tracheotomy because of the swelling in your throat from the first intubation."

Another slice across my throat. Not pleasant but better than being forced to lie back on a hospital bed. I needed to sit up. I just had to get up.

I'm covered in scars, what's one more?

Jeremy cleared his throat. "She says that she doesn't care if she gets another scar."

The doctor looked between us, clearly unamused, but considering. "One hour without the ventilator, and we'll pull the tube."

A whole hour?

"She's hoping to get it out sooner," Jeremy said.

"One full hour. Even that is negligent."

Jeremy looked to me as if to ask if that was okay.

It wasn't ideal. But if it was medically necessary, it was medically necessary. Not that I held much merit to doctors these days, but this guy seemed nice. I'd waited three months to kiss my fiancé, I could wait another hour. In the meantime, I could talk to him through my thoughts.

I gave a slow nod. Jeremy looked back to the doctor. "She says okay."

He came over to the machine beside me. "Now Laila, as the machine stops breathing for you and you breathe on your own for the first time, you might feel a wind knocked out of you sort of sensation for a second. If it lasts longer than a second, we're turning it back on. Got it?"

I gave a nod against the abnormally soft pillow behind me. Damn, I'd all but forgotten how nice pillows were.

Jeremy lowered himself to the bed beside me, gently rubbing his hand over mine. "This is actually a major step in the ICU, you know," the doctor said. "Getting off the ventilator usually means you're over the worst of it."

I knew that was hardly the case. I had a long ass road ahead of me.

"Okay, so I'm slowly turning the ventilator down now. How do you feel?" he asked. I nodded slowly, still feeling okay at first. "We're almost off now so don't be surprised if you feel out of breath for a second. Just stay calm, I'm not going to let you die."

I nodded again. Jeremy caressed my cheek. It was just like a said. A sudden siphon within my chest, like the wind had just been knocked out of me. I struggled in a gasp. But Jeremy's hand held my cheek gently. The other soothed my tense knuckles. "You're okay. Just breathe. Just breathe, baby. You're okay."

As he spoke, I felt my heart rate gradually decrease. I knew it was him fucking around in my thoughts, but I didn't mind that time. I wanted that damn tube out.

"How are you feeling, Laila?" the doctor asked.

I gave a nod, continuing to gaze at the man I'd dreamed of touching for three months.

He looked different. Happy, clearly. But broken. His once clean shaved jaw was covered in thick scruff nearly two inches long. His electric blue eyes still vibrated with excitement, but the deep bags beneath them were black as night. The corners were red and chafing from tears. But his chapped lips held the sweetest smile.

I just wanted him to hold me. I didn't want to be hooked up to wires or tubes anymore. I wanted to be free.

"Can we go outside in an hour after you pull the tube out?" Jeremy asked, still holding my gaze as he spoke to the doctor.

"I'd prefer if we could closely monitor Laila for a few hours first so that we're sure she isn't having any breathing problems before she's moved." He studied my numbers on the screen to the left of me.

I'll just teleport you after he takes it out whether he likes it or not, Jeremy said into my mind.

I smiled through the tube in my mouth. He smiled back.

"I'm going to make sure a nurse is stationed right outside your door here with a crash cart just in case."

"Sounds like a plan, doc," Jeremy said, still gazing at me.

The doctor chuckled. "Let's give them a minute of privacy, everyone."

Funny, I hadn't realized anyone else was in the room.

I heard pitter-patters toward the door. Then a quiet click as it shut. With a grimace, I thought, *Can you crack that door?*

Jeremy kissed my hand and stood. "Yeah. Yeah, of course, baby."

I watched him walk past the wall that was beside the door and for a moment, my heart sunk. I knew he wasn't going anywhere. But I didn't want to be here, and his hand around mine gave me a sense of security that nothing else did. Especially with how trapped the tube and wires and IVs made me feel.

I heard the click of the doorknob and it sent chills down my spine. My eyes pulled shut.

"What's wrong?" Jeremy rushed toward me. He took my hand in his.

I made what I could of a smile. Why the sound of a doorknob made me uneasy wasn't something I wanted to get into. I hadn't seen the love of my life in three months. I just wanted to talk to him.

I like the beard, I thought.

He laughed and rubbed it. "It's really bad. I need to shave."

Don't shave, it's cute. I like it.

He smiled wider, reaching out to touch my face. "I'm so happy you're back."

Jeremy had no clue. This moment was all I'd been dreaming of. Didn't exactly picture the tubes and wires playing a part, but at least I was out.

Can you ask everyone to stay out until they pull the tube?

"Baby, nobody cares about that. They just want to see you."

I can't talk to them anyway. And I don't even want you to see me like this.

He was quiet for a moment. "Okay, I'll tell Hannah to let everyone know."

Thank you.

He gently squeezed my hand.

How is everybody? I asked.

He smiled. "Everyone's okay. Worried about you, but otherwise, okay. Hannah and Wyatt and Celena graduated a couple weeks ago, they're really happy about that."

I missed their graduation?

His sweet smile fell, but he pulled it back up. "They all looked like ants anyway."

Shit. I guessed that make sense. It was late June. Obviously, that meant I'd missed their graduation. But damn.

I made a gesture for him to go on.

He cleared his throat. "Your mom and Jenna have been good. I was keeping your Mom updated as everything unraveled. We kept each other sane sometimes."

I smiled through the tube. Sounded about right. The son she'd always wanted, as she'd made a habit of stating over the years.

"And Kai and Hannah seem to be pretty serious, so that's good, I guess. Let's see." He paused, thinking. "Oh, Moe's is doing really good. Our profits have stayed level since you..." He paused again, unsure how to carefully tiptoe around the word kidnap. "Since you've been gone. And I finished the painting in the living room, it looks really nice. I started on the retiling of the shower last week, but then shit kind of blew up all at once, so I didn't get very far, but I'm working on it."

He tried to keep the conversation light. It was nice, it made me feel normal for a second. I missed small talk. I especially missed hearing his voice.

"I just took the car for its first oil change and they rotated the tires too. I would have done it myself, but it was covered with the warranty, so I figured why not. I wasn't going to have them rotate the tires, but I was already there, and you know how much of a bitch it is to make another trip so I got something to eat while I waited." He paused again. "I'm sorry. You don't care about all that."

I squeezed his hand. *Please don't stop talking.*

It was literal music in my ears. I missed that voice so much. Until the night before, I'd almost forgotten it.

He smiled and ran the palm of his other hand against the back of mine. "Okay, what else. Oh, um, I got a new chef's special for Tuesdays. Everyone was getting sick of that ham soup and Max said he had this bomb recipe for homemade tomato soup, and it's been a huge hit. We actually ran out of seats two weeks ago. Some of the waitresses are saying we need to get a hostess, but I think we're a little too small for that."

I smiled and gave a nod. I agreed though, we didn't have room for a hostess stand anyway.

"Also, do you remember that one time when we first started dating and you told me I had to try putting cinnamon on my popcorn and I said it sounded disgusting?" I nodded. "Well, I tried it a few months ago by accident. I thought it was the salt, but it was that little shaker with sugar and cinnamon you use for your oatmeal. And needless to say, you were right, it was amazing. I should have listened years ago."

My lips made what they could of a smile. A random offhand comment, but it wa sweet. Honestly, he could've told me about the shits he'd taken over the last three months and I'd still smile.

But I had to ask.

I squeezed his hand. *And what about you? How have you been?*

He smiled. "I'm better now."

Liar.

His smile widened for a second. Then it lowered and he glanced away. "It's been pretty tough."

I'm sorry, Jeremy—

"Baby, stop apologizing." He touched my face and leaned in a bit closer. "Please stop apologizing. You have nothing to apologize for." His eyes moved back and forth between mine as he held my cheeks between his palms. "None of this was your fault. None of it, okay?"

It was one hundred percent my fault. We both knew that good and damn well. But he'd never admit it aloud.

I wanted to chew my cheek or maybe swallow the lump in my throat, but all I could do was nervously tap my foot. *I wish it weren't.*

"Shh." He pushed hair behind my ear. "You were amazing, Laila. Do you know how many people are going or already went home to people they love because of you?"

I shook my head.

"Two hundred and twenty-four. You helped so many people, baby. You saved so many lives. You're amazing."

He meant it when he said it. His eyes lit up, his lips lifted in a smile. He did, he meant it. But I didn't save the lives that meant the most to both of us.

My teeth trembled around the tube. *I didn't save Chris.*

His eyes softened. "It's not your fault, Laila. You did everything that you could. We all did."

Tears burned down my cheeks, and he frowned. "It's okay, baby. Please don't cry, you'll strain your lungs."

I'm so sorry.

"It's okay." He leaned down in the best, most awkward hug he could for the odd angle.

I hooked my arms around his back, and he soothed his hand against my hair. "It's okay, Lai. Everything's okay. You're home, it's okay."

CHAPTER FOUR

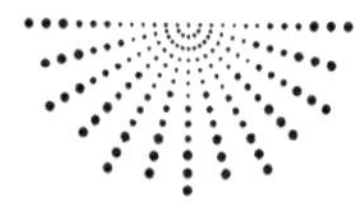

LAILA

The doctor rambled a bunch of medical jargon as he prepared to remove the tube, but none of it registered. I didn't want to think about what could go wrong whatsoever. I wanted to think about going home, snuggling in bed with my fiance, and doing everything in my power to block out the last few months.

So when he pulled the thing from my throat, the moment I finished coughing, I shot forward and wrapped my arms around Jeremy's body as tight as I could. He laughed. Then he squeezed me even harder. He gently pressed his hand against the back of my head and kissed my cheek.

The doctor chuckled again. "Still breathing okay, Laila?"

I nodded and closed my eyes against Jeremy's shoulder. I don't know how long it was before I let go, only that it couldn't have been long enough. It felt so good. Warm, and safe. Like home.

Jeremy turned up to the doctor. "Can I take her outside now?"

The doctor considered long and hard for a moment. "You can teleport, right?"

"If anything happens, we will be right back in this bed," Jeremy said.

"I suppose so. Just no smoking."

"Thank you," I made out in a scratchy voice, smiling.

"Just be careful, alright? Undo all the wires first but bring the IV. I don't want to see you getting dehydrated."

"Sure," I muttered.

I just couldn't wait to feel fresh air again. I couldn't wait to see the sky. Wasn't a fan of the plastic hanging out of my hand, but I'd do anything to feel the sun again.

As the doctor headed from the room, Jeremy wrapped his arms around me in another tight embrace. "I missed you so much," he whispered in my ear.

"I missed you more." I took in the smell of his two-day old cologne on his dusty T-shirt.

"That's not possible." Eyes glistening with joy, he leaned in slowly and touched his lips to mine. He practically cradled my face in his palms, holding me tight, like I was the most precious thing he'd ever touched.

Warmth radiated through my body, pleasant goosebumps lifting over my arms. His breath tasted awful, I'm sure mine did too, but it felt so good. So safe.

I closed my eyes and kissed him back, hand lifting to his furry jaw. His beard made his lips feel different against mine, but not in a bad way. In a great way. After Peterson, I'd never want my lips to touch a clean shaved mouth again.

His lips opened gently on mine, carefully grazing but trying not to be too pushy. I kissed him back, letting the moisture of his mouth soften my cracking lips.

It was slow and sweet. Maybe one of the best kisses we ever shared. No intent of more, just soft, gentle intimacy. My body flooded with warmth, and butterflies flew in my belly. I felt safe. For the first time in three months, I felt safe.

I pulled back a minute later, resting my forehead against his. He still cupped my face in his hand. He opened his eyes to meet my gaze. His lips heightened in a smile. "I'm so happy you're home."

I smiled. My eyes closed. For a moment, I simply enjoyed the feel of his warm hand against my cheek. I basked in the feel of his breath against my face. I drew in the smell of his musty body odor mixing with our laundry detergent and cologne. I just took it in for a moment.

It was real.

I was out. I was going home. I was back where I belonged.

He pulled away and met my gaze with a warm smile. He ran his hand along my hair. "Do you want to go outside?"

The biggest smile of my life stretched across my lips. I started to my feet, but he caught my hand. "I don't want you to fall. We're going to sit anyway." He lifted the blanket into the air and whooshed it around my shoulders.

I was a little woozy. As much as I wanted to get up, I didn't wanna bust my head open and end up in here for any longer.

"That's probably a good idea," I said. "I don't feel great about walking right now anyway."

He placed one hand on mine and the other on my IV drip. And we spun through the air.

I missed that sensation. The feeling that always reminded me of freedom. Knowing we could go anywhere in the world. The liberating vibration of spinning on a merry-go-round and sitting still at the same time.

We landed outside on a small, stone bench. His arm wrapped around my shoulders and he pulled me tight against him. I lay my head against his chest, breathing in a slow, deep drag of the first fresh air I'd smelled in months. It was crisp and cool, yet somehow still warmer than that temperature-controlled cell. The moonlight shined down over a large empty field lined with trees. I felt a weight lift off of my shoulders as I gazed around in awe of the openness.

I was out.

"It's so warm," I murmured.

"A little chilly." He laughed. "But there has been a bit of a heat wave recently."

I rested my head against his shoulder. There was silence for a moment, but a comforting sort of silence. The silence that paired beautifully with whistling wind and cricket chirps. The kind of silence that joined in with the soft thumps of Jeremy's heart beneath my ear to form a quiet melody.

Stillness was a better word for it, I supposed. Before, I would've called this silence, but the white noise of my cell had been true silence.

This was still, not silent.

Eventually, I broke it with, "Thank you for not giving up on me."

He held me a tighter and kissed my forehead. "I could never give up on you."

A sweet sentiment. But given what I'd done, I wouldn't blame him if he had.

"Just... thank you."

He leaned down and pressed his lips to my forehead again for a long moment. I basked in the comfort of his body. *He* was home.

But fuck, I needed out of this hospital gown. It felt stiff against my skin. Scratchy. I wanted something soft, like the fabric of his hoodie against my cheek.

"When we go back inside, do you think you could run to the house and get me a couple things?" I asked quietly.

"Yeah, of course, baby. What do you need?"

"Clothes. Your clothes preferably. They're comfy," I said. "And my slippers. And I need shower stuff. Oh, and food. So much food."

"I'll write a list when we get inside."

My hand found his and squeezed it hard.

I sat there quietly, just frozen in that spot for a moment. Part of me was trying to fathom if it was even real. It all felt like a dream I didn't want to wake up from. Almost as good as the dream I *had* awoken from.

"You aren't dreaming," he whispered against my head." You're home, baby. You're home."

I knew that. I knew this was real. It just didn't feel like it was.

I was gazing out over the humid, misty green field. The air was thick and muggy. I used to hate humidity. It irritated my allergies. But I loved that thick feeling in my throat. Even the postnasal drip that ran down my esophagus. It felt like being alive. Like being a person instead of a lab rat.

I smelled the dew in the air as I took in another slow deep breath. I actually felt like I could breathe again. It wasn't mechanically filtered, recycled air. It smelled like earth opposed to imprisonment. For the first time in my life, I genuinely loved the fact that I needed a Zyrtec.

As I looked at the budding trees and flowers in the distance, a thought dawned on me.

That sweet little girl with a bullet in her chest.

My heart thudded. I turned up to meet Jeremy's gaze. "Is Lydia okay?"

"Kai healed her. She's fine. Ray's with her. They're scheduled to have her implants removed tomorrow afternoon and then she can go home."

A tear of joy streamed from the corner of my eye. I smiled. "She's okay."

He smiled back. "She's okay."

"And Haley? How is Haley?"

"She was the girl in the cell beside yours, right?" Jeremy asked. I nodded. "She's doing great. She's being discharged today."

I smiled wide, letting out a half laugh. "She didn't believe we'd ever get out. I kept telling her, but she said I was crazy." He smiled, waiting for me to go on. "I just had to get them out. As many people as I could. I just had to get them out."

And I did. But there had been close to four hundred. He'd said I saved two hundred and...

I counted on my fingers. "How many didn't get out?"

He licked his lips. "Don't think about that right now, Laila."

I did the mental math for a moment. "A hundred and fifty?" I asked.

"Something like that from what we saw on the other side of the building."

I looked down. All that and I didn't even get them all. I lost Micah for this, and I still didn't save them all.

Jeremy's voice was a quiet plea. "Please try not to think about that right now."

"Did we lose any of our people?" I asked.

"Just a few minor injuries. Nothing Kai and Celena couldn't take care of."

That was reassuring. I may not have gotten everyone, but I was far from done. They still had my brother-in-law. It wasn't over. But I'd done it once without losing any of my own and I would do it again. That gave me hope.

"Not a single casualty."

"Not on our end. Your plan was amazing. No one else could have pulled that off the way that you did."

Something between a huff and a laugh left me. Yeah, it was great that none of our people went down. But it wasn't exactly 'amazing.' "Could have been better."

He tilted my chin up to face him. "You were right, Laila. If I would have come sooner, God only knows what would have happened. You were on the fourth floor and that place was almost impenetrable. I definitely wouldn't have gotten half the people out that you did." He held my gaze, sincerely looking from my left eye to my right. "I would have run in guns blazing. I would have gone straight to you. And I *may* have gotten you out. But I wouldn't have managed to get anyone else. I wouldn't have even tried, you were all I was thinking about. And I would have been in such a fog of adrenaline, I probably would have gotten myself killed. I might have gotten you killed too," he said. "I couldn't have done what you did. You were amazing, Laila. You had to be the hero this time." He managed a smile. "You didn't need me to save you. You needed to save *them*."

I forced a smile back. "But I wish I would have saved them *all*." I rubbed my temple." I didn't even get to Peterson."

Any joy in his expression vanished, growing serious. Seemingly without thought, his hand around mine tightened, as did his grip around my waist. "That's who was in charge? Peterson?"

"Doctor Robert Peterson," I said. "He was the brains of it all."

"He may have gotten away, but that doesn't mean anything." Jeremy clenched his jaw. "They still have my brother. We're not done."

"You just read my mind." I chomped on my lower lip and turned away. "But I should have killed him when I had the chance."

Jeremy gritted his teeth together for a second. He looked down. "I... I don't know how to ask this."

I pulled away a bit so that I sat upright. I knew what he was trying to ask. But I didn't know how to say it either. So, I tried to say it between the lines. "He wasn't *just* the brains. He did everything except for the stress tests, but that was intentional so he wouldn't get killed."

"Stress tests?" Jeremy asked.

"The torture," I muttered.

He gazed at our hands in his lap for a few heart beats. "Was he... Was he the one who..."

I wasn't able to verbalize it either, so I nodded. "He was, or is, I guess, like..." This wasn't any easier for me to say than it was for him to hear. "He's monomaniacal about the Fae. He treated us different than everyone else. Especially Amy. But me too. In a dramatically different way but... It's complicated."

"You can explain it to me," he said softly. "Or not, if you don't want to."

My gaze turned up from the field to meet his. He looked down at me, expression ginger, but there was a hair of fear in his gaze. Like he was tiptoeing on hot hand. Did he really want to know? I didn't want to say it either way, especially not to him. It'd hurt. I knew it would. And I didn't want him to hurt any more from all of this than he already was.

"I just need some time," I said.

"Take all the time you need." His eyes looked so sad. Angry, too. Not at me; I knew that. He was angry at what Peterson had done.

"You don't have to do that."

"Don't have to do what?"

I pulled a smile to my lips in attempt to lighten the mood. "Be so understanding. You're allowed to want to know what happened."

"I do." His eyes slid between mine. "But I already know a lot. And I wish you would have been able to tell me about what happened to you in your own time, when you were ready. I can wait until you're ready on the details, Lai."

I chewed on my lip. By the look on his face, he didn't seem the least bit curious. Angry, but he didn't want to know it all. Not yet. He had his own theories, and regardless of why they did what they did, he knew *what* they did. The what was hard enough to fathom, the why might have been even harder.

And I didn't want him to know either. I knew I'd have to figure out some way to talk about it. I had so much information trapped away in my brain that we would need to bring Chris home. But I wasn't ready to verbalize my experiences yet. We both knew what Jeremy was referring to, and neither of us wanted to think about that.

CHAPTER FIVE

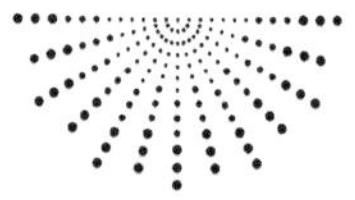

LAILA

A knock sounded at the open door. "Hey," Hannah said.

I turned that way, and a warm smile came to my lips.

Dark purple underlined her bright blue eyes, water seeping from the corners. She held a small bouquet of sunflowers on top of a pale pink box. Her messy black hair was knotted into a bun at the back of her skull.

"Come here." I opened my arms.

Hannah dropped the flowers and box to the small, wheeling hospital table, darted across the room, and wrapped her arms around me. "I'm so glad you're back."

I laughed, trying to breathe through her firm grasp. "Thank you for forcing me to stay."

She pulled back with a smile. "I couldn't let you leave."

"I'm glad you didn't."

She just stared at me for a long moment. Her lip quivered. Then the quiet tears turned to sobs. "I'm so sorry, Laila. I—You should have let them kill me. I—I—That would have been best. You-you should have—"

"No." I hugged her again. She clutched her arms around my back, holding me like she'd never let go. "I couldn't let that happen." I lowered my voice so it wouldn't crack. "I know you would have given your life for us, but I chose. I couldn't let anything happen to you."

Part of me wished I had. Only a part. But it wasn't her fault. It was mine.

Still, if I would've let her die, we would've lost our key to the afterlife. That hadn't been the reason that I got into the van, but it was one way that I rationalized why it was the right decision.

"But you should have," she wept. I closed my eyes, holding her body against mine. She was there. She was alive, weeping in my arms, but she was alive.

"I didn't make the wrong choice," I said quietly. I fought the memory of Micah in my arms.

He'd be there instead if I let her die. But he wasn't and she was.

So were two hundred and twenty-four other people.

That's what I had to look at. That's what I had to think about.

"I made the right choice," I murmured.

Truthfully, I wasn't sure if I was trying to assure her or myself.

She pulled back a bit, gesturing to the bed. "Can we sit?"

I should have thought to hold the hospital gown together as I walked but it completely slipped my mind. Until I sat down on the bed and saw Hannah's face. She was practically holding her breath. Her eyes were wide. It was probably the same face I made when I saw Daniel's back for the first time.

"They don't hurt anymore." She opened her mouth to talk but seemed to choke on her words. I just smiled and gestured to the pink box on the table. "So, whatcha got there?"

After an awkward moment of quiet, she grabbed it and set it on my lap. "It's a bunch of pastries from Beverly's."

I lifted the container to my nose, closed my eyes, and inhaled. I smelled it all, the chocolate, cinnamon, the yeast and brown sugar. Each hint hit off of my taste buds and sent my mouth to a drooling water. I smiled, set it on my lap, and pulled up the lid.

Hannah gazed at me with an awkward smile. I laughed. "Sorry, was that weird?"

She chuckled. "Maybe a little. But you've never exactly been normal."

I laughed, pushed her shoulder, and lifted out a chocolate chip cookie. "It just smells so good." Her eyes shifted over me, and her lips curled down. I lowered the cookie from my lips. "Please don't do that."

She cocked her head to the side. "Do what?"

"That look," I said. "I don't want anyone's pity. I'm not just a victim, okay? I didn't just sit there and take it, Hannah. I did everything I could to make it stop and then to break out. I could have before I did, but I knew I had to be ready if I wanted anyone other than me to get out alive."

"I know," she said. "I'm sorry, I didn't mean anything by it."

"No, I'm sorry. I'm not trying to be a bitch. I just..." I paused. "I don't want people to think about what happened to me. I want them to think about what I *did*."

"You weren't being a bitch. I understand completely. I'm sorry," she said. "It wasn't even pity, you know."

"No?" I asked.

"It was guilt. I just..." Hannah bit her lip. "I just saw your back, and I thought about the baby, and I know you don't want to hear this, but it should have been me. It shouldn't have been you."

I looked away and took a bite. The chocolate made my taste buds feel like they were going to explode. I closed my eyes for a second, taking in the magnificent rush of flavor I'd missed so deeply.

It occurred to me in that moment. It had crossed my mind inside a few times, but now that I was out, I was sure.

It was never going to be Hannah.

If I hadn't gotten inside, they would have killed her. Then they would've shot me with a few tranquilizers and tossed me inside either way.

"It had to be me. I don't know if it was fate, or God, or the fucking piece of shit Council up there. But to save those people, for things to have worked out the way they did, it had to be me. You can't tell me that shit wasn't planned. Someone or something put me in that place for a reason."

"Yeah," Hannah said. "A torturing, murdering sociopath."

I gazed off into the trees out the window. I took another bite of my cookie.

One of the first things Daniel ate after we picked him up was a chocolate chip cookie from Beverly's too. It was nearly poetic and too coincidental to be a coincidence.

Maybe it sounded crazy, but I couldn't crack it all up to chance. It was just too weird.

Jeremy so happens to have a soulmate who's the most powerful hybrid anyone's ever seen. Said soulmate, the only one with capabilities of being on the inside and the outside of the structure at the same time—not to mention the fact that her abilities made destroying the complex seem like a leisurely stroll—was kidnapped by the same people who took Chris while carrying the most powerful child the world has seen in nearly a millennium.

It was meticulously calculated.

This was bigger than Peterson. He was a speck in the grand scheme. There had to be some reason for what he was doing to all of us. It wasn't that he was just psychotic or some supernatural fearing bigot. If anything, he genuinely loved us. But he wanted something from us besides the pleasure of cruelty.

"Laila." Hannah shook my shoulder a bit. "Are you okay?"

"Huh?" I turned to meet her gaze.

"You just went all quiet," she said.

"Sorry," I said. "My mind's just somewhere else."

Just behind the hallway by the bathroom, I heard a tap-tap. Adam's head peeped around the corner with a mile-wide smile.

Grinning, I stood and started toward him. He darted across the room, wrapped his arms around my back, and lifted me into the air. I tried to laugh but he squeezed so hard that I struggled to breathe.

"Don't ever scare us like that again," he said. "When Hannah called, I was sure it'd be bad news."

"Well, you sure were wrong." I laid my head against his big chest.

He chuckled and gripped me tighter. "Jesus, you're skinny now."

I laughed as I pulled back. "Yeah, well. The starvation diet is pretty promising, as you can see."

He chuckled and gestured to the scar at my neck. But he didn't stare, he just glanced. It didn't even bother me, really. There was no pity. "They didn't take yours out yet?"

"No. I think I was too unstable."

"Makes sense."

Another head bobbed around the corner. A smile came to my lips and I brushed past Adam to Brody.

I threw my arms around his big shoulders, and his went to my waist. "Hey," he whispered. He squeezed a bit too tight, but I just smiled and hugged him back.

"Hey." Meeting his gaze, arms still around his back, I did my best to give him a smile. "Almost got him."

"Almost," he murmured, lips pulling down.

But I just willed my lips higher. That was me and Brody's thing. He'd frown and I'd laugh until he did. "It's nice to see you, you know. Not covered in my blood."

"Think we both look better like this."

"I'd say so." I laughed.

Just behind Brody's shoulder, Leah's purple hair bounced toward me. I moved past him to her. She smiled, but we both knew it was a façade. I wanted to tell her how sorry I was that I let her down. That I had Chris, and that I lost him. But she knew it as I thought it.

She opened her arms and she stepped closer, wrapping them around me in a tight embrace. "We've missed you so much," she said near my ear.

"I missed you more," I whispered, hugging her close.

I didn't expect her to argue. I knew she was upset. I wasn't the face she expected to see, and her heart was broken all over again.

"I'm just glad you're back."

I closed my eyes against her shoulder. "I'm sorry Chris isn't."

CHAPTER SIX

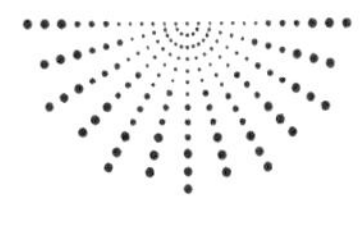

LAILA

We all huddled around the bed talking for a while. They talked mostly, and I listened. It's not like I had all that much to say. They knew what I'd been doing for the last three months. But they filled me in on their lives.

Hannah talked about how she finished high school with a four-point-o GPA. Brody said how grateful he was for summer break. Leah mentioned that work was boring but going well. Adam said he'd watched the last three episodes of season one of *Carnival Row* without me and I hit him.

We fell right back into our groove.

"Have you talked to your mom yet?" Leah asked.

"Not yet. She's on a flight here with Jenna but it's taking her a while. Jeremy said she spent the whole day looking for her passport, it was a great big mess."

"Thank God for teleportation." Brody chewed a corner off of a scone.

"Hey, guys." Jeremy appeared in the room near the door with a bag over his shoulder. He walked to me, kissed me quickly, and leaned forward to take a bite of my cookie. I chuckled. He grinned, pulled away, and set the bag down on the chair beside the bed. "I got everything you asked for, but I didn't get you food because everything back home is closed still. I thought about making you a burger and fries at the diner, but Max would be pissed I fucked up his clean kitchen."

I laughed. "That's okay, I have cookies."

He lowered himself beside me, mumbling an apology to Hannah as she scooched over to make room for him. Once he was situated on the bed, he wrapped an arm around my back and moved the other in front of my waist. His fingers locked together at my hip. I leaned against his chest and he kissed my forehead.

"You two are adorable." Hannah smiled.

I chuckled and took another bite of my cookie. Jeremy burrowed his head closer to mine, kissing my cheek.

"So how are you doing, Lai?" Leah asked quietly.

The room fell silent. But I just shrugged. "I'm better than I was." I glanced at Jeremy to ask him to pass me my Coke, but he was already out. I laughed. "That was quick."

"Guy hasn't slept in days." Adam glanced at him. "Maybe weeks. I don't even know."

I believed it. His hair was the greasiest I'd ever seen it, probably a lot like mine. Not that he ever had to actually *do* anything to make it look so great. He had a perfect mane from a bottle of three in one shampoo, body wash, and conditioner. Lucky bastard.

I leaned in and softly kissed his forehead.

Leah said, "Was it as bad as I imagine it was?"

I didn't want to go into the details. But I understood how badly they wanted to know.

"It was mostly pretty quiet actually. Spent a lot of time staring at a wall. I mean, it was hell when it wasn't quiet. But I guess it was hell when it was too." I broke the cookie into chunks between my fingers. "I don't know, there were a few highlights. I met Chris."

She smiled. "That's what Jeremy said."

"His cell was next to mine. I don't know if he did that out of kindness, or torture, but..." I trailed off. "I don't know. But he was really levelheaded. I mostly was too, but he was just... So graceful about it all. As bizarre as that sounds."

"Sounds like Chris." Adam smiled.

I smiled back. Then it slowly fell. "He talked about you guys a lot. More than he talked about anything else. He... he said it was nice to get to know what you're like now through me. I'm not sure if you wanted to know that but I think he would want you to know that."

"Of course we want to know that." Hannah clutched my hand. I sent her a quick smile. Then I looked back down.

I stared at the cookie in my hands, thinking about how he should have been in that room too. He should've been "fucking up" a buckeye as I chomped on my cookie. I wanted to smile at that memory of him, but I couldn't.

Just a few weeks prior, I sat in a cell, swearing to him that I'd get him out. Swearing to him he could tell his family everything he wanted to when we got out of there. I listened to him tell a sweet anecdote for each of them, begging me to give them each the message if he wasn't able to get it to them himself.

And there I sat, surrounded by them, yet completely silent. I could remember what he wanted me to tell them, but it wasn't there in my conscious mind. It would have been a beautiful moment to tell them all how much he loved them and the sweet little personalized message for each of them. But I couldn't find the words.

"Hey, are you okay?" Hannah laid her hand on my thigh.

"Yeah, I'm sorry." I sat up straight. "Chris is..." We were going to find him one day, and they had to know what to expect when we did. "He's a lot like you described. At least, his character is. But he's..." I chewed my lip. "He's vastly different than the person you remember."

Brody quietly chimed in. "I couldn't see that great when I saw him, but..." I looked up to meet his gaze. "His eyes..."

"Yeah. He's blind."

Leah's jaw dropped. "What? What happened?"

"It was a long time ago, I guess. Shortly after he was taken. Peterson was studying teleportation and hypothesized that teleporters couldn't teleport if they couldn't see where they were going. It obviously didn't make an impact on his abilities but..."

"They took out his eyes?" Brody murmured from the foot of the bed.

I didn't even know how to respond. So I stared at my cookie and nodded.

Leah cleared her throat. "Peterson," she said. I looked up and met her gaze. "Who is that?"

"Doctor Robert Peterson." My tongue ran along my teeth. "I wish I knew more about him than I do, but that's all I really know. At least, as far as things that would help us track him down go."

"You know *nothing* else about him?" Leah asked.

I had to think for a moment, unsure of how to respond. "He's a sadist. He's insane. He's infatuated with the Fae, the Elites especially, and yours truly in particular." My thumb and forefinger broke off a piece of my cookie. I raised it to my lips. "He's too much of a pussy to murder, but he gets a fucking kick out of seeing us do it."

"Is that who..." Brody began quietly.

"Who what?"

Brody swallowed hard. Adam looked away, and Hannah glanced down.

My stomach sunk. They knew too.

I looked at Jeremy sleeping against my shoulder. I was about to wake him up just to punch him in the face.

But Leah closed her eyes. "I was in Jeremy's head the night that it happened. I wasn't thinking. It kind of slipped."

Licking my teeth, I felt my brows fall. "Really wasn't any of your business to blurt to the public, Leah."

Her eyes turned down. "I know. I'm sorry."

"She couldn't really cover it up," Adam said. "Her reaction to Jeremy's thoughts made it pretty clear what had happened. We already knew what face she made when he felt them torture you and it wasn't the same."

I couldn't make them unknow it. And the bite at my neck made it pretty clear anyway.

I broke another corner off my cookie. "Yeah, Brody. Peterson's the one who raped me."

It was bizarre how the word sent a shock through the room. Nearly everyone grimaced in their own way. Hannah, a pull at the center of her brows. Adam, a hard swallow. Leah, an absent-minded shake of the head. Brody, a gaze of sympathy tied up in disgust.

"Is that a typical thing he does?" Leah asked quietly.

"I only knew one other girl in there, but it didn't happen to her. And the OB was pretty shocked when I told her. So, I guess it's not his typical method of torture." I chewed my cookie. "Seemed to be a heat of the moment thing for him."

"Then why did he?" Brody asked.

"What does rape always boil down to?" I asked.

"Power," Leah muttered.

"Control. Dominance." I reached into the box of baked goods and pulled out yet another cookie. "Whatever you want to call it. One of the only ways he had left to hurt me."

"Sick fuck," Brody said.

"To put it mildly," I muttered. "He was... " I paused, trying to find a way to say the words aloud. "I think he really believes that he's in love with me."

Leah made a face. "What do you mean?"

"I don't know. It's hard to explain. It's all kind of a blur right now," I said. "He said things about Jeremy, and our baby... He said I was his. And then I..." Tears welled in my eyes and phantom pains soared through my lower abdomen. "I'm sorry, I don't want to talk about this, guys."

"I'm sorry, I shouldn't have brought it up," Brody said.

"No, it's okay. Just kind of a lot right now."

"We should probably get going anyway, Lai," Adam said. He pulled on a smile. "We'll be back in the morning though."

"Sure. I think I want to get a shower anyway. I miss shampoo."

Hannah chuckled. "I had Jeremy grab some of yours when he left so you don't have to use that icky hospital kind."

"Any soap is better than no soap," I said. "But thank you."

"And I'll bring you your favorite coffee when we come in the morning. And breakfast. Oh, and Celena and Kai. I didn't want to wake them earlier but—"

"That sounds great, Han." I smiled. "Thank you, but you don't need to do all of that."

"You'd do it for me." She leaned down and wrapped her arms around me.

Adam approached with a quick side hug. "You better not die before I see you again."

I smiled. "I don't plan on dying any time soon."

"Well, everything else might suck, but at least there's that."

I laughed as Leah got between us. She put her arms around my shoulders. "I really am so glad you're back."

It meant a lot to hear her say that. I knew she was. But hearing her say it felt good.

I grasped her narrow shoulders in a hug. "You have no idea."

"Don't ever disappear on us again." She pulled away and wagged a finger.

"I'm not going anywhere but home."

"I'll see you guys in the morning, okay?" Brody said beside Leah.

"We'll be here." I smiled and reached my arms upward for the hug he was too embarrassed to initiate. His smile lifted to a more legitimate grin. He leaned down, put his arms around me, and kissed the top of my head. "I'm so happy you're okay."

I forced a smile. "Me too."

As they disappeared, and my gaze caught on my shadowy reflection in the window, I had to wonder.

Was I happy that I was okay? Not really. Yeah, a big part of me was grateful that I was alive.

But I didn't have my baby. I didn't have Chris. And over a hundred people were still missing.

It was a failed mission if I'd ever seen one.

I did have something that made life feel a little bit worth living.

I turned my gaze back to Jeremy and his arm still wrapped around me. Not resting, but literally still grasping my hip. He was out cold, and still, unable to let me go. I guess I would have felt the same way if the roles were reversed.

My hand raised to his cheek. I cupped it gently. I ran my thumb against his beard, enjoying the warmth of his body radiating toward my skin. I'd been far too cold for far too long. I missed the way his body felt against mine more than anything.

I missed it almost as much as I missed normal clothes.

The kind that didn't leave my skin raw where the seams had rubbed or a rash between my thighs where they met. The kind that smelled like roses and daisies instead of bleach and other sanitizing agents. The kind with soft fleece instead of little over washed lint balls.

The doctors said they wanted to keep an eye on me for a few more days, which I'd reluctantly agreed to. But I'd be damned before I spent that time in another hospital gown.

I gently moved Jeremy's hand from my hip and slowly began to sit up. Then he sprung forward. "What's wrong?"

I turned and met his droopy red eyes. I gave a smile and pushed hair behind his ear. "I just want to get a shower and change into those clothes you brought me."

"Do you need help?" He sat the rest of the way up.

"Baby, why would I need help with a shower?"

He blinked hard a few times, still exhausted and disoriented. "Right. I'm sorry."

"It's okay." I smiled. "Just get some rest. I'll be back in a couple minutes."

He laid his head back to the pillow and gazed at me under heavy eyelids. As I reached down to grab the bag, I still felt his eyes on me.

I looked up with an awkward grin. "What?"

His lips pulled at the edges a bit. "You're just beautiful."

I laughed. "I look like I'm dead."

He bit his grinning lip, shaking his head against the fluffy white pillow. "You're beautiful."

One of the many reasons I loved that man. No matter how awful I looked, he always made me feel pretty. Even though I definitely looked dead.

I smiled. I leaned down to press my lips to his. "I love you."

"I love you too." His deep, raspy voice was softer than it'd ever been. "Just call for me if you need me."

I laughed. "I'm walking, like, six feet away from you. I'm fine, Jeremy."

"But if you do."

I gave a smile and turned to the bathroom. As I made it through the doorway, I faced the small, tile hospital shower. But when I turned to the mirror—as one reflexively does when they enter a bathroom—I nearly dropped my bag.

My stomach sunk.

It was the first time I'd really seen myself since it all started.

A different person stared back at me. I didn't recognize her. She was cold and tortured. Her big, round green eyes were pulled down by dark blue bags. Her cheeks were hollowed in toward her tongue. Her cheekbones looked higher than ever before. Her jaw line was so sharp it could cut glass.

Her throat and arms were littered with scary, painful scars. Her bones poked from beneath her skin like it could rip the flesh to shreds. Her tiny shoulders hung low toward her stomach as she stood like she had no spine.

She was me. But she wasn't me.

How could just over three months turn me into her?

I was planning on leaving the door open as I showered, but I was in tears then and didn't want Jeremy to see me cry. I gently pushed it shut. My eyes washed over myself in the mirror a minute longer. I walked closer, pulling the gown down at my neck to see the scar just above my collar bone better.

My mind ran around different ways that I could cover them up.

I can wear long sleeves. It might be a little hot in the summer, but I spend most of my time indoors during the summer anyway. And chokers, I'll be investing in chokers.

I closed my eyes and shook my head, then walked to the shower. I turned the knob to adjust the temperature until it was comfortable. Hot, so hot that steam slithered off of it. Cold showers had been one of the things I hated the most in there. I wanted that water boiling. Then I turned back to the mirror and pulled off the hospital gown.

I was more shocked to see my naked body than my face. I couldn't find a thing on it that looked the way it did before. Not a single thing.

I was a little chubby before. Not very big, just on the larger side of the spectrum than smack dab in the middle. My thighs were jiggly, I had a pouch and love handles above my skinny jeans. But it was never something I felt uncomfortable about. I always liked my body before. I wasn't curvy or thick, but I wasn't skinny either. I was just me.

But now, I fell past skinny into unhealthy. I was clearly malnourished. Before that moment, I hadn't even realized how small my hips really were beneath my chunk. Suddenly, I could make out the shape of every bone beneath my skin.

My ribs were like speed bumps in a parking lot. For the first time in my life, I had a gap between my thighs. My poor chicken legs appeared to be bending in support of my upper half.

Not that any of those things were particularly bad if achieved in a healthy way, but it didn't look like me. I looked generally unwell. I looked like I was on my last leg. There's no better word to describe it than deathly.

And the stretch marks.

They brought me to a sob. I stifled it into my palm to keep Jeremy from hearing, but they hurt the worst.

Not because they were ugly. I didn't particularly love the way they looked, but it hurt because they were for nothing. If I had my baby in my arms, I'd love them. But they were going to be a daily reminder of what I'd lost.

Looking at myself felt like I was sliding backwards down a slippery slope that landed me back on that metal table at the bottom of a dark abyss.

I couldn't go back to that table.

So, I looked away and stepped into the shower.

CHAPTER SEVEN

LAILA

Before I went to bed, I thought my biggest problem about adjusting to normal life would be finding clothes that covered my scars. A naïve notion, I suppose. But that was before I had my first nightmare.

In that cell, I didn't have bad dreams. My dreams were almost always good. Sometimes they were about Thanksgiving dinner with my parents before dad died. Sometimes they were about having sex with Jeremy. Sometimes they were about our life with our son. They always brought me to the happier moments. But I guess when you're in hell, you create a version of heaven in your dreams to help you cope with reality.

Once you're out, nothing terrifies you more than going back in. And even when you forget about it for a while, that fear is always living in a little box inside your mind. It's like the moment that you close your eyes, that little box creaks open and the fear escapes.

I didn't even remember the dream, not really. His face was clear. The terror as he cut my wrist open was as vivid as the day it happened, but the dream itself was a fuzzy mess. All that I remembered was being afraid.

When I awoke, I had a hard time telling what was real and what wasn't. I heard someone saying my name but I couldn't absorb the flames in my hands. Not until I smelled burnt flesh, felt his pain, and heard him say, "Baby, it was a dream. It was a dream. It's okay, you're okay."

I blinked through the darkness in an attempt to make out what was unfolding in front of me. The only light in the room came from my palms and the blinking monitors. I gazed at my violet flames. My heart raced, watching Jeremy's hand raise to mine. He touched his hand to my flaming fingers and gently threaded his through mine.

I jumped backward, shaking my head. Smoke ascended from his skin as my hand burned from his pain. I tried to yank my hand back, but he held it tighter. "It's okay, Lai—"

"I'm so sorry. Oh my god, I'm so sorry. I didn't mean to—"

"It's okay."

"No." Tears beading down my cheeks, I took his fingers in mine and held a white light over it to heal the still smoking flesh. "I'm so sorry. I didn't mean to do that. I—I was just—"

"Laila." He gently took my face in his hands. "Baby, I'm okay."

"I hurt you." My chest grew heavy and my breaths came out in short, hyperventilating gasps. "I could have killed you. I didn't mean to hurt you."

"Shh," he whispered. "It's okay. I'm okay, Laila. I'm okay."

"I didn't mean to—"

"I know. Come here," he whispered, holding his arms out for me. As I collapsed into his chest, nuzzling my head into his shirt, he hugged me tight. "It's okay."

"I'm sorry," I whispered again. "I'm so sorry."

I'm not sure why it bothered me so much. It's not like it was the first time I'd accidentally burned him. Maybe it was because I'd already hurt him so much over the last few months. Maybe it was because I'd killed so many people, so quickly, at that compound and I was terrified I could do that to him without realizing what I'd done. The burns always hurt before, but that day, my fire incinerated on contact. I could've killed him so fast. I could've woken up to a pile of ash beside me.

"It's okay." He soothed my damp hair and held me close. "Everything's okay."

I tightened my arms around his neck.

A light turned on and a voice said, "Is everyone okay in here?"

Jeremy pulled back. I turned to the nurse. "Yeah, we're fine."

She looked between us. "We heard screaming, what happened?"

I looked away and wiped my watering eyes. Fuck, I needed out of there. I knew that I was a mess, I knew that I'd be a mess for a long time. But it was bad enough Jeremy had to see that. I didn't want the whole world to.

Jeremy looked to me and then the nurse. "Just a bad dream. Everything's fine, thank you."

"Are you sure?" she asked.

I gave a nod, avoiding her eyes. She walked toward me and lowered herself to try and meet my gaze. I knew she was trying to be nice, but I was embarrassed. I just wanted to be left alone.

"Do you want me to see if we can get something to help you sleep?" she asked.

"No. Thank you."

"We could just get you a low dose of—"

"No," I said, firmer that time. "I don't want anything. I'm fine. Thank you."

She hovered a few inches before my face, eyes burning into the side of my head. When she realized I wouldn't meet them, she raised herself back up. She turned to Jeremy. "Just let us know if you need anything."

"We'll be fine," Jeremy said. "Thank you."

She headed from the room. I heard the door shut behind her and pulled a gust of wind through to prop it back open.

Jeremy put his hand on my back, gently sliding up and down. "Are you okay?"

I nodded, staring out the window. The sun was turning the sky an orangish gray in the distance. I was tired of looking at the sun through a sheet of glass. It was better than the foggy, glass block one, but it was still like being in a cage.

His thumb moved just a little too slowly and caught a second longer than I liked on a large scar on my back. With a grimace, I pushed his hand away.

"I'm sorry," he murmured.

"Don't apologize."

In the windows reflection, I saw him fumble with his hands. He'd reach forward and then pull them back. He wanted to comfort me and didn't know how.

What I'd been through was as hard on him as it was for me. I knew that. And I hated that it hurt him. I hate that *I* hurt him.

"You have nothing to apologize for," I said.

"I don't know what to do," he whispered. "Please tell me what to do."

The way those words left his lips made my stomach sink, butterflies dance within it, and my chest tighten. I was hurting him. I didn't want to. I didn't mean to. But I was.

I turned over my shoulder to meet his gaze. Tears bubbled in my eyes. "I don't know what to do either."

Jeremy sat forward, putting one leg was on the ground and curling the other beneath his thigh. He opened his palm and turned it up to me. "Is it okay if I hold your hand?"

Fuck, I hated that he felt like he had to ask. I loved that he did, but I hated that he felt obligated to. He was my fiancé. We'd spent more than the last three years of our lives together.

I gave a small smile, blinking away the water that formed in my eyes. His hand found mine. He looked up and smiled back.

I leaned my head into his hand, shaking it a bit. "I'm pathetic."

"No," he said. "No, you're amazing. You're just going through something awful. It's gonna be okay though, you just need time. That's all. You're gonna be okay."

It didn't feel like I was ever going to be okay. "I don't feel like myself."

"You don't have to. Not after what you've been through."

He was right, I knew that. But it sucked.

Every time I fantasized about getting out, I didn't think about this. I felt powerless in there, and I thought that as soon as I got out, I'd feel strong again. But I didn't. I felt small, and useless, and *scared.*

Scared of hurting him. Scared for the people I didn't get out. Scared of ending up back inside.

I was just so *scared.*

More tears invaded my eyes. I nodded once more.

He frowned and gently caressed my cheek. "You're gonna be okay."

I wasn't sure I believed that. I didn't think I'd ever be okay again. I didn't think I'd ever be the happy, bubbly waitress he fell for again. I wasn't even sure if he could love the person I'd become.

"Who are you trying to convince? Me or you?" I asked.

"I know you're going to be fine." His voice softened, tinging with hope. "You can make it through anything, Laila Callidy."

Tears welled in my eyes once more. But I smiled, and he smiled back. Then I looked down and grew quiet for a moment. "I really didn't mean to burn you."

He laughed. "I'm fine, baby."

I looked down at our hands against that scratchy hospital blanket. It was better than none at all, but I wanted mine. I should have told him to grab one. It was on the list of first things I'd do when I got home, but I'd almost forgotten what that list consisted of. I couldn't forget the most important thing of all.

I turned back up. "When do you think I can go home?"

"I'm not sure, we'll have to check with the doctor."

"I want to go home."

"I know," he said. "I'll talk to the doctor when he gets in, okay?"

For a second, I felt trapped all over again. I knew that wasn't his fault. And I knew no one was trying to hurt me. But I needed to be at home. I needed my couch, and my bed, and my blankets.

"I'm fine, Jeremy. Really, I'm okay. And either way, I'm allowed to check myself out at any time." I spoke quickly. "*I need to go home.*"

His thumb brushed my cheek. "Of course you can, baby. And you will. But you're safe here, no one's going to hurt you."

I anxiously tapped my feet, as though preparing to bolt out of that door. "I'm glad I'm not there anymore, but I don't want to be here either. I want to go *home*."

He wasn't responsible for this, I knew that. But I needed out. I needed comfort and the smell of coffee and eucalyptus. I needed to hear Max banging around in the kitchen downstairs. I couldn't be locked up again, and that's how this felt.

"I know, Lai, I want that too. And you can. But you just started breathing on your own a few hours ago. We have to make sure you're okay, alright?"

My gaze slid from him to the door. "I'm okay. I'm fine, I just—"

"Please." He gently cupped my cheek. "Let's just make sure you're okay."

He didn't add a "For me?" but his face did. And I'd put him through enough already. I knew I was fine physically but if he needed to hear a professional okay it, then I'd concede.

I swallowed hard, and Jeremy gave my hand a squeeze. "How about we go sit outside again? Would that be better?"

Just the thought made my belly flip. Suddenly, I remembered something else from the list. And as soon as I did, a craving unlike anything flooded over me.

"And maybe get some coffee?" I asked. "I really want coffee."

<hr>

The soft morning scent of dew filled my nose. I lifted my knees onto the stone barrier of the hospital's retaining wall, resting my head against the cool building. I didn't appreciate cold, but this was nice. Cold, but warmed with humidity. Beautiful orange and pinkish rays shined against the green grass of the field, pretty blue morning glories spreading their blooms for the early birds.

"Be careful." Jeremy handed me a small styrofoam cup. "It's really hot, I almost burned the shit out of myself."

I smirked. "Takes a lot to burn me."

His brows pulled together over his smile. "Obviously, huh? I'm sorry, I don't know why I said that."

"I didn't realize I was that easy to forget." I gave a playful smile, pulling my hands into the sleeves of Jeremy's hoody and lifting the coffee to my lips.

I took my first sip. It was diluted, cheap hospital coffee. Probably the worst in the country, yet at that moment, it was the best coffee I ever had.

"Things would've been a lot easier if you were."

"Ouch." I grinned. "That sounded like it *could* have been a compliment."

He paused, retracing his words. Then his eyes widened a little. "It was definitely intended as a compliment." He shook his head. "I'm sorry, I don't know why I'm being like this."

"You're like a fourteen-year-old boy on his first date." My grin widened. "It's kinda cute."

A half laugh left him. "It's just surreal."

"Can't say I disagree."

He smiled, but something about it looked sad. "I feel like I'm meeting a new version of you."

I swallowed my sip of coffee and set it down on the retaining wall. "Well, I think it'd be fair to say I'm not the same as I was before I was taken. So, I guess you kind of are."

He was quiet for a moment. "Before you go home, you're going to need to know some things."

"Uh-oh." I picked up my coffee. "That doesn't sound promising."

He rubbed his eyes again. "We had to involve the police when you went missing. I was against it, but Hannah was injured, and Daniel was dead, so we had to file a missing person's report to cover our asses."

"Yeah, kind of figured. It'd be too hard to explain why I just dropped off the face of the earth. Especially with Moe's and everything. And you knew I wasn't dead, but you didn't know how long I'd be gone or if I was coming back. You had to do what you had to do."

His gaze hardened. "I knew you were coming back."

I smiled. "Just go on."

He gave a bare smile. But it fell as he continued, "Your face was on everything. It still is. You went viral."

"Oof." I raised my coffee and took a sip.

"Hannah had a fundraiser in your honor, and I performed in it."

I grimaced. "Bigger oof."

"I knew you'd say that," he said in a matter of fact, *damn it*, kind of tone.

I laughed. "No, I'm sure it was sweet. But big oof."

It was just a weird concept for me. Couldn't have gone viral for something cute or funny. Had to be my kidnapping.

"The money went to some human trafficking organization or something though."

"Super awkward, but that's cool. So I guess that means I'm going to have to lie to a cop."

"Yeah, pretty much. But Ray said it was the same FBI agent that interviewed me, and she was really nice."

"FBI?" I asked. "It got that much attention?"

"Well, yeah. Pretty, twenty-one-year-old, pregnant, white girl goes missing and the whole East Coast loses their shit. The kidnapping itself scared the shit out of a lot of people after what happened to Daniel and everything. You were just fostering some kid and then... Yeah, it's been a big deal."

I took another gulp of my coffee and turned down to it. "She's going to ask about the baby."

Silence fell between us. I felt his gaze on me. But I stared intently at the lid of my coffee cup. I shouldn't have said that. I'm not sure why I did. It was the first thought that came to mind, and as usual for my dumb ass, it just spilled right out of my lips.

"Lai."

"Hmm." I fidgeted with a piece of stray plastic on the side of my cup.

I knew what he was about to ask. And he had every right to know. But I couldn't even say Micah's name aloud. I pushed him to the back of my mind because it hurt so much. It hurt like nothing ever hurt before. If I let myself think about it, I'd want to go slit my wrists.

"Can you tell me what happened to the baby?" he whispered.

I shook my head a bit and pulled at the plastic on the lid.

He reached out and gently steadied my hand that shakily held the coffee. I stared down. "I can't talk about it. I want to tell you, but I just can't. Not without falling apart. And I don't want to fall apart right now."

He watched me carefully for a few seconds. I felt his gaze, but I couldn't meet it. I knew how much it hurt him, and I couldn't see that look on his face. I'd want to kill myself if I did.

He lifted the coffee from my fumbling hand and set it down on the cement retaining wall. "It's okay."

It wasn't okay. It really fucking wasn't.

He moved his hand to mine, just barely touching our skin. "Can I ask you one thing though?" he whispered.

He had to know. I hated myself for it, but he had the right to know. If the roles were reversed, I'd expect at least that much.

So, I looked up to meet his desperate gaze.

"Is he gone?" he asked.

His gaze was full of hope. As if I was hiding him away somewhere in my feeble body. As if he didn't feel me birth him. And when I saw that expression, I just crumbled.

My lip quivered, and my throat tightened. Tears rapidly poured from my eyes. But I managed a nod.

His eyes filled with water too. He wrapped his arms tight around my shoulders, pulling my suddenly trembling body against his in a tight embrace.

"I'm sorry," I whispered, hardly audible through my sobs. "I'm so sorry."

He held me closer, shaking his head. "Don't apologize. It's not your fault."

I almost hated how understanding he was. I loved it, but he shouldn't have been. He should have hated me. *I* hated me.

It *was* my fault.

CHAPTER EIGHT

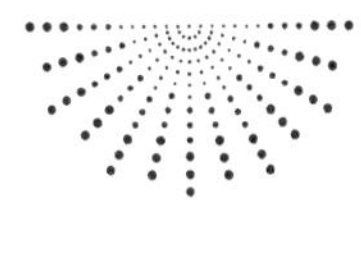

LAILA

A knock sounded at the doorway. Then a middle-aged woman peeped her head around the hallway beside the door.

"Hello." She gave a gentle smile. "Are you Laila Callidy?"

"That's me."

She started across the room carrying a messenger bag over her shoulder. "It's a pleasure to finally meet you. I've heard so much, it's nice to put a name to a face."

Hadn't been exactly looking forward to this moment. But I'd hoped Jeremy would've been there when it happened. However, my hopes rarely became reality.

She did seem nice though. There was a sweetness in her warm brown eyes. But a sweetness like mine. You could tell she'd seen some shit. Probably killed a couple people. But still, a gentleness. Not quite motherly, but kind regardless.

"And I've heard close to nothing about you." I stood, holding my smile. "Are you the FBI agent Jeremy was talking about?"

She extended her palm. "Tina Davis."

"Laila Callidy." I shook her hand. "Nice to meet you."

"Oh, no. Please, the pleasure is all mine." She gently lowered herself to the chair beside the bed. I sat down and dangled my legs off the edge. "Can I be honest with you, Laila?"

"Hmm?"

"I was worried you'd be another one we never found. Although, I guess we didn't find you, did we?" she asked.

"I guess not." My eyes wandered to the table near the bed where a small bag of chocolate candy sat. I grabbed it, sat them on my lap, pulled one out, and unraveled it. "Do you want one?"

"No, I'm okay," she said. "Thank you."

"Are you sure?" I extended one toward her. "Not gonna lie, it feels a little weird eating in front of people these days. I have plenty."

She smiled and extended her hand. "Sure, thank you."

I didn't love talking to cops. But I was good at it. I made them feel comfortable. I had a sweet smile and a friendly face, even when I looked like I was dying. I knew it and I used it. Not that I prided myself in it, but I've always been a pretty good liar. I knew just how to dance around the truth enough to make my lies sound believable.

I popped the chocolate into my mouth. "So, where do we start?"

"Wherever you'd like."

"I'd rather not talk about any of it, really."

"Unfortunately, I'm not sure that's an option."

"Be pretty cool if it was."

She chuckled. "In a perfect world."

I chewed on the chocolate for a minute. Where *was* a good place to start? When I got in the van? When I woke up in the cell? When he gave me the scars?

"I really don't know where to begin."

Tina sat forward. "Maybe at the beginning. Maybe how Lydia Ramirez ended up in all of this."

Definitely not where I wanted to start.

I licked my teeth. "That."

"That seems important."

"What did Ray tell you? Because, that."

She laughed. "It doesn't work that way."

"Well, Ray and I started developing a friendship after he investigated my friend's murder. We started talking about different things and over time, his family came up. Then Jeremy's brother came up, and… We just started doing some research. Nothing notable, anyway. Not really. But right after we found something, Daniel showed up. We didn't know for sure if the two were related then."

Like I said. I danced around the truth. Didn't lie. Nothing I said was untrue. It just wasn't the *whole* truth.

She clicked her pen and opened up her notebook. "And you know that they are now?"

"My little getaway tied up a lot of loose ends," I muttered. "It's complicated. It's all kind of a blur now, anyway."

"Do you remember the night you were taken?" she asked.

"I remember *being* taken. I don't remember the trip. They shot me up with benzos. Said it was safer for the baby. I don't know how I got in there. I have no recollection of the transportation itself."

"So, you remember what happened to Daniel and your fiancé's sister?" she asked.

"Yeah, I remember every second of it."

"Can you describe it to me?"

I looked up and furrowed my brows. "What—To confirm Hannah's story?"

"We're just checking on loose ends of our own," she said.

I ran my tongue along my teeth. It pissed me off. I didn't want to repeat what had happened. But whatever. The sooner I could get her to leave me alone, the better.

"Somebody cut us off and then slammed on the brakes. I rear ended them, we crashed. I got out. They pulled a gun on me and forced Hannah and Daniel out." I grabbed another candy and fiddled with the wrapper. "They said they'd let the two of them go if I got in their car. And I saw them put the knife down from Daniel's throat, and he let Hannah go, so I got in and then, like just as the door shut… I saw them snap Daniel's neck. I was screaming, and then it kind of just faded away."

I couldn't let myself think about it too hard. Maybe breaking down to that agent would have helped my story. But I refused to fall apart in front of her. I had to stay strong. If I didn't, I'd fall into a nasty pit I had no clue how to climb out of.

She scribbled in her note pad. "What happened after that?"

"I don't remember."

"Well, what *do* you remember?" she asked.

"I don't know."

Every detail was permanently etched into my brain. Every cut and whip, each needle prick, every now-healed wound. There was a memory attached to every permanent mark left on my body as well as the ones that didn't leave a scar at all. But I had no idea how to say it out loud, especially to a human.

Tina chewed the inside of her cheek. She shifted in her chair as I fiddled with the silver aluminum wrapper in my hand. "Laila, I understand that you've been through a lot. But if you don't tell me what happened, I can't help."

"You can't help any way." I ironed the wrapper between my fingertips. "You guys didn't even find us. You didn't get us out."

"Let's talk about that then."

"I'd rather not."

"Can you tell me about the abuse then?"

I huffed. "What about it?"

"The scars have made it abundantly clear that the abuse was constant and calculated," she said. "But we'd like to have more detail to go on to build a better case against the people responsible."

"He called them stress tests," I chewed on my cheek and opened another candy. "Every few days, they'd drug us, and we'd wake up in the testing room. He hooked up wires and monitors to our heads, and our chests." I paused. "They put a shit ton on my belly to monitor the baby too."

"And then he'd torture you?"

"Not him. Peterson stayed in some room nearby and watched. He'd chime in over the intercom sometimes, but he was never in the room."

"Peterson?" She wrote in her pad. "Is that who was in charge?"

"Doctor Robert Peterson. I don't know if that's his real name, but that's what he told me it was. Seems pretty common though so I doubt you'll be able to track him down by it even if it is the real thing."

"Okay, we'll come back to that. Who was torturing you while he watched?" she asked.

"Lots of different people. They were, like, guards or something? I don't know. I never even saw their faces. They were just pawns."

She continued scribbling. "So, what do you know about the doctor?"

"More than I want to and nothing that will help."

"You'd be amazed at the things that could help." Her eyes shifted over me.

"I don't know, I really don't know much about him. He... He was confusing. I don't know, it's hard to explain. He wasn't innately evil. I mean, he was awful. But I don't think he was evil. He... He wanted something from us. I don't really know what but..." I took another breath and rubbed my eyes. "God, it's hard to explain."

"Why don't we talk about his appearance? What did he look like?"

"He has a friendly face. You wouldn't expect him to be who he is. He has a big smile, sweet eyes." His face flashed behind my eyelids and my stomach clenched. "Early middle aged, maybe mid to late forties. I can't see him being more than fifty. White, dark hair, dark eyes." I closed my eyes. "Salt and pepper hair. Sometimes he was clean shaved, others he had some scruff, but never a beard. Geeky looking, but not hideous. Attractive, actually. He doesn't look like the type of person he is. You'd think... If you saw him walking down the street, you'd think he was respectable. You might even wish he'd ask you on a date."

"That's not uncommon for guys like him," she murmured. "Would you be willing to give a more detailed description to a sketch artist?"

"Yeah. Sure."

She looked up from her papers and met my gaze. "You said they gave you benzodiazepines?"

"They used them like a sedative. I guess what they gave everyone else wasn't safe for the baby. Once I... when I wasn't pregnant anymore, he made a comment. 'Trazodone, beautiful drug.'"

"He cared about the baby?" she asked. I fought the tears that began to sting my eyes. I nodded. "Laila, what happened to him?" I shook my head, tears lodging in my throat.

Tina grabbed a tissue from the side table and handed it to me. I lifted it to my face and wiped my eyes. "Did they kill him?"

"They didn't have to," I whispered. "He didn't cry."

"When he was born?" She sat on the bed beside me. "Can we talk about that?"

I shook my head and unwrapped another candy. Fuck, I didn't want to talk about this. I either wanted my baby in my arms, or I wanted to pretend it never happened. One or the other. But I guess she had to know.

"How far along were you?"

"Just after thirty-one weeks. Or thirty-two, maybe." That was actually the first lie I'd told. Everything else was an omission. He was born less than ten days prior, on June 22, 2019. "I don't know."

"Was anyone with you?" she asked softly.

"Just me. Well, Haley was in her cell across from mine and Chris was in the one beside mine. But I was alone in my cell," I said. "Maybe I should have called for help. Maybe he would have lived. I don't know."

"What happened after he was born?" she asked.

I licked my teeth. "I don't know. I started bleeding. A lot of bleeding. And I... I don't know. I fainted, I guess. Then I woke up tied to a table a few days later."

"What happened then?" she asked.

"Peterson told me how sorry he was," I muttered. "He... I don't know."

"It's okay, take your time," she murmured.

"He told me I should have called for help. That Micah would still be here if I had." I sucked my teeth. "Actually, he said that *our* son would still be here if I had."

"What do you mean?"

My sorrow started to morph into fury. I had to close my eyes and recollect myself to make sure they didn't glow. "He said that a lot. That it was his baby. That I was *his*," I said. "He talked about Jeremy sometimes, almost like he was trying to make himself sound better than him. Like he was trying to talk himself up."

"So, he knew things about you."

"They'd been watching me. He knew all kinds of things he couldn't have unless they had."

She stared at me for a moment, watching for my reaction. "Would you say that you were special to him?"

"You could say that."

"Were there any other types of assault?" she asked.

"That's one way to put it."

She fell silent. I popped another candy into my mouth. Didn't really want to have this conversation either, but maybe it wasn't a bad thing for the FBI to know. "I don't think he did it often, if ever before me."

"What makes you say that?" she asked.

"I don't know. He made comments sometimes, things about us being a family and all kinds of weird shit." I licked my dry lips. "That day, the day that he um..." A lump started to form in my throat and I cleared it away. "I got shot because I managed to get out of the restraints during one of the stress tests. He seemed to feel... Almost guilty for it. The shooting, I mean, but I—I was livid. Everything hurt and I... When I woke up after they fixed up my bullet wound... I don't know, I just wanted out. I just wanted to get out, even if that meant he killed me. My smart mouth started going. I don't even remember what I said now, but I was... I was egging him on. I wanted to hurt him, even if it was just with words. I just, I wanted him to hurt too."

She handed me another tissue. Funny, I hadn't realized my eyes were watering. I took it and wiped them again.

"I said something about how worthless he was, or something like that. I don't know," I muttered. "I told him that I'd never be his, and my son would never be his, and he... It was like some kind of punishment, I guess. He knew it was wrong, even for him. After that, they didn't do the stress tests on me again. He said it was because I was getting too close to the end of my pregnancy, but I think he just didn't want me to go through it anymore."

She studied me carefully for a moment. I felt her heavy eyes on the side of my face. And I opened another candy. "What happened after that?"

"I was beginning to realize that no one was going to find me. So I decided I was going to set myself free. And as many others as I could get. I didn't know how many of us there were at first, but I started paying more attention. I listened to the guards, and the nurses, and I... I just started planning." I took in a slow breath and licked my teeth. "I didn't want to die in there. I didn't want my baby to die in there."

"What was your plan?" she asked quietly.

"I hadn't crossed all the t's and dotted all the i's, but I knew if I could open my cell, I could open Haley's and Chris's. So I did. I managed to crack the door just enough to get out and... I don't know. I... Somehow, I knocked a guard unconscious and got his gun. Then I just remember shooting the hinges off of doors and opening them. But it's all kind of a blur after that."

"The explosion, was that after you made it out?" she asked.

"Maybe. I don't know. It was... It was happening in slow motion and instant replay at the same time, if that makes any sense."

"It does. Is there anything you can think of that might help us find him?"

"He's a genius. I'm sure he had a backup plan in case something like this happened. But maybe he didn't, he was pretty far from modest."

"I do have another question." I looked up to meet her gaze. "Why doesn't Lydia Ramirez have the same scars as the rest of you? On her back, I mean."

"I should really talk to Ray first."

"None of this will be public information, Laila. The case is ongoing, everything you tell me is confidential. And considering the overlap with his family being included in this mess, he's no longer on the case."

"He isn't in trouble, is he?" I asked.

"Not currently."

"Good," I muttered.

"But that does depend on the information I gather here today." Her eyes moved over me. "I don't think he did anything wrong. But I need to know how she ties into this. Why she stands out."

"He didn't do anything wrong. He just wanted to find his family."

"I believe you. But it has to look believable on paper too and the little girl isn't talking. Do you know why Lydia wasn't tortured like the rest of you?" she asked.

I hated Amy. But she was his wife. And if I had to incriminate someone, I'd rather it be her than him.

"I think you do, Laila. And I need to know."

"Amy... I think she had Stockholm's or something," I muttered. "She... She worked with him."

"What do you mean?"

"She referred to him as her family. She got to wear normal clothes, and she wore makeup, and she ate real food. She had her own little apartment, and..." I closed my eyes at the memory. "There was a window in her apartment that overlooked the stress test room." Tina's mouth fell open. "I think he gave her the same spiel he gave me. *You're mine*, or whatever. I don't know. But I do know that Ray and Lydia are innocent in all of this. I know that for a fact."

Her eyes moved between mine, as if scanning them for a lie. Then she scribbled in her pad for a long moment. "I'll be in contact as more questions arise, but in the meantime, if you think of anything that might help, please give me a call." She tore out the long sheet of notebook paper with her name, phone number, and email address on it. "But I think you should get some counseling. You may not realize it yet but adjusting to normal life again won't be easy. Don't be afraid to ask for help."

Probably a good idea. Was I gonna do it? Probably not.

"Sure. Thanks," I muttered.

"Please, don't be afraid to ask for help, Laila. You're not alone anymore."

CHAPTER NINE

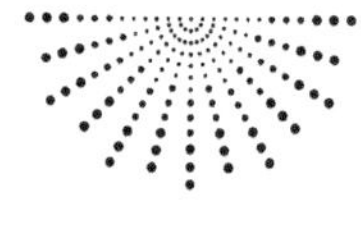

LAILA

My head rested against the cushy pillow. Jeremy's arm twisted around the back of my neck. I fidgeted with a hole on his shirt. It was so soft. Familiar. And it smelled like home.

He gazed down at me, twirling a piece of my hair between his fingertips, smiling. I turned to face him better. With a laugh, I said, "What?"

"You're just beautiful."

"Shut up." I rolled my eyes and laid my head back onto his shoulder.

"What do you mean?" He tilted my chin up to meet his gaze.

My eyes met his, and I laughed. "I look awful."

"You're beautiful."

I rolled my eyes and I turned back down. Sweet, but a lie. I'd seen myself. I was beautiful once, but I wasn't now. Cute that he still thought so though.

"Laila," I heard from the door. The sound of her voice brought an instant smile to my lips. Then I raised my head and met her gaze.

She smiled back, but tears poured from her green eyes when she looked me over. I got it. I would have cried if I saw my baby in the shape I was in too. But I just held my smile because she needed to know that I was okay.

"Hey, Mom."

She darted across the room, put her arms around my back, and held me tighter than I knew she was capable of. "Baby," she whispered. "God, I missed you so much. I was so worried."

"I'm okay, Mom." I squeezed her shoulders. Then I saw my sister, the one that I was raised with, meander in from the hall.

"Jenna." I smiled over Mom's shoulder. She started to cry. She hurried across the room to me in less than a second. Then she joined in on the hug.

"Hey, sissy." Her arms overlapped Mom's around my shoulders.

My big sister. My sweet, bitchy big sister. I hadn't thought much about what my capture had done to her. She'd only crossed my mind a handful of times in there. We hadn't been close since we were very young. But that "sissy" made me feel like the little girl I used to be. It almost brought tears to my eyes.

"Leah said you weren't doing good." Mom pulled back a bit while I hugged Jenna a moment longer. Then she leaned back too, gripping my shoulders, eyeing me carefully. "You look okay though. I mean, you look like shit, but you look okay."

"Thanks." I laughed, shoving her shoulder. "I wasn't, I guess. But I'm okay now."

"She woke up last night," Jeremy said. "Just started breathing on her own and everything."

"I'm alright. Don't really understand it all, but I'm okay."

Jenna's eyes grazed over me in either fear or pity. I couldn't quite tell. Her blue eyes traveled over my scars and I watched as questions started to spin behind them.

Fuck, I hated that look. I should've told Jeremy to bring me a turtle neck, damn it.

I cleared my throat and turned to Jeremy. "Could you go get me another cup of coffee, baby?"

He kissed my cheek and started to his feet. "Sure. I'll be right back."

I smiled at him. Mom sat beside me on the bed, Jenna sat at the foot. Her eyes were practically cemented to the scar at the base of my neck. I touched it, and she looked away with a shake of her head. "Sorry, I wasn't trying to stare."

Everyone else had been watching me with a tube down my throat. The initial shock of how I looked now had worn off. But Jenna was seeing the new me for the first time. And as she did, a realization dawned on me. If my big sister who'd known me all my life stared, so would everyone else. I was going to have to get used to it.

I forced a smile. "It's okay. I know it's hard to look at."

"No. It isn't…"

I smiled again. "It's okay, Jen."

A few heartbeats of silence passed. "What happened to you?"

I looked down and my smile faded. The reality was, I couldn't tell her. She couldn't know everything. She didn't even know what I was, she couldn't make sense of everything that had happened. And even if she would understand it all, I wasn't ready for that conversation.

"More than I care to talk about."

Mom reached out and took my hand. Her thumb traced over the scar at my wrist for a moment before she squeezed it. "Are you okay, baby?"

I looked up to meet her gaze. Then I plastered a smile against my mouth. "Yeah. I'm okay, Mom."

She glanced at my stomach and then back to my eyes. I fought the lump in my throat. Another thing I wasn't prepared to talk about. Something I wouldn't be ready to talk about for a very long time.

I just shook my head. Her eyes glossed over, and her lip quivered. Then she leaned forward and wrapped her arms around my shoulders. She hugged me tight before pressing her lips to my cheek. I closed my eyes and took in the familiar smell of her laundry detergent and shampoo.

It smelled like home.

I just wanted to go home.

I wanted to erase the past three months and just *go home.*

"So how long until you get out of here?" Jenna asked. She had her back against the bottom of the hospital bed, poking my waist with her foot. "This place is weird."

"The doctor said it shouldn't be long." I sipped my coffee. "They have a small procedure to perform before I'm good to go, but everything looks good. My vitals are stable, I feel normal. They'll release me once it's done."

"The doctors are saying late tonight or early tomorrow," Jeremy said from the chair beside the bed. "Everything else can be done outpatient. Mainly just routine tests."

"What kind of procedure?" Mom asked.

"To remove the trackers," I muttered.

"Trackers?" Jenna's lower eyelids tensed as her lips pulled down at either end. "As in, GPS trackers?"

I gestured to the slit at my throat and wrists. "That's what these are from."

"Jesus," she muttered. "That's gonna hurt."

"It's got to be easier going out than they were coming in. I wonder if they'll be able to cut along the scar that's already there or if I'll have another one."

"They're pretty cool actually." She brought a smile to her lips. "Makes you look like a badass."

I forced a laugh. "I look like a failed suicide attempt."

"No, you don't," Jeremy said. "You're beautiful."

I rolled my eyes and took another sip from my coffee. "You guys don't have to pretend that I look normal. This" —I gestured to my throat and then to the scars over my arms— "these aren't normal."

"They're battle scars," Jeremy said quietly. "They're beautiful. *You're* beautiful."

Beautiful. Beautiful my ass.

That was a cheesy, worn out phrase I would hear frequently for the rest of my life.

It was sweet though. I'd give him that—it was sweet.

I took another gulp from my coffee. "Is this coffee actually half-way decent or did I just *really* miss coffee?"

"Nah." Jenna sipped hers. "It's pretty gross."

"Yeah, it's bad," Jeremy muttered.

I took another sip. "I kinda like it."

Mom's gaze found mine, frowning. "What were you eating in there?"

"I don't know, some nasty mush. When I was too hungry not to eat, anyway."

"That's why you haven't stopped snacking since we got here." Jenna grinned and grabbed a candy from the bag in my lap. "That was probably the hardest part of it all for your fat ass."

"Certainly one of the not-so-great aspects."

Mom smacked her leg and shot her a look. Then Jenna said, "I'm sorry, that was insensitive, huh?"

I smiled. "It's okay."

I heard a knock at the door and turned that way. Quiet steps made it through the little hall. When I saw her face in the light from the window, a big smile pulled at my cheeks. She smiled back.

"So I guess I owe you," she said, turning her cheek my way. "I'm wide open. Come smack me."

"Haley." I grinned and jumped to my feet. I practically ran toward her, taking her in for the first time.

Her black hair was pulled into a messy puff at the back of her head. Her obsidian skin had pale undertones beneath it from the years without sunlight. Her big brown eyes were heavy, filled with grief and guilt between her small ski slope nose above her plump, dry lips.

"I'm so glad you made it out." I wrapped my arms around her narrow shoulders. She squeezed hers around me, holding tighter than anyone else had aside from Jeremy.

"Who's that?" I heard Jenna say quietly behind me.

"A new friend, I think," Jeremy murmured. "We should probably give them some space. Do you guys want to come find a vending machine with me?"

"Sure," Mom said.

I felt Jeremy's hand touch my back as they brushed past us. Once they were gone, I continued hugging Haley until she pulled away.

There were tears in her eyes. "I don't know how he got away from me. He was, he was right behind me. I had his hand, and then everyone started jumping and somehow, we-we just got separated and I-I tried to find him, but he wasn't on the ground with the rest of us and I—I couldn't find him. He was just, he was—"

"It's okay." I forced a smile. "It's okay, Haley."

CHAPTER TEN

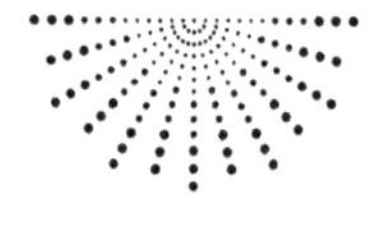

LAILA

"Did it hurt?" I gestured to the gauze on Haley's wrist.

She unwrapped a candy and tossed it in her mouth. "Nothing really hurts any more, you know?"

"That I do."

She was right. I hated that IV in my arm but only because it was a PTSD trigger. I hated the feel as they hooked a vial to it and extracted my blood, but only because it reminded me of Peterson. I hated it all. But it didn't hurt. The only thing that hurt, then, was inside of me. Physical pain didn't feel the way it used to.

"You really scared us, you know," she said. "Not waking up after you were healed and everything."

"I didn't realize I was asleep. I just thought all of this shit was a bad dream."

"I've had the same one."

I grabbed another candy from the bag. "I haven't really grasped the whole being out thing yet." I dropped the chocolate to my tongue. "I just keep thinking I'm going to wake up on that table, ya know?"

"It doesn't feel real yet. I don't know if it ever will. Maybe once we're home though." Haley twiddled the wrapper between her fingertips. "I don't know how the hell you pulled it off, but somehow, you did it."

"Not really."

"You got two hundred of us out, Laila." Her serious gaze moved between mine. "You saved us. You're a hero."

"Not all of us." I swallowed the chocolate. "I'm no hero."

"Try telling that to all the survivors. They want to meet you, you know. Everybody keeps talking about the girl that rescued them. They want to meet their savior."

I laughed. "I'm not Jesus."

"You did more for us than he did," she said.

Fair enough. Even I prayed to that fucker in there. But who saved me? Myself.

"I guess so."

"We all wanted to come pay our respects when we thought you were dying, but your man wouldn't let us come in. Said you needed time, or whatever."

I smiled. "Sounds like Jeremy."

"I talked to him in the hallway after they admitted you. I knew it was him because of the look on his face. Like his world was ending. That, and how much he looks like Chris. I mean, aside from..." She shook her head, and I nodded. "It was right after you coded the first time. I told him what you did in there and a little about Chris. You should have seen the look on his face. So proud and heartbroken at the same time. You know, I thought you were being dramatic when you talked about how much you loved each other back there. But then I met him." I laughed. "He's so in love with you that it's almost sad, dude."

I shrugged, still holding my smile. "He's my world."

"You're clearly his too." She grinned. After a moment, her smile began to fall. "Have you told him about Micah?"

"A little bit. He knows he didn't make it." I paused, eyes shifting down. "It's hard to think about."

"And harder to talk about."

"It's easier to talk to you than them."

"They weren't there, you know? They don't get it. They think they do, but…"

"They don't," I said. "I mean, how could they? It's almost too horrible to actually imagine."

"'Til they see the scars," she muttered. "Then everyone looks at you like you're broken."

I let out an ironic laugh. "Like what we went through made us weak or something."

She chuckled. "It's funny, isn't it? Looking at us like we need their pity when we survived their worst nightmares?"

"Definitely a double-edged sword." I laughed. "So, when are you getting out of here?"

"I'm good to go whenever." She sat up. "Just trying to figure out how to get home. Mom's going to piss herself when I show up at her door."

"I could have Jeremy teleport you, if you want."

"No. No, I couldn't ask that."

I laughed. "Don't be ridiculous, it'd only take him a second."

"Really, Laila. After everything you did, I can't—"

"Oh, shut up. I only did what any of us would have done with the opportunity at hand. Just take the damn lift."

"Alright. Thanks."

"Any time."

Then she fell silent. Her teeth chomped on her lower lip.

"What?" I asked.

"You're wrong, Laila. Not everyone would have done what you did. I wouldn't have. I would've run straight to the door and said to hell with the rest of you. Let alone pull it off." A smile pulled at her lips. "Was beautiful though. Watching those cells fly into the air was like watching the shackles fall off our feet."

I pushed a smile. "I couldn't have done it alone, so thank you."

"You practically did though," she said. "I knew you were powerful and everything, but I didn't know you were *that* powerful."

Honestly, neither did I until I did it. I'd always known I had potential. But I didn't know I could do that until I did it.

I chuckled. "I wish I would have had the power to be in two places at once. I only got a little more than half of us out."

"Not only, Laila," she said. "You got half of us out."

"I guess."

But not the two lives in there that meant more to me than anyone else.

When Jeremy came back to the room, I asked him to take Haley home. He nodded happily and did as I asked, as he almost always did. Mom and Jenna stayed around a while longer until a few nurses came in and asked if I was ready for my procedure. I practically jumped with joy.

I couldn't wait to get those fucking lumps of rock out. I guess I thought I'd feel better, somehow more disguised, if they couldn't track me.

Jeremy asked if I wanted him with me when they removed the implants. I insisted that I would be fine. I didn't want him there. I knew he didn't want to leave me, but I just didn't want to see the look on his face as the scalpel cut through my scars. The pain was bearable. His expression wasn't.

First, they suggested a mild anesthesia for the procedure. I told them I'd be fine awake. Then they said we could just do small, local anesthetic at the site of each stone. Again, I declined. The doctor highly recommended I take something; a muscle relaxer or an anxiety medication to deal with the pain. But again, I told them I was fine. They insisted that I couldn't possibly want them to cut into my flesh without any numbing agents. I literally couldn't stop laughing when they said it like it was the scariest thing imaginable.

The doctor reluctantly agreed, telling me that they'd be prepared in case the pain was too much to bear. I chuckled and assured them I would be fine.

I wasn't comfortable in that hospital. I would never find comfort in a hospital again. But being given drugs that lowered my ability to defend myself in a hospital was terrifying. After blacking out for days on end and waking up with new cuts on my body day after day, being mentally unaware in a place like that was more unnerving than the torture itself. Not knowing what happened to me scared me more than anything.

As they began slicing my arm to remove the implants, one of the nurses watched me carefully to see if I was going to panic. I looked back at her completely unshaken. She retorted some comment about how I was a perfect patient to which I couldn't help but smile.

I was by far the worst patient Peterson ever had. It brought me a great deal of satisfaction. Maybe things hadn't gone exactly as I hoped, but one thing was obvious. I did what he never thought any of us were capable of. I ended his righteous list of victories. I chopped his list of prisoners in more than half.

The doctor gave me discharge information shortly after the procedure was complete and Leah healed the incisions.

I couldn't wait to go home after that last cut was closed. I couldn't wait to cuddle up in my big, comfy bed. I couldn't wait to sit on the steps outside the diner and watch the sun set. I couldn't wait to cook myself something to eat. I couldn't wait to get back to normal.

When I was wheeled back to my room, Jeremy said that Celena, Kai, and Wyatt wanted to come visit. But since Jenna was there, and she didn't know about our abilities, I figured it might be a little too hard to explain. I told them to just come by the diner tomorrow morning after I got to sleep in my bed.

Jeremy smiled, saying something like, "Whatever you want, baby."

He was overcompensating a bit, constantly running to and from the vending machine, and then back home to grab some miscellaneous object I mentioned. His hand hadn't left one part of my body or another since I got back except when he left the room. His eyes were constantly looking over me, checking me like an infant for SIDS.

It made me feel like shit to know how full of pain he must have been in while I was gone. Then even worse when I remembered that not only had he lost me, but he lost a child too. I was the only consolation prize I could offer him since Micah was gone.

CHAPTER ELEVEN

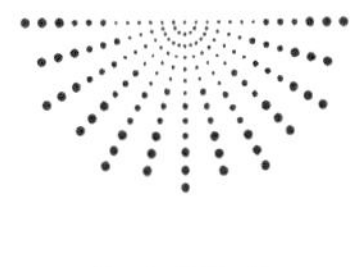

LAILA

As I pulled my hoody tighter around my hips, Jeremy delicately took my hand. "Are you ready to go home?"

I smiled so wide that my cheeks hurt. "You have no idea how ready I am."

Smiling, he stood, lifted my bag from the bed around his shoulder, and tucked his arms around my waist in a gentle hug. "Let's do it then."

Then we disappeared.

As we landed at the door to our apartment, my senses went into overdrive.

Pots and pans banged in the kitchen and the cacophony of customers' voices over soft rock music as they ate their meals, filled my ears. Salt and grease from the burgers and French fries filled my nostril as the scents wafted toward me from the kitchen. I salivated at the thought of chomping into the delicious food.

The old paneling that lined the steps from the diner downstairs I'd been bitching about for ages, was gone and replaced with drywall painted a soft, peaceful shade of yellow. A shade I'd picked out at the end of the last year. The steps had been redone too, no longer coated in cheap Berber carpet, but a light, cedar colored vinyl plank. Another feature I'd picked. The ugly wooden handrail had been replaced with a thick, white plastic railing. Something we talked about but hadn't yet decided on. Jeremy was right though, the plastic railing looked beautiful.

Tears formed in my eyes, and a lump thickened in my throat. I'm not sure why a coat of paint and new floors made me so emotional, but it could have been the tapering hormones from Micah's birth.

"What's wrong, baby?" Jeremy pulled back to meet my gaze.

I bit my unwilling, smiling lip. "Nothing. It's just so different."

I didn't have to read his mind to see his guilt. "I'm sorry, I should have waited to do all this. I didn't even think—"

"No," I said. "No, baby. It looks beautiful. Everything looks beautiful. Thank you so much. You did amazing."

"I didn't even think about how I was changing everything in your house, I was just—"

"I wanted you to do this stuff." I locked my arm around his and leaned my head against his bicep. "It's beautiful. You did amazing. I'm just going to be crying a lot for a while."

He gave a sad smile and kissed my forehead. "I'm sorry, I don't know how to go about all of this. I don't know what I'm supposed to say or do, and I don't want to do anything wrong. I just want you to be happy."

I smiled. "I will be. Stop apologizing, okay? Don't worry about me."

"I'm always going to worry about you."

As he opened the door to our apartment, my stomach dropped. We had been in the middle of renovating when I disappeared. Honestly, I'm not sure what I expected to see. But it wasn't the masterpiece Jeremy carefully created in my absence.

Jeremy had just finished all the floors before I left, but we hadn't gotten around to the painting, trim or arranging all the IKEA furniture that sat around in boxes. But I guess Jeremy had a lot of time on his hands while I was gone because it was perfect.

I looked in from the doorway at the expensive shag rug I'd ordered once the floors were finished. It was coming from somewhere in Europe and took two months to arrive. But now it laid against the couch under the coffee table. The grayish blue paint we'd picked out now shined around the little place, brightening the room to a welcoming, homey vibe. My gaze shifted to the impeccable white of the baseboards and window frames.

The new granite countertops were situated carefully on top of the bright white, recently painted cabinets. My new farm sink sat below the window, letting in light from the sun setting in the distance.

I couldn't help the tears that rushed from my eyes and flooded like a river over my face. It was exactly as I'd wanted it to be. Every single thing was perfect. From the new chandelier to the new TV stand. It was flawless.

And it made me feel like shit.

I didn't deserve it. I did *nothing* to deserve it. Moe just handed me all of that money, that place, and I loved it, and I was grateful for it, but I didn't deserve it.

I didn't deserve to live so comfortably when so many other people had so little. I didn't deserve a soft plushy rug beneath my toes or the impeccable new light fixtures. I didn't deserve to be happy when they were still in cells.

"Baby." Jeremy put his hand on my shoulder. "Baby, it's okay."

"It's beautiful." I wiped my eyes. "It's perfect."

He made a disgruntled expression, watching me carefully. "Tears of joy?"

I forced a smile. "Yeah. Yeah, baby. Tears of joy."

He knew I was lying but he kissed my hair anyway. Then he stepped through the door and held it open for me. I walked into the room and he began to close the door behind us, but I turned. "Leave it open, please."

He did so. "Right."

I walked through the living room and took in a whiff of my spa scented wax melts. I turned with a smile. "You've been changing out the wax."

He grinned, walked to the kitchen, and leaned against the counter. "I smoke a lot of weed, and there's a business being run downstairs so."

He shrugged. "And I knew you were coming home, so I cleaned up a little."

"You're so sweet." I smiled.

Then I kicked off my slippers. I pulled off my socks, threw them to the couch, and stepped onto my new rug. I smiled at the soft, plushy fabric between my toes.

Jeremy laughed. "What are you doing?"

"I've been wondering how my feet would feel on this rug for months."

He smiled. "Did it live up to your expectations?"

"No, it's not as soft as I thought it'd be."

"Well, I think we're past the return window."

"Unfortunate," I muttered. I walked to the bay window and gazed outside. My eyes shifted over the full parking lot. "We've got a pretty full house down there tonight, huh?"

"It's been like that for a while. Right around the time you went missing actually." He blew out a slow breath. "I guess any publicity is good publicity."

"Hmm." I unlocked the window and spun the knob to open it. As it creaked open wider with each turn, I smiled, taking in a breath of warm, humid summer air. "I can't believe I missed spring."

"There's always next year." He sat on the couch a few feet away.

I sat on the cushion below the window and gazed outside. Propping my face in my hand, I leaned against the wall beside the screen and just watched.

In the far-left end of the parking lot, I saw a small family unloading from their car. They were young, maybe late twenties or early thirties. The woman piled up baby toy upon baby toy on the diaper bag as the man struggled to pop the stroller into place. I watched as he opened the back door, lifted a cute red and black car seat into the air, and set it on top of the stroller. They joined hands and started toward our entrance.

All that I could think was *that's supposed to be us.*

"You aren't going to jump, are you?" Jeremy asked.

"No. I'm not going to jump." He tried to look happy, but pounds of pain were shrouded behind those joyful eyes. "What's wrong?"

He shook his head.

"Jeremy, what is it?"

He sent me a sad smile. "I'm just so scared of losing you again."

Bringing a smile to my lips, I stood and walked to the couch. Gazing into those compassionate, caring blue eyes, I leaned down and touched our lips together. "I'm not going anywhere."

As he kissed me back, he hesitated. He began to reach up to my hip, then pulled his hand away. He started to reach toward my waist, but the angle was awkward, and he pulled back again.

It was as if it was the first time he'd touched me. It was like we were strangers again. Somehow, it was like we'd pressed reset on everything that had happened in the last three and a half years. As if we didn't know each other until I woke up yesterday. Like he hadn't seen me pop pimples, or take a shit, or all the other simple, less romantic parts of a relationship no one likes to talk about.

Tugging back to meet his gaze, I gave a smile. "I'm not a balloon, you know. I'm not going to pop if you squeeze me too hard."

"I just." He closed his eyes. "I'm sorry."

"Stop apologizing," I said gently. "You didn't do anything."

"I just, I don't know what's okay and what isn't." His expression softened a bit. "I don't want to be too forward, or too withdrawn, or too—"

I cut him off with a kiss again. This time, his fingers found my cheeks, and he held them tightly, but I wanted to send him a message. I wanted him to know he could touch more than my face.

Grazing his shoulders, bracing them for support, I kneeled around him. His breaths grew short and uneven as I settled in on his lap. His worry was still prevalent, fingers laying on the outsides of my knees.

Lips still pressed together, I slid my hands down his arms to his fingers and gently lifted them to my waist. Once they settled there, I rested my forehead on his, took his cheek, and brushed my thumb along his lower lip.

As much as his caution was appreciated, I didn't want him to think

I was afraid of him. I wasn't, and I never would be. I trusted Jeremy in a way that I trusted no one else.

"I'll let you know if it's too much, okay?"

His breathing was slow and heavy, as if he'd just run a mile. Fingers tightening just a bit around my waist, he laughed and gave a gentle nod. "That's a good idea."

CHAPTER TWELVE

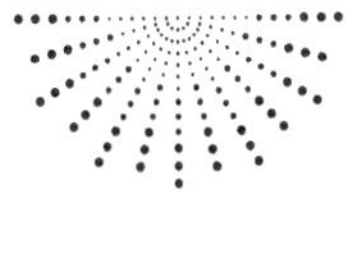

LAILA

Jeremy went downstairs to get our dinner around seven o'clock. I heard Max excitedly start toward the steps when Jeremy gave him our order. Then I heard his quiet murmurs about me not being ready to talk to people yet.

I'm sure it seemed overbearing, maybe even controlling, from an outside perspective. But it was the best thing he could have done for me. I didn't need to tell him I wasn't ready to talk to my friends for him to know. He could see that I didn't want to be around them. Not yet anyway. I appreciated that he was willing to let people be pissy with him rather than force me to hurt their feelings when they realized I didn't want to talk to them.

We ate dinner followed by apple pie and dozed off on the couch. Or at least, Jeremy dozed off on the couch. I couldn't get my eyes to close. Part of me, a very tiny fraction of a fraction wished I were back there. Because as uncomfortable as that table was, at least I got some fucking sleep.

I was exhausted. But my mind wouldn't stop racing.

My baby was dead. I was the reason my baby was dead. Chris was still trapped inside, Micah was dead, and I had failed.

I failed.

Those two phrases repeated in my mind like a skipping record.

I failed, and my baby is dead.

It hurt. It hurt so bad but I couldn't even cry. All that I could do was think those words, over and over and over. I knew it, and it hurt, but somehow, it didn't feel real. If I closed my eyes long enough, I could still feel his little toes hooking around my rib. I could still feel his hiccups inside of me.

How could he be dead?

I lay there with my head curled against Jeremy's lap. I pulled at a string on my fleece snowflake blanket while I gazed mindlessly at the TV. I wasn't even paying attention to it. Not until I heard my name.

Laila Callidy, the missing pregnant woman from Somerset County, was found alive following the over three-month investigation into her disappearance. Very little information has been released by authorities, but we're told she was being held captive by still unknown assailants since March. She, as well as her friends and family, have not yet been available for comment, although we have learned that Laila was only one of many people who were being held captive. Nearly two hundred missing people, or people believed to have been dead, going back more than a decade were found as well, presumably because of the same kidnappers. Unfortunately, whoever was responsible has yet to have been found or identified. We're hoping to have more information by the morning, but it really is quite a story.

I licked my teeth as they flashed one of my maternity pictures on the screen. Jesus. I *definitely* wasn't ready to see people, especially not after seeing that.

Everyone in town was talking about me. As soon as they saw my scars, I would forever be imprinted in their minds as a victim. All I ever would be to them was a victim. Not a survivor. Not a hero.

A victim.

All that shit I went through, all the people I helped get out, just to be viewed as another victim. I didn't want to be a hero, but I wanted to be a victim even less.

It's funny how when something awful happens, people view us as the result of something awful instead of the powerful, badass survivor the awful forced us to become. They act like we're something to be pitied and cared for. But we don't want pity.

We don't want thoughts or prayers. We don't want to hear people say, "I'm sorry you had to go through that."

We want people to say, "I'm glad you lived to tell the tale."

And then to shut their god damned mouths.

The screen flashed to a new story. Bold white letters on a red back drop read, **Breaking News.**

Fire fighters out of Westmoreland County have been battling a massive house fire in an apartment complex for about forty-five minutes now. We're told the fire started as the result of a malfunctioning furnace in one of the tenant's homes. She says that she reported the issue to her landlord three times in the past six months and was told it had been repaired each time.

The screen flashed to a police officer.

At this time, we have six people hospitalized as a result of this fire, including two children who suffered severe burns. We know that there are still people inside, and we're doing everything we can to get them out. We're having some issues getting through parts of the building that are no longer structurally sound, but we're praying that the coroner is done here.

Behind him, I saw people huddled together crying. Others held their phones toward the fire a few hundred yards away.

People were burning while I sat there wallowing in self-pity over the lives I couldn't save.

Those people on the screen, holding their breaths as they waited for their loved ones to walk out of that burning building, I could help.

I couldn't bring Micah back. I couldn't save Chris. But I could save them.

CHAPTER THIRTEEN

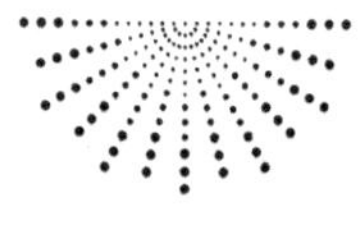

LAILA

At the time, I hadn't learned to teleport. But I did have one form of transportation that was still faster than driving.

I'd never done it, but I knew I could.

What was the worst that could happen? I guessed I could die. But I thought, fuck it. If I died trying to help someone, at least I'd die trying to do the right thing.

I could have taken the steps. It would've been a little less dramatic. But it would have taken more time that I didn't want to waste. Plus, I always had a thing for drama.

I went to my bedroom window, knowing it was the biggest and easiest to fit out of. I pried the glass open and crawled out onto the ledge. My bare toes wrapped around the edge of the brick. I tried not to look down.

I pulled the air around me below, almost imagining it as a tornado beneath me. Then I held my breath, closed my eyes, and jumped.

Although, it wasn't much of a leap. The wind did exactly as I thought it would. I gazed at the ground as the wind whistled through my ears.

I stared down in pride for a second. I did it. I was flying.

But I didn't have time for self-appreciation. I headed northwest, creating a shield of air around me that prevented bugs and dust from hitting me in the face and another that moved me through the air.

As I flew, I thought of nothing. I genuinely had no thoughts. Not of the air soaring beneath me, not of the clouds I slammed through. I thought of nothing. Only reaching my destination.

And that this was freedom. I really was free.

I took off way faster than I realized I could. It took me maybe five minutes to get to a place that would have taken forty-five by car.

Before I saw, or even smelled, the fire in the distance, I could *feel* it. It was similar to the way I felt when I met another supernatural creature for the first time. It was this bizarre sense of knowing that's almost impossible to describe. Kind of like when you feel someone looking at you before you see it.

I knew the landing would be the tricky part. Not because landing would actually be hard, but because I wasn't sure how I could get inside of the building without being spotted once I arrived.

Once the fire came into view, I got as close as I could without being immediately spotted. There, on the roof top, was a doorway.

That was my way in.

I moved through the atmosphere as quickly as possible, creating a cushion of wind just above the roof. I couldn't land on my feet without being spotted, so I dropped to my side, exhaled out a heavy breath and prepared for the impact.

But my powers knew exactly what to do. I didn't have to brace at all. The air caught me before I hit the ground.

As I landed on my side, still levitating above the ground, I gazed down at my body in awe. I fucking did it.

But I didn't have time to waste. I dropped the air, bolted to my feet, and ran to the door in a full sprint. Luckily, the door wasn't locked.

I started down the linoleum stairs, taking two steps at a time. As I ran, I felt the heat getting warmer and warmer against my skin. The smoke got thicker and I pulled my shirt up to my nose to block the thick smog from my lungs. Then I heard the first scream.

A man cried out for help, coughing between each cry. "Please," he begged. "Please! Somebody help!"

"Where are you?" I yelled.

"In here!" he screamed. "In here! I'm in here!"

"Keep yelling, I'll follow the sound of your voice," I called.

"I'm in here! The third floor, second apartment on the right from the stairwell. Please hurry. God, please hurry. I'm bleeding." His voice cracked and he began to cry. "God, there's so much blood."

"What's hurt?" I continued down the steps to the next doorway. "Can you move?"

"No." He coughed between heartbreaking, ear piercing cries. "I can't fucking move, man. I'm gonna die in here. I'm gonna die."

"No, you're not." I pushed the door open with a large 3 printed on it. I couldn't make out much through the smog, so I gripped the wall for guidance. "You've got to stay with me, alright? Keep talking to me, I'm coming for you."

"I was trying to get my ferret," he cried. "Now we're both going to fucking die. Fuck, I should have listened. I didn't need a fucking ferret. Polly was right, I shouldn't have gotten the fucking ferret."

"It's okay." I made it to the second door on the right that he described. When the handle didn't budge, I pushed a gust of wind at it and let it fly open.

There he was, lying on the rug riddled with debris. A massive metal beam laid on top of his stomach, trapping him beneath it. I rushed toward him, trying to think of a way to get the pole off of him.

Fuck. I should have woken Jeremy. He could have teleported him out from under it.

I dropped to the ground beside him. "I'm going to die," the middle-aged man cried. "I'm going to die."

I raised my hand to his sweaty, clammy face. "You're going to live."

"I can't feel my legs. I don't want to live without my legs."

I knew there was no way in hell I could carry the two-hundred-pound man down three flights of stairs. But I could heal him. If I could heal him, I could get him out. But I had to get that pole off of him first.

It started at the ceiling and ended somewhere inside of his stomach, basically holding his organs inside of him now that his skin couldn't.

"Here." I grabbed a blanket off the armchair. "I'm gonna cover you up so nothing gets in your eyes, alright?"

He cried, unable—or maybe just unwilling—to reply, as he continued to mumble that he was going to die.

I hoped like hell that it wouldn't kill him. At least if it did, it'd be a quicker death than suffocating from the smoke in the air.

I made the air spin until it created something of a vortex. Carefully, I directed the tunnel toward the base of the pole near the man's stomach. It slowly lifted and he screamed louder, more ear piercing than before. I kept lifting until it was out of him. Then I dropped it onto the couch.

He screamed the worst, nails on a chalkboard sort of scream. Blood began to pour from his stomach. Then it went dead silent. My heart raced as I lifted my hands above his wounds and radiated healing energy into his body.

He wasn't screaming yet, but the skin began to close. He was still alive. It would work.

Fuck, it had to work.

I continued holding the heat against him. Then he woke up screaming bloody murder again. It was the best noise I ever heard.

Once his skin was closed, his body writhed in pain and I knew I'd done it. I'd restored his ability to walk.

Flames filled the room, but once he was healed, I knew that I could get him out. He struggled to sit up. I scurried to my feet.

I squinted through the flames, the cage in the corner was littered with broken dry wall and ash. But no fire.

I hurried to the ferret, flicked the metal bar open, and reached inside. The little guy was barely moving, but he was alive.

I ran back to the man with his ferret in my hand. He stared at me in amazement as I set the little guy in the man's arms. "Polly was wrong. He's a cutie."

"Who are you?"

I smiled. "Let's get you out of here."

I took his other hand, pulled him to his feet, and ran from the room. He followed close behind me. But then I heard another scream.

I was torn. Should I take him out first? Or go to the next person who needed my help?

My heart raced against my ribs. I prayed desperately for some way to get them both out.

It was almost simultaneous.

I thought it, so it was.

We stood just outside the building at the rear entrance. The man lurched over vomiting as my jaw dropped.

Holy shit.

I did it.

I teleported.

As the man continued to puke, holding his ferret close to his chest, I did it again.

I stood in the same hallway I had been in just a second before.

Then, I heard the quiet, heart wrenching little cry for help.

It was without thought.

Suddenly, I stood beside a scared child covering their head with a blanket curled up in a closet.

I didn't even see if they were a little boy or girl, I just grabbed their shoulders and teleported again.

Then again, and again.

Four people. Four people who would get to see their families again because I hadn't fallen asleep yet while I lay there watching the news. Five lives, if you count the ferret.

I hated what happened to me. I hated what Peterson did and especially the way he did it.

But I managed to save two hundred and twenty-nine people in a three-day time span because of the abilities I could use now.

It didn't bring Micah back. It didn't bring Chris back.
But fuck, it was better than nothing.
At least all that torture wasn't for nothing.

CHAPTER FOURTEEN

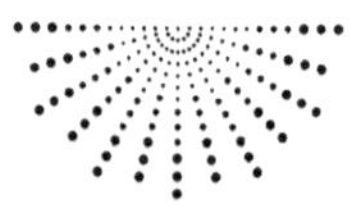

LAILA

When I finished at the fire, I teleported back home. My heart was still racing, and my blood was nearly boiling with excitement. I was overwhelmed with glee. I made a difference. *I made a fucking difference.*

I landed in the kitchen, steadying myself against the counter before I regained my balance. Once I was level, a wide smile pulled at my lips and I found myself happily jumping in a circle.

"Laila," I heard Jeremy say. Then he gasped and rushed toward me from the living room. He grabbed my shoulders, wide eyes moving between mine. "Are you okay? What happened? Where were you?"

"Yeah, I'm fine." I smiled. "I'm great actually."

"What happened?" He touched my cheek, face screwing up in confusion as he wiped some smog away. "Is that smoke?"

"It is."

"What the hell happened?"

"I—I don't know. I was watching the news, and they said—They said there were people trapped in a fire at an apartment complex. I don't know, I just, I couldn't sit there and wait to hear that they died. So, I just... I just went."

"You went," he repeated. I nodded. He cocked his head to the side. "You just rushed into a burning building?"

"I guess I did."

His breaths became a bit uneven. "You're okay, right? You look okay, are you okay?"

I smiled. "I feel great."

His expression fell somewhere between concerned and furious. Just as I was about to say something about how he better not try and tell me I did the wrong thing, he reached forward and quickly put his arms around my back in a tight embrace.

"I was so scared," he whispered.

Of course he was scared. Just a few hours prior, his exact words to me were, 'I'm just so scared I'm going to lose you again.' And what'd I do? Ran into a burning building.

Squeezing him as tight as my arms allowed, I whispered, "I'm sorry, I didn't mean to scare you."

"How did you get there?" He pulled back to meet my gaze. "And how did you get back?"

My lips pulled into a smile. "I flew there, and then I teleported home."

His jaw dropped. "You can teleport? And you can *fly*?" I smiled wide and gave a nod. "You can *fly* and you didn't tell me?"

"It was just a theory before tonight. I just thought about Kai, and how he levitated everyone out the other day. And I knew that was a thing. I can manipulate air. If you can move air, you can move yourself *through* air. And I—I don't know, I just figured it was worth a shot."

He looked over me for a moment. "You could have died."

"But I didn't." I smiled wide.

He gazed over me with his hands still on my upper arms. "You didn't," he murmured. His eyes shifted over me a moment longer. Then he smiled. "When did you learn to teleport?"

"Like." I glanced at the clock on the stove. "Fifteen minutes ago?"

His eyes widened a bit. "You unlocked another one that easily?"

"I guess. I just, I was scared. I heard a kid crying, and I already had someone that I just healed with me, and I thought about how I wished I could teleport, and I just…"

"Teleported." His eyes widened in amazement. "You can teleport."

"I can teleport."

"Huh." He huffed, smiling. "You never cease to amaze me."

I grinned. "That's a compliment, right?"

"Certainly a compliment."

I moved my hands to his arms and his slid to my hips. "You aren't jealous, are you?"

"A little bit." He chuckled and pulled me closer. "But just a little."

I laughed, enjoying the rush of adrenaline and endorphins coursing through my veins. "I'm really proud of myself."

"You should be." He raised his hand to my hair and pinched a piece of ash between his thumb and forefinger. "I'm proud *for* you. You've come so far."

"I have. I saved four people. And a ferret."

He laughed. "A ferret, huh?"

"A ferret."

Still smiling, he kissed my forehead. He pulled my body closer to his, tightening his arms around my back. "I know you're dealing with a lot right now, and I know it isn't going to be easy on you. But can you do one thing to make things a little easier on me too?"

I looked up from his chest and met his gaze.

"Leave me a note or something if you're gonna fly off into battle like Superman," he said. "I almost shit myself when I looked around and you weren't here. I can't lose you like that again."

After what I'd put him through for the last three months, grief crept through my joyous body. It wasn't fair. Of course he wasn't going to get mad and demand anything given my state. But what I'd just done wasn't fair to him.

Had I died, he would have never forgiven himself. I did the right thing, but I should have been more considerate. He would have flown in with me if I'd woken him. Leaving a note was the least I could have done.

"I'm sorry, baby. I thought you'd be asleep."

"It's okay, just please let me know. I thought... God, I don't know what I thought. I was just so scared. I get it, and I'm not mad. But please don't scare me like that again. I can't lose you, too. Not again."

Before I was kidnapped, I always took the little things for granted. I looked at a tile shower and just saw a place to clean yourself. Then, I stared at each tile Jeremy had meticulously placed against the wall like a piece of art.

I'd said once, the first time I saw the Skoulda house to be exact, that I liked the way the tile looked turned sideways to sit like a diamond. Going on four years later and Jeremy remembered.

He'd turned every little one inch by one inch tile to face upward, pointing to the sky.

I'd said we should just throw up a new acrylic surround, but he said tile would be better and I reluctantly agreed. I didn't realize why the tiles were so important to him then, but as I lay my head against the half-finished product, I smiled. That was the sort of thing Jeremy did. Cute little things that I might not even notice if I wasn't paying close attention. But I noticed and it made me happy. Even if it was just for a second, I was happy.

As the water got cold, I turned off the spigot and stepped from the shower.

After walking onto the memory foam bathmat, I hurried into my clothes before I got the chance to look at my naked body and kill my own buzz. I stepped into a pair of fuzzy Eeyore pajama pants and a bright yellow Volkswagen T-shirt. Tacky combination, I'll admit. But I missed color. I didn't realize how dull life was without it until I was stuck in navy blue and gray for months.

I slipped on some purple socks and slid into my unicorn slippers. Wiggling my toes, I smiled at the silly little childish antics I was glad still brought me a shred of joy.

After my trip into that burning building, I felt like myself. Not that I was one hundred percent the girl I'd once been. But I didn't feel like a zombie on autopilot. I felt like I did something decent enough to deserve to smile.

I turned my eyes to the ground before I could meet my gaze in the mirror. Then I started from the bathroom down the hall to the living room. Jeremy sat at the couch leaning over the coffee table.

"Whatcha doing?" I made my way around the sofa and sat beside him.

"Rolling a blunt." He fiddled with the corner of a brown cylinder before ripping the end of the paper. "Or trying to. This shit isn't cooperating."

"Scooch." I pushed him with my hip. "You suck at this."

"Just blunts. I can roll a damn good joint." He set it down on the table.

"Sure, baby." I grinned as I picked it up.

"Are you suggesting I can't roll a good joint?" He gave a smile and angry, furrowed brows. I laughed, grabbed the other cigar wrap off the table, and split it in half to make it thinner. "Because I can roll a great joint."

"You can roll a *smokable* joint." I chuckled and met his gaze.

He smiled and his jaw dropped. "You're mean."

I smiled and poured the herbs from the torn paper into the fresh one. "I'm sorry."

"No, you're not."

A laugh escaped my grinning lips. "Yeah, I'm really not."

He laughed too. I rolled the paper between my fingertips. I tucked the end into the inside to meet the other side of the paper. I raised it to my lips, licked the end, and pressed my finger along it to seal it. I grabbed a paper clip off the table and pushed the stray pieces tighter together. Then I took a small nug from the table and gently pushed it inside as a mouthpiece. Then I pushed in the stray herbs on the other end and rolled it together between my fingertips to create a point.

I gazed at my masterpiece. "Just like riding a bike."

Jeremy took it from my hand and looked over it. "I don't understand how it's so easy for you."

"Years and years of practice, my friend." I grinned and leaned back onto the couch.

He held it to his lips and tapped his pants for a lighter. I brought a flame to the tip of my pointer finger and held it up to his mouth. He smiled, held the blunt to it, and gently blew outward a few times to get it burning.

"I know you told the nurses and everything that you didn't want any drugs, and I completely get that. Probably better than anyone." He took a long hit and blew the smoke upward. The smell filled the air and I breathed it in. My mouth practically watered. "But does weed count?"

"I don't know," I said. "It's kind of hard to explain, I don't know."

He brought his knee onto the couch and faced me. "I'll listen if you want to talk about it. Or we can talk about something else."

"It's not drugs themselves that freak me out. I mean, I've done them all, just about anyway, and have a positive memory with each. It's more the setting than anything," I said. "I don't know if that makes any sense."

"It does."

"I mean, I'll probably never touch Xanax again, but I don't know," I said. "Like, I want to relax. I want to sleep. But I don't want to be comatose. I have to be alert."

"You don't *have* to be alert, baby."

"I do. At least for now. I just... Three days ago, I was..." I raised my hand to my eyes and rubbed them.

Some part of me wanted to open up about it. I did want to talk. I just didn't want to talk about it with Jeremy. All of it was disturbing enough, I didn't want him to think about me like that.

He lived it too. In his own way, he lived through just as much torture as I had. But it was different because I was the *reason* he was tortured. And that hurt. It hurt me to know that I hurt him.

"You were in hell," Jeremy said quietly. "I know, baby."

I paused. "But it's just weed."

"Shitty weed too."

"Damn, really?"

"Max has been off his game lately. I don't know, a couple big guys got busted so his dudes were out, so he had to go off someone else. It's practically shwag."

I lifted the bag from the table, held it beneath my nose, and took in a long whiff. "It doesn't smell too bad."

"But look at it, there's a billion seeds." He took another hit.

I put my hand inside and picked up the dry, barely green leaves. "Ew." I set it back on the table.

"We should just get medical cards," he said. "We definitely could. I'm a heroin addict and you have PTSD."

"But I like being a law breaker." I smiled. "Rebellion, end prohibition, all that patriotic shit."

Jeremy grinned. "I think breaking the law is basically the polar opposite of being a patriot."

My head shook. "No, we were founded on rebellion. America's history starts at the brink of a revolutionary war. Our country literally exists because of saying 'fuck the men in power.'"

"This is true." He took another hit off the blunt.

I gazed down at it in his hand. My stomach danced with butterflies. I was actually nervous about smoking weed. There was a time I was going through a quarter pound of weed in a month. And suddenly, the thought of a little micro hit off a blunt gave me anxiety. But it also made my mouth salivate.

"Do you want a hit?" He extended it to me.

"I do."

He held it out further, but I reluctantly gazed at it. His hand receded back to his mouth and he took in a slow, long drag. "But you don't?"

"It sucks, because I love weed. I *love* weed. And I quit smoking because I got pregnant, so my tolerance went down. And now, I'm not, and I want to, but I'm also kind of stressed about getting too high. But I also really *want* to get high," I said. "It doesn't make any sense, I'm sorry."

"No, it does. I get it." He bit his lower lip. "Ultimately, whatever you do is entirely up to you. But do you want my opinion?" I gave a nod, and he sat forward. "Okay, so we both know weed can cause anxiety, but it's also about your mind set. And I know you're still—"

"A mess?" I grinned.

"I was going to say adjusting."

"Mhmm," I said.

"You're still adjusting, and I know you're anxious. But if you're worried something's going to happen to you because you're too high to defend yourself, I'm here. And I won't let anything happen to you." His eyes gently held mine, yet still in a firm, protective manner. He threaded our fingers together and squeezed tight. "I'll never let anyone hurt you again, Lai. I promise."

I already knew it, but to hear him say it aloud brought a layer of warmth to my heavy heart. Even Peterson said once that he wouldn't have been able to get to me if Jeremy would have been there instead of Hannah. If I had one thing for Jeremy, it was trust that he would keep me safe. Especially after the hell he'd been through when I was gone.

"If you don't want to, then don't. There's nothing wrong with being sober." He took another hit to keep it from going out. As he exhaled, he went on, "But if the only reason you don't is because you're scared as a result of what *he* did to you, then smoke. Don't let him take something else that you love away. Don't let him continue to hurt you. Do what *you* want to do."

I ran my tongue along my teeth in thought. He was right. That fucker took everything from me. He took my child, he took the girl I was, he took my right to choose.

And I fucking loved weed. At least then. I'd outgrow that passion one day.

But it was almost symbolic in that moment. If I didn't hit that blunt, Peterson would have taken yet another thing I loved away from me.

"It'll probably help me sleep, huh?"

"But it won't knock you out."

"I do need to sleep," I murmured.

"But don't think I'm trying to pressure you. If you don't want to, you don't have to. You don't have to do anything you don't want to." He squeezed my hand tighter. "Never."

I reached out, took the blunt from his hand, and lifted it to my lips. I breathed in a slow, deep drag. My eyes closed as the familiar burn made its way into my lungs. The taste tingled on the tip of my tongue and the warm nicotine of the paper numbed my lips.

I held it in for a moment, staring down at the small pieces of herbs that gradually turned red.

"This tastes like 2014." I laughed and flicked the charred paper into the ash tray on the table.

Jeremy chuckled and I handed it to him. "Like middle school middies."

I smiled as I felt it sink in. The tingly sensation over my skin. My body started to feel lighter. My stiff joints and muscles began to loosen, like standing for the first time after a long Netflix binge. My thoughts started to line up beside each other, no longer grouped in a messy array of spider webs that overlapped and twisted together.

Everything began to soften around the edges. Not dull, but soften. Clean straight lines looked less perfect and a bit more fluid. The new chandelier above the dining table cast a soft, yellowish hue on the room around us, almost making me feel warm.

What I loved about weed was the way it allowed me to feel the euphoria without being completely out of my head. It's not the kind of drug that knocks you out or disables you from reality. It just softens the way you think. It's like a warm iron over a wrinkled shirt.

"You alright?" Jeremy asked, watching me gaze up at the light.

I smiled as I turned. "Yeah, I'm good."

He gave a sweet smile. "I'm good, just put it out when you're done."

I held it to my lips and took another hit. Pulling my legs from the ground onto the seat, I nuzzled them sideways against the cushion. I leaned back into the comfort of the couch. I gazed at the bluish gray smoke coming off the end of the blunt.

That couch was like a big, fluffy cloud. It practically held me. The texture was soft against my palm, the cushions were thick and plushy. I practically melted into it.

I turned my gaze to Jeremy. "Have you written anything recently?"

"Nothing worth mentioning."

He always said that, and he was always wrong. Any music he wrote tended to be soft and slow, and I think in his mind, that equated to bad. He was into Nine Inch Nails and Blue October. He never managed to write a song as heavy as *Light You Up* or *Closer.* He could cover them beautifully, but he couldn't write one of his own.

But that was one thing I loved about his music. It was him. It was soft and gentle and soothing. That's who he was, that's who he'd always been. He could be angry, he could be mean. But at the depth of his soul, he was light and airy. Like the aura of a star in the deepest part of space.

"Can you play me something?" I took another hit. "It doesn't have to be new or anything."

He huffed, half smile inching up his lips. "If you really want me to."

I smiled. "I missed hearing your voice." I felt my smile fall. "When I was in there, I just... You know how when you get a haircut, you kind of forget what you looked like before you cut it?

"I... I tried really hard to remember, I didn't want to forget. I remembered the way things made me feel. I remembered the way I *felt* when you sang, but I couldn't hear your voice in my head anymore. Even your face kind of started to blur."

His eyes softened, lips curling down for a moment. "I'll play you whatever you want, baby."

I smiled. "It doesn't matter. Just sing me something."

He swiveled his legs off of the couch onto the floor, stood, and walked to his acoustic guitar hanging on the wall by the window. I smiled, watching him gently grip the neck and pull it off the metal hook. I'd never understand what I found so attractive about a guy with a guitar in his hand, but even now, it still makes my stomach flip.

I leaned my head against the plushy couch pillow. He sat beside me and set the hollow piece of wood to his lap. He didn't take the time to tune it, he just started strumming.

Butterflies danced in my stomach as he began singing. I wasn't even paying attention to the words, I just listened to his voice. I closed my eyes as the gentle melody bounced off my ear drums and drowned out my thoughts.

Everything slowly drifted away when he slid his fingertips against the long wires. It was almost like a dance. An elegant, soft and sweet little dance.

I lay my head on his shoulder and felt the vibration of his voice beneath my ear. It was the sweetest sound I ever heard. I wanted to stay in that moment for eternity.

That sound, and the weed, put me into the softest, most peaceful sleep I'd had in months.

CHAPTER FIFTEEN

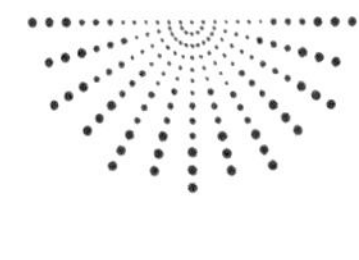

LAILA

"She's still sleeping, but I'll tell her you wanted to see her when she wakes up." I heard Jeremy say from the doorway.

"Oh, okay," Max said quietly. "Is she okay? Like health wise? She's not going to code again or anything?"

"No. No, she's alright," Jeremy said. "The doctors still aren't sure what caused all of that, but she's physically back to normal now."

"And... mentally?" Max said. I opened my eyes and gazed at the suede couch.

"She's gonna be okay," Jeremy said. "She just has a lot to work through."

He had more faith in me than I had in myself. I genuinely didn't know if I'd ever be okay again. But his hope was sweet.

I heard Max sigh. "But she's home."

"She's home," Jeremy repeated. I could practically hear the smile at the edge of his voice. "I'm sorry if I'm being a little domineering, but she's just..."

"No, I get it, man. She literally just got home. I know you missed her more than anyone." He paused. "Celena mentioned something about her looking different. What did she mean by that?"

"She looks like Laila," Jeremy said.

"Right, but…"

Jeremy huffed in annoyance. "She has some scars."

"Oh," Max said.

"It's probably best if you don't say it like that when you see her." There was a tone to his voice I'd only heard before he slit a Demon's throat or slammed a blade through a vamp's chest. Defensive and angry. He never used that tone with me, even when we fought.

I really appreciated that. I was more insecure about those scars than I'd ever been about anything in my life. And I was dreading the look on my best friend's face when he saw them.

"Right," Max muttered.

"Look, she's going to have to deal with everyone in this town looking at her like she's some poor, little baby deer alone in the woods. But she isn't, dude. She's Laila. She's who she's always been. She doesn't want anyone's sympathy. So be her friend. Don't treat her like she's broken. All that's going to do is push her away."

A smile touched my lips. He may have been sweet and careful with me, but he didn't see me as wounded. He saw me as strong.

"Sure," Max said. "Yeah, of course."

I could practically hear Jeremy's frown. "Sorry, I'm really not trying to be a dick—"

"No, I get it, man. I'm working until six, so if she's ready for company, just tell her to come down."

"She'll probably want you to come up. I don't think she's ready for a crowd."

"Right," he muttered. "Well, just let me know."

I winced as I heard the door creaking shut behind me. Then Jeremy pulled it back open. "She's got this thing about leaving doors open."

"Oh," Max muttered. "Sure, okay."

I heard Max's heavy feet trot down the steps. I rolled over to look at Jeremy.

He didn't realize I was awake and hadn't put on his façade of positivity yet. That was the first, and maybe only, glance I got into the stress my capture caused him too.

He rubbed the bridge of his nose for a moment. His thumb and forefinger parted against his cheeks and slowly drifted to his mouth. His messy waves of black fell along his stiff jaw and rested against his shoulders, tangling up in the curls of his beard. His shoulders hung beneath his head like they were carrying the weight of the world.

He was trying so hard to be everything I needed. I was grateful for it, but the guilt heavily outweighed the appreciation. My pain was still hurting him. So, I put on my façade too.

"Morning." I smiled.

He looked over and brought a smile to his lips. He started toward me. Then he sat on the coffee table. He took my hand and raised my knuckles to his lips. "Hey, beautiful."

"Thank you." I gestured toward the doorway where he'd stood.

"I didn't do anything."

I squeezed his hand. "Just thank you."

He gave a gentle smile back, leaned forward, and kissed me. "What do you want to do today?"

"Maybe go see Kai and Celena? I haven't seen them since everything happened, and I want to tell them how grateful I am for their help. They didn't have to do that, but they did and I really appreciate it."

"That sounds good. She's called a couple times. Leah and Hannah made breakfast and invited us over, but I wanted to check with you before I told them yes."

Most crowds, I didn't want to be around. But they were family. And they knew. They knew everything. I didn't have to sugarcoat shit.

"Yeah, I just want to get dressed first. I think I'm going to try to contact Mary at some point today too though."

"Really?"

"I wouldn't have been able to do it without her," I said. "If that's okay with you, I mean. I know that after everything—"

"She's your mom," he said. "Of course it's okay with me."

"I don't know if I'd go as far as to call her my 'mom.' But I do want to thank her."

"I do too. She was a big help. I talked to her while you were gone too. Actually had a nice little heart to heart. I'm not... ya know, over the things that she did. But she is a part of our lives. And I think it'd be good for you guys to talk."

I smiled.

That wasn't the whole truth in why I wanted to see her.

When I was in there, I'd thought about the things she said after she killed Moe. About how Jeremy was perfect for me, but I needed to leave him. How I needed to run away. That I should abort my baby before it was too late and save myself the heart ache.

I hadn't known what she meant at that time, but I was pretty sure I did then.

She knew I was going to be taken. And I wanted to know how because Angels are not psychics. But if she wouldn't tell me how she knew, maybe she'd at least tell me something else about what the future had in store for me.

Stumbling a bit as we appeared in the living room, Jeremy caught my arm with a laugh. "Got to work on the landing a bit, Lai."

"At least we aren't inside the wall, okay?"

He chuckled and let go of my arm. I gazed around the old room I'd sat in thousands of times. A smile inched up my lips. "Nothing's changed." I ran my hand against the little table behind the couch.

"Things have been pretty docile these days," Jeremy said as I meandered around.

The room was a near-perfect temperature, although a bit cool for my liking. But just as it always was. The sun radiated in from the large windows, casting an almost heavenly glow and reflecting like a mirror against the mahogany floors. The smell of warm apples filled my nostrils, bringing with it a million memories.

The bacon sizzling in the kitchen made me smile before I started toward it. My fingers grazed the delicate swirls on the wall as I made it through the doorway. Leah sat at the counter in front of her computer just as she had been for months before I was taken. Brody, Adam,

Hannah, and Kai huddled around the breakfast nook, mumbling amongst themselves.

I teleported to the bench beside Kai and threw my arms around his shoulders. He jumped and spilled his tea on his lap and consequently mine. But he didn't care. Neither did I.

"Laila." Kai laughed. His chest shifted toward mine and his arms tightened around my shoulders.

Adam and Brody bickered, saying something along the lines of "how in the hell can she teleport now?" And "that isn't fair." But I just focused on the warmth of my brother's arms around me, hugging him a while longer. He squeezed me so tight that bringing in a full breath was almost impossible, but I didn't care. I always loved hugging Kai. We hadn't even known one another for a year yet he felt like home, too. But an older home.

"I'm so glad ye're back," he said quietly in my ear. "I'm so glad."

I smiled and squeezed him harder. "Me too."

We stayed tightly wrapped up with each other for a moment or so, the same way we had as fetuses.

"I couldn't have done it without you, Kai," I murmured at his ear. "Thank you so much."

"Thank you for fighting." His arms got even tighter around me.

"Laila," I heard in the doorway.

I released Kai, turned with a smile, and hurried to my feet. "Hey, Celena."

She rushed toward me, hurriedly put her arms around my waist, and pulled me into her in a tight embrace. I knew that hug was more for me than her. She hated physical contact. But that's what I loved about my baby sister. She'd do what was best for someone else even if she didn't particularly enjoy it. "I'm so happy to see you without a tube down your throat."

"You have no idea." I laughed.

She pulled back and gazed over me with large blue eyes. "Jesus Christ, you're tiny."

"Hopefully not for long."

"Come get some food." Leah stood. "And there's coffee in the pot."

"I made orange juice." Hannah grinned, scooting over Kai and bringing herself to her feet. "Leah wouldn't let me touch the cast iron skillet, so I didn't get to cook, but the orange juice is really good."

My gaze shifted to the island. It was like a buffet. Eggs, bacon, sausage, toast, fruit salad. You name it, it was there.

"You guys didn't have to do all this."

"We did actually." Leah gave a gentle smile. "Seriously, get something to eat. But use a paper plate because I don't feel like loading the dishwasher."

Smiling, I started toward the cabinet above the coffee maker and grabbed a cup.

This was what home felt like. Fixing a plate with my brothers and sisters, breathing in the smell of coffee and bacon, and watching the sun shine in through the French doors. I loved my apartment, but this was home.

"So have you decided which college you're going to in the fall?" I asked Hannah. She perched herself onto the island, kicked her legs back and forth like a kid on a rollercoaster, and shrugged.

"Penn State," she said.

I grabbed a piece of bacon off the plate on the counter. "Not U Penn?" I asked. She shook her head. "Why not?"

"Yeah, why not, Hannah?" Leah asked.

"Well, if I go to U Penn, I have to move out to Philly," Hannah said.

"And you love Philadelphia," Jeremy said.

"Yes, but I love it here. And I'd have to live on campus, which doesn't seem like a good idea considering all the craziness in our lives."

"That's exactly why you should move away." Adam laughed.

I chuckled. Couldn't say I disagreed. But I also understood why she wanted to stay close. Our family was as tight knit as they came. I'd never want to move away. And I didn't want her to move far either.

"But that means I have to pay for my dorm, and a meal plan, and why would I do all that when I can live here for free and be in thousands of dollars less debt?" Hannah said. "Plus, I'd miss you guys too much."

"There's literally" —Celena began counting us— "literally four out of nine people in this room can teleport anywhere in the world at any time."

"But not her man," Brody said.

"I don't care what Penn she goes to so long as she's happy," Kai said. "Don't bring me into it."

I laughed and Wyatt chimed in. "Penn State's a good school."

"U Penn's better," Leah said.

"Yeah, ivy league, better," Jeremy said.

"If money's the issue, I can help, Hannah," I said. Jeremy came behind me and placed his hands gently on my hips. I glanced at him over my shoulder. "We can afford to help, right?"

"Oh, yeah," he said. "We're good."

"Money isn't the issue," Leah said. "Mémé and Papy are paying for it. Plus, U Penn's average tuition is a few thousand dollars cheaper than Penn State."

I furrowed my brows at Hannah. "You're going to turn down a chance at an Ivy League education that you aren't even paying for? That's just stupid."

"Thank you!" Leah exclaimed, typing away on her laptop.

"It's too late now anyway, I'm already enrolled at Penn State," Hannah said. "It's not even about Kai. It's about the fact that I'm not ready to leave home."

"Little birdy with a broken wing." Adam gave a mock crying face, rocking his fist back and forth beside his eye.

She rolled her eyes. "It just makes more sense. I can live here, I can get a car, and a job. Which actually reminds me. Laila, do you have any shifts open at the diner?"

I turned back to Jeremy. "Not unless we cut you guys' hours." He gestured between Wyatt and Celena.

"Bitch, I don't have a Mémé and Papy paying for my school and shit." Celena made a face.

"That's no beuno, Han," Wyatt said.

"What about bartending downstairs on the weekends?" Hannah asked.

I turned to Jeremy as he said, "I really don't like the idea of my eighteen-year-old little sister bartending."

"I second that notion." Adam bit into an apple.

"But it's less work on your plate," Hannah said.

Celena raised her hand. "Actually, she can take my hours if you let me bartend."

"That's less cringey," Adam said.

"So what, you guys are perfectly content with *my* eighteen year old little sister bartending?" I glanced between Adam and Jeremy.

"Celena's different," Adam said.

"Yeah, Celena's a Werewolf. No one's fucking with her," Jeremy said. "And if they do, she'll just eat them. Hannah doesn't eat people."

"And Fae." Celena sparked a flame at the tips of her fingers. "Eating someone sounds fun though."

"It actually isn't," Wyatt muttered. "The organs are good and all but ya feel kinda gross when it's over."

"See? Not vulnerable at all," Jeremy said.

Hannah's eyes grew dismal, falling to the floor. My heart ached for her. I was alive because of her. She was stronger than any of her siblings in her own way, and they always treated her like she was powerless.

"Hey, Hannah is not vulnerable," I said. "And you guys are acting like Moe's is a slum biker bar or something. The only audience we get is middle aged couples, hipsters, and preteens."

"That's fair," Leah said. "I agree with Laila. We need to stop stigmatizing women as being vulnerable and unable to care for themselves. Hannah can carry a taser and pepper spray just like every other woman in America."

"It's not her being a woman that concerns me," Jeremy said. "It's this fucking disaster of a life we live. Not even four months ago—" He stopped abruptly.

The room fell quiet and all of our gazes turned to him. My jaw tightened.

"Yeah, probably better you don't go there." Leah looked up at him and licked her teeth.

My gaze caught Hannah's and my heart broke once more. Her eyes fell in shame, tears puddling in the corners.

She hated that her only power was necromancy and no one but her, Kai, and I knew. To everyone else, she was the powerless Skoulda kid. After what happened to me, not only did she blame herself, but she was viewed as even more of a damsel than she'd ever been.

"I didn't mean it like that, Han," Jeremy said. "I just don't want anything to happen to you. You're my baby sister, that's all."

She stood from the bar stool and started toward the maid steps.

"C'mon, Hannah, don't leave," I said. Kai stood and followed behind her.

"Hannah, come on," Jeremy called. He released my waist and walked toward the stairs. "Hannah, don't be like this. Just come back down."

"She's a teenager, let her sulk," Adam said.

As Jeremy treaded back toward me, my brows furrowed. "Don't do that."

He creased his the same way. "Don't do what?"

"Try to use what happened to me as a way to prove how impotent she is."

"I didn't say that—"

"But that's what you meant. That if she had powers, this would have never happened. But that's not fair, Jeremy. She was stronger than almost anyone I know that day. She begged me to let them kill her. *I'm* the reason they got to me. I'm the one who insisted on keeping Daniel, I'm the one who wouldn't risk killing Hannah to kill the guard, I'm the reason it happened. Blame me, don't blame her."

"I don't blame anyone except for the piece of shit who did it, Laila," he said. "Not you, not Daniel, not Hannah. She blames herself, that's something she has to deal with on her own."

"Well, you're not helping," I said. "You weren't there. You don't know what happened."

His jaw tightened. A slow breath eased from his nostrils. "Fine. You're right. I won't do it again."

"Good." I took a sip from my coffee. "Because—"

"Umm," Leah said. "Laila."

I met her gaze. "What?"

"What the fuck is this?" She turned the computer to face me. I leaned forward to read the print on the news article.

Four People In Apartment Fire Says Guardian Angel Saved Them From Certain Death

Oops.

"James Carson says he was pinned under a steel beam during a fire that took firefighters nearly five hours to extinguish early this morning in Westmoreland County. James says he couldn't feel anything below his waist when a young girl found him and lifted the beam from his body. He alleges that she then healed his wound with a bright white light that radiated from her hands. The story wouldn't hold much merit if it weren't for the large quantity of blood found in the man's apartment once the fire was put out. Watch the interview here," Leah read aloud.

I sipped my coffee once more as the man's voice played over the speakers.

"I was trying to get my ferret out of its cage before I left, and this beam just went down from the ceiling. It fell at an angle and knocked me down and lodged right here in my stomach. It was, like, pinning me to the ground. The only thing keeping me alive was that beam inside here." He patted his beer belly. "And I was screaming for help for a while, and then I heard her voice. She told me to keep yelling so she could find me, and then my door just swung open. And she came in, and she got on the floor beside me and there was this giant wind all of a sudden and the beam just started to lift up. I started bleeding and I fainted but when I woke up, I just saw this bright light. Everything was on fire, and it really hurt but then a second or two later, it was done and I was normal again. Then she grabbed my ferret from his cage, brought him over to me and we were just standing outside. It was amazing."

"What did she look like?" the interviewer asked.

"I don't know, it was hard to see. But I know she had bright green eyes. It was almost like they were light bulbs or something. She was beautiful though, exactly what you'd think an Angel would look like."

"Well, I mean... He's right about the Angel part."

"Are you serious right now?" Leah made a face. "You seriously risked exposure?"

"It wasn't like that," I said. "I was watching the news, and they said they were having a hard time getting everyone out, and I could see how scared everyone was, so I just—"

"You risked exposing us. You risked exposing yourself." Her eyes darted between mine. "You haven't even been out of your fucking death coma for two days and you're already going to make my life hell again."

"We're Guardians, Leah," I said. "It's our job to protect humanity. It's bred into us. I'm not going to apologize for saving lives."

She laughed.

"What?"

"Uh-oh," I heard Adam mutter under his breath.

"Why didn't you care this much about your *own* people a week ago? Or better yet, a month ago? You had contact with Jeremy, you could have knocked the wall down in your head—"

"You don't have a clue what you're talking about," I snapped.

Honestly, I got it. Yes, I did risk exposure. I could have gone about it completely different. But I was in a bad place, and I needed to feel good. Saving people did just that. Leah had been looking for a reason to pick a fight with me. She didn't have a reason to before that would seem justified, but after that, she definitely had just cause.

Still, my blood boiled. She wasn't there, she didn't understand. I knew we wouldn't have come out on the other end if I hadn't done things exactly as I had. Jeremy would have died, I may have too, and there was a good chance that all the people who helped would have as well.

"I've been in your fucking head, dude. I know you've thought it. You had the opportunity to give Jeremy your location and you didn't. You could have fucking—"

"Shut up, Leah," Brody said, watching me clench my hands to fists and grind my teeth together.

"You could have saved everyone. And you could have done it sooner. We could have come for you. We could have gotten you, and Chris, and the baby, and—"

"Seriously, shut the fuck up, Leah," Jeremy said.

"We could have saved you all, but you had to be the hero, right?" Leah said. "You just *had* to prove something. Had to show the world what Laila Callidy is capable of now that all of her superpowers have been tortured out of her—"

"You weren't even there," I barked. "Celena has only known me for six months, never even met Chris, and she was fucking there. But where the hell were you? Pressing buttons and fighting battles behind a fucking screen—"

"Fighting battles behind a screen?!" Her eyes glowed and she leaned over the counter. "I hacked into the chips installed in your bodies and disabled them. I did what I fucking could."

"So did I!" I screamed, eyes glowing with warmth. "If I didn't do it the way I did, people would have fucking died. *Our* people would have died."

"You don't know that—"

"And neither do you!"

She gritted her teeth together. "I know that you could have saved all of them if you would have used your fucking head for once. My brother would be here if you wouldn't have fucked up. Your son would be alive right now if you—"

"Shut your mouth, Leah," Jeremy said behind gritted teeth.

She clenched her teeth together as I tried to steady my fast, anxious breaths. "You could have done better."

"Fuck you. Up on your high horse like you have any room to talk. You didn't even know your brother was alive. You *wouldn't* have known if it weren't for me. And yeah, you know what, things could have turned out better than they did. I'll never say that I'm happy with this outcome because it's fucking bullshit, Leah. All of this is fucking bullshit. But at least I fucking did something. You didn't. You weren't out there with us opening doors. You didn't go through what we did. You'll never understand what I'm fucking feeling right now. But don't go casting stones like you've never fucked up." I pushed my trembling teeth together. I turned to Jeremy. "I'll see you at home."

"Wait, baby—" he began, but I was already gone.

CHAPTER SIXTEEN

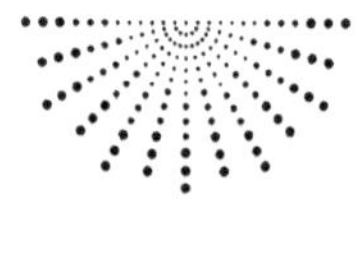

LAILA

I sat on the floor of my bathroom with my back against the door and my hands cupped over my mouth. For the past four hours, I hadn't been able to stop crying. I'm not sure what the worst part was.

Was it the stress everyone at home was under while I was gone? Was it that Hannah blamed herself for the whole ordeal? Was it because I could have saved Chris and failed?

Was it because I was the reason my son died before he even got to live?

It was all horrible and I hated myself for every bit of it. I couldn't even bring myself to look in the God damned mirror. I hated myself.

It wasn't just one of those moments in life where I could let my mistakes fade away.

I was the reason my son was dead.

That fight with Leah dissolved the numbness and reality set in.

My son died in my arms, but still managed to save me before I bled out. How did I fail him when he gave his life for mine? How did I let him die? How did I leave his uncle trapped inside? How could I be so powerful and yet still so weak?

I ran my fingers through my hair on either side of my head and squeezed at the roots until I felt painful pressure around my skull. As I lifted my hands to my head, I saw the scars on both of my wrists and wanted to vomit.

It was all my fault.

Every bit of it could have been avoided.

I could've been anxiously waiting for my water to break at that moment, instead, I was struggling to catch my breath as I mourned the loss of my son on the bathroom floor.

I didn't even want to be alive. I pushed that thought to a far corner of my mind when I was under the impression that I was the only one who thought it was my fault. I started to believe it wasn't, that it was Peterson's, but Leah was right.

I could have let them come. A lot of people probably would have died just trying to get inside, but maybe Micah would be alive. Maybe.

"Baby," Jeremy said outside the door with a quiet knock. "Baby, can you talk to me?"

"I'm fine," I managed out, forcing myself to stop crying. "Please just leave me alone."

"Laila, please let me in," he whispered.

I knew he could feel my tears, that he wanted to help, but I didn't want him to see me. I felt pathetic enough already.

"That was horrible, I don't know why she said all of that. She didn't mean it."

"She did," I murmured, holding my jaw to keep it from shaking.

"Well, even if she did. She was wrong. You did what you had to do; I know you did. I was there, I saw you. It was the most amazing thing I've ever seen. You fought harder than any of us have ever fought for anything."

I felt his hand tap against the door at my back.

It reminded me of Chris tapping on the wall against my bed from his cell. I'd heat my hand and press it against the cool steel. It wasn't much, but it was the closest thing to human touch Chris had felt in almost seven years.

And that just made it hurt worse.

I held my hand to my face and covered my mouth to prevent a desperate, pathetic shriek from leaving my lips.

"Laila, please don't shut me out. Let me be here for you." His voice was a gentle plea. "Please, baby."

"I just need to be alone right now."

A moment passed. "Alright. I'm going to go to the store, do you need anything?"

"I'm okay. Thank you," I muttered.

"Okay. Your phone's on the table. Just let me know if you change your mind, alright?"

"Mhmm," I said, still holding my hand over my mouth.

"I love you," he said.

"I love you too," I murmured.

After half an hour or so more of crying, I heard a knock at the door from the steps. "Jeremy? Laila? Anybody home?"

Max.

At least he didn't know what I did.

"I'm in the bathroom, hang on a second," I called.

I brought myself to my feet and wiped my cheeks with my hands to clean up the tears, but it wasn't enough. I resorted to the box of tissues on the edge of the counter. My hands angrily wiped salty water and snot from my face. Then I reached for the door handle, spun it and walked down the hall to the living room. Max leaned against the couch facing the window with a patient gaze.

"Sorry I'm such a mess." I wiped my hands against my red leggings.

He turned with a wide smile. He didn't even glance at my scars or bony cheeks. He just smiled. "I'm so happy to see you."

Tears welled in my eyes at the sincerity in his voice.

"I missed you." I rushed toward him and put my arms around his big, chunky shoulders. He moved his around my waist and pulled me up against him.

Max was the oldest, and only human, friend I had outside of Mom and Jenna. We'd met so long ago that I couldn't even remember it. He was just always there. Grade school? Middle school? I couldn't be sure.

We were the typical small-town kids you see in the movies. We went bowling, hiking through the local woods to get high, movie theaters, day trips to the city and high school dances together.

He was one of the only people left who didn't know what I was. It fed me the illusion that I still had humanity hanging on inside somewhere.

He pulled back to meet my gaze and frowned. "You're home now. You've got to turn that frown upside down."

I forced a smile. My lip began to tremble, and tears started to gush from my eyes again. "Damn." He hugged me tight. "You aren't doing too good, are you?"

I shook my head against his chest.

He hugged me back for a moment. Then he said the words that always left Max's lips in a moment of turmoil. "Do you want to get high?"

I pulled away with a smile, nodded, and wiped my cheeks. "Got any booze too?"

He chuckled. "I don't, but you've got a full bar downstairs."

"Want to get drunk with me?"

"Are you sure *you* want to get drunk?"

"I just want to forget."

"This is your first drink since October, huh?" Max opened a bottle of Crown Royal and poured it into a short glass cup.

"Yup."

He poured she short glass it about two finger lengths high. He set the bottle down and began to screw the lid back on. I reached across the counter, pulled the bottle from his hand, and poured my glass until it was three quarters of the way full.

"No way you're drinking all that."

"Wanna put money on it?" I asked.

"Five bucks you can't drink that at once."

"I bet you ten that I can drink it without a chaser." My grin heightened.

He smirked, reached in his pocket, and threw a ten on the bar. "Bet."

"Alright. Bet." I raised the glass to my lips and tilted my head back. I shuddered as it hit my tongue but kept chugging anyway.

Truthfully, I wanted nothing more in that moment than to get black-out-drunk. I wanted to forget my entire existence. I wanted to climb inside of that bottle and drown myself within it. I wanted that numb feeling back because it was better than the agony of knowing what I'd done.

"Oh no." Max frowned as I gulped. "Shit, I needed that for gas."

The whiskey slid down like rain against the window on a dreary day, gradually burning its path down my throat until I felt a warm tingly sensation in my belly. I used my tongue to lick the last drop off the edge of the cup. Then I slammed it to the bar. I shivered, making an awkward gag face.

He laughed. "Sure you don't want a chaser?"

"Nah, I'm good. But keep your ten bucks, I just wanted to prove a point."

He slid the ten toward me. "A bet's a bet."

I left the cash but grabbed the bottle. I took another sip and walked through the room. My gaze caught one of the poles supporting the building where a flyer hung, taped up like a lost dog poster. My face with **STILL MISSING** written below it.

I grabbed the paper and ripped it from the pole. Then I took another gulp from the bottle, already feeling my vision getting distorted around the edges.

"Here." Max took the bottle of Crown from my hand and replaced it with a bottle of red wine.

"True friendship," I said.

I glanced above him at the giant poster, at least three feet wide and five feet tall that hung to the right of the stage. My face.

"Did you guys have to turn this entire place into a shrine of me?" I started toward it, took a gulp from the bottle, and set it on a table.

"We were worried," he said.

I grabbed a chair from a table, pulled it against the wall, and wobbled my way onto it until I stood. I grabbed the top corner, ripped it down, and jumped to the ground with it. Then I started walking around and yanking down every picture of me that was plastered over the walls.

"This is supposed to be a positive, creative space." I tore down another one. "Nobody wants to look at some dead girl's face while they're trying to have a good time."

Max caught my shoulder and forced me to meet his gaze. "But you aren't dead, Laila."

"I might as well be," I muttered. Then I turned back toward the wall. My nail lifted to scratch the tape down.

"Don't say that." Max frowned, dragging a chair and ushered for me to sit. He lowered himself to the chair across from mine. I reluctantly joined him, exhaling as my ass hit the chair. "We were so scared you were gone forever, Laila."

"Yeah, me too," I muttered.

"I know I'm not supposed to ask, and if you don't want to tell me, you don't have to."

"Ask away," I mumbled. "I'm drunk now anyway, so I'm an open book."

He stroked his chin and chewed his bottom lip. "What happened to you?"

What happened to me? What happened to me. So much. So much more than I could say aloud.

I let out an ironic laugh. "I don't even know where to start."

He gestured toward my throat. "Maybe there?"

I raised my hand to touch the, now healed, scar from the removal of my implants. "GPS tracker so I could be found if I escaped." He gestured to my wrists. "More trackers. They put them everywhere so we couldn't cut them out. Might be able to get a few but you're more likely to bleed out searching before you get them all."

His face was emotionless, and I appreciated that. Then he raised his fingertip to the side of my neck and grazed the bite shaped scar. I pushed his hand away and tucked my hair in front of it. "Is it that obvious?"

"Not with your hair there."

"Guess I'm never getting a bob again," I muttered. "Where's my wine?"

He stood from his chair, grabbed my wine off a table a bit closer to the stage, then handed it to me. As he sat, in a level tone, he said, "Is that what it looks like?"

"Yup." I held the glass to my lips and tilted my head back.

"Was that... Were you pregnant then?" he asked.

"Twenty-six weeks, I think."

"Sick fuck," he mumbled.

"You don't know the half of it." An ironic laugh. "You know what's funny?"

"Hmm?" he asked.

"Emotionally, I felt better in there than I do out here," I said. "I don't even know what normal is anymore. Definitely not me, I'm far from normal."

"You always have been." He smiled.

"But I don't know. I do feel normal for a second, and then it just kind of fizzles out, you know? I don't know, it's hard to explain."

"Honestly, you don't seem that different to me, man," he said. "I mean, aside from the scars and everything. You're you. An angrier, maybe a little sadder, version of you. But still. You."

I smiled. "Well, I'm glad you see it that way."

He smiled back. Then he took the bottle from my hand, drank for a moment, and set it on the table. "Jeremy made it sound like you had a shit ton of scars. I mean, not in a bad way but..."

"I do. He hasn't even seen them all. Or maybe he did when I was in the hospital. I don't know."

"Are they that bad?" he asked.

"I don't know. The one on my thigh's pretty gnarly, but I haven't brought myself to look at my back."

"Your back?"

I lifted the bottle to my lips and took a slow, long gulp. "I don't really want to talk about it."

"It's alright."

A smile came to my lips. Most of them made me feel weak, but not this one. This one I'd gotten for fighting back. "Want to see the one on my leg though?"

"Sure."

I pulled at the base of my once tight legging that now effortlessly stretched around my knee cap up my tiny thigh. "Holy shit." He poked the circle in the middle. "Were you shot?"

I nodded and pulled my pant leg back down. "Not a good time, man."

"Well, yeah, I can fucking imagine." He took the bottle from my hand and drank a long gulp. He burped. "You're a badass, dude."

I laughed. "I ain't shit."

"You were shot and lived to tell the tale. You're a badass."

"It was all for nothing anyway."

"What do you mean?" he asked.

"Look at me, Max. I'm supposed to be thirty-seven weeks pregnant." I grabbed the bottle and took another gulp. "Now I'm just a bunch of scar tissue."

Silence crept in for a moment. And I just kept chugging. The words were spilling out like vomit, and it felt good. Not good, I suppose. More like relief. But damn, it was just nice to talk to someone who wasn't looking at me like I was broken. He wanted to know things, but he wasn't tiptoeing. He was just... being my best friend. Talking to me like he always had.

"What happened?" he asked quietly. "To the baby, I mean."

I tightened my hand around the glass bottle and lifted it to my lips. I drank it down until I had at least a fourth of the liter in my belly. "He died."

"Damn," he said. "I'm so sorry, man. I know how excited you and Jeremy were."

I bit the raw skin beneath my lip. "It's fucking awful. Worst thing I've ever felt in my life." Another ironic laugh.

It wasn't funny. But that was my thing. When I was hurting, I laughed. Tried to look on the bright side. It was a very tiny, figment of fraction of light in this case. But still. Something.

"But at least I can drink. And legally, too. How 'bout that?" He gave a wan smile. "Don't look at me like that, okay? I'm not anyone's charity case."

"That's not what that face was."

"No?"

"I mean, yeah. I guess it was out of pity, but not for you," he said. "More for Jeremy, to be honest."

"How was he?" I asked. "When I was gone and everything."

"Not good," he murmured. "Real bad, man."

"How bad are we talking here?" I leaned over the table.

"I don't know if I should put my nose where it doesn't belong."

My heart sunk. "He relapsed, didn't he?"

Of course he had. He was a recovering addict who felt his pregnant fiancé being tortured for months, then raped. I'd just gotten into an argument with his sister and I was already a bottle in. I may have been a serious abuser, but I wasn't an addict. And I wanted nothing more than to get fucked up. Surely, he'd felt the same way.

Max scratched his head. "I mean, he wasn't banging dope or anything. But he was drinking. Like, drinking more than you."

I ironically lifted the bottle to my lips. "Can't say I blame him."

"Neither do I," he muttered. "Honestly, I don't know why he didn't go back to heroin. If I were in his shoes, I would have."

Max didn't even know that Jeremy was feeling every awful thing that happened to me while I was in there.

"It was depressing. I don't know. He was like a different person," he said. "He still did a good job around here though. He was spiking his morning coffee with booze, but he still made sure to write out the schedule, and fill out quarterlies, and make phone calls, and do pay roll." He scratched his head. "The guy does well under pressure."

"Like a lump of coal." I smiled. "Push him hard enough and you'll get a diamond."

He smiled. "Speaking of those. Are you guys still getting married?"

I paused. "I don't know. I mean, I would think so, right? My abduction doesn't rescind his offer, does it?"

"I wouldn't think so." He laughed. "I mean, he still refers to you as his fiancé. So I guess you're still engaged?"

"I should check on that," I muttered. I glanced around the room. "It's so quiet."

"Want me to put some music on?" he asked.

"I'll handle the music. Can you go upstairs and get my weed and papers?"

"We're going to smoke down here?"

"We're closed for the night, why not? I'm sure people do anyway. It's not like we search people at the door before shows."

He laughed, stood, and headed to the stairs. "Well, you're the boss."

I stood and reached into my back pocket to pull out my phone. It was actually the first time I looked at it since I was home. As I slid it open, I saw a notification for nearly every app installed. One hundred and fifty-six emails, eighty-four missed calls, seven hundred and thirty-eight Facebook notifications, and one hundred and twenty-seven texts. That was just on the home screen. Clearly, Jeremy wasn't the type to go through his partner's phone, even if I was practically dead.

I rubbed my eyes. No part of me wanted to open a single one of them. I knew what most of them would be or at least the ones for social media.

I miss you so much!

Please come home),:

Why do bad things happen to good people? Missing my girl so much today.

Don't let the police forget! She's still missing!

Missing her so bad! I only met her once at a party when she was throwing up in the bathroom after drinking ten Four Lokos and a cut of shrooms but if I could go back to that night and tell her this would happen, I totally would!

None of them actually gave a damn. The only people who did knew where I was and wouldn't waste their time on some stupid paragraph on the internet because they knew it wouldn't make a difference.

If we, a group of legendary, super powered creatures couldn't get a single lead on Peterson's operations in all the months we were searching, there was no way in hell a bunch of lazy cops would. Everyone else just wanted to jump on the viral bandwagon in failing attempts to find the poor, helpless pregnant girl they met a handful of times.

CHAPTER SEVENTEEN

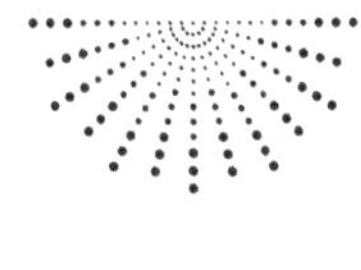

LAILA

Deciding which song to listen to after not hearing music for so long was like trying to pick my favorite blossom from a field of sunflowers. They were all so beautiful. Deciding on just one didn't seem fair.

I wanted to pick just the right one before settling on a classic. *Come On Eileen* by Dexy's Midnight Runners.

The violin picked up and I turned the volume knob as high as it could go, enjoying the vibration in my chest. I headed toward the open dance floor, lifted the bottle to my lips, and tilted my head back. My hips drunkenly swayed, and despite how horrible I was at this, it was relieving.

Suddenly, I felt a hand at my waist from behind. The startle sent me about three feet forward, clutching my chest and spilling wine all over myself. I turned with a laugh and met Jeremy's gaze.

He smiled, yelling over the music, "I didn't mean to scare you."

I laughed, set the bottle to a table, and took his hands. He pulled me toward him and placed his at my hips.

"I thought you couldn't dance." He grinned, spinning me in a circle with a sweet smile.

"Only when I'm sober."

He forced a smile. He held my hips and swayed, gently dancing through the rest of the song with me.

I knew what he was thinking without having to read his mind.

But, Laila. You were nervous about smoking a little weed, how could you possibly want to get drunk?

I wanted to tell him that I knew it didn't make sense. I wanted to explain it, but I didn't know how.

It was self-destructive, I knew that. It's not like I was proud to drown myself in my sorrows. But at that moment, I needed an escape. I needed to lose touch with reality for a while. I needed to stop wanting to die for a little bit. It was far from a healthy scapegoat, but an escape regardless.

Whether it was the abyss at the bottom of a green glass bottle or flying into that burning building, I just wanted to feel something that didn't hurt. Even if that meant becoming completely numb.

I was tired of thinking. I wanted to burn my thoughts alive. I hated them. I hated what they were telling me about myself. And I would do anything to shut them up, even if I couldn't kill them for good. Even if it only lasted for a short while. Anything to make the pain stop was better than nothing at all.

As the song ended, Jeremy pushed hair from my face and gently cupped my cheek. "You're drinking alone?"

"I sent Max upstairs to get the weed and papers."

"And you're okay?"

I smiled. "I'm alright."

"Well, I'm sure you guys have a lot of catching up to do. I still have a good bit of work to do in the bathroom, so I think I'll head upstairs. Let me know if you need anything though, okay?"

"Will do, baby."

I think he knew how refreshing it was for me to be around Max. He wouldn't say 'enjoy being around someone who doesn't know what you did' but I knew that's what he meant. And I appreciated it.

He kissed my forehead before he began to pull away, but I caught his hand. I rolled onto the tips of my toes, grasped the side of his neck and pushed my lips to his for a long, peaceful moment. His hand made it to the small of my back and tugged my body close against his. It wasn't one of those extremely passionate, sexual kisses. It was one of those sweet, gentle ones that leaves you hoping for more.

But I pulled away and wrapped my arms around his chest. I didn't want more yet. I just wanted that moment. Just the feeling of his arms around me and the vibration of his heart beneath my ear.

"I missed this." I closed my eyes and breathed in the smell of his cologne I'd been trying to remember for months.

He kissed my hair and rested his head against mine. He didn't say anything, he just held me. And I felt like I was floating. Then again, that could have been the hooch.

"Oh, shit." I heard Max say from the steps. "Sorry, I didn't mean to interrupt."

Jeremy chuckled and we pulled apart. "No, you're good, man. I'm gonna head upstairs, you guys have fun."

Max gave a nod and Jeremy started up the steps. I headed to my phone attached to the AUX cord and turned to Max. "Okay, are you ready for the throwest of throwbacks?"

"Throw it at me." He plopped to a chair and set my bag and papers on the table. I went to the search bar and typed in *Miss Murder* by A.F.I.

As the intro started, his lips lifted in the biggest smile. We both excitedly screamed the lyrics with grins, mumbling our way through the lines we couldn't remember. We jumped around, laughing as we passed the bottle back and forth. We danced ridiculously, pumping our fists in the air, yelling the lyrics into each other's faces with laughs and grins.

It was one of those moments that made me feel alive when most of me wanted to die. Two old friends practically time-travelling to their early adolescence through the sound of drums, a guitar, and a voice.

When the song ended, I wiped sweat from my brow, hopped onto the bar, and dangled my feet off the ledge with a laugh. Max smiled. He sat at a bar stool a few feet from me and poured another glass of Crown.

"Remember when we went to that show?" he asked.

"First concert either of us went to after Adrian went missing."

He took a sip, eyes a bit distant. "Our little group doesn't have the best of luck, does it?"

It wasn't the group so much as it was me. People I loved had a habit of dying.

"Any reason you played that song in particular?" he asked.

I met his gaze. "Are you asking if I want to kill myself?"

"I wasn't gonna say it like that, but sure. Do you want to kill yourself?" He pulled a vape pen from his pocket and handed it to me.

"No. I don't want to kill myself." I pulled a hit deep into my chest and handed it back. "But I don't really want to be alive either."

Max turned away and took another sip of his whiskey. "Yeah, I can relate."

"I just hate my life. I hate myself. I hate what's happened. I'm an overflowing tub of hate. There's still plenty of things I love, you know. Like, I'm relieved that I'm home. I'm relieved that I get to see you, and my mom, and my sister, and Jeremy... But it's just that. Relief. Not happy or pleased. Just relieved. I love you guys, and I love all of this." I gestured around. "I mean, there's a moment or two here and there where I feel happy, but mostly it's just..."

"Relief," he said. "Yeah, I get it."

I was quiet for a moment. "So, this is depression."

"Pretty much." Max laughed and took another gulp. "I've been on antidepressants for a few months and they've really helped. Maybe you should talk to your doctor."

"I don't think antidepressants are it for me, man. I'm not against them or anything. I know they literally save people's lives. I don't know. I... Me and drugs aren't on good terms these days."

"You just hit a THC vape and drank half a bottle of wine." He laughed.

"It's different. I don't know. Neither of them are pharmaceuticals, you know?"

And I still feel that way. Drugs work for some. But I didn't want to be dependent on anything. The withdrawals from the benzos was horrendous. SSRIs may have been easier to get off of, but I still never wanted to experience anything like that again.

"I know big pharma is evil and everything, but like you said, medication saves lives."

"That's how they controlled us, Max," I said suddenly. "They shot us up with tranquilizers and benzos so we couldn't fight back. Do you know how many times I woke up with a new surgical wound of some kind? Do you know how many times I got stabbed with a needle full of some drug I wasn't able to identify and woke up somewhere that I didn't fall asleep?"

His muddy brown eyes softened. "No. I didn't."

I clenched my jaw. "I didn't even let them sedate me when they removed the implants. I can't even look at a needle without my hands shaking and my vision getting fuzzy. Why do you think I left the hospital hours after waking up from a coma, Max?"

"I didn't know."

I released my tense jaw and shook my head. "I'm really not a fan of doctors these days."

He paused. "So that's what they were doing? Experimenting on you?"

I hoisted the bottle of whiskey to my lips and tilted my head back, guzzling until I drank at least three shots worth. "Something like that."

"What do you mean?" he asked.

I laughed, hopped from the counter, and steadied my now drunken body against the counter. "You wouldn't believe me if I told you."

"Try me," he said.

I laughed again, raised the bottle back to my lips, and drank for a moment.

The taste didn't bother me anymore. My mouth, along with the rest of my body, was completely numb. I drank and drank, not even stopping for a breath until the bottle was nearly gone.

That's when things started getting past buzzed onto full blown drunk. My legs swayed beneath me, nearly unable to support my upper half. The room started to spin, and my mouth grew as dry as it would if I were sucking on cotton balls.

I was in no state to be babbling about my life to a human.

"You don't want to know, man," I slurred.

"If you want to tell me, I want to know," he said.

"I want to tell you, but I know you don't want to know."

"Why don't you let me be the judge of that?" he asked.

I laughed, grabbed the bottle off the counter and finished what was left. "You really want to know? Because once you do, it's kind of hard to forget."

CHAPTER EIGHTEEN

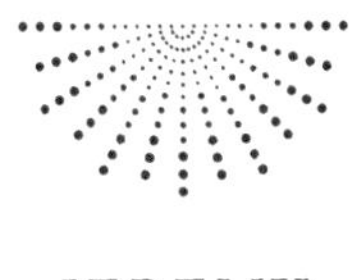

JEREMY

I sang quietly to myself, shimmying a piece of trim into place. It jammed against the edge of the tub and I shook it back and forth a bit. Becoming frustrated, I smacked the corner with the back of my hand. It didn't want to budge so I picked up the hammer from the floor by the toilet. I grabbed a rag from the towel rack, covered the painted piece of wood, and tapped it into place with the hammer.

I hadn't been doing great. Truthfully, having Laila back was almost as hard as her being gone. Every smile she gave looked forced, her arms around me felt obligatory, and things just weren't as they'd been.

I knew they wouldn't be. Rationally, I knew that. But I hoped I was wrong. I hoped we could fall right back to the groove we'd been in.

But we'd never be the people we were before she left again. Things would get better, but they'd never be the same. Which wasn't bad. We'd grown and growing is what we're all meant to do. Things just changed so rapidly, and I wasn't sure how to adjust.

My phone buzzed in my pocket. Setting the hammer down with one hand, I reached into my pants and pulled out my phone with the other. Leah's picture lit up my screen. I rolled my eyes and slid the reject button, plopping to my ass.

I'd already flipped out on her. Although I was in too much of an angry haze to recall exactly what I'd said, I knew selfish bitch and cunt were in there somewhere. The last thing I wanted was to share another word with her.

My phone vibrated again. Leah.

If I knew one thing about my big sister, it was that she wouldn't stop until she got out what she had to say. I didn't want to fight with her, but I didn't have the energy to keep rejecting her calls either.

I accepted the call and held my phone to my ear. "What?"

"You're seriously going to bitch button my call when you're on *my* family plan?" she said.

"Take me off the plan then." I pulled the phone away and clicked the end call button.

It rang again and I clicked accept. "What do you want, Leah?"

"I want to talk about what happened earlier," she said.

"You mean when you told Laila she was the reason our son was dead?" I snapped. "She hasn't even been home for a full day yet and you already jump down her throat? You're supposed to be her friend. No fucking friend would treat someone like that."

"Oh, come on. Laila's my best friend. She knows I'm a cunt—"

"That was fucking different, Leah," I almost yelled. "And you know it. You know that was a different level of fucked up. That was the worst thing you could have ever told her. You knew that and you said it anyway."

"I was just saying what everyone else was thinking."

She wasn't really wrong. It wasn't that I *blamed* Laila for what happened to our son. But I definitely wondered why she was certain I couldn't have helped before he was born. And I wanted to know. I wanted to understand why she did things the way she did. But not at the expense of her healing.

"Fuck you." I clicked the end call button.

It buzzed again and I answered it with a furious slide of my finger. "We both know this has nothing to do with her plan. If she hadn't gotten shot, she would have pulled it off. She would have gotten everyone out and you know it. Maybe her saving those people last night was reckless, but she's fucking hurting, Leah. She did everything she could to save as many people as possible and she still wasn't able to and she's killing herself over it. She fucking *hates* herself for it. She just wanted to help someone who needed it. Chris isn't her brother, Hannah isn't her sister, and she put both her and my son's life on the line to protect them. You have no fucking right to treat her like she did anything wrong," I said practically in one breath.

She began to talk but I continued, "No, this whole fight is because you're jealous. You wish it were Chris. You'd rather it have been him than her and I get it. I fucking get it, Leah. I miss my brother too, but you have no clue how hard the past three months have been for her or me. You think you do because you got a few glimpses into my head, but you don't fucking know. You didn't live it. You don't know what it's like to feel that god damned helpless. You can pretend to, you can act like it's the same because you saw it in my mind, but you don't have a clue. You got to escape it, but I didn't. She didn't."

I paused for a breath as my angry, shaking hand gripped the phone. I was pissed and I had so much more to say. She started to say something, but I cut her off again. "And she lost our baby, and you don't even know the context, and you're going to tell her it was her fault? You're going to blame her for her son's death when she was too weak to prevent it? You're going to make her hate herself more than she already does for something she couldn't help? She did everything in her power to keep as much of *our* family alive as she could. She gave my child's life to protect our sister.

"Chris was the second person she let out, did you know that? I must have walked right past him. He was in the cell next to hers, he was on the top floor, and somehow, we all missed him. And I didn't see you up there trying to bring him home. But Laila tried to get him out first. She did, she got him out and somehow, they got him back. She killed so many guards while Kai and Adam and Brody were getting people out. Not a single *one* of our people was hurt because of what she did. She saved more people in one fail swoop than we've saved in our entire life, Leah. You aren't mad because she did the wrong thing, you're mad because she didn't save the right person."

"Jeremy—"

"You didn't just hurt her today, you hurt me. My son is gone, and I don't even know what happened to him because she can't even talk about him without hysterically crying. I don't even know what she named him. And you made that worse. You just forced her to put up another fucking wall I'll probably never be able to break through. She spent the entire day crying. And now she's wasted blasting screamo music in the basement and it's your fault. Don't call me, quit texting me. Just leave me the fuck alone. If you want to talk to Laila, try and get ahold of her. But I'm done. I'm so fucking sick of you acting like you can say whatever you want and fuck how it makes everyone else feel. I'm done, Leah. Seriously, quit calling or I'm going to turn my phone off."

I pulled the phone from my ear and pressed the end call button. As I sat there trying to catch my breath and steady my shaking hands, I half-expected it to ring again. It wasn't like Leah to back down from an argument.

After a minute or two without a call, I realized that she must have felt guilty. I wondered if I'd been too harsh, but I quickly concluded that I hadn't.

She was right. At some point or another, we all wondered why Laila didn't let me come sooner. But the more I thought about it, the more sense it made.

She went into labor a month early. She thought she had more time for her wounds to heal. She said she was too weak to fight for a reason. There was a massive hole in her thigh from a bullet. She had to be able to move around.

If she had me come any sooner, we wouldn't have been able to get inside without casualties. That's if we were able to get in at all.

Had she let me come while she was *in* labor, she would have been one of the first people they carried out and flew away. No way in hell were they letting her go.

She had to be strong enough to fight her way out. How was she supposed to fight anyone or anything with a baby cramping his way out of her vagina?

She did everything she could in an impossible situation. She fought harder than I ever could have dreamed to. She did everything she fucking could. It infuriated me that Leah cared more about Chris than all the others Laila *did* manage to save.

I loved my brother more than most things. But Laila wasn't one of them. I didn't love anyone as much as I loved her and that baby. I never wanted to admit she was more important to me than my siblings, but it was true. Maybe it was because of the bond, but maybe it was just because I loved harder than I should have.

Either way, no matter how much I missed Chris, I couldn't be upset that she was back. I couldn't be upset with her. She was amazing. She saved so many people. She saved herself.

She just couldn't save everyone.

I lay my head against the wall chewing my lip and shaking my head. My eyes closed, stinging with tears.

I wasn't *happy* with the outcome. But I could have lost her too. I had to be grateful she was back.

As it always did, her pain came out of nowhere and tenfold. A throbbing, stabbing pain in the left side of my forehead that would have knocked me off my feet if I wasn't already sitting. My head quaked, pulsating like it was expanding and contracting against my skull.

Fear rang through me in more agony than the pain itself. I didn't care that it hurt. All that I cared about was finding her.

What if they'd come back? What if that bastard was trying to hurt her again? What if I was about to lose her again?

I grasped my head and pulled myself to my feet. The pain throbbed for a second as I teleported to the bottom of the steps. Then I darted through the kitchen of the diner and called her name.

But Max was already running toward me, yelling something about Laila falling outside. I barely heard him, I just had to get to her. I bolted past him, nearly knocked him over, and hurried out of the diner. Max was close at my tail. After barreling through the front door, I immediately saw her.

She lay on the gravel of the parking lot with a large rock below her head like a pillow. Blood drained against it, forming a slow growing puddle beside her shoulder. Her eyes fluttered open and closed, trying to focus. I collapsed to the ground beside her.

"Laila." I grabbed her face.

"I fell." She laughed. As she opened her mouth, a whiff of alcohol as strong as a doctor would use to sterilize equipment filled my nostrils.

"Jesus, Lai," I whispered. I tucked a hand behind her head and the other below her knees. I lifted her into my arms, heart beating against my chest, and started back to the diner. Her hand grasped my shirt, squeezing it like a handle. Her eyes closed. "Baby, you got to stay awake for me, okay?"

"She—She drank so much." Max held the door open while I turned sideways to keep her head from banging the wall. "She... she was—Oh, god I don't even know. She—She—"

"I told him," she mumbled.

I started through the dining area. "What do you mean? What did you tell him?"

Her glazed eyes fluttered shut. "Everything."

I stopped cold and turned to Max. "What did she tell you?"

He blinked a few times, as if still in awe. "She flew. How—How did she fly?"

Laila. My lovely, beautiful soulmate. The only person in the world who could tell a human what we were and wouldn't send me into a furious frenzy.

I wanted to. I wanted to yell and tell her how stupid what she just did was. But she was Laila. She was the only person in the universe I could never stay angry at for more than a second.

My heart pounded even harder against my chest. "I'll explain everything tomorrow. Go home."

"But, Jeremy—" he began.

"My hands are a little full at the moment, Max, I don't have time to explain," I barked, gesturing to Laila in my arms. "Go home. We'll talk tomorrow. And keep your mouth shut until then."

CHAPTER NINETEEN

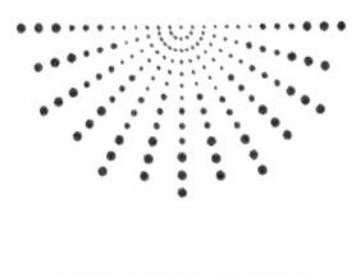

JEREMY

"Hey, I'm sorry if I woke you," I said into the phone. I gently pushed a towel into the gash on Laila's head. "Were you asleep?"

"No, I was just getting ready for bed," Celena said. "What's up? Is everything okay?"

I frowned, shaking my head and gazing over Laila's closed eyes. Blood poured from her head like a leaky sink, little streams sliding past her brow against her eyelids and down her cheeks. "No, not really. I would have called Leah but we're not really talking after today."

"Completely understandable," she muttered. "What's going on? Is someone hurt?"

"Yeah. Laila got really drunk with Max and I don't know what happened exactly, but I guess she fell and cracked her head open. I was going to take her to the hospital, but she told me no and I figured—"

"Shit, okay. Let me get dressed. I'll be over in ten or fifteen minutes."

"No. No, I'll call Adam and have him come grab you. She's bleeding a good bit so the sooner the better. I'd just come get you, but I don't want to leave her."

"Right. Sure. Let me get my shoes on."

"Okay, thank you. I'll see you soon."

"No problem," she said.

I ended the call and dialed Adam's number.

"This better be important," he answered. "I was having a damn good dream."

"I need you to bring Celena over here. Like asap. Laila cracked her head open and she's bleeding a lot, and I don't want to leave her or move her and—"

"Fuck," Adam mumbled. "Guess I'm up now. Alright. I'm coming." He hung up and I tossed my phone to the coffee table.

I started counting the little breaths that billowed from her narrow, fragile chest. But it was hard to hear them over the sound of my heart slamming against my ear drums.

She looked so small that night. So human. Four days before, I watched her lift an entire floor off the ground and throw it in the air like a basketball. And that night, she lay practically lifeless in front of me. Yet again.

I wondered if I'd ever get used to seeing her as the dramatized oxymoron that she was. The strongest creature to ever walk Earth's green grass while still being the softest, most delicate thing I'd ever laid eyes on.

She was so worried about the scars and how skinny she was now as if it mattered. But even like that, dripping in her own blood with nearly purple lips and pale as paper skin, no one else compared to her. She was still the most beautiful thing I'd ever seen.

It broke my heart to look at the scars, but only because I wished I would have been able to protect her. Not because they were ugly. There'd never come a time when I looked at her and thought the word ugly. Never, not once.

She was broken and hurting, maybe even dying a little inside, but still the most beautiful thing I'd ever seen. In fairness though, that may have had something to do with my hero, damsel in distress complex.

"Jesus Christ, Lai," Adam said behind me.

I stood to make room for Celena to reach her. "I'm sorry I woke you guys up."

Adam frowned, gazing down at her. "Don't worry about it."

Celena kneeled beside Laila's head. "Laila." She gently shook her shoulder.

Her eyes fluttered open a bit and she smiled. "Hey, sissy."

Celena laughed. "Got yourself pretty good there, huh?" Laila closed her bloodshot eyes again. "I'm going to heal this up for you, okay?" Laila gave another slow nod and dozed back off.

"Come here." Adam gestured toward the kitchen.

I teleported after him. "What?"

"Is she alright?" Adam's concerned eyes met mine. "I haven't really gotten a chance to talk to you since she woke up."

"I don't know. She seemed okay, better than I expected, anyway. Until Leah said all that shit. Then she locked herself in the bathroom and cried for like five hours. Then she went downstairs and got drunk with Max."

"Jesus." He rubbed his tired eyes. "That was horrible, I don't know why she has to be such a cunt."

"Maybe you guys should do something. You and Laila, I mean. She's… I don't know, she's having a hard time talking to me. She tells me some things, but not much. I know she'd talk to Leah if she weren't being such a bitch to her. But she's not going to talk to Hannah about it because she knows how guilty she feels over everything and doesn't want to burden her with how she's feeling too. And you've known her longer than any of us, you might be our best bet at getting through to her. Maybe you and Brody can take her out somewhere, or do something here, or…" I rubbed my eyes with my thumb and forefinger. "God, I don't know. I just want her to talk to someone."

"I think she needs therapy, dude," Adam said. "I mean, yeah, I'll definitely talk to her. I want to hang out, I'm sure Brody does. But I don't think it's going to make a difference, man. She needs serious psychiatric help. Maybe even meds."

"She's not going to take any pills," I said. "But I agree. She needs to see a professional. She's been through some of the worst trauma imaginable, and…" I paused. "I don't know how to help her. I don't know what to do. It's like a piece of her died in there."

"Part of her did, Jeremy," Adam said quietly. "Her baby, your son... He's gone. Laila cries when she sees roadkill. What this is doing to her head... God, all I've got to say is that I'm glad I'm not a telepath. I don't even want to know what's going on between her ears."

"I guess I just have to be here for her, right? I mean, we know she's going to do what she wants regardless—"

"Hey, guys," Laila's drunken voice said behind me.

I turned. She grabbed the dining table. Celena stood behind her with her arms outstretched, waiting for Laila to hit the ground.

"Hey, baby." I walked toward her and put my hands on either of her hips. She laid her head against my chest, radiating warmth against me like a little personal heater. I steadied her drunken body against mine.

"Hey, Lai." Adam smiled. "Looks like you had a good night."

She chuckled. "I've seen better days."

I leaned down and kissed her sweat dampened scalp. I saw his smile fall before he forced it back up.

"It amazes me how you can fight a bunch of lunatics with guns and Demons with superpowers but can't manage to win a fight with the ground." He smiled wider. "I can think of at least four different occasions where you cracked your head open now. Not even doing anything impressive, just walking or standing up or something."

She laughed. "Gravity's my worst enemy. Mostly when I'm drunk though."

"Thank you, guys, for coming." I laced my fingers around her lower back.

"Don't mention it." Celena gazed over Laila's swaying body as I struggled to keep her vertical.

"Do you want to do something soon, Lai? Maybe go on a hike or something?" Adam asked.

"That'd be nice."

"It's a date. You get a good night's sleep, alright?"

She yawned. "Sounds good."

"We should get going, though," Celena said. "I'm opening tomorrow."

"Thanks again." I rested my chin on top of Laila's head.

"Good night." Laila drunken eyes closed against my chest.

Celena smiled. She held my gaze for a moment. "Take care of her, alright?"

"I got her." I held her body a bit tighter to mine. Celena gave a nod. Adam teleported to her. He placed his hand on her shoulder and they disappeared.

"I need a bath." Laila started to pull away.

"Baby." I slightly tightened my hands around her. She looked up to meet my gaze with big, pouty emerald eyes. "You're really drunk. How 'bout you just lie down?"

"I don't want to sleep in my blood again."

Those words sent a shiver up my spine and phantom pains over my extremities. She'd slept in her own blood for three months. Obviously, she didn't want to sleep in the freshly made sheets doused in blood.

I frowned. "I don't want you to fall and get hurt again either."

She laid her head back on my chest. "Can you help me then?"

I was a little surprised she was willing to get naked in front of me. She hated shut doors, but had made sure to close the bathroom's each time she went inside. She carefully held her gown together when she stood at the hospital. I knew she didn't want me to see her back, and I didn't blame her, so I didn't push the issue.

When I didn't reply, she looked up and met my gaze. "You don't have to, I guess that was a silly question."

"No. No, it's okay. I'll help you." I smiled and brushed hair from her face.

She laid her head back down. "I haven't been able to look."

"What do you mean?" I ran my palm over the back of her head.

"My back," she whispered. "You can tell me how ugly it is now."

I closed my eyes. Quietly, I said, "You're beautiful."

CHAPTER TWENTY

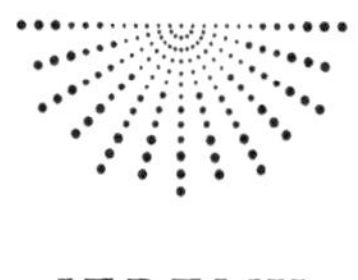

JEREMY

Her feet bowed outward as I kept my arms beneath her shoulders. I'd tried to pick her up, but she insisted she could walk. It left me practically carrying her like a toddler learning to take its first steps.

As we made it to the bathroom, I carefully helped her to the toilet. She leaned back and rested her head against the wall behind it.

"Here." I delicately tucked my thumbs into the waist band of her pants. When I began to tug them down, I noticed a big, wet crimson spot on the crotch and felt my heart begin to race.

She gazed down at it. Tears beaded from the edges of her eyes. "I'm still bleeding from the baby."

My heart's rhythm leveled out. I lowered myself to the edge of the tub. "Postpartum bleeding's normal. I think it should start slowing down soon."

She angrily wiped her tears away. Her lip quivered and her head shook. "I don't want to be postpartum."

My chest tightened and my stomach sunk. Water tried to burn across my eyes, but I held it in. I knew how much this was hurting her because it was hurting me just as bad. But to hear her say it...

"I know, baby."

Her gaze met mine. "I'm sorry." Her lip trembled beneath her big teary eyes. "I'm so sorry."

I kneeled in front of her. "Don't apologize. It isn't your fault."

"It is." Tears trickled from her eyes. "It is."

"No." I tucked blood drenched hair behind her ear. "You did everything you could."

"Not really. Leah was right, I could have done more. I could have done better."

I blinked tears of my own away. "You did everything you could, amour."

I thought it'd make her smile. She always had before when I spoke in French. But her head shook and a soft sob escaped her.

"Leah was right. I could have done better. I could have saved him. I could have... I-I failed him. I failed you. I failed Chris, I failed Leah, and—And I-I failed everyone." Her jaw trembled. The tears fell harder, and her breaths became uneven. "I should have healed him; he shouldn't have healed me. I was supposed to protect him and I failed him. I fucking failed."

I gently thumbed her tears away. "Baby, you didn't choose any of this. You didn't ask to be taken. What happened after that, what you went through... To accomplish what you did, you had to think. There was too much on the line not to. Things could have ended better than they did, yes. But they also could have not ended at all. If you weren't as smart as you were, you might still be there. More than two hundred other people would *still* be there. But you saved them, you saved yourself."

Her cries got closer together. I took her hands in mine. Her lips were trembling, the once snow soft, ample cheeks were as red as apples and more hollow than an abandoned house. Her eyes were practically begging for help, and I didn't know how.

I didn't know how to help. All I wanted to do was take her pain away and I didn't know how.

I was right back to where I was a month ago. She was hurting and there was nothing to do. All I could do was be there.

"You did everything you could," I said again.

"I didn't." Her cries got harder and her teeth clamored together. "I didn't. I had one job. I had to keep him safe and I fucked up. My baby is gone. He's dead because of me." I could barely hear her through the sobs but she was talking and I wouldn't tell her to slow or calm down. At least she was talking. "I should have let you come sooner. I shouldn't have waited. I—I..." She stuttered and slurred as she spoke. It was like watching an artifact fall to the ground and shatter in slow motion. Her glazed over green eyes met mine. "Please don't hate me. Please don't."

"No." I reached out and put my arms around her shoulders. I pulled her tight. My head shook. "I could never hate you, baby."

Laila's cries were so deep that she struggled to breathe, let alone speak. "You should. You shouldn't love me after what I did. You—You should hate me. It's all my fault. Micah's gone and it's my fault. It's all my fault."

His name. That was the first time I heard her say his name.

A tear formed in the corner of my eye. I pulled back to look at her and brought a sad smile to my lips, wiping the salty water from her cheeks with my thumbs. "You decided on Micah?"

I was trying to change the subject without really changing the subject. Desperately attempting to get the conversation away from how much she hated herself was easier said than done. No matter what I brought up, it always came back to her failures. It was like a balancing act. I was constantly trying to support her as she walked a tight rope of sorrow and grief without getting too close, because if I did, I knew she'd just push me away. When you're walking a rope like that, just one strong gust of wind can send you plummeting downward, let alone a physical push.

She wiped her cheeks with the back of her hands. "Micah Christopher Skoulda."

I smiled. "How did Chris feel about that?"

She chuckled through her trembling lips. "I don't know. He was excited," she mumbled. "But he was scared I'd lose him."

"Was he okay?" I asked quietly, trying to get the subject off of Micah because I knew how much that hurt her, but also because I missed my brother and wanted to hear about him. "Chris. In there, I mean."

Her voice was quiet. She gazed at the ground. "No one's okay in there. But he was better than most."

I smiled. "He always was an optimist."

She stared off into the distance. "He doesn't deserve what's happened to him."

"Neither do you," I whispered.

Her trembling lip shook worse. She rocked her head from side to side. "I'm not innocent any more, Jeremy. I deserve to hurt."

I knew she was right; she was far from innocent. But no matter how many lives she'd taken, she didn't deserve that pain. No one deserves the pain of losing a child.

"Nothing you did when you were in there was unjustified, Laila." I pushed hair behind her ear. "You did everything you could to save as many lives as you could. You took some too, I know that. But that doesn't mean anything. You aren't heartless, you just aren't helpless. You did everything you could, baby. I know you did."

"I didn't save them." Her teeth clanged off of each other as her breaths got further apart. "I ruined everything. It was all for nothing. Micah died for *nothing*."

I hugged her tighter, shaking my head. "No, it wasn't."

She was on the verge of a panic attack; I could see it. Her lips quivered, her drunken hands shook, her teeth chattered. If she'd been standing, she would have already hit the ground.

All I could think to do was hug her. I didn't know what else to say or actions to take that would help. All I did know was that when I held her tight enough, the shaking got less violent. She wasn't okay. She was anything but okay. But it was all that I could do.

"None of this is your fault. None of it."

She cried into the nape of my neck. Her hands shook around my body. I held her a while longer. Just letting her cry against me.

"I'm so sorry," she said again.

"Shh." I kissed the top of her head. Then I whispered in her ear, "I love you."

"I love you too," she murmured. "I love you so much."

"It's okay." I soothed my hands through her hair. "It's okay."

It wasn't okay. It wouldn't be okay for a really long time. There'd be many more nights like that before she was remotely close to level again.

Like all things, it was going to get worse before it got better. We were past the absolute worst of it, but it wasn't close to over.

We had been through a lot of shit together. But nothing, and I mean *nothing*, was as bad as those few months. Nothing touched the damage those three months did to her. It wasn't even those few months inside, but the past two weeks since she lost the baby.

Nothing could ever destroy her the way that losing him did.

CHAPTER TWENTY-ONE

JEREMY

After a few long minutes, she was able to regain her composure. She pulled away wiping her cheeks. Then she exhaled a slow, calming breath. "I should get cleaned up, huh?"

I nodded, stood, and turned to the bathtub. I adjusted the temperature, threw some body wash into the water, and spun it around until it created bubbles.

As I turned back to her, she gazed up at me with lips curled downward. "I don't want you to see them."

I was afraid to see them too. Not because of the way they looked. I didn't care how they looked. But I knew it'd hurt. She hated them for their appearance. I hated them because that was evidence of my inability to protect her.

"I'm going to see them sooner or later, baby. But you don't have to do this, you can just lay down and go to bed if you want."

Her head shook. "I've spent too many nights covered in my blood." She gazed down at her hands for a moment. "I know they're ugly."

I lifted her chin to meet my gaze. "You are the most beautiful person I have ever seen, Laila. No scar is ever going to change that."

"I used to be. Beautiful, I mean."

I sat on the edge of the tub and took her hands in mine. "They're scars, baby. You're not any different. You're just as beautiful as you've always been."

"I remember the look on your face when you saw Daniel's back."

"That was different," I said. "It was the shock. He was a little kid, and I hit him with a car." She sniffled snot back up her nose, and I cradled her cheek in my hand. "I know you have scars and it doesn't change the way I see you."

She slowly raised her hand to her neck and traced the scar at the base of her throat. "You made the same face when you saw this."

I was quiet for a moment. "I did, huh?"

Her eyes steadily held my gaze. "You did."

"I just..." I paused. "I didn't think about the scars in that moment. I was just focused on seeing you. I... I heard your voice, and I just... I had to see you." I smiled and ran my thumb along her jaw. "It startled me a little, but it doesn't mean anything." I gently thumbed her pretty lip. "You're still the most beautiful thing I've ever seen."

She looked away. "You have to say that."

I lifted her chin, leaned forward, and molded my mouth with hers, cupping her face in my hand. Telling her she was beautiful didn't come from a place of obligation. I said so because to me, she was everything. Even when she was a catastrophe, she was *my* beautiful catastrophe.

Last night when I'd been scared and uncertain, her kiss had assured me that she meant the words that left her lips, and I prayed mine did the same.

She kissed me back, hand tracing down the side of my bicep, leaning into it. It was soft, close to innocent even. Relief washed over me, filling me with ease and comfort, but my dick wasn't so pure.

My thoughts began to wander, and I had to fight them. It had been *months* since I could even think about getting hard. But now she was here, and I wanted her. I wanted to rip her shirt off and fuck her right there on the toilet. But there were about a million reasons that I couldn't, and I felt guilty for even thinking it.

It had been barely a week since she'd given birth. She was still healing, not to mention bleeding. Not that the blood mattered, it wouldn't have been the first time.

But she didn't even want me to see her without her clothes on. I understood but it sucked. It almost hurt. I'd seen her naked a million times. I loved seeing her naked. But suddenly, she was beyond insecure over something that I didn't even care about.

Aside from it all, she was traumatized. Not only from the physical violence but the rape. There's no way she wanted to have sex after all the shit she'd just been through. Sex after rape is a complex thing. I didn't even know what she would like. She was always pretty kinky, but I doubted she'd want me to bite her or choke her again.

Plus, she was shit faced. So shit faced that she told Max. The one thing she never should have told him, she told him. Obviously, she wasn't capable of making responsible decisions in her current state of inebriation.

It was complicated.

Everything was so complicated.

As things started to get more intense, at least for me, I pulled my lips from hers. She leaned forward and tried to kiss me again, but I pulled back and struggled to catch my breath. My forehead touched hers. I laughed softly.

"Why'd you stop?" Her vibrant, shining green eyes met mine.

I chuckled and cupped her face in my hand. "Because I didn't want to."

Her glowing irises began to dull. "What do you mean?"

I sat on the edge of the tub and laced my fingers between hers. "It's been a while, babe."

She turned her head to the side, then her gaze traveled to my crotch, and she laughed. When she looked back up, her eyes shot open. She stumbled to her feet and reached past me to turn off the faucet. Her chest brushed my shoulder, and her drunken foot began to slide out from under her.

I grasping her hips before she had the chance to fall again.

"You almost flooded our bathroom." She gestured to the tub nearly at its brim as I steadied her.

"And you almost fell. Again." I smiled.

Her cheeks got red. "I drank a lot."

"I can tell."

She circled her arms around my shoulders. "I thought it'd help."

I knew what that was like better than anyone. Anything to numb the pain. Anything to think about something that wasn't hurting.

"Did it?" I asked.

"For a little."

"Usually how it works."

She was quiet for a moment. "I should get cleaned up."

My eyes met hers, and I couldn't place her expression. It wasn't pained but scared. Like she wasn't sure what she was thinking. "Do you want me to leave?"

She leaned back a bit, eyes meeting mine as she tucked some of the hair that hadn't made it into my ponytail behind my ear. She just looked at me for a long moment, considering.

It was incredibly difficult to go from seeing someone naked every day to them being afraid to take their clothes off in front of you. I was being as understanding as I could, and I would have left if she asked me to, but I was in an endless loop. No matter what I did, it could have been interpreted poorly. I didn't want to stare at her and have her think that I found her repulsive now. On the other hand, I didn't want to walk away and leave her believing that I didn't want to see her naked.

It was a damned if I do, damned if I don't kind of situation.

We'd been faced with a lot of those recently.

"No," she said. One of her hands was still wrapped around my back and the other rested on the side of my neck. "I don't want you to leave."

I smiled. "Good, 'cause I didn't want to."

She smiled back, a half-laugh leaving her lips.

It was one of those sensual, intimate life moments. The kind that you look back on in twenty years and still remember the way your stomach danced and your heart raced.

There was nothing sexual about it. I'd pulled her shirt up over her shoulders and through her arms a thousand times before, but when I think back on the most important time, it was that night.

Because it wasn't about being naked. It wasn't about sex. It was the moment she let her guard down. She allowed herself to be vulnerable with me. It didn't last long, but I enjoyed it as long as I could.

As I dropped her shirt to the floor, she leaned down, pulled her pants to her ankles and sloppily kicked them off her feet. She was too close to get a good look at her body, but what I could see was just as beautiful as it'd always been. Just a little different.

My hand found hers to keep her balance. She straightened up and met my gaze.

I cradled her cheek with one hand and held her steady with the other around her waist.

My heart drummed against my ribs, holding her naked body in my hands for the first time in three months. And I wanted more. I wanted *so* much more. But I just leaned to her height and kissed. That'd be enough. It had to be enough.

She reached onto her tip toes, pushed her bare chest to mine, and rested her hands against my shoulders. Maybe it was because I hadn't so much as jerked off in more than three months, but in that moment, it felt like the most intense kiss we'd ever had. It sent the same rush of blood through my body as the first but was shrouded by the comfort we'd gained in the past three and a half years. It was all of the wonder of our first with all of the normalcy of the thousand others.

I slid my hand to the small of her back and pulled her even closer. For the first time, I felt them. The long, nearly swollen raised lines of flesh. I felt goosebumps swell beneath my fingertips and squeezed tighter, trying to make sure she knew I wasn't any less attracted to her.

Because I wasn't. No part of me found her unattractive. Honestly, the scars made her a little sexier. I wasn't sure why, but they did.

We stayed like that for a while longer, kissing innocently like middle school kids on their first date. She was naked, of course, but the gentleness to it, the lack of intent to go past it, couldn't have been more virtuous. Still, my dick wasn't as innocent, and my thoughts definitely wouldn't be when she fell asleep, but I ignored it while I held her.

A moment or two later, she pulled back. Her long dark hair rested over her shoulders, coasting down her body like a blanket. "Just try not to look disgusted, okay?"

I could never use disgust and Laila in the same sentence.

My heart still raced. My hand slid from her back to her waist. It gently coasted down the seamless, now even more pronounced curve that dipped beneath her rib and flared out at her hip.

"You're perfect," I murmured.

Laila took my hand, bracing herself against the wall with the other, and stepped beside me. I watched carefully, ready to grab her hip if she began to slip. Then she raised her right leg into the old cast iron tub, and I saw the one on her thigh. I remembered that scar vividly.

They beat her and I felt the pain stop for a moment or two. Then, the stabbing, almost indescribable pain in her thigh began. And it hurt for almost a month after.

But it was the last time they beat her. I think it was the first time she scared him. He'd spend the rest of his life fearing her after that.

And it made me proud. I didn't know what happened, but that day changed everything for her. It brought out a strength in her she didn't realize she had.

As she raised her left leg inside, I got my first glimpse of her back.

In all actuality, it wasn't as bad as I expected it to be. It wasn't nearly as bad as Daniel's had been. I didn't know the exact number, but at least forty scars descended her spine. Some were only a few inches long while others were nearly the length of her torso. Some were thinner than others, some were more raised. Some even seemed to recede into the skin.

But they weren't ugly.

If anything, they were kind of sexy. They showed how strong she was. They showed the pain that she could withstand and still be able to keep fighting.

She fumbled a bit, foot slipping slightly. I gripped her hip tighter. She caught herself against my hand and the wall, then slowly lowered herself to the bubbles.

Then she splashed a handful of water to her face. The water beaded down her cheeks to her neck. It slid to the gap in her clavicle, then toward her breasts. I watched as it travelled to her nipples and they hardened. And so did my dick.

As she engulfed her body in the water, she met my gaze with a serious expression. "I haven't looked at them yet so please be honest."

"Hmm?" I asked.

"Are they as bad as I think they are?" she asked quietly.

A smile pulled at my lips. I kneeled beside her, dipped her rag in the water, and wrung it out against her thigh. "They're nowhere close to as bad as you think they are."

She pulled her knees to her chest and wrapped her arms around them. "I know there's a lot."

"There are. But they're not the way you're envisioning them."

"And how's that?" she asked.

I raised the rag to her face and wiped the dried blood from her forehead. "Like they make you look like a monster." I dipped the rag in the water to moisten it. Then I raised it back to the dried blood on her cheek. "Like they're Daniel's. And they're not."

She studied me. Like she was waiting for me to show some sign of pity or disgust. When I didn't, she said, "How do they make me look then?"

"Like you've been through some awful shit." I slid the rag down the blood's path that traveled from her neck onto her shoulder. I turned my gaze back up to meet hers. "And like you didn't give up."

A soft smile pulled at the corners of her lips. "I love you."

I smiled. "I love you, too."

CHAPTER TWENTY-TWO

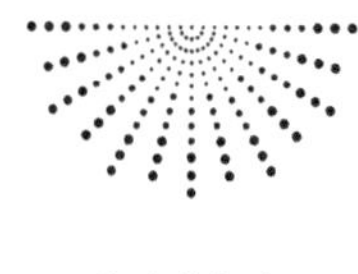

LAILA

By the time Jeremy helped me into bed, I'd begun to sober up. The room was still spinning. My words were still slurring. But mentally, I was getting closer to my normal self.

He pulled the blanket down, holding my swaying body against him with the other. I rested my head against his chest that was now damp from my wet hair.

"Here." He gently ushered me toward the bed.

I squeezed him a bit tighter first. He chuckled. His lips met my forehead. "Lie down, baby. I'm gonna go get you some water. You're gonna need it."

I pulled away and fell backwards into the some ridiculous number thread count sheets Hannah insisted I *had* to get when we were shopping to furnish the apartment. She said they'd change my life. They didn't. But they were soft.

Jeremy chuckled as I nuzzled my head into the pillow. "Can you try to not fall off in the time it takes me to walk to the kitchen?"

"I will try." I lifted my feet onto the bed and beneath the sheets. "But I can't make any promises."

He laughed and disappeared. I pulled the comforter up to my face and breathed in the smell of the clean cloth. Jeremy must have changed them when he cleaned up the house because they smelled like they were fresh out of the dryer. Then again, it could have just been that I hadn't had truly clean linens in months.

It was almost surreal. All the comfort I used to take for granted. I didn't realize how lucky I was to sleep in a bed with a blanket until I slept on a hard table in the freezing cold for months.

"Baby." Jeremy sat on the bed beside me. He handed me a glass of water and set a bottle of aspirin down in his lap. "You don't have to take these if you don't want, but you do need to drink the water."

"It's not aspirin I have a problem with." I sat forward and extended my hand to him. He opened the bottle and set two in my palm. I popped them in my mouth and chugged.

He set the glass on the side table. "There's another bottle of water right here and I brought the trash can over in case you need to puke."

"I'm not going to puke."

"You always say that."

"Yeah, and I've only puked, like, two times," I slurred.

"That is definitely not true." He gave a genuine laugh.

"Um, it definitely is," I said. "I can handle my liquor like a boss."

"Says the one who has busted her head open while drunk three times in the nearly four years we've been together." He grinned.

"Okay, the first time, I have no excuse for. I was drunk and I fell. The second time, I was a disaster over what happened to Moe. And tonight... Well, tonight I was just sloppy," I muttered. "But considering how much I drank, it's impressive that I'm still functioning."

He gave a smile and handed me the other bottle of water off of the table. "Hydrate, babe."

I twisted off the cap, raised the bottle to my lips, and chugged for a moment. When I was about halfway through the bottle, I set it in my lap and burped. "I'm hydrated. Are you happy?"

"I mean, you're probably still pretty dehydrated because you're supposed to have a glass of water for every alcoholic beverage you drink. But yeah, just don't drink it too fast or you'll make yourself puke."

"Drink more water, but don't drink too fast, he says." I reached for his hand and smiled. "I can't win with you."

He smiled. "You'll thank me when you don't wake up in the middle of the night with a pounding headache."

I squeezed his hand.

It seemed as good a time as ever. At least with how drunk I was, he knew I wouldn't be judging him. "First-hand experience?"

His smile gradually lowered. "So, Max told you."

"I asked. Don't be mad at him, he wasn't trying to be a snitch or anything. It just came up."

"No, it's okay. I wasn't hiding it. Everyone knows. I just didn't want you to worry about it."

I held his hand a bit tighter. "You don't have to pretend like this was easy on you. I can't imagine how you were feeling."

"Yeah. Yeah, I know. I just don't want you to worry about it happening again. It was stupid and I know that. It's not going to happen again."

"When *did* it happen?" I ran my thumb over his. He looked down at our hands. "I don't blame you, baby. I would have had to get high too if I were in your shoes."

He rubbed his eyes, exhaling slowly. "The night you went missing, Leah said something was wrong, and Daniel was just murdered... Wyatt and Ray were arguing about how the APB wouldn't make a difference because there's no way they were going to let you out of their car and I... I just... I didn't even think. I just picked up the bottle and..."

He expected me to be upset. And not that I was happy but, clearly, I had no right to point fingers when it came to substance abuse. Plus, I'd just lost his kid because of the decision I'd made. I was in no position to be angry at him for much of anything.

I pulled his hand from his face and laced our fingers together. "Was that it? Just alcohol?"

"No." He cleared his throat. "I did oxies the night that..." He looked up to meet my gaze. "The night that you were raped."

For some reason, it sounded different when he said it than when I did. Sadder, maybe? Less angry?

It didn't hurt to hear him say it. Not me, at least. But it looked like it hurt him.

"But that was it," he continued. "And that was the last time I drank too. After I could talk to you again, even though our communication was the most insane, painful way to write love letters." I smiled, and he did too. "But I knew you were okay. You weren't where you should have been, but you were okay."

"Have you been to any meetings?"

He laughed. "The NA way is not the only way. I was clean for years and I didn't go to any meetings then either."

"I know I'm not the best person to preach about sobriety, but please tell me if it happens again. Or if you're thinking about relapsing again. Please, just... Don't keep it from me to protect me, alright? I know that I'm not in a great place. But I can still be here for you."

"I know."

I took his hand, collapsed backward onto the bed, and yanked him with me. He laughed on the way down.

As I curled my hands up against the pillow, turning to look at him, my gaze caught on my left hand. More specifically, on my empty ring finger.

"Baby." I raised my hand to his and twined our fingers together.

"Hmm?" His gaze found mine.

"Do you still want to marry me?" I asked.

He knitted his brows, but a smile played at his lips. "You really have to ask?"

"I don't know, I just wasn't sure."

His smile widened, tugging my face toward his and leaning in to kiss me. His lips parted against mine, curly scruff gently scratching my chin and upper lip.

I hadn't gotten butterflies in so long, but that moment brought them back. It was so gentle and soft that it made me want to melt into him. In fact, that's exactly how it felt. Like we were one, moving within each other like food coloring mixing into a cup of water.

It almost made me forget about everything. All of the horrible things that happened, all of the stupid decisions I made. They faded into the background, far from my conscious mind into the blur of feelings I pushed as far down as they would go.

His hand at my back gently thumbed through the ends of my long hair that laid messily on the sheet behind me. "There is never going to come a time when I don't want to be married to you, Laila."

My stomach flipped and I smiled. "Shouldn't I put on my ring then?"

His eyes cascaded a beautiful, genuine smile. "Am I supposed to get down on one knee again?"

"I don't like that ritual. I like being eye to eye."

He pulled his hand from my neck and a small white box appeared in his palm. Then he yanked the blanket from his legs, teleported to the ground beside me and dramatically flipped the box open, grinning. "Will you marry me, Laila Callidy?"

"Just give me the damn ring." I laughed and snatched the box.

He laughed, teleported to the bed beside me, and stole it from my grasp. "I'm supposed to put it on you."

"Sounds kinky." I grinned.

He lifted the ring and took my hand with the other. "So that is a yes, right?"

I smiled and gazed up at his messy black hair hanging in his bright blue eyes. "Yes. I will marry you, Jeremy Skoulda."

Smiling, he slid the ring onto my finger and laced his fingers between my left hand. "I love you."

"Shut up and kiss me." I smiled.

He grinned, lowered his face to mine, and gently held my hand.

"But I love you too," I murmured against his mouth.

I felt his lips curve into a smile, and he kissed me harder. He moved his hand from mine to my back and pulled me against him. I touched his face, feeling his strong jaw beneath my palms. Then he lowered his chest to mine and pulled my body up to his.

And the romance disappeared.

It was replaced with a desperate urge to push him away. It was like

I couldn't breathe, and I needed him to get off of me. I wasn't in a flashback—I was well aware of who I was kissing. I knew he would never hurt me, and I knew, rationally, that I had no reason to be afraid.

I didn't like it though, and I wanted him to get off of me.

But I didn't know how to say that. The moment I verbalized it, he'd jolt back and apologize, but I didn't want him to because this wasn't his fault. He wasn't doing anything wrong.

I enjoyed it a few minutes before in the bathroom. In fact, I didn't want him to stop. I wanted to like what he was doing now, and my body said that I did. My soaking underwear were proof of that. But the other part of me was scared.

I didn't want to be. I tried hard not to be, and I tried even harder not to show it. Not because I felt obligated to fuck him, I knew he wouldn't care if I told him to back off. But I didn't want him to think that I was afraid of him. I loved him with every piece of me and I trusted him just as much. I didn't want him to believe otherwise for a heartbeat.

Somehow though, he must've known, because he leaned away, eyes softening. "Are you okay?"

I nodded and forced a smile.

Jeremy didn't quite frown, but he saw that I was lying, and I could see the pain behind his eyes. He moved beside me instead, and that weight of terror disintegrated.

I hated that. It wasn't fair. He hadn't done anything wrong. He was the love of my life. I knew he wouldn't hurt me. I knew he'd never force me into something I didn't want, but my instincts didn't seem to understand.

I was scared, and he saw it.

He forced a smile. "You don't have to lie to me, Lai. I understand."

"I'm not lying."

He laced our fingers together, brought my knuckles to his lips, and kissed them gently. "It's okay, baby."

"It's not that I don't want to kiss you. I... I want to, I just... Earlier, in the bathroom when we were kissing... I didn't feel like this."

Touch softer than flower petals, he said, "Maybe because I wasn't on top of you?"

The moment he'd pulled away, that fear was gone. "Maybe."

"I won't do it again then," he whispered, twirling a piece of my hair. "You take the lead, okay? I'll follow."

My heart expanded, stomach flipping.

He was perfect. So gentle, so considerate, so careful. This was why I loved him, this was why I wanted to spend the rest of my life with him. He wanted to do whatever it took to make me happy, because that made him happy.

I leaned forward and touched my lips to his. Gently, Jeremy touched my cheek, almost afraid to touch anything else. The gentle, tenderness of his lips on mine was so soft, and yet so passionate at the same time.

As I kissed him, I felt my stomach flip again. I even lifted my leg around him and tightened it around his waist.

It didn't feel quite the same as it used to. I was still nervous, but like a teenager getting past a peck for the first time. The fear was gone. Still, if I wasn't wearing a pad to catch the blood that was still leaking out of me, my pants would've been soaked.

My body wanted him, but my mind wouldn't allow it to get past that. It was like a war within myself. I felt his dick getting hard against my pelvis, and it made me want him more, but not enough to actually satisfy the desire that danced between our bodies.

A moment or so later, Jeremy pulled away. His breaths were short, and he closed his eyes. "Okay, give me a minute here."

I smiled, nudged him to his back, and kneeled around him. "Are you alright?"

He laughed. "Not really."

I bit my bottom lip and grinned. "I'm sorry."

"Stop apologizing." He shook his head, hands sliding to my hips.

"I want to, I just don't think I'm ready."

He nodded, still trying to catch his breath. "No, I know. That's fine, baby. We have the rest of our lives." He rubbed his eyes. "I just don't want to jizz in my pants. Kinda gross."

I laughed. "Really?"

"Besides pissing, my dick hasn't been touched since the day before you were taken. So yeah, I'm uh…" He glanced down my body. "Okay, you've got to get off of me."

I laughed, spun my leg around, and plopped down beside him. "You didn't jerk off once?"

"The last thing I was worried about was coming, Laila."

"That makes me feel special." I grinned. He chuckled. "You can, you know. There's nothing wrong with getting yourself off."

"Can we not talk about masturbating?" His tone was somewhere between uncomfortable and playful. "Not unless you're going to and let me watch."

I laughed. "Subject change, then."

CHAPTER TWENTY-THREE

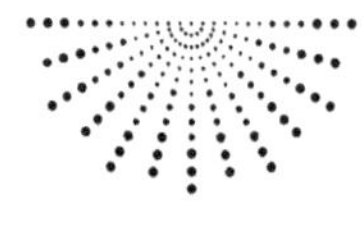

LAILA

After a full night's rest, I awoke peacefully in Jeremy's arms. The sun shined in from the open window. Birds chirping outside filled the room. The warm, humid summer breeze pushed the curtains toward me. I felt a bead of water leave my eye as the pollen entered my nostrils.

Jeremy's slow, warm breaths teased my shoulder and his cozy arm held me close to his chest.

It was a new day.

Hopefully, a better day than the last.

It was the day I pressed resume on the life I was torn away from ninety some odd days ago.

I was going to get up. I was going to get dressed. I was going to run a comb through my hair. I was going to put on makeup. I was going to find a choker and some bracelets that covered my scars. I was going to make a pot of coffee. I was going to grab the newspaper. I was going to sit on the back steps with my fresh cup of joe and today's paper. I was going to try to remember what it meant to feel normal.

I was going to be positive.

I was going to make it through the day without breaking down.

But first, I was going to lie there a while longer in his arms.

Just as I finished putting on my red lipstick, Jeremy spoke at the bathroom door. "You're gorgeous."

I turned to him and smiled. "Is the choker a little too goth?"

"Not at all. It looks good with that shirt. Is it new?"

"Kind of. I bought it right before I got pregnant but then I was too fat to wear it. And now it's loose."

"It isn't actually. Your boobs look huge. And you were never fat."

I waved him off. Like I'd said before, I knew how I'd looked before captivity. Maybe fat wasn't the descriptor he would've used, but I wasn't exactly small. I had no shame in that—I missed it, actually—but the fact remained. I was on the upper end of midsized before I was kidnapped.

I turned sideways in the mirror to look at my back. That side of the black shirt was sheer at the top, but the color was dark enough that it covered the scars. "At least I had an ass."

"You still have an ass, it's just a little smaller. But proportionally speaking, it looks the same as it did before."

I dramatically put my hand to my chest. "That's the sweetest thing anyone has ever said to me."

He laughed. "Can I piss?"

"Yeah, I'm done anyway."

I shoved my makeup back into its bag and started out of the bathroom. As I stepped through the threshold, Jeremy caught my waist and pulled me against him. His other hand moved to the side of my neck. He lowered his lips to mine. I lifted my hand to his chest, kissed him back for a moment, and pulled away.

Biting my lip, I met his gaze. "I need to talk to Max."

"Oh, shit. Yeah," he said. "Why did you tell him anyway?"

"I don't know. I was drunk. I didn't want to lie to him."

Jeremy sighed. "Worst case scenario, you can wipe his memory."

"Yeah, I know."

He pushed messy hair from his face. "I'm gonna get a shower and then I'll be down. I have to make the schedule for next week."

"I can do the schedule."

"I'm glad you're ready to jump back into things, baby, but it's summer and everyone's schedules have changed. There's a lot we should go over together first."

"I guess that's fair." Biting my lip, I gave a smile. "Thank you for taking care of everything while I couldn't, by the way. You did a damn good job."

He smiled back, took my hand, and squeezed it. "I know how important this place is to you. But I can't take all the credit. Max helped a lot. He deserves a raise actually."

I turned from the steps into the kitchen. Max stood over the gas range flipping a pancake.

"Hey," I said.

He looked up and met my gaze. Greasy brown hair fell in front of the deep purple bags resting beneath his brown eyes. "You look better than you did last night."

"And you look like you haven't slept in weeks."

"Yeah, well, I've slept better."

I was quiet for a moment, searching for the words. "Can we talk? In private?"

He plopped the pancake onto a plate. Patting his hand against his apron, he walked across the galley kitchen to set the meal on the serving hatch. "I need a cigarette anyway."

I grabbed a pot of coffee, poured myself a glass, and started to the back door, snatching a few sugar packs off the counter on my way. Then I pushed the door open with my hip. I lowered myself to the steps and sat on the cement. Max closed the door and sat beside me.

He pulled a cigarette from his pack and searched for a lighter. I smiled, brought a small flame to my fingertip, and held it out to him.

He gazed at it for a moment. Then he huffed and leaned forward to spark it.

I watched him take in a long drag before leaning back on his palms.

He gazed off into the green trees, chewing his lip as he exhaled smoke from his nose. "What are you?"

"I'm a hybrid. Mostly Angel, but a little Fae, and a little Guardian too."

He grew quiet. "I have a million questions."

"I've got all day." I gave a smile.

"So, all that shit. All the fairy tales we were told as kids. They weren't..." He gazed off into the distance.

"As real as the air we're breathing. Details are skewed, but just about anything you've heard a story about exists in some capacity. Never seen a dragon though."

He huffed again. "And you're... God, what are you again?"

"My mom, my real Mom, not the one you know," I said slowly. "She's an Angel."

"I'm going to assume you don't mean like the ones we see in Catholic churches." He took a long hit off his cigarette and flicked an ash to the cement.

"They're definitely not little naked babies with wings, if that's what you're asking."

"What about wings?" He glanced at me. "I saw you fly but I didn't see any wings."

"I fly through my ability to manipulate air. Wings are symbolic for being able to pass from the realm of Heaven onto the Earth realm," I said. "It isn't literal. Angels don't fly."

"And your dad. Was he your real dad?"

"He was. He's where most of my abilities come from."

"What all can you do?" He turned to meet my gaze. "I know about the air thing, and now fire. What else?"

I laughed. "Do you want me to go down the whole list?"

"There's a *list*?"

"I... I have more powers than most."

Another tick of silence. "Jeremy and Adam, all of them. They're not human, are they?"

"No."

"Have you always been like this?"

"I always had powers," I said. "But I didn't know until about three and a half years ago."

Max paused, thinking. "When you met Jeremy."

"When I met Jeremy."

He raised his cigarette to his lips and took in another long drag. "I never really understood why Jeremy is the way he is about you until last night."

"The way he is?" I asked.

"Yeah. Really protective, you know? Not controlling, just protective. Almost comes off controlling though."

"I really don't need his protection. Not anymore, anyway."

He looked from the trees back to me. "That's why they took you. Because of what you are." I gave a nod. He took another hit off his cigarette. "You're a big deal, aren't you?"

I took his cigarette from his fingers and held it to my lips. I breathed in a deep drag and handed it back to him. "You could say that."

"Jenna said something once, about the way you were taken, and the way Daniel was killed. Something about it being too carefully done to take someone so simple. That stuff like that happens to big people. Politicians and royalty. Are you royalty or something?"

"Hardly. I'm just really powerful."

He chewed his lip. "Do I even want to know what all you can do?"

"Might be a little sensory overload at the moment," I said. He stared off into the distance. "If you wish you didn't know, if you want to forget about all of this, I can take it away."

He cocked his head to the side. "You can take away my memories?"

"Not exactly. But I can push them out of your conscious mind."

I didn't want to. I wanted him to know. I wanted my best friend to know who I really was. But if he didn't *want* to know, I wouldn't force him to.

"Have you ever done that to me before?"

"No. I've only ever done it to people who asked me to. And you never have," I said. "But I will if you ask me to."

"No. I don't want to forget. It ties a lot of loose ends together. Like why you disappear all the time and why you got more distant after you and Jeremy got together. I thought it was just because you were getting serious or whatever. I guess you were just trying to keep me out of this." He turned and met my gaze. "You know what happened to Adrian, don't you?"

I looked away.

"Always thought you might," he muttered.

I tried not to let that comment hurt but it did. I loved Adrian, and I would have never hurt her. But I did help cover up her murder to protect my friend. And I'd do it again.

"You don't have to go into the details. But she's not going to come home, is she?"

I was quiet for a moment. "No. She's not coming home."

CHAPTER TWENTY-FOUR

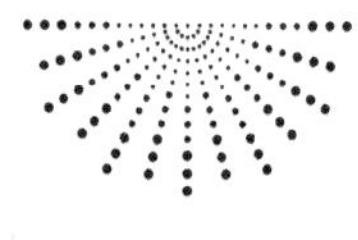

LAILA

The smell of coffee, pancakes, and bacon wafted up my nose. Quiet, soft rock played in the corners of the room. Warm air brushed around me, bringing a pleasant spin to my belly.

Damn, it felt good to be home. The apartment was home, the main house was home, but this was home too. Moe's Diner. Easily my favorite place in the world.

The bell rang above the front door while I started a fresh pot of coffee. "Go ahead and have a seat wherever you like, I'll be with you in one second." I scratched the screen of the filter holder, trying to knock loose a stubborn granule.

"Take your time," Leah said.

I turned around. Our gazes met as she sat at the bar.

Was I hurt by what she'd said? Of course. But did I hate her? No. I wasn't one to hold a grudge. We were both mad. Shit comes out when you're angry. We had to get over it.

I pulled a gentle smile to my lips. "Hey."

"Hey." She managed a smile too. "I like the choker."

"A means to an end."

"Well, it looks good." She smiled. "You look more like yourself today."

"Thanks." I put my hands at my hips. "Do you want a cup of coffee? Or something to eat?"

"I just ate but yeah, I could go for coffee."

I walked back to the coffee maker, put a filter into the strainer, and scooped a few spoons of grounds into it. "So, what made you decide to come out here?"

"I wanted to talk about yesterday." I turned back to face her. "You and Jeremy aren't taking my calls and I..." She paused. "I don't blame you, or anything. I was a cunt. I..." She took in a slow deep breath as if the words couldn't make their way out of her mouth. "I owe you an apology."

I met her gaze. "It was kind of shitty."

"More than just kind of. I shouldn't have said all of that. It was mean, and unfair and..." She paused. "Can we talk somewhere private?"

"Sure. Let's go to the back."

She stood and trailed behind me. We made our way through the little kitchen into my office. She closed the door behind her. I leaned against the desk and she turned back to me.

A slow breath left her O-shaped lips. "I'm sorry I was such a bitch. You were right, I wasn't there. I don't have the right to act like I can even begin to understand why you did what you did."

I smiled. "How'd those words taste coming out of your mouth?"

"Like bleach." She huffed. "I mean it though. I am, I'm sorry."

I rubbed beneath my eyes. "Look, Leah, I get why you feel the way you do. As you know, I feel the same way. I have a million regrets about how things turned out. It was far from the outcome I was expecting."

"But I shouldn't have said it like that."

I scooted onto the edge of the desk. "Well, it wasn't a lie."

Her eyes shifted between mine. "Can I be honest with you, Lai?" I nodded. "I wasn't just wrong, I didn't mean what I said. Not really. I have a lot of unanswered questions and I don't understand the choices you made, but I don't blame you for what happened."

I gave a smile. "It's okay, Leah. You were right. I could have done better."

"What I said came from a place of jealousy, Laila. You're home. You get to see Jeremy, and your mom, and your sisters, and brother. And Chris is still there. And you got to see him. *You* got to talk to him, and you got to know him, and I'm mad. I'm mad he's gone. I'm mad that I can't figure out where he is. I'm mad I can't save him. I'm mad I wasn't there to help him get out. Hell, I'm mad it was you that got taken because you got to see him. You got to talk to him and I didn't." A tear formed in the corner of her eye. She angrily wiped it away. "I'm so glad you're back. I'm so happy that you're okay. I really am. But..."

"You wish it would have been him instead of me?"

"No. No, it isn't that," she said.

"It's okay, Leah. Really. I wish it were him too."

Another tear welled in her eye. "It's not that I'm not happy you're home."

"I know."

She grew quiet for a moment, struggling to hold my gaze. "Why didn't you push the psychic out of your head sooner?"

"It wasn't that simple"

"If you aren't ready to talk about it, I'll wait. I just... I want to understand."

I got more comfortable on the desk. I wasn't ready to talk about it with Jeremy. It'd take years before he heard the whole story. But Leah was my best friend, and I *was* ready to tell her.

"It was complicated. It's going to take some time to explain." I gestured to the seat. She lowered herself to it.

I pulled my legs up onto the desk and crossed them lotus style. "I should probably start at the day of my last stress test."

"Stress test?" she asked.

"Every few days, they'd torture us. It was..."

And so, I explained. She didn't say much as I talked, only asked a question here or there. I told her about what they did to us, I told her about how he called Micah his, I told her about how they'd shot me in the leg. I explained that it rendered me damn near defenseless, and that I needed two feet to get us out.

"Peterson stopped doing stress tests on me, so I had an opportunity that no one else did. I am a Fae so I knew as soon as I left my cell, I could use my powers to get other people out. But to do that, I had to be able to walk. I had to be able to fight. I knew you guys wouldn't be able to get inside without people dying. The place was littered with barrier spells like a maze to teleporters. You couldn't teleport inside, you could only teleport to the border. Then you'd have to *break* in. And there were hundreds of guards. They'd snipe anyone who got too close, I knew they would. These were the same people that laughed as they tore a pregnant woman's back to shreds and made jokes about how cute her naked ass was as they whipped her. They're ruthless, Leah. And I couldn't. I couldn't be the reason anyone I loved died. I had to be smart. You guys couldn't come in from the main entrances, so I had to make one. I needed back up to move people somewhere safe and I had to have the ability to move around so I could handle the guards as you guys got people to safety."

Her harsh green eyes looked so soft as I told that story. I'd never seen her look so gentle in my life.

"That's why I decided to wait. I figured around thirty-six weeks, I'd be healed enough to maneuver around and still be able to be home for Micah to be born. That was my plan. Week thirty-six."

"But he came early," she murmured.

"But he came early. And I wasn't healed yet. Not really. And I couldn't have you come while I was in labor. Even if you guys were able to get past the guards, they would have been carting me out of there at any and all costs. Jeremy wouldn't have been able to fight, I wouldn't have been able to fight. So I breathed through the pain, and I had my son."

A sad smiled pulled at my lips. Then it fell. "I was in this tiny, dark cell. And he came out in this giant orb of white light that shined so bright that Haley started panicking. Chris felt this massive surge of energy. It was... It was tragically beautiful. Because he didn't cry. He just... He wouldn't cry."

She wiped a tear from her eye, continuing to gaze at me carefully.

"I didn't even notice all the blood at first. Not until I was fainting." Shaking my head, I used the tips of my fingers to wipe along the water line of each eye. "I laid him on my leg and just passed out. I didn't even realize what was happening until after it happened, you know? I heard Chris and Haley banging on their doors when I stopped responding. They were calling for the guards but then it was all just... black."

She gazed at me gently, waiting for me to go on. "When I woke up, I was in his personal office. He apologized for my loss at first. *Our* loss, he said, actually. Then I said it was all his fault. And he... I don't know. I don't remember it that well. We argued. I don't know if I even realized I was healed at that moment. I was just so angry and hurt and I wanted to fucking kill him. Then he kissed me, and I bit a good chunk out of his lip." I laughed. She gave a bare smile. "He made some comment about how at least now that I wasn't pregnant, he could give me trazodone. And he did."

"You were healed?" she asked.

"Micah healed me. Every bit of me. My leg, whatever hadn't healed on my back, even my vagina. I'm still bleeding but..." The smile that'd come to my lips when I thought about him drizzled as I wiped a tear from my cheek. "He... He literally gave his life for me. And I couldn't waste it. I had to save them. So when I woke up, that's when I gave Jeremy the signal."

"But how did you get out?" she asked.

"I'd been studying the guards for a while. Picking up what I could from their thoughts about the building. I'd wait until after rounds, open my door through the hole they fed us from with a little gust of wind. Then I waited for a guard to come so I could get his hand to open the double door."

"His hand?"

"It was pretty high tech. They used handprints to open up the double doors. To get anywhere important, really. So, I needed a hand."

"Makes sense."

"So I killed the guy. Then I opened Haley and Chris's cells. Didn't have a knife, but Haley's a wolf so I had her get me my hand. She chewed it off."

"Naturally." She rested her chin on her palm.

"Then we made it to the next unit, and the next and the next. And then onto the next wing. We let everyone out on our side of the top floor and moved to the hall that adjoined the two wings. I had everyone duck and cover their heads. And I just... I made a big wind and just blew the roof off."

"That was the way in."

"And then I heard guards, and I saw Kai and Jeremy, so I figured they could get them out while I moved to the next floor and took care of the guards."

She watched me carefully. "You thought Chris was out. So you went back for the others."

"I thought he was out."

A knock sounded at the door. It creaked open. Celena stood there, awkwardly gazing between Leah and I. "Hey, I'm sorry to interrupt. But someone's here, Laila. She asked for you."

"Did you get a name?"

"No, but she looks official. Maybe a cop or something?"

"Alright, I'll be out in one minute."

"Sorry again, guys." Celena pulled the door shut

I turned back to Leah. "Look, Leah. If you could keep that stuff between you and I for now—"

"Of course," she said. "And that's another thing I want to apologize for, by the way."

"I get it. They saw Jeremy's reaction. They knew something was wrong. You felt it, you knew what was happening. It's alright, Leah."

"Either way."

I gave a smile. "I'll see you later, alright?"

"Actually, I wanted to ask you something."

I adjusted my jeans, pulling them higher up my waist. "What's up?"

A smile moved up her cheeks. "I'm so happy you're back. And I was already planning you a welcome home party when you were in the hospital. I know you're just getting back in the groove of things, but I...

I want to celebrate you coming home. I want to sip wine, and eat cake, and gawk over that rock on your finger and have fun and with my best friend."

Pleasant chills rose over my skin. Our family parties were always so fun. It'd be a good way to keep my mind busy.

I smiled. "When is it?"

"It was supposed to be a surprise tonight so it times out with your mom and sister getting back from Canada. Jeremy didn't even know yet. I hadn't gotten the chance to talk to him before that fight yesterday. And now he won't take my calls. So, I had to invite you to your own surprise party."

"Am I still supposed to act surprised?"

"No. That's okay. But it starts at six."

I smiled. "I'll be there."

As I started from the room, a weight fell off of my shoulders. Talking to someone genuinely helped. It really did. I didn't have to lie; I didn't have to sugarcoat it.

Leah understood. And that made me feel a little less self-hatred. Just a little. But a little was better than nothing.

CHAPTER TWENTY-FIVE

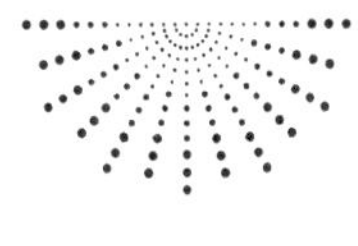

LAILA

The moment I saw her, I knew what it was about. Tina Davis. She sat at a booth in the otherwise empty diner besides Celena, Leah and I.

There were about a million things about my story that didn't add up. I knew that but I'd hoped she wasn't going to dig too deep.

"Hi, Tina." I smiled and extended my hand out to hers. "Nice to see you."

She gave an almost surprised smile. Then she stood from the booth and shook my hand. "Likewise, Laila. You look great."

"I'm a mess, but red lipstick and a nice necklace work wonders for a girl."

"Right. Are you busy? Could we sit for a moment?"

"Sure." I lowered myself to the bench across from her. "Celena, could you get us a couple cups of coffee?"

She looked at me from the bar. "Course."

I turned back to Tina and smiled. "So, what's this all about?"

"There's a lot of issues trying to get information from the Canadian government on your case. The other survivors haven't been..." She set a file on the table. "I'm just having a hell of a time getting anything out of anyone."

Kinda figured as much. Jeremy and the family had spread the message loud and clear. 'You heard nothing, you saw nothing, you know nothing.' It wasn't a human matter. The cops, even the feds, had no clue what they were up against. And if they had too much information, they'd only get in our way once we *did* have another lead.

"What do you want to know?"

Celena set our cups and a small container of creamer in front of us. She sent a darting gaze toward Tina before turning to me. "Let me know if you need anything, Lai."

Tina gazed at me, eyes scrunching a bit as she studied the look we exchanged. While Celena walked back to the bar, Tina's heavy eyes watched mine.

"Why are they calling you the savior?" she asked.

"I don't know." I shrugged, trying to not let my discomfort shine through. "Probably because I opened the cell doors."

"Right."

I watched her for a moment. She thumbed something inside her case file. Her fingers almost trembled. "This is a sketch drawn from the various descriptions we've received. You said that he had a special interest in you, and the people who gave these descriptions only saw him a couple of times. I'd like you to tell me how close to your captor's appearance this is, if you're comfortable with that."

Biting my lip, I grabbed the container of creamer and poured some into my black coffee. My fingers found the sugar packs at the end of the table, ripped them open, and dumped them into my coffee. I grabbed the spoon from the rolled silverware on the table and stirred my cream and sugar into my coffee.

"Laila?" Tina asked.

I lifted the cup to my lips and set it back down. "Sure. You can show it to me."

She flipped open the file and lifted the page into the air. Then she turned it to face me. When my eyes met the image, my stomach sunk. My breathing became uneven. It was as if he had posed for it.

The strong jaw with his salt and pepper five o'clock shadow. The intense eyes behind his framed glasses. The prominent nose on his paper white skin. The sick, almost Joker-like smile across his lips that forced themselves onto mine.

I felt nauseous and turned away. Tears stung my eyes. I cupped my hand over my mouth. My heart slammed against my ribs. It was as if he was standing right in front of me.

I knew it'd be hard to see. But I didn't think it'd hurt. It physically *hurt* to look at that image. My stomach ached. My chest got tight.

It was like he was right there.

"Laila." She reached across the table to take my hand.

I pulled it back. I took in a breath, still looking at the wall as she put the image back into the file. "Yeah, that's a good depiction. Looks just like him."

"I'm sorry, Laila. I know this can be hard—"

"I'm alright." I closed my eyes, wiping black mascara tears from beneath them. "I'm okay, just give me a second."

"Sure."

I took some slow deep breaths. I counted in for seven seconds, held the breath for three, and exhaled for five. A few moments later, I regained my composure and turned back to her. "I'm sorry, I didn't think it would affect me like that."

She raised the cream and poured it into her coffee. "You see his face behind your eyes every time you close them, but actually seeing it... In a picture, or in person..." It was as if she was speaking from firsthand experience. "It does something to you."

I reached for my coffee with shaking hands. "One in four, right?"

"Support groups help."

I managed a smile. "Maybe for some people."

"They helped me," she said softly.

I gave an understanding nod. "I'm okay. In most regards, anyway. So, what else do you need to know?"

"Right," she muttered. "How did you guys get to the hospital?"

I hadn't thought up a cover for that. "I don't really know. It all happened so fast, it's kind of a blur. I just remember running."

"The place you were being held was on a small island. It could only be reached by boat."

My heart raced. "Right. Yeah, we took a boat from the pier. We made a few trips, getting everyone off the island, I mean. Then we just... We just ran."

She wrote in her notepad. "How did your fiancé get there so soon?"

"What?"

"Jeremy. I spoke with nurses at the hospital. They talked about how sweet he was." She sipped her coffee and set it back down. "How he hadn't left your side since you got there. That he carried you in."

My hands trembled around my coffee mug, spilling som liquid to the tabletop. I cleared my throat and rubbed the tops of my thighs.

After everything I'd put him through, suddenly I made him a suspect in all of it too. I had to come up with a lie to protect him, but I couldn't think of any. It caught me off guard so quick, I didn't have the chance.

"I guess, what I'm really wondering here is..." She paused. Her breathing nearly stopped. She looked between my eyes. "Did Jeremy have anything to do with your captivity?"

"What?" I asked. "No. No, of course not. How could you even say that? After what..." I gritted my teeth together. "No, Jeremy isn't *capable* of hurting me. Let alone all of the..." I bit my lip until I tasted blood on my tongue.

"Then how did he get to you from almost three thousand miles away as you simultaneously escaped, Laila?"

I hadn't thought of a rational excuse for that. There really wasn't one.

"And I'm trying to wrap my mind around those things they put into your bodies. They aren't normal GPS trackers, they're primarily some type of crystal. And I can't really grasp why. Normal trackers are easier to access and require less resources. And I especially can't understand why some of you have the scars on your backs and others don't, yet you all seem to have been treated with the same negligent abuse, to say the least. I'm not trying to attack you, Laila, I just want to get to the bottom of this. Whoever is doing this, they have to be stopped. And you're the only one who will talk to me."

"Baby," Jeremy's voice rang through my ears. His hand touched my shoulder. He gazed down at me, tilting his head to the side. "Are you alright?"

I nodded. He pulled his hand away. He turned to Tina, plastered a smile on his lips, and reached across the table. "Nice to see you, Tina."

"I'm glad you're here, Jeremy." Tina smiled. "Do you have a moment? Could you sit with us?"

My stomach sunk and my heart raced faster than it did when I blew the roof off of that building. Losing him was my worst nightmare next to losing my baby. But the latter had already occurred. I couldn't lose him too, but I didn't know how to protect him.

"Sure." Jeremy gave his familiar, friendly smile. He lowered himself beside me. It was fake, but it didn't look fake. I only knew the difference because I knew what he looked like when he was genuinely happy.

She's asking a lot of questions, I said into his mind.

"How are you?" he asked with a gentle smile.

What kind of questions? he said in my thoughts.

Like how you made it all the way to Canada so fast. How you carried me into the hospital. If you had something to do with my disappearance. Why we had morion and hematite implanted under our skin. Why some of us have scars on our backs and others don't.

You have to erase the memories.

I can erase, but I don't know how to distort them, Jeremy. Not with something this complex.

Suddenly, Leah made her way to the table. She stood at the end, quickly grabbing Tina's hand from her cup and squeezing it tight. Tina tried to yank it away, but Leah smiled and began to speak. "It's alright, Tina. I'm not hurting you."

In a slow, trance like state, Tina said, "You're not hurting me."

"Those questions you were asking, about Laila's captivity, those may have been a little out of line, don't you think?" Leah lowered herself into the booth beside her.

"They were."

"Clearly, you can see that Jeremy would never hurt Laila. Just look at them," Leah murmured. Tina turned, looking between the two of us.

"They love each other more than anything. Not in the way that your ex loved you. You see that, don't you?"

"I do."

"You were just projecting," Leah murmured. "It wasn't about Jeremy, you like Jeremy. You think he's a nice kid, don't you?"

Tina nodded.

"You remember how distraught he was the day you met. He was heartbroken over Laila's disappearance; you know that wasn't an act. He loves her more than he loves himself."

"Sadly true," Jeremy muttered.

"I remember."

"And the conversations you overheard at the hospital, about Jeremy carrying Laila in, you must have misunderstood. He stayed by her bedside from the moment he arrived, but he didn't rescue her. He only made it there quicker than you because another survivor told the hospital to call him. Jeremy's grandparents have a lot of money, as you know from your research. They arranged a private flight for him the moment he was notified of her disappearance. So was Hannah, she wanted to be there because she felt responsible for Laila's capture. They're simply privileged, not suspicious."

"Sure. They're just privileged."

"Laila was treated just as badly as everyone there; she doesn't know why her captor used the GPS trackers that he did or why some got abused worse than others. Maybe he's psychotic and obsessed with crystals, who knows? Not Laila, because she was a victim," Leah said.

"Right."

"And as far as how they ended up at the hospital goes, it doesn't matter. They were scared and they escaped. They didn't know where they were going or how long it would take to get there, but they were out. That's all that matters."

"Sure," Tina repeated.

"These two have been through so much since this all started. They need space to heal. Laila has answered your questions and now you need to leave her alone."

"Of course." Tina gazed between Jeremy and I.

"And you're going to do whatever it takes to keep this out of the media. No details of the case need to be released."

"Sure."

"So, you're done here then," Leah murmured. "Laila and Jeremy are traumatized over the horrible things they've been through and you know they did nothing wrong. You're going to let them pick up the pieces of their lives."

"Right."

"Now, I'm going to go back to the counter, and you're going to forget that the two of us spoke today. You'll wave and say goodbye, but that will be the only conversation of ours you will remember from today. All of the things we've discussed, you'll remember as conclusions you came to on your own. You'll forget Laila's reaction when you asked how she managed to run off the island and her reaction to asking how Jeremy got to her so fast. The clearest memory you will have from today is Laila's reaction when you showed her that sketch. The look of horror on her face. You will remember her as the victim she is in all of this."

"Right," Tina said. "Laila's a victim."

Hated to hear that, but hey, it covered our ass.

"When I leave, you're going to apologize for inconveniencing Jeremy and Laila's day and be on your way." Leah met my gaze.

"Of course," Tina muttered. Leah released her hands and stood from the booth.

Tina remained quiet as Leah returned back to the counter. Once she was behind it, Tina said, "I'm sorry for taking time out of your day. I'm sure you're anxious to get back to your life. Thank you regardless, I feel a lot better after speaking with you."

"No problem at all. Thank you for all of your hard work."

She smiled at Jeremy as she stood. When she lifted the file to her hands, she fumbled a bit and that picture of Peterson daintily fell to the ground, as if a feather off the wing of a pigeon on a windy day.

Jeremy looked at it as it landed on the shiny, checkered tile. I watched his teeth grind and his hands clench. He lifted it from the ground and took a long gaze. I didn't look at the photo, but I studied his face. His nostrils flared, his breathing got fast and heavy, his scruffy jaw grew tight. He reached up and handed it to Tina. Then his gaze turned to mine.

I probably looked like a deer in headlights. I felt my sweaty palms trembling with my lower teeth. But I clenched them together and looked back to Tina. "If you're ever in the neighborhood, you're always welcome to a cup of Joe. On the house."

"That's very kind of you, Laila. Thank you."

"Sure. Anything for our public servants."

She smiled, lifted a five dollar bill from her jacket pocket, and set it on the table. "Thanks again."

She waved and said goodbye to Leah. Then the bell rang above her head as she made it outside.

My heart still hammered in my chest. Jeremy reached out for my hand, but I pulled mine away. "Can you move please? I need—I need a minute."

"Sure, baby," he murmured, standing from the booth.

I rushed from the bench to my feet. "Thanks, Leah."

I brushed past the counter, through the swinging door, past the stove in the kitchen and out the back door. I clenched my racing heart, taking a long breath of humid air into my lungs. My heart was thudding so fast, I thought it would shoot out of my chest like an old cartoon.

I gripped the dumpster for support as I breathed in and out. My stomach churned. That drawing flashed behind my eyes. Then that same face in my memories. I struggled to get my breaths back to normal. When breathing exercises didn't work, I bent over to grasp my knees.

"You're okay," I murmured to myself. "You're okay. You're out, you're home. You're safe. You're okay."

I heard the door of the diner creak open. Then it clicked shut. Jeremy stood there biting his lip, looking me over.

I straightened up and met his gaze. "I'm alright. I just need a minute."

"Do you want me to go inside?"

"No. No, it's alright. I just…" I grasped the edge of the dumpster. "I just needed some air. I'm okay."

He lowered himself to the step. "Alright, baby."

I breathed heavily for a moment. I brought myself down to the gravel. My lips felt dry, and my teeth were chattering. I rested my head against the metal dumpster.

In for seven, hold for three, and out for five. Or was it in for five, hold for three, out for seven? No, maybe it was in for three, hold for five, out for seven.

Jeremy turned his gaze away. He pulled a joint and lighter from his jacket pocket. He lit it and gazed out over the trees.

After a few drags, his gaze met mine. "Do you want to hit this?"

"Only if you bring it to me," I whispered, feeling too unstable to walk.

Managing a weak smile, he walked closer, cutting away at the distance between us. He sat beside me, and the tips of his fingers grazed mine. I lifted it to my lips and took in a long, deep drag.

After a few hits, and about half the joint, Jeremy softly broke the silence. "So that was him."

I gazed out in front of me. I took another hit off the joint. "That was him."

He nodded, staying quiet for a second or two. "He didn't look the way I pictured him."

"He doesn't look like what he's capable of."

He was quiet again. "Neither do you."

Something between a huff and a chuckle left my lips. "Yeah, I guess so."

He grew quiet for a moment. Then he handed me the joint. "It's weird…" he murmured. "I've seen a lot of scary shit. But he's caused more pain than any beast I've ever seen."

"That's what keeps him safe. He's soft spoken and personable… He seems so normal."

CHAPTER TWENTY-SIX

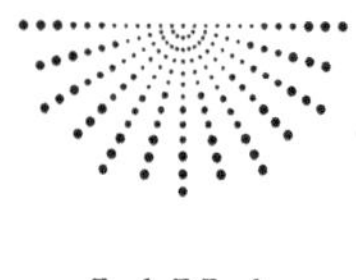

LAILA

"Do I *have* to come?" Jeremy gently squeezed my knee as I started the ignition.

I pulled my seat belt over my chest and clicked it into place. "Do you really not want to?"

"I mean, I do," he said. "I just don't want to see Leah."

"She apologized, you know."

"An apology doesn't change what she said." Jeremy gingerly ran his hand along my thigh.

"Tensions are high right now," I said. "She was harsh, and it was mean. And yeah, it hurt to hear her say how she really felt. But she was right, Jeremy. My plan wasn't flawless. I could have done better."

"No, she wasn't," he said.

I put the car into drive. "I want you with me. I want to be around all the people I love, Jeremy." I turned to meet his gaze, holding my foot on the break. "Can you just play nice for the night?"

"I guess. For you."

I smiled. "Thank you."

"Mhmm," he murmured.

As I let off the break and started out of my parking space, I glanced at Jeremy. "I'm sorry about last night."

"What are you apologizing for?"

I looked back to the road. "I was really drunk."

Jeremy laughed. His hand found mine, fingers lacing together. "Wasn't the first time, I doubt it'll be the last."

Eh, not wrong. Still, not something I'd boast about. I was a basket case. A weak, pitiful, whiny little bitch.

"I just... I said a lot of things. And I was sloppy. Not my proudest moment."

He squeezed my hand. "I'm happy you talked to me."

"I don't remember most of what I said. I just, I was hurt. And I just... I don't know."

"Baby," he said softly.

I met his gentle gaze as we stopped at a red light. "What?"

He just looked at me for a second. "I don't want you to think you have to feel guilty for talking about what's going on in your head. I want you to talk to me about what's wrong. Like you always have."

I managed a smile. "It was pathetic."

"It was the opposite of pathetic." His blue eyes locked with mine. "You opened up, Laila. That takes courage."

"Liquid courage, in my case," I muttered.

He leaned forward, grazed the side of my neck with his hand, and touched our lips together. I kissed him back. I relaxed into his embrace for a moment, holding on the break.

Maybe he was right. It did feel good to talk to Leah. Maybe he'd handle it better than I thought.

A honk sounded behind me.

I started to reach back to the steering wheel, but he pulled my face to his again. The car kept beeping, but he kissed me longer, softly, but in a way that made me feel safe. So familiar, so homey.

As the car passed us laying on its horn, Jeremy held my chin, rested his forehead against mine, and looked between my eyes. "Never apologize for telling me how you feel."

The Skoulda home looked a little darker somehow. Dreary, would be a good word for it.

Everything was the same. The old stone hadn't been painted. The flowers bloomed in the front gardens the way they always had. The water in the fountain still shot up and rained back into the small pool beneath it. It was just as pretty as it had always been. The inside felt like home. But the outside felt haunted.

Maybe it was me that was haunted.

"Are you sure you want to do this?" Jeremy asked as if he thought I would say no.

I looked his way and grinned. "If you really want to go home, you can."

He reached across the center console, and pushed hair from my eyes behind my ear. Then he twirled a piece of it between his fingers. "No, I'll stay. I just wanted to make sure."

"Let's go in then."

He unbuckled his seat belt, I unbuckled mine, and we started outside. I hopped to my feet and gazed around, starting toward the house.

I had so many pleasant memories there. The acres upon acres of woods, the little streams scattered through the property, the little cabin Jeremy and I made love in for the first time.

But so many bad ones too. The spot where Adrian stabbed me, and where Adam killed her. Throwing Jeremy into the stone wall off the back porch when I thought he'd cheated on me. Burning the siren's body in the back yard.

Jeremy took my hand. He raised it to his lips and gently kissed the back of my knuckles. I smiled and he smiled back. Then he lifted an arm around the back of my neck, still holding my hand in his. My head rested against his shoulder as we started up the small stone staircase.

The familiar scent of cinnamon apple filled the air when we walked through the threshold. Everything was freshly cleaned, even the little dust bunny under the end table in the foyer that had been there for as long as I'd been with Jeremy was gone.

But it was strangely quiet. This house was always a little rowdy.

Damn it. I was going to have to act surprised.

"Oh, good. You're here." Adam jogged his way down the steps. "Follow me."

"That's not at all cryptic," Jeremy said.

I chuckled as we started down the hall. "You know that I know, right?"

"Just follow me." Adam glanced over his shoulder with a grin.

I rolled my eyes. Surely, Leah told him that I knew. Hell, I just did. But whatever. I'd act surprised if that'd make them happy.

As we made it through the kitchen, Adam said, "Okay, Jeremy. Cover her eyes."

"Really?" I asked. "I get that it's a surprise party and everything, but—"

"Just shut up and close your eyes," he said playfully.

Jeremy stepped behind me and placed his hands over my eyes. "Alright, my eyes are closed."

"Okay, come this way."

"Don't let me fall," I muttered.

Jeremy guided my steps. He chuckled and kissed the side of my head. "Do I ever let you fall?"

"Not yet," I murmured.

"Okay, a few more steps," Adam said.

I heard the back door creak open.

"Watch your step," Jeremy muttered.

I stepped onto the wooden porch. "Yeah, yeah."

"Okay, open your eyes," Adam said.

Jeremy pulled his hands away.

My eyes began to water almost instantly. I cupped my hand over my mouth. I knew about the party. But that wasn't the surprise.

A small, white tent sat a few feet from the steps of the porch. Above the last stair hung a gold banner that read, "Welcome Home" but aside from some printed napkins and a few more banners, the decorations were relatively menial.

What brought me to tears were the guests.

At least a hundred and fifty people stood around, holding a drink or a plate and smiling up at me.

I wouldn't have known who they were if it weren't for their scars.

Smiling, I started to sob, still cupping my hands over my mouth. Had Jeremy's hand not held my hip, I may have hit the ground. It was a beautiful kind of overwhelming.

Looking out over them, noticing each of their faces, I felt like it hadn't been so useless after all.

They weren't just a number. They were people. They were *my* people. People who wouldn't be standing there if it weren't for me.

Leah made her way up the steps and handed me a glass of red wine. She smiled. "Welcome home, babe. There's a lot of people who want to meet you."

CHAPTER TWENTY-SEVEN

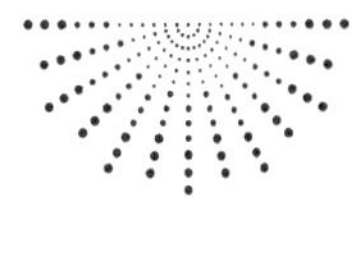

LAILA

t was somehow one of the most heart wrenching, yet empowering moments of my life. Each of the survivors had their own story, and they were all so beautiful. They were all so strong. They'd been through so much and they were so thrilled to simply breathe fresh air again.

They hugged me. They kissed my cheeks. They cried on my shoulder and I cried on theirs. We wiped each other's tears and exchanged phone numbers and names to contact each other later. I couldn't remember all of their names then, but I tried. It would take time, but eventually, I would remember them all. I would know and love every person my son gave his life for.

I sat on the bottom of the steps, sipping my second glass of wine. I watched everyone mingle before me. Jeremy huddled near Adam and Brody a few feet away, glancing at me with a smile from time to time. I'd shoot him a silly face and his smile would widen before he turned back to his brothers.

Surrounded by them, all of those beautiful creatures, ranging from four to fifty-year-olds, all with different colored skin and hair, I couldn't help but feel happy. They were here. This was their welcome home party too.

We made it home.

Chris may not have. Micah may not have.

But we survived.

I felt a soft little tap on my shoulder. I turned. A beautiful little girl in a pink blouse with tight brown curls hanging in front of her blue eyes gazed up at me.

"Lydia." I smiled.

"Hi, Laila." She raised her fingers to her mouth and chewed her nails.

"How are you doing, sweetie?" I grinned and shifted to face her better.

She gave a shrug. I ushered her to sit on the step beside me. She did so, twirling a curl between her fingers.

She was out too. My friend had his daughter back. I didn't have my kid, but he had his. And that made me feel a little bit better.

Most of me still wished it were Micah beside me on the steps that day. Most of me hated myself for what I'd done. But one way or the other, it wasn't for nothing. That little girl had a life yet to live, and my son gave her that opportunity.

"Can I tell you something, Lydia?" She only looked at me, waiting for me to say more. "I was worried you didn't really like me."

"Why?"

"Well, when we met... Or rather, when I saw you for the first time, I'm sure that was scary."

"You weren't scary."

"No?"

"What Mom and the doctor did to you guys was scary."

I was quiet for a moment, unsure how to respond. "I'm sorry you had to see those things. No one should have to live like that. Especially not a kid."

She frowned, still twirling that curl around her finger. After a few heartbeats, she said, "I miss my mom."

I raised my glass to my lips. "I miss my baby."

"I don't know why they did that. You would have been a good mom."

I managed a smile. "I wish I knew, sweetie."

She held my gaze. "But why did Mom do that to *me*?"

My throat tightened. I fought the urge to cry. I bit my trembling lip. I cleared my throat, unable to keep a few tears from leaving my eye. "I don't know."

Lydia grew quiet once more.

Part of me was congruent with Amy. I was the reason my son was dead. She shot her daughter in the chest. But I didn't knowingly make the choice to end my son's life. The decisions I made led to that outcome, but I didn't do it intentionally. She did.

That's what separated her from me.

And I couldn't wrap my head around it.

"Do you think she loves me?" Lydia asked quietly.

I fought the urge to wipe my eyes. My heart was splitting inside of my chest.

I could never hurt a child. Let alone shoot my own. I still didn't understand it. In fact, I never would. There would never be a way to rationalize what that cunt did. Stockholm's or not. Killing your own daughter is another kind of evil. In that sense, she was worse than Peterson.

"I know your daddy loves you more than anything in the world." I forced a smile. "He's been looking for you since the day you disappeared."

"He told me that."

Grateful for the subject change, my smile grew more genuine. "Are you happy to be home with him?"

"Yeah, I like him. My room's brown, but he says we can paint it any color I want."

"That's nice," I said.

"And I get to go to school now." A small smile pulled at her lips. It was the first time I saw the little girl with so much as a half smirk. "But not until the fall because school's out for the summer."

"Of course." I smiled back.

"And we got ice cream last night when we got home from the hospital," she said. "Daddy let me get as many toppings as I wanted."

"I bet he did."

I tried to keep my eyes from watering. That poor little girl. All the horror she'd seen in her own living room. All the evil.

And now, she was back to the real world. She could have a normal life again. She could be a child.

Thanks to Micah. Even at birth, my kid was a hero.

"Hey, you," Ray said behind me.

I stood and turned to meet his gaze. "Hey, Ray."

"Get over here." He opened his arms and stepped to the ground beside me. I hugged him, struggling to bring in air with how tight he squeezed. But I smiled, despite the pain, because I was happy for him, and, aside from Lydia, he had no one to celebrate with.

"Thank you so much," he said at my ear.

A tear escaped my eye. "I'm sorry I couldn't bring them both."

He gave his head a small shake and glanced down at Lydia. "Why don't you go play for a while, honey? I'll be over in a minute."

She nodded, stood, and looked up at me. "I'll see you soon, okay, Laila?"

I smiled. "I'll definitely be seeing you soon."

She almost smiled. Not quite, but almost. I ran my fingers along her little shoulder as she started off toward a group of kids on the far right of the field a few hundred feet from the tent.

I watched her walk away for a moment. The little green monster strived to climb out of me and I struggled to push it down. I just couldn't help but wish that it were my son running off to play with the other children in the yard.

It wasn't though. No number of wishes would change that reality.

So, I breathed out a slow sigh. "She's beautiful, Ray."

"She is." He gave the sweetest, most joyful smile I'd ever seen. We both watched her walk away, smiling as her little curls bounced with each step.

"I'm sorry, Laila."

I turned back to him and tilted my head in question.

"It can't be easy." He placed his hand on my upper arm. "Seeing all these kids, I mean."

"It helps, actually." I lowered myself back to the porch step. He sat beside me. I raised my glass of wine to my lips, took a slow sip, and held it between my pointer and index finger.

"Really?" he asked.

"It isn't going to bring him back. It doesn't make me a mom." I glanced around. "But they wouldn't be here if it weren't for me. If it weren't for Micah. It wasn't all for nothing, you know?" I smiled and turned to meet his gaze. "They're the reason I'm still standing."

"That's a good outlook."

I took another sip of my wine. Gazing out over the crowd filled me with a fuzzy feeling. It hurt a little too, but I still felt better than I had the night before.

"Laila," Ray said.

I turned to meet his gaze and knew what he wanted to ask. The look on his face said it all. "You don't understand what happened with Amy?"

He was quiet for a moment. "Can you explain it to me?"

"I don't really know enough to explain it. But I can show you."

"Do I want to see it?"

"No. But you should know. She isn't the person that disappeared all those years ago anymore, Ray. And I don't think you'll believe it unless you see it for yourself."

He extended his hands toward me. I placed mine on top and allowed the memories to flow into him. When I escaped during the stress test. The soft, almost pleased expression on her face as the bullet entered my thigh.

Then her apartment as I searched for Lydia. The window that overlooked the stress test room.

Then the expression on her face in the strobing red lights as the gun fired straight through Lydia into me.

"I am home, Laila. As far as I'm concerned, Ray is dead. I have a family right here." Her voice echoed through my mind, then through Ray's.

He ripped his shaking hands back. Tears poured from his eyes. He nearly held his breath to retain his composure.

I gazed at him for a moment. He didn't even reach up to wipe his face, he just sobbed in silence.

My heart ached for him. He spent all those years thinking the worst. Little did he realize his wife was willingly holding his daughter in that prison.

I gently placed my hand on his arm. "I'm sorry it isn't the outcome you expected."

"How..." He looked at his daughter in the crowd. "Our baby... How could she..."

"Maybe she was aiming for me."

"She lowered the gun, Laila," he said. "She had a clear shot of your head, and she lowered the gun."

He was right. That's exactly what she did. There was no denying the intention of that shot. I only said it in hopes of giving him some peace.

"She shot our daughter to save *him*." He scrunched up his nose. "I wouldn't shoot my daughter for anyone or anything. And she shot my baby in the chest to protect that piece of fucking shit."

"I don't understand it either, Ray. All I know is that your baby is home."

He gazed at her in silence, licking his teeth and clenching his hand to a fist.

"Your baby is home and mine is dead." I caught his attention. He turned and met my gaze. "Fuck that bitch. You got your baby back."

CHAPTER TWENTY-EIGHT

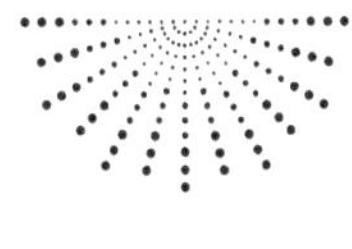

LAILA

The warm summer air drifted around me. I breathed in the scent of barbecue, relaxing in the sweet taste of wine that lingered on my tongue. Music from a portable speaker vibrated into my ears. The sun was setting in the distance, casting beautiful hues of pink and orange over the tent tops.

My gaze shifted over the party. I smiled. People danced. They ate, they drank, they hugged one another. It truly was a beautiful moment. I wished I could freeze time and live in that instant forever.

"Hey, baby." Mom plopped onto the stair beside me.

I smiled and set my glass to the ground. "Hey, Mama."

She wrapped her arms around my neck an awkward side hug and kissed my hair. "You look beautiful today."

I laughed. "You're full of shit."

"Don't talk to your mother like that." She released her hold and placed an arm gently around my shoulders.

"How was your trip home?" I shifted to look at her.

She stifled a yawn. "Longer than yours."

I smiled. "Well, in all fairness, I probably wanted to come home more than you."

She gave a bare smile and pushed hair from my face. "I'm sure you did."

Fuck, I could only imagine what these last few months had done to her. "I missed you so much, Mom."

Her smile grew a bit more convincing. "I missed you so much more, Laila."

"Normally, I'd argue that. But after losing a kid... Yeah. Yeah, you probably did miss me more."

She frowned.

I reached down to grab my glass of wine. Without thought, I raised it to my lips. Then her mouth fell agape.

She grasped my hand and held it close to her face. A laugh made its way from my lips. "Oh my God, the picture did not do it justice."

"It's pretty, isn't it?" I smiled.

"Absolutely gorgeous." She studied it carefully. "Dear lord, how much did you spend on this thing?"

"A couple thousand," I said. "We paid more for the cultured diamond."

She stared at it in awe. "The hell is a cultured diamond?"

"They're grown in a lab. They're the exact same as a regular diamond except little kids in Africa aren't dying in an attempt to mine them."

I lifted my hand out in front of us and gazed at it for a moment. I watched the princess cut rock glimmer in the dawning sunlight. It really was pretty. Kind of a waste of money, but I did love it. My hand didn't feel so empty now.

She chuckled. "Everything is a point of pride with you, huh?"

"The diamond industry is a scam anyway. You know diamonds actually have very little value? We spend so much for the—"

"It's about marketing and demand." She rolled her eyes. "Yeah, I know. You've told me a hundred times."

I sipped my wine and gazed off into the distance. "Is Jenna here?"

"Around here somewhere. She said she was looking for you, but I guess I got to you first."

The wind must have fluttered my hair. Because Mom pulled it back more carefully to examine my neck. I tugged it back to my face.

"Is that…"

I lifted my wine to my lips, chugging my fresh glass in a few gulps. "It's what it looks like."

"Does that mean…" she asked. "Oh, God."

"I'm okay, Mom."

Tears bubbled in her eyes. "You… Were you…"

I turned to meet her gaze, and my expression must've answered the question she couldn't bring herself to ask.

"Baby—"

"I'm okay, Mom. Really. I'm okay."

It was like her heart was breaking. If the bite mark hurt her this bad, I could only imagine what she would think of my back.

"Were you pregnant?" she asked.

I turned my gaze to the ground.

She didn't even know what to say. There really wasn't anything to say.

Sorry you were raped.

Sorry you were tortured for three months.

Sorry your baby died.

There was no good response. There was nothing she could say that would make it better. Nothing could turn back time and keep it from happening. It was a part of my life and we both had to accept that.

I forced a smile. "I'm okay, Mom."

"Do you want a hug?" she asked.

"I've had enough hugs to last a lifetime tonight. Really, Mom. I'm okay."

"How about another glass of wine then?"

"Sure. That'd be great. Thanks, Mom."

"I'll be right back." She started to her feet.

I went back to staring at the crowd, trying not to think about the awkward conversation I'd just had.

Instead, I focused only on the smiling faces in the crowd. I didn't realize then what I was *actually* looking at. All that I knew was that a bunch of people who'd been through absolute hell were safe. They were home, and they wouldn't have been had it not been for me.

That's what I *had* to think about. I had to look at the positive. Because whether I'd admit it then or not, I did the right thing.

Jeremy lowered himself to the step above me. "How's your night going, ma chérie?"

I lay my head backward onto his lap. He moved his legs around my waist. With a smile, I said, "Pretty good, actually."

"Oh, yeah?" He ran his fingers through my hair.

"It's nice," I said. "Seeing everyone here. All these people."

"All the people who are alive because of you?"

A gentle smile coasted up my cheeks. I gazed up at him. The stars were just becoming visible, twinkling around his face. His eyes glistened like those beautiful balls of light, so happy to see me happy. "This was sweet of Leah."

"It was."

"Did you guys make up yet?" I asked.

"Not exactly."

"Well, you should. She's your sister."

"Yeah, yeah," he muttered.

"Excuse me," a voice said in front of me. I sat forward and met the man's gaze. "Laila?"

I extended my hand. "That'd be me."

He smiled and shook my hand. "It's a pleasure to meet you."

I knew those brown eyes from somewhere. That cleaned shaved jaw looked familiar. He was a huskier guy, and that should've been the dead giveaway. The rest of us were abnormally thin. But there were family members to the survivors here.

"We've met though, haven't we?"

"Maybe you saw me when we were getting out. I know I saw you."

"Maybe." I stood so I was at eye level. "I don't know, you look really familiar though. Like I know you from somewhere."

"I don't know. But this is a really great party, I'm happy to be here."

Jeremy stood and made his way beside me. He put an arm around my waist.

"I'm happy you could come. It's beautiful, I'm so glad to meet you all. This made my night," I said.

He smiled. Then he huffed. "Not like it really matters though."

"I'm sorry?"

He laughed. "C'mon, Laila. We both know this is just a distraction. It's not going to bring our son back to you."

"Excuse me?" Jeremy's brows quickly fell over his eyes.

The man laughed, and I remembered. I couldn't forget that stupid fucking laugh.

Day thirty-six. He opened my cell door and shot me with a tranquilizing dart. I remember the sound of his snicker as I fell to the ground and slammed my head off the corner of my bed. It left me with a goose egg for three weeks.

"What did you just say?" Jeremy took a step forward.

"It didn't have to be like this."

Screams began pulsating in my mind. Throbbing and splitting pain stabbed through my skull. Agonized moans cried out between my ears.

It was so loud that the music and bustle became silent. It was like when I had a bad day, turned my car speakers as loud as they could go, and forgot to turn it down before I got out. Then I got back in the next morning, started the car, and the speakers screamed into my ears.

But the difference was, this hurt.

Then a slash sliced down my spine. The screams got louder with each whip.

I lurched over in pain, heart beating in my chest too fast to breathe correctly.

That voice. Those screams. I'd never heard him yell like that, but I knew his voice.

Chris.

"You betrayed me, Laila. You destroyed what I created. What I created *for you*." His eyes glossed over. I struggled to stay on my feet, grasping Jeremy's arm to stay vertical. "I offered you the world and you destroyed it. Now, see what happened? Do you hear it? Do you hear him screaming? Do you feel his pain?"

I squeezed my scalp. Angry tears began to pour from my eyes.

"How are you doing this?!" I bellowed over and gripped the handrail. Jeremy struggled to hold me up by my waist.

"Amy really is a wonderful partner. I have an excellent Witch too." He smiled. "You would have been, too. A wonderful partner, I mean. I would've told you everything and you would have understood. I tried to give you that opportunity. I tried to be kind to you. I even brought everyone pizza because you wanted me to, do you remember that?"

I curled my nose up in disgust, stomach churning.

"Fuck you," I said between trembling teeth.

He smiled. "I already did, remember?"

I lunged forward to punch him. I knew that it wasn't him but fuck. He was right there, he was right in front of me. He wasn't him, but he was, and I wanted to rip his throat out. But I stumbled. Jeremy grasped my hip to hold me up.

"I helped you, Laila. I know I hurt you, but I helped you too. I'm the reason you have that variety pack of powers in your pocket." He gazed at me longingly. "We could have been great. I could have given you anything you ever wanted. I would have shown you; I would have. And you would have understood why it was all necessary. Because it was, Laila. Every single thing was *needed*. I didn't do what I did for pleasure, I did it because it *had* to be done. But now you'll have to learn the hard way. You should have just listened."

"I wanted freedom," I snarled. "I wanted to be a mother."

"I could have given you that," he said.

"What the fuck is going on?" Celena said behind me.

His gaze turned up to her and he smiled. "This is your sister, right? She's a hybrid too, isn't she?"

"Don't even fucking look at her," I said between gritted teeth.

I wanted to reach out and do something but the pain in my mind was unfathomable. I could barely stand. My heart was racing a mile a minute, and Chris's screams were still echoing through my ears. Jeremy must have felt it too, and he was too busy holding me upright to do anything either way.

He turned back to me with a smile. "I can see the resemblance.

Something in the lips." His hand raised toward my face, but Jeremy caught it with his free hand.

He bent his fingers backward, eyes darting between the guard's. "You're never going to fucking touch her again."

The guard smiled and painlessly pulled his hand away. How did he do that? Jeremy wasn't weak by any means. He surely broke those fingers.

"A little jealous, Jeremy?" He grinned.

His hands shook and his shoulders stiffened. If he didn't know it was a waste of energy, he would have killed him.

"Coming from the pussy who has to wear someone else's face to look me in the eye," Jeremy growled.

He let out a laugh, shaking his head. Then he turned back to me. "We could have done great things, Laila. We could have had the world together."

The screams in my head began to quiet. The stabbing pain softened to a dull throb.

My gaze narrowed. "I hate you. I fucking *hate* you."

"And I love you. An unfortunate repeating cycle in my life." He sighed. "I wish you would have given me a chance, Laila. I wish you would have let me show you how much you mean to me. But after this, after what you've done... I don't know how to heal from this."

"I'm going to kill you." My eyes warmed in their sockets. "I'm going to fucking kill you."

"One day," he said. "You will. I know that. Accepted it long, *long* ago. But not any time soon. You don't even know where I am." He chuckled. "And the next time you do know where I am, it'll be because I want you to. One day, I *will* have you again. We'll be side by side. Even if you're tied to a table, you'll be by my side."

"You're never taking her again." Jeremy's hands defensively clenched my hips.

The guard laughed. "The thing is, you think that you've seen the worst of it. But our story is just beginning. See, you destroyed my work. You took years of time and effort and love from me. I'm going to destroy your hard work too. I'm going to take what you love too." He reached into his pocket as he spoke. "I'll see you soon, Laila. Farther away than I'd like, but still. Soon enough. But just remember. This is perhaps the most important lesson I will ever teach you, so listen carefully. You'll never be able to save them all."

He pulled a small remote from his pocket.

Jeremy hurdled himself in front of me.

I didn't even put two and two together until I heard the boom. By the time I heard it, it was too late to stop it.

It was just damage control.

CHAPTER TWENTY-NINE

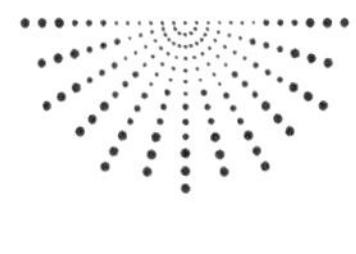

LAILA

Jeremy's hands gripped my waist, but behind his head, just before he teleported, I watched the explosion in slow motion. It was on the far-right end of the tent near the picnic buffet. I saw the orange and yellow light flash. It left my vision a blur of black stars for a moment. But it wasn't the light that would haunt me.

It was the people flying through the air. Blood spraying and falling from the sky as rain. Limbs soaring through the wind like a game of volleyball on the beach.

I held my breath, eyes wide with shock as their screams began. I was almost frozen in time in that moment. I couldn't process or really grasp what was happening.

We landed near the tree line with Jeremy holding me against him.

And then, it fell into place. I realized what I was witnessing, and I realized what he meant.

He did this to prove a fucking point. That I may have won a battle, but I was still losing the war. He had Chris. He was the reason my baby was dead. And now, he was the reason people who had come to celebrate our freedom were dead too.

"No!" I screamed. "No. No, no. No, no, no."

It was all I could make out. I couldn't speak anything else. I couldn't even think another word.

I went to teleport into the disaster, but Jeremy caught my hand. "Baby."

I turned to meet his gaze. Blood dribbled from the side of his mouth. His body started to sway in my arms.

My jaw trembled. I gripped his biceps, gazing at him with eyes wide. *Not him too.*

It didn't feel real. I didn't even feel his pain. It had to be a dream. It was a bad dream and I just had to wake up.

Then my eyes caught on his abdomen.

He began to fumble to the ground. He struggled, using my arms to steady himself. "I can't feel my legs."

I helped him to the ground and dropped beside him. Tears poured from my eyes. My teeth clambered together so loud that I could barely hear the pleas in the distance.

A piece of metal protruded from his chest.

"No," was all I could manage out.

"Heal me," he said between gurgles.

It was instinctive. I didn't even think about it. I just couldn't let him die.

I couldn't let him die, too.

That piece of shit took my baby from me. He took Chris again. He just killed... I wasn't even sure how many people.

But he wouldn't take Jeremy.

No one would *ever* take Jeremy from me. Never.

I ripped the piece of metal from his chest, threw it to the ground, and held my glowing hands above the wound in his chest. My head shook, tears pouring from my eyes like waterfalls. His hand held my thigh. He grimaced and closed his eyes in agony. I felt it too, but I kept going because I had no other choice.

Once his wound shut, he met my gaze and said, "Go. I'm right behind you."

None of what Peterson said even processed. None of it. It wouldn't, not until well after the dust settled. The only thing that did was the line about destroying my hard work. Because that was exactly what he did.

He took the only ounce of joy I had. He hurt me by hurting the survivors. The people my son had given his life to protect. He blew them up for no reason other than to hurt me.

I teleported into the catastrophe.

There were so many screams. So many people lying on the ground. So many bloodied bodies. So many detached limbs.

I didn't know where to start so I dropped beside the person closest to me. I began healing whatever wounds I saw that bled the hardest. He was a young kid, no more than sixteen, screaming in agony as blood poured from the joint where his arm once hung.

I cried, telling him how sorry I was as I sealed the gushing arteries. He screamed. His body rolled and quaked in agony. As the wound closed, I hurried to my feet.

"Laila!" Adam screamed. "Laila!"

"Over here!" I called.

Suddenly, he was in front of me. He grasped my arm and we spun through the air. "It's Leah. Heal Leah."

I dropped to the ground beside her. She was on the outskirts of the tent on the left side, thankfully.

She lay in the green grass unconscious, blood streaming from her pink lips. Shrapnel protruded from her chest, but it didn't go the whole way through like Jeremy's had. It was probably five inches into her left breast.

I grabbed whatever it was that stuck out of her and ripped it from her torso. She screamed, her eyes opened, and I began healing. The white light radiated from my hands. Adam collapsed on top of her, holding her arms against the ground. She screamed and writhed against me, but I kept going. She wasn't going to die on me too. That bastard wasn't going to take my best friend.

As I finished, Adam helped her to her feet. "Can you heal them?" I asked.

"Yeah. Where're Kai and Celena?"

"I don't know."

"I'll find them," Adam said. "Just start healing people."

I started toward a group that screamed on the ground. Then I paused for a split second. I'd already lost my son. I wasn't going to lose the other most important people in my life. Maybe it was fucked up that I thought about my loved ones when a family huddled around some dying loved one of their own. But I learned another lesson in there. If I didn't take care of my family first, I'd never forgive myself.

My gaze met Adam's. "Find Jenna and my mom. If they're hurt, you call for me."

"Jenna went to the bathroom and your mom was getting drinks in the kitchen. They're fine. Just go."

I disappeared to the group closest to me. A group of people kneeled crying over a young girl near my age.

"Help, Laila!" an older woman cried over the body.

I stumbled to the grass. "Move." I pushed past them to get to the girl. Blood formed a puddle around her gray, smog covered blond hair. She wasn't breathing. I put my hand to her neck but didn't feel a pulse. "Do you know CPR?"

She shook her head.

I said, "It's easy, alright? Make a fist with both of your hands and start pumping right here." I gripped her shaking hands and put them to the girl's chest and pushed down. "As I count, you push down, alright? To the beat of *Stayin' Alive*, okay?"

She nodded fast. I shifted upward and put my hand to the girl's head. I turned it to the side and began counting. There was a lot of blood, but no brain matter. I began healing the wound as she pumped.

I don't know how long it took, probably only thirty seconds. But it felt like a lifetime waiting for her to open her eyes.

But she did. Her eyes flung open like she was rising from a nightmare.

I didn't waste time to make sure they were okay once she was healed. I just moved onto the next group.

The next person had a large piece of glass stuck in his throat, but no one had pulled it out so he was still alive. He was older than the last girl, maybe closer to Leah's age. That was a quick way to bleed out. I'd have to move fast. And even then, the chances were still slim.

His panicked, teary eyes shifted between the older man's that held his hand.

"I'm going to take the glass out and heal you, okay?" I said.

He shook his head as best he could, eyes watering profusely. The man beside him panted heavily.

"It's going to hurt." I pushed bloody hair from his cheek. "It's going to hurt a lot, but you're going to live. You just stay with me. I'll do everything I can. But you have to want to live. You don't die on me, okay?" His lips trembled. "You've been through too much to die like this."

His honey eyes stared up at me. But he managed a slow nod.

I gripped the glass and tore it out. Blood sprayed up at me and I quickly moved my hand over the wound, holding in as much blood as I could as the white-hot light radiated into his body.

He writhed in agony, and I climbed on top of him to pin him in place. The wound began to close but still dribbled blood between my fingers.

Once the blood stopped pouring from my hands, I stood and ran to the next victim.

The first kid I saw who was injured.

It hit different than the others.

He didn't have the scars. He must have been there for a family member who did. His mother laid on the ground beside his cold little body.

"Help me," she begged with eyes that poured tears. "Please help me. Don't let my baby die." Her eyes locked with mine. "Save my baby. Don't let him die."

I fell to the ground beside her and held my hands above his body. The white light shined against his dark skin. It didn't help that he looked like Daniel, either. I put every ounce of energy I had into him. I poured and poured whatever life force still remained in me into that small child, telling myself I had to save him. Another child couldn't die because of me.

My hands shook when it didn't work, but I kept trying. I couldn't stop. I had to save him.

I couldn't let another child die. Not another baby. I couldn't let another mother feel the way I did. I couldn't. I had to save him. I had to.

The mother's cries grew louder. He remained unresponsive, his yellow SpongeBob shirt smiled up at me in irony. No, he couldn't die. He couldn't die.

He had to go home with his mom. He had to live. He had to fucking live.

The white light got brighter. I strained, body quaking. Water rolled down my cheeks.

Leah grabbed my shoulder. "He's gone, Laila."

I focused every fragment of energy I had into his body. "I have to save him."

"There's nothing left to save," she said softly. "You're wasting time, there's so many more people who need help. We can't let them die."

"No." I shook my head again, white light still radiating against him. "No, he has to live. I have to save him."

"You can't, Laila," Leah said. "He's gone. You have to save someone else."

My tears fell down, crashing against his soft, still little cheeks.

She gripped my shoulder. "You can't save him, Laila," she said again. "Save someone else."

But just remember... You'll never be able to save them all.

I hated him. I always hated him, but after that, I hated him so much more.

I fought with everything I had to save those people. And I did. I fucking did. I saved over two-hundred lives. Then a little boy who should have never even been a part of it died because that fucker was right.

I'd never be able to save them all.

I turned to the mother, tears gushing down my cheeks. The light receded from my hands. "I'm sorry. I'm so sorry."

CHAPTER THIRTY

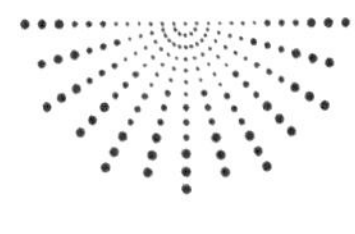

LAILA

I sat on the bottom step. My blood covered, shaking hands gripped a bottle of wine. I gazed out over the yard, watching the police as they covered another body with a white sheet. I counted each one.

Twelve.

Twelve corpses lay around the blood and debris littered grass.

Funny. Earlier that night, I'd looked over the crowd and thought about how they weren't numbers. But there I was. Counting.

I wasn't sure who called 911. The explosion and smoke may have signaled someone from the highway nearby. Or maybe it was Ray.

It *was* caused by a human. We didn't have to cover it up.

At least one part of it was easy.

"Laila Callidy?" a voice said to my left.

I didn't turn. I just lifted the bottle to my lips and drank another long gulp. "That's me."

He extended his hand. "Deputy Fred Carlson."

I raised the bottle back to my lips, still staring out in front of me. He dropped his hand back to his side.

"Can you tell me anything about what happened tonight?" he asked.

I raised the bottle back to my lips and chugged. "Do you know anything about my case?"

"That's FBI, a little above my pay grade."

"I'm not going to repeat it then." I took another gulp. "I'll talk to Tina Davis."

"She's not going to be here until the morning. Could you just answer a few questions?"

I huffed. "What do you want to know?"

"Do you know who did this?" he asked.

"Robert Peterson."

He began jotting in his tablet. "That's who set off the bomb?"

"No. One of his guards did."

"His guards?"

I rolled my eyes. "I'm not repeating it all. This is why I said I'd talk to Tina."

"Alright. Well, do you know why this happened?"

"To prove a point. To hurt me. To show it isn't over."

"How do you know that?"

"That's what the guard said," I muttered.

"He said that this was to prove a point?"

"In a manner of speaking."

"You're going to have to give me a little more than that, sweetie," he began.

"You're going to have to fuck off, *sweetie*." I tilted my head back and finished off the bottle.

"Excuse me?"

"I said fuck off."

"There's no reason to use that kind of language with me—" he said.

"Fred," Ray interjected nearby. He jogged toward us. "Fred, it's been a hell of a night."

He turned his gaze back to me. I chewed my jaw. As they spoke, I watched them cover the thirteenth body.

Two hundred and twenty-four minus thirteen. Two hundred and eleven. Maybe less after they finished collecting the bodies.

"I was here, man. I'll give you a detailed statement. She's only been home for a couple days; this was her welcome home party. She needs to catch her breath." Ray patted his co-worker's shoulder.

Fred turned to me, then back to Ray. "I'll meet you down at the station once we're done here."

"Thanks, Fred." He turned away. Ray lowered himself in front of me. "Are you okay?"

What was the use in even asking that question? Obviously I wasn't fucking okay.

"Nope."

"Where's Jeremy? Is he alright?" he asked.

"I don't know, but I healed him. He's okay."

"Your mom wanted to see you, but I told her she should go home. She wants you to call her."

Good move. I didn't want to see her. I didn't want to see anyone. The only person I wanted to see was Peterson so that I could skin him alive. So that I could rip his throat out. So I could cut off his dick and shove it down his throat.

There were a million awful murder methods running through my mind.

Ray pushed long, blood crusted hair behind my ear. I slapped his hand away. "This wasn't your fault."

"It wouldn't have happened if it weren't for me."

"They'd still be in that place if it weren't for you," he said softly.

I slammed to my feet. "It wasn't just survivors that died tonight, Ray! Their families were killed. They were amputated, they bled out, they watched their loved ones get blown to pieces at *my* welcome home party!" My eyes rapidly shifted between his. "Tell me again how this wasn't my fault, Ray. Fucking explain to me how this wasn't because of me."

He glanced at the cops whose gazes settled on me. But I couldn't give a shit less. People could stare and gawk at the crazy bitch screaming all they wanted, what difference did it make? Why would I care? After what I'd just witnessed, I was allowed to be angry. I was allowed to scream and curse and stomp my feet.

And even if I wasn't. What difference did their stares make?

I lifted the wine to my lips and tilted my head back. Only drops fell to my tongue.

"Fuck, I need alcohol." I started up the steps.

As I stumbled, he grasped my elbow. "Alright, but I'm gonna help you."

I yanked my arm away. "I don't need any God damned help."

He raised his hand in surrender. I continued up the stairs. I drunkenly swayed my way to the patio door, now cracked from some projectile during the explosion. Ray was right behind me, probably preparing to catch me.

As I made it into the kitchen, my gaze traveled to the counter where large bins filled with ice held bottles of wine and liquors. I lifted the whiskey. Ray grabbed it from my hand and passed me a bottle of wine.

Fair enough. I was already two bottles in. Hard liquor was probably a bad idea.

I took it reluctantly, unscrewed the metal cap, and raised it to my lips.

"Take it easy, Lai," Brody said from the breakfast nook.

I flipped him off and chugged. My head tilted back as far as it could go. The burn slid down my throat and settled in the pit of my stomach. When I drank just under half of the bottle, I set it back to the counter. My fingers twisted around its neck. I gripped the counter with my other hand.

"Where's Jeremy?" I gazed down at the bottle.

"In the basement," Adam muttered. "He got the guard."

I steadied myself against the counter.

Leah gazed out over the yard behind me. She grabbed the whiskey Ray took from my hand, screwed off the lid, lifted it to her lips and took a long swig.

"Well," she murmured, "I'm not getting my security deposit back on the tent."

I almost laughed. Almost. Then I lifted the bottle of wine and took another sip.

The basement door opened, and Jeremy made his way through it. "Hey." His voice was soft as velvet as he walked toward me.

I didn't say anything, I just took another drink from the bottle.

"The cops want to talk to you, Jeremy," Celena said beside Brody in the breakfast nook. "You heard what the guard said before the bomb went off. I told them what I gathered, but I chimed in at the last second."

He gently kissed my head. I wanted to find some relief in that kiss, but nothing could bring me relief in that moment. I think he knew that.

Jeremy started outside. "He's gagged and cuffed, so don't let anyone in the basement."

As the patio door shut, Hannah quietly said, "What do we do now?"

"I don't know," Leah said.

Neither did fucking I.

All I knew was that I didn't want to be alive anymore. I didn't want to see what the future had in store for me. I didn't want to keep watching people I helped get murdered.

The only reason I didn't teleport a thousand feet into the atmosphere and drop to my death was because of that fucking catch-phrase of his.

One day.

One day, I'd kill him. Even he knew that. And that was the only reason I wanted to live. Just to take his worthless, disgusting fucking life.

CHAPTER THIRTY-ONE

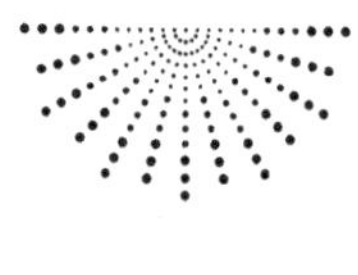

JEREMY

"You were there when the man who detonated the bomb approached your fiancé, correct?" The cop jotted down on a note pad.

"Yeah. Laila thought it was another survivor."

"Can you tell me what he said?" he asked.

I ran my fingers through my messy hair. "I can try. It's kind of a blur."

"That's okay. Take your time." He waited for me to continue.

"She said something about recognizing him and he said that they must have met when they were escaping. Then he said it was a nice party, and Laila agreed. But then he said something about how it didn't matter. Nothing was going to bring the baby back, or something like that." My fingers found the bridge of my nose. I rubbed between it down to my beard. Not exactly what he said but close enough. "It took a second before we realized what he meant. Then he said that she ruined his work, that she took what he loved from him and that he was going to do the same to her," I said. "Then he pulled a little detonator from his pocket and I jumped in front of Laila, and he ran, and it's a bunch of noise after that."

The wrote for a while longer in his note pad. "Did you see which direction he ran in?"

"I wish I did. I was just worried about her. I didn't even think to follow him."

"Could you come down to the station and make an official statement?" He continued writing.

"Yeah. Sure, anything I can do to help. But Laila's... She's pretty messed up right now and she drove here. I don't think she could shift the car into drive if she tried. Is it alright if I come down in the morning?"

The cop patted my upper arm in a father-like fashion. "Sure thing. Thank you for the help, kid. I hope things get better for you."

"Yeah, me too. Thanks. I'm gonna get back in there and see what's going on. Is there anything you need?"

"We just have to go over some things with the owner of the property. Do you know who that is?" he asked.

"Yeah, my sister. Leah Boucher. I'll tell her to come out."

"Thanks, kid. You have a safe trip home."

I pushed a smile. "Thanks, officer. Have a nice night."

Kid. It killed me how people saw me as a child because I was young. I was polite regardless, but it pissed me off. I'd seen more shit than every cop there aside from a few that served. Most of those small-town cops hadn't seen more than a few overdoses and some domestic disputes. Yet, I was the one looked at as a child.

Although, I supposed it was to my benefit. They didn't suspect me of anything. I was a sweet kid who worked at the little diner in town with his fiancé. I had a friendly smile and a soft demeanor.

You'd never think that I just beat the shit out of some guy and tied him up in my sister's basement.

As I made it back into the kitchen, I met Leah's gaze and said, "The cops need to talk to you."

She raised a glass of some brown drink to her lips and finished it off. "Knew that was coming."

Leah started toward the door. But before she did, she caught my arm and met my gaze. "She's in a really bad place, Jeremy. I can't see her coming out of it any time soon. Be patient with her."

"Yeah. Yeah, I know."

"No, dude. I was in her head. It's bad. Just be ready."

"I will."

I began to brush past her, but she squeezed my bicep. "*Watch* her."

"What do you mean?"

She searched for the words. "Hide the knives type of shit."

My confusion turned to fear. "I'll watch her."

Her green eyes met mine. After a moment, she brushed past me onto the patio.

"Where is she?" I asked Adam.

He gestured toward the powder room in the hall. "Puking."

I started through the kitchen. As I drew closer to the bathroom, the smell of stomach acid and alcohol filled my nostrils. I practically had to hold my breath the closer I got.

Laila was sprawled out on the floor, her head resting on the toilet seat. Brody hovered behind her, tucking hair from her face behind her shoulder.

"Thanks, man." I gestured to her on the ground.

"Any time. Are you all good here?"

"Yeah. Yeah, I got her. Thanks."

"Just take care of her."

"You know I will."

"I'm going to get a shower. Can you do me a favor and let me know when you guys get home and she's all settled in?"

"Sure."

He disappeared. I brought myself to my knees beside her. I brushed hairs that hung loosely around her face behind her ear. "Hey, baby."

She opened her eyes for a second and met my gaze through black, mascara mixed tears. "You're okay, right? I healed you the whole way?"

I smiled. "I'm good as new."

She closed her eyes again. "Good."

I placed my hand on her back and delicately rubbed her shoulders. "Are you ready to go home?" She nodded slow. "Can you walk?" She shook her head. "That's okay. I'll just carry you to the car."

Laila sat up and stumbled sideways a bit. I caught her shoulder and helped her off of her knees onto her butt. I tucked my arm beneath her knees and wrapped my other arm around the back of her chest. I teleported to a standing position. She nuzzled her head into me, holding my shirt in her hand like it was a rope that fastened her body from a dangling cliff. I kissed her forehead and turned sideways to get through the door without hitting her head off of anything.

As I walked to the car, I thought about what Leah said. I didn't know what I would do if she was gone again. Especially if she left the world willingly like my dad did.

I wasn't even sure I would physically survive if she killed herself. Legend has it that when one of us dies, so does the other. I didn't know if it was true, but a lot of us didn't know if any of the par animo myths were true at all. I did though. We were proof.

I was certain about one thing though. I'd definitely get dope if she died. Fuck, I wanted to get high so bad after the night we'd had. It was selfish and I didn't want to think it. But life was fucking hard and I wanted to get away. I couldn't though. I had to be there for her.

It wasn't that I wanted to get away from Laila, just from the disaster we called our lives. I wanted my girl back. I wanted our life back. I wanted her to be her again.

But I wasn't sure that would ever happen. I didn't think she'd ever be that girl again. I caught a few glimpses of her the day before and a few more that morning, but it was just a couple flashes. She still had this heartbroken look in her eyes that just wouldn't budge.

I didn't blame her. If I was dealing with what happened to Micah instead of burying it deep in the archives of my mind, I'd probably have that same gaze.

I set her into the passenger seat and clicked the seat belt into place. As I set her down, I gazed at her sad, hurting little body. Her cheeks were stained black with watery mascara. Dried blood turning brown covered her nearly head to toe.

She turned over onto her side and cupped her bloody hands

beneath her head as a makeshift pillow. I guessed I'd have to shower her again.

———

The ride home was quiet. So quiet that I could hear the crickets and cicadas chirping in the trees through the open window.

As we made it to the lot, I decided it'd be best to carry her in through the back door. It was easier than carrying her messy body through the entire restaurant.

I shifted the car into park near the dumpster. I headed to the door, pulled it open and ran up the steps to open our apartment because it'd be too difficult to fuck with the handles while she lay in my arms. Then I tossed a throw blanket over the couch, knowing she'd kill me tomorrow if I laid her bloody body on the suede.

I went back to the car, opened her door, and carefully hoisted her into my arms. Her body curled against mine like two magnets coming together. I kissed her forehead and started inside, carrying her tiny body as easily as a sack of potatoes.

We made it through the doorway, and I set her down on the couch. Her eyes fluttered open when I walked to the kitchen and got a bottle of water off the top of the fridge. By the time I made my way back into the living room, she was pulling herself to a sitting position. I sat on the coffee table and handed her the bottle.

She unscrewed the lid. "Thanks."

I wanted to say something. But what could I say? I could've asked if she was okay, but we both knew she wasn't. I could've told her I was sorry, but she didn't want to hear that either. I could've told her it would all be okay, but I didn't know that it would. I could've begged her to stay with me, to find a reason to live, but she didn't want to hear that.

There was nothing to say. All I could do was be there.

Laila brought the bottle to her lips and chugged. When the bottle was gone, she yawned and rubbed her eyes. "I need a shower."

"Probably not a bad idea." She started to her feet and I said, "Are you okay to walk?"

She avoided my gaze. "Yeah, I'm alright. Barfing and that nap sobered me up some."

"Just call for me if you need me."

She started to the bathroom.

When I heard the door shut, I hung my head low. I put my hands to my face and rubbed my eyes.

All the shit needed to end. We were all miserable.

I reached for my bowl on the table. I took a long, slow hit. Burning ashes shot down my throat. I spit it out and wiped my hand across my tongue.

I stood and made my way to the entertainment stand. I reached in for the bag of weed. But my hand caught on a piece of paper. I leaned down to see what it was.

A pink post-it was stuck to the inside of the cabinet with Laila's messy handwriting scribbled over it in black sharpie. On top of it sat a small, perfectly symmetrical, impeccably rolled white joint. I lifted it and pulled the paper to my hand.

I hope this made you smile
I love you
<3

A smile pulled at my lips. Tears welled in my eyes.

Just a flash. Only a glimpse. But it was enough to remind me that she was still the girl I fell in love with. She was a little rougher around the edges, but she was still Laila.

I held the joint to my lips, sparked the lighter to a flame, and took a puff.

Plopping back onto the couch, I dazed off into space. Everything was a mess. Our life was one fucking catastrophe after the next. It never ended. We were stuck in a cycle it seemed we would never break.

After a few minutes, I heard her leave the bathroom and go into the bedroom. I stood because I wanted the chance to talk to her about the night's disaster before she passed out. Or, if she didn't want to talk, at least to hold her for a moment. That may not have been her love language, but it was mine, and I needed her too.

As I entered the bedroom, I softly said, "Hey."

She glanced over her shoulder as she ran a comb through her hair. She gave a sad, slight smile. I sat beside her on the bed. I reached to put my hand on hers, but she pulled it away.

My heart sunk. "Baby." I brought my hand back to my lap.

"I'm sorry," she muttered. "I just... I need some time. It's not you, I just..." she whispered. "I don't want to be comforted right now."

I didn't know what to say. Usually, I'd reach out and hug her. But she didn't want that. She didn't want me to touch her and it broke my heart. I wanted to be held just as bad as I wanted to hold her. Realizing she didn't, felt like someone just kicked a hole through my chest.

CHAPTER THIRTY-TWO

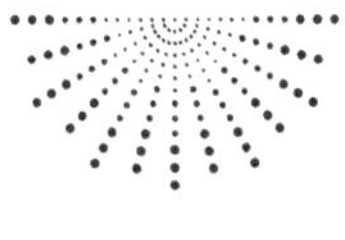

LAILA

My eyes fluttered open, sun shining in them.

But I couldn't find the will to stand up. It wasn't the hangover. Physically, I felt fine. It was just everything else. I couldn't find the energy to so much as take a piss. I just lay there staring vacantly out the window.

It was a new day. But I had nothing to look forward to. I just wanted to die.

Jeremy ran his hand gently down my arm. "Good morning."

I shook it off and continued looking out the window.

It looked like it was going to be a pretty day. The sky was the softest shade of blue. Wind rustled the full treetops. The sun was bright and warm. Inviting.

But I didn't want to move.

What if I went to the store and another bomb went off just because I was there? What if I went for a walk at the park and watched a dozen kids get blown to pieces? Or maybe worse, what if I enjoyed the walk? What if I was happy? That would be worse. After what I witnessed last night, I shouldn't be.

I didn't want to be happy. I didn't *deserve* to be happy.

He was staring at me. I felt his eyes on my back, but I couldn't bring myself to look at him. I knew I was hurting him. It wasn't the goal; it was just collateral damage. But knowing I was hurting him made me hurt worse.

Fuck, I just wanted to fucking die. I just kept thinking it. I kept running over and over through my mind. It was like I was entirely incapable of thinking anything aside from *I want to die.*

A minute or two later, Jeremy said, "I have to go down to the police station and give a statement. Do you want to come?"

I shook my head. He fell silent again.

"Do you want me to get you something to eat?" he asked softly.

I shook my head again.

"Can I kiss you before I go?"

I turned over to meet his sad, begging gaze. I leaned forward and touched my lips to his. His hand made its way to my neck, delicately holding my face in his palm.

Then I pulled back. He looked at me with big, droopy blue eyes. "Do you want me to see if Leah or Celena want to come over and spend some time with you?"

"No. I just want to be alone."

"Are you going to be okay until I get back?"

"Why wouldn't I be?"

Jeremy was quiet for a moment. "I... I just don't want anything to happen to you."

"I'm fine." I rolled over and looked back out the window.

The bed swayed as he stood. I pulled the blankets up closer to my face. He made his way around the bed, reached into his dresser, and pulled out a pair of jeans. As he stepped into them, I chewed my lip to keep from crying.

I didn't want to cry in front of him. I was hurting him enough already; I didn't want him to hurt any worse.

He said that I could tell him anything. He insisted that he wanted me to open up. But that wasn't true. He didn't want that pain. He just wanted me to be happy. I loved him for that, I wanted to be happy too.

But he wanted me to be the sweet, bubbly, fun-loving girl I was six months before. And that Laila was dead. Maybe she'd resurrect some-day, but it wasn't going to happen overnight.

Once he had his pants on, he walked toward me and sat on the bed in front of me. When his gaze locked on me, I looked away.

"I'll be back soon," he said. "I love you."

"I love you too," I murmured.

He leaned down and kissed my cheek. Then he turned toward the door and headed out. When I heard his footsteps start down the stairs, I let the tears fall.

I held my pillow close to my face in a tight embrace, sobbing into it to muffle the sound of my dry heaves and coughs.

Those people, those families, were gone because of me.

Sure, I wasn't the one who detonated the bomb. But it was *because* of me. It was to hurt *me*.

Mission accomplished, Peterson.

I was fucking hurting. My heart was broken.

Everything I'd done to save them was worthless. I guess most of them lived, but the ones that didn't were led from hell, to freedom, straight into their deaths. *I* led them to their deaths.

More sets of blood on my hands.

Chris's screams.

His fucking screams would haunt my nightmares for years. He didn't deserve that.

It should have been him who made it out. Not me.

He'd have been grateful enough to enjoy it.

I was more miserable than I'd ever been, even in there. The hole in my chest hurt worse than the slashes on my back.

Survivor's guilt fucking sucks. Depression fucking sucks. Living fucking sucks.

There was one thing I'd been wanting to do since I'd gotten home but hadn't gotten around to. Jeremy was out of the house for the morning. And I had a million questions. I needed answers.

I sat up in the bed. I had to do it, but I was dreading it.

"Alright, bitch. I know you can hear me. We need to talk." I looked around the room.

Mary appeared in doorway. "I have a name, you know."

"Bitch is an endearing term, get with the times," I said.

She gave a smile. "How are you, Laila?"

"I'm pretty sure you know." I sat further up and adjusted the blanket.

She gestured to the end of the bed. "May I sit?"

I scooted back and made room for her on the bed. She walked across the room and gracefully lowered herself to the mattress. She crossed her ankles in front of her but turned her gaze to mine.

"You knew," I said.

She remained silent. Her hazel eyes held mine. The lack of response was enough of a response.

"You knew that all of this would happen," I said again.

"Not all of it. I didn't know what would happen last night."

"But you knew I'd be taken."

Her eyes grew somber. After a moment, she said, "I did."

I gritted my teeth together. "You knew and you let it happen anyway."

"I didn't know all of the details, Laila. I just knew that it would happen. I didn't know when. I didn't know where you'd be captured. I just knew that you would."

"That's what you meant at the funeral. You said something about my pregnancy ending badly," I said. "That I should listen. I should run."

"Yes."

"And when you killed Moe, you did that so I could have a fresh start somewhere else."

"And to keep my identity concealed. But you figured that part out on your own."

"You had that siren rape Jeremy so that I would break up with him before I got pregnant."

"That was the plan. I guess my math was a little off. Although, again, I didn't know all of the details."

"And when you saw that he and I hadn't ended things, at least not entirely, you tried to kill him."

"I really wasn't trying to kill him, Laila."

"No?"

I hadn't believed that, but I was starting to. Now that I lost a kid, I'd do anything to bring him back. Almost anything, anyway. But I wouldn't kill one of my children to save the other. That was my line.

Mary frowned. "No. I just wanted to slow him down. I wanted to get rid of Ally before he had the chance to talk to her and figure it out. But I had to be careful with her death so that the Council didn't realize I killed her. The maids are endangered, we're only allowed to kill them in self-defense. I thought that if she died in her home with no obvious signs of foul play, no one would notice. She was a pretty young girl who spent a lot of time at bars and concerts. It'd be chalked up to her reckless behavior and no one would bat an eye. It's not like anyone was looking for her."

It did make sense. Not that I would have done everything that Mary did, but that would've been how I killed her too. The less mess the better.

"Then you killed her before she could tell us your plan."

"I did."

"Why didn't you just tell me?" I asked. "Why didn't you just tell me that I was going to lose the baby anyway? Why didn't you just tell me not to look into what happened to Chris and Ray's family?"

She chewed her lip and let out a slow breath. Now I know why. Because she knew much more than she was able to say. I get it now, but I didn't then.

"I tried to." She wrung her hands together. "I warned all of you not to look for Chris. But as you kids would say, I lost my cool. I slipped up for a minute and you figured me out. My plan was already falling apart, I couldn't change your pregnancy. But I hoped once you realized" —she breathed out a slow, heavy breath— "I hoped you'd get an abortion. At least that would have saved you from most of your pain. Then I hoped you wouldn't keep digging into Chris's disappearance. Although my reaction is probably what made you guys so set on finding him in the first place."

"You cared for all of them most of their lives. How... How could you let Chris continue to suffer in there?"

"Laila, if I knew how to save him, I would. If I would have known where you were, I would have saved you too. But I didn't have all of the information, and he..." She bit her tongue, as if she had something to say but had to do it carefully. "If Chris staying there would have saved you from all of this pain, I would have left him there for an eternity. I would have killed Jeremy if it meant all of this could have been avoided. And you can tell me I'm awful for that if you want. You can hate me for it if you like. But as a mother... " She paused. Her gaze firmly locked with mine. "You would kill anyone to keep your child safe, wouldn't you? Even if you loved them?"

I didn't want to face that fact. But it was true. It always would be. I would burn the world to ash if it meant my son was safe.

Changed my perspective on her though. She loved me more than she loved them. And I got it. I loved a child I didn't get to raise too. Even now, I would have let Daniel die that night if it meant Micah got to live. Not because I didn't love that child. Just because I loved my own more.

"I'm not proud of what I did, Laila. Knowing what I know now, that all of this was inevitable... I wouldn't do it again. But if it could have been avoided, if I could have ever kept you and Jeremy from meeting, I would have. Unfortunately though, it was a necessary evil. Or at least, that's what I thought at the time."

The sentence sounded like an oxymoron. I replayed it through my thoughts, trying to make it make sense. But it didn't. It wouldn't, not for a very long time.

"What do you mean none of this could have been avoided?"

She looked away. "I've already said too much."

"No, Mary, what do you mean?" She kept her gaze away from me. "I need answers. I need to understand. I'm having a really hard time accepting all of this. And I... I hate myself for what happened."

"I know you do."

"And you... You can help me. You can help me understand."

She gave a slow shake of her head. "I don't even understand it all, Laila."

"But you—You said..."

"It took me a long time to develop that plan, Laila. It was nearly flawless. And reality shifted around it. Reality changed as I planned to prevent it. Don't you see?"

"I don't."

"You can't fight what is meant to be. By trying to create a new future for you, I gave you the reality I was trying to prevent." Her omnipresent frown remained. "Destiny will always have what it wants. It does not care about what we want or what we think is right. Destiny has forever, and will always, win." Her gaze softened. "You can't elude destiny."

"I don't believe in destiny."

"Neither did I," she muttered. "Not until I fought her. And she won. She always wins."

Clearly, Mary knew more than I did. Still, that was only a sliver of the big picture.

"How did you know all of this?" I asked. "Angels aren't psychic, you don't have premonitions."

She turned her gaze out the window.

"Mary." I grasped her shoulder. "Mary, how did you know all of this?"

Her gaze turned back to me. "I wish that I could tell you, Laila."

"You can," I said. "I won't tell anyone, I swear. Please, just..." I licked my dry lips. "Please just explain it to me."

Her eyes were soft. "I'm not worried about you telling anyone, Laila. I'm worried about you knowing too soon."

"What does that mean?"

"You'll understand one day," she said softly. "But you have many battles to fight before that time comes."

My heart thudded in my chest.

One day.

One day.

That was his catchphrase.

Were they working together? Was she the equivalent to one of his guards? Is that how she knew?

"What do you mean 'one day?' When? Soon?" I asked. "He-he said that. He says that all the time. One day. Do you—do you work for him?"

Her brows furrowed. "No. I'd kill that man if I ever got the chance." Her gaze hardened. "No, I do not work for him. But we both know things. And that's all that I can tell you, Laila."

Those hazel eyes were more sincere than they'd ever been. She was telling me the truth.

"What do you know?" I begged. "Please, Mary. If you love me, please tell me. I need to know. I need to know what comes next."

She gave a smile. "What comes next is healing, Laila. And the rest... You'll understand it all one day."

"But, Mary—"

"Laila, I can't tell you any more than I already have. Just have faith. What's meant to be will be."

"Fuck fate."

Her smile widened. "I hope so."

I made a face. "Now what the hell does that mean?"

She chuckled. Her head shook again. "If you need me, just give a call."

"Mary, no. Wait—"

"Things will get better, Laila. I know you think you're stuck in the hell you're feeling forever, but I promise you that isn't the case."

"No, don't leave—" I began, but she was already gone.

I stared at the empty room.

I hoped that conversation would give me answers. Closure maybe. But instead, I was left with more questions.

CHAPTER THIRTY-THREE

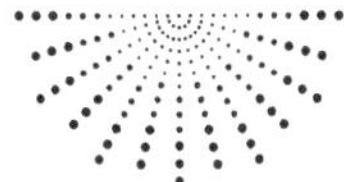

AUGUST 18, 2019 - JEREMY

The past seven weeks had been just as hard as the three months Laila was gone. If I thought she was broken after escaping her capture, she was shattered after the bombing. She was there but, mentally, she was still imprisoned.

No matter how hard I tried, nothing helped. I didn't know if I was trying too hard or if I wasn't trying hard enough. I didn't know what I was supposed to do or say, and she wasn't exactly giving me guidance.

At one point, our souls slid into one another's and flooded back into ourselves and created this massive cycle of fluidity. We'd mix up within one another the way the Atlantic floods into the Pacific. We passed a bit of ourselves into the other—constantly and effortlessly fueling whatever each of us needed with whatever the other had to give.

Now we were like oil and water.

The harder I tried to get close to her, the more she pushed me away. I was close, resting just on the outside of where I wanted to be. But no matter how close I got, we just couldn't meld into each other anymore.

She barely spoke a word since it happened. I understood that she had been through something awful. But she put an impenetrable wall around her heart, and no ladder was tall enough to climb past it.

Laila would say bye when I left to take care of the business down-stairs, she'd tell me she loved me before bed, she'd ask me if there was any coffee left, but that was the extent of our conversations. Anything else I said, she flat out ignored. I was able to hold a better conversation with her when we were a thousand miles apart carving words into our limbs to communicate.

She wouldn't even let me touch her. It just didn't make sense. I understood that after rape, a lot of victims didn't like physical contact, so I didn't push the issue. But she was perfectly content with making out when she first escaped. I couldn't wrap my head around why it changed. And I didn't get why she wouldn't hold my hand. I didn't get why she didn't even want me to hug her.

As shallow as it sounded, that may have been the hardest part. But I was hurting too. She wasn't the only one mourning a child she didn't get to meet. I just wanted an ounce of comfort from my fiancé.

It wasn't just her son that died. He was mine too. And I wanted to be a parent more than her from the get-go. As time went on, that shifted, but it didn't change the fact that I was hurting too.

She got time with him that I didn't. She got to feel him wiggle around inside of her belly. She got to feel when he hiccuped. She got to see him come into the world. Even if he was only here for a second, she got to see him. She got to hold him.

Not that I was really upset about that. It wasn't her fault that things went down the way they did. But I was jealous. And that jealousy turned to resentment when she blocked me out of her world. I wanted to be there for her, and I kept trying to be what she needed, but it was like she didn't want me around.

She wouldn't talk to me. She wouldn't touch me. We shared a bed, but we didn't feel like a couple. We didn't even feel like friends. I was trying, I was *really* trying. But our apartment had been virtually silent for the last seven weeks. I knew she'd gone through a lot, and I was trying to be understanding. But I needed someone too.

I needed what I was offering her. She wasn't the only one fucking hurting.

I'd tried to accept Micah's death by saying, "At least I have Laila."

But I didn't. She was gone. She was right there beside me, and she was fucking gone. I was just as alone as I had been while she was in captivity.

She had not left the apartment since that day. When the FBI asked to get her recollection of events from the bombing, she insisted that Tina come to us. Then she made me leave the room when they talked.

She refused to go visit her mom or her sisters. She hadn't visited my family. She hadn't gone to the grocery store or out to dinner. She wouldn't even go outside to pick up the newspaper or grab the mail.

It was like she imprisoned herself all over again. I couldn't put my head around why she was torturing herself the way she was. She was so excited to go outside when we got to the hospital and now, I couldn't get her to walk out the door to save her life.

It was ironic. When she first got out, she couldn't even leave a door closed without swinging it back open. Now she'd built a fence around her so big there was no way to climb it.

Our house was going to shit. I didn't expect her to be a housewife but she hadn't lifted a finger. The dishes piled up at the sink until I washed them, the garbage overflowed until I took it out, the furniture stayed dusty until I wiped it. It wasn't that big of a deal; I didn't mind cleaning up after her. But she wasn't talking to me. She barely even acknowledged my existence.

I knew she was depressed. I understood that. After what she'd been through, she had every right to be. But when I'd mentioned talking to a psychiatrist in one of the underground hospitals, she told me to fuck off and shut the bedroom door in my face. Aside from asking if there was any coffee left, that was the first time she talked to me that day.

It hurt. And it was incredibly unfair. I was putting in a hundred and ten percent while she didn't put in so much as a fraction of a decimal.

The drinking was driving me crazy too. She was drunk every single day. And I got it. I'd want to forget my life if I were in her shoes too. But it just made me want to get high so bad.

The worst part was that it wasn't Laila's usual drunkenness. That, I would have happily dealt with. But she wasn't happy and bubbly, laughing and trying to touch my dick at every chance she got. She just sat there in bed, headphones in her ears, taking shot after shot after shot. When I tried to talk to her, she either ignored me or gave me a one-word answer.

I was just so frustrated. But I kept staying quiet because I did understand. She'd been through one horrible event after the next. She needed to heal. I really did, I understood. But damn it. She wasn't taking any steps *to* heal.

I never felt so alone in my entire life.

Everyone told me she just needed time. I knew it had only been a couple weeks. But in that time, she acted like I meant nothing to her. Like her feelings were the only ones that mattered. And it fucking hurt.

Looking back on it now, I know that I was being a whiny little bitch and should have given her the time she needed. She had been through the worst shit imaginable. I was being selfish. I know that, and I regret it.

But I was a person too. I should have done better, she deserved better, but I was spiraling just as hard as she was.

I sat at the dining table drowning in tax forms I didn't understand how to complete. There was 1040 Schedule C, a 1040 Schedule F, a 1065, an 1120, and an 1120 S form laid out in front of me. I didn't have a clue what to do with them.

My chest was tight, and my palms were sweaty. They should have been done months ago and I knew we could be audited if I didn't complete them soon.

I chewed my lip, scrolling wiki-how on my phone. But Jesus Christ, I didn't even know what half of these words meant.

Then I heard her laugh from the bedroom.

My heart skipped. For a second, I thought maybe she was climbing out of the hole she'd dug herself into. It gave me hope.

Just the sound brought a smile to my face. Thinking it would be a good time to try and talk to her, I started to the bedroom. As I drew closer, I started picking up on parts of her conversation. I couldn't make out much, but I heard her say Brody's name.

It wasn't that Brody making her laugh bothered me. It was that I couldn't, and he could.

I knew it was childish and I tried to suppress it. She didn't have feelings for Brody, he was her friend. I knew that.

So I tried to be a big boy. I pulled on a smile.

She had a bare smile on her lips at my first glance into the bedroom. But it seemed that as my gaze met hers, it faded. Maybe it wasn't intentional, but it stung.

I smiled anyway.

Laila pulled the phone from her cheek and put her headphone back in.

"Who was that?" I asked.

She grabbed her coffee from the side table and took a sip. "Just Brody."

"Oh yeah? What did he want?" I asked.

"He had a question about his business class."

It shouldn't have made me upset. I should have been happy she held a conversation with someone, even if it wasn't me. But there I'd been, scouring the internet to figure out the tax forms for our business.

It wasn't that I minded doing the work. I loved Moe's too. But I didn't even have a title. She wouldn't talk about anything, let alone the wedding we were supposed to be planning. I was far from being a partner. Yet, I was the one busting my ass to keep the place going while she laid in bed ignoring me.

Talking to my brother, who we both knew was in love with her, and ignoring me.

"What was so funny?" I asked.

She creased her brows over the rim of her mug and set it down. "What?"

"You were laughing." I leaned against the door frame.

An awkward, almost sympathetic half smile pulled at her lips. "I didn't realize I was laughing if I did." I licked my teeth and gave a nod. She said, "Is something wrong?"

"Yeah, Laila. Something is wrong."

"What is it?" she asked.

"You're somewhere else."

Her eyes flicked between mine, waiting for me to say more. When I didn't, she said, "What are you talking about?"

"The way you're acting. This isn't you." I gestured toward her. "You're completely blocking me out and it isn't fair."

"I'm not blocking you out." She pulled her headphone from her ear and dropped it to the bed.

"Really?" A half laugh left me. "You've barely said a word to me in weeks."

"That's not true."

"C'mon, don't act like I'm being crazy. We both know that you've pushed me so far away that I need a rocket to get close enough to even see you."

"Well, sorry if I've been a little distant but—"

I laughed. "A little? A *little* distant? You ignore me at every chance you get. You act like I don't even exist, Laila," I said. "If there's a but, it isn't an apology. You're the one who always says that. But I don't even want an apology, I just want you back."

"I am back."

"No, you really aren't," I said. "You haven't left this house in more than seven fucking weeks, Laila. You have a giant mountain of coffee cups piling up beside the bed. You haven't showered in what—five days?"

She huffed and licked her teeth. "Well, I'm sorry I'm such a burden, Jeremy."

My tense jaw softened. I didn't actually want a fight. I just wanted to move forward. I wanted to get on with our futures. I definitely didn't want her to think I saw her as a burden. I just wanted to move on.

I ran my hand over my mouth. "It's not that you're a burden, Lai. You're depressed. I get it. I don't mind picking up the slack. I'll always help with anything you need, but you're acting like I don't even exist. It's like I mean nothing to you."

"That's ridiculous."

"How? How is that ridiculous?"

"You mean more to me than anything, Jeremy. You know that." Her words were decent, but her eyes were piercing. "I don't even know where this is coming from."

"It doesn't feel like it," I said. "You literally ignore me half the time that I talk to you. Then Brody calls you, and you actually have a conversation with him?"

"Are you serious?" Her voice raised. Then she laughed. She laughed again. But that time, mocking me. "What—Are you jealous or something?"

I huffed. "You know what? Yeah, I am. I'm jealous that I can't get more out of you than an 'I love you' before bed and a 'Is there any more coffee?' but he gets actual communication. I can't even get a smile and he gets a laugh."

"Do you think I have something for Brody?" she asked. "Because I don't. He's my friend, Jeremy. He's your brother, he's going to be my brother—"

"Really? Is he? We're getting married? Because you haven't even let me touch you in weeks unless you were too drunk to stand on your own. You push me away any time I get remotely close, and don't act like you don't. We both know you're a fucking mess—which would be fine if you would let me fucking be here for you. But you won't. You act like I'm not even here. You just keep pushing and pushing and pushing. It feels like you don't want to be with me. I don't even know what the fuck I'm here for anymore, Laila."

"That's not true—"

"Yes, it is, and you know it." I closed my eyes and ran my fingers through my hair. I was angry, and I needed to calm down before she actually did tell me to leave. So, I tried to lower my voice. "I know you're going through a lot of shit, but you aren't the only one who's hurting."

She sucked her teeth. Her eyes glowed. "You have no idea how bad this hurts."

"Right, because I didn't feel every single thing you went through or anything."

"No, clearly you didn't."

I narrowed my gaze. "*My* brother is still trapped in that place. *Our* son died in there. You don't think that fucking hurts me?"

"You weren't there, Jeremy." Her eyes glowed brighter.

"I didn't witness it so it shouldn't hurt?" I asked. "Are you saying it doesn't hurt me that my son is dead?"

"Yeah, I am. Because it doesn't, not like it hurts me."

When she said that, my heart picked up to a mile a minute. Ultimately, she was right. What she went through was harder than what I had to deal with. But it still hurt because it proved what I already suspected she thought. She didn't care that I was hurting too.

"Right. Because no one else's pain can possibly compare to Laila's."

"Fuck you," she said. "Leave me alone."

"No, that's what you said. It's my brother locked up in there but you're the one who's *really* hurting, right?"

"You don't think I fucking know that?" she barked. "Everyone was counting on me and I failed. *I'm* the reason my son is dead. *I'm* the reason Chris is still there. *I'm* the reason all those people died at the party. You heard him, Jeremy. He did this to hurt me and—"

"So, you're going to let him keep controlling you?!" I yelled. "Drop the fucking pity party and do something. You were locked up in that place for months and you're still in fucking prison. You're wasting your life away, Laila."

"I'm mourning the death of my son!" Angry tears rolled down her cheeks.

"So am I!" I yelled.

My jaw tightened, and my eyes burned with tears.

So alone.

I felt so fucking alone.

"I fucking lost him too, but at least I had you. At least you came home. But you didn't. You're still locked in that fucking cell. Only now, the door's open, and you won't fucking get up to see what's on the other side," I said. "You lost a son. I lost a brother *and* a son." My eyes travelled over her. "And I lost you. You still have me, but I don't have you. That might just be the worst part. Because I'm trying so damn hard to be here, and you just keep pushing me and pushing me. I lost all of you at once."

The glowing in her eyes softened, growing silent.

She didn't know what to say, and neither did I. We just stared at each other. After a long moment, she said, "I just need time, Jeremy."

"And I just need you," I said. "But take all the time you need."

"Jeremy—" she said.

"No, I get it. Do what you have to do. Lie here in this bed for another month. Or two, or three, or four. Hate your fucking life if you think that's going to help. It won't, but if you want to be miserable, be miserable, baby. But you keep pushing me away, and one of these days I'm gonna be too tired to keep running after you."

She opened her mouth to say something, but I was already gone. Sitting in the driver's seat of our car outside.

I raised my hand to my face and rubbed my eye for a second. Then I dropped my head to the steering wheel.

Instantly, I regretted about half of what I'd just said.

I should have kept most of that shit inside my skull. But I'd been walking on broken glass since she got back.

The spark that lit the powder barrel was stupid, but the argument wasn't. I could have handled it better. I could have been kinder. But damn it, she essentially said I didn't deserve to hurt over the death of my son.

I was angry, and frustrated, and lonely. I should have just gone to the house and bitched to Leah or Adam, but I didn't want to hear "She just needs time."

It was selfish and I should have thought about the consequences of my actions before I jumped on them.

But fuck it. Fuck being sober.

I reached into my pocket and pulled out my phone. I slid through my contacts, found her name, and clicked the call button.

After three rings, she answered. "Hey, stranger. What's up?"

"Are you busy?" I asked.

"Not really, I'm just heading home from work. Do you want to come by?"

I wanted to say no, but it came out of my mouth almost involuntarily. "Yeah, if you don't mind."

"Yeah, of course. I'll be home in like fifteen minutes. You can just go in. I don't want a neighbor to see you teleport into my front yard or something."

"Alright, cool. I'll see you soon, Liv."

It wasn't that I wanted to see her. I wanted what I knew I could get from her.

I wanted to get high.

CHAPTER THIRTY-FOUR

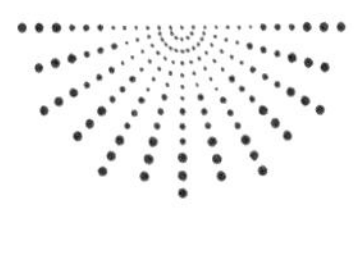

LAILA

I grabbed a tissue from the side table to wipe my eyes and blow my nose.

Jeremy never talked to me like that before. All the times I'd been a bitch to him, even when I broke up with him last October, I never saw that look on his face. He meant it when he said he'd leave me.

As the thought entered my head, that hole in my chest got bigger. It was pathetic. All the shit I'd been through and my fiancé saying he might leave me still managed to bring me to tears.

Maybe that's not what brought me to tears. Maybe what brought me to tears was the fact that not a single word that left his mouth was untrue.

I'd been a cunt and I knew it. It's not that I was trying to. But I knew he was hurting, and I ignored it. I was too caught up in my own pain to think about anyone else's.

He was right. I was wasting my life away. I was *allowing* Peterson to continue to hurt me.

Instead of trying to improve my situation, I'd spent the last month wallowing in self-pity. I'd told him not to tiptoe around my feelings when I got back but then I forced him to. No wonder he blew up. He'd been far too understanding for far too long.

All beautiful things in life are fragile. Family, love, friendships. They're easier to break than they are to hold onto. If they crack or chip, you might be able to handle it just a bit more carefully and hold onto it a while longer. But if it shatters to a million pieces, it can't be saved. If you kneel down to try and piece it back together, you're more likely to cut yourself than save what's already destroyed.

After cutting myself on the pieces for long enough, I became so bloody that the shards slid right out of my wet, bloody fingertips. They sliced new cuts as I struggled to keep them steady enough to piece it all back together.

At some point, I had to move onto holding some other fragile thing tightly. But I had to be careful holding it until my cuts healed or I'd shatter it too.

And that's what I'd done. I shattered Micah first, and there was no piecing that disaster back together. Then I shattered Jeremy too.

Yeah, he could have said it in a kinder manner than he did. But he'd tried and I kept shutting him out. He'd been kind every day. He did everything but wipe my ass for me. He was literally *bathing* me when I was too drunk to do it myself.

He was right. I had to get up. I had to climb out of it. I wasn't ready to go back to how things were before I was taken but I couldn't just keep sitting in that bed. I had to do *something*.

Not even for Jeremy, but for me.

For Micah.

He healed me. He was the reason I was able to break out. He saved me. Even if I couldn't save him.

I couldn't waste the gift of freedom he'd given me.

Standing was the hardest part. But once I was vertical, I just put one foot in front of the other. That was all that I could do.

Just lifting the coffee cups from the nightstand to the kitchen was a task. It felt as straining as running a marathon.

It was tragic, really. I could lift half a building into the air but dusting and scrubbing a few dishes was somehow more difficult. I didn't understand why those simple things felt so impossible. I didn't understand why I was so drained. But it was just so hard.

Taking care of my house had never been a difficult task before. In fact, I enjoyed cleaning my home. I typically kept things nearly spotless. I'd dust the little jewels that hung off the chandelier, the frame of the clock at the top of the steps, the air conditioning register vents. All of those little details that usually get overlooked until you're moving or preparing to sell your house. They used to be so important to me. Even when I lived with Mom, and then just as tediously, if not even more so, when I lived with Jeremy and his siblings.

But then, it felt like I was told to build an arc without the whispering words of a man in the sky.

Depression's a funny thing in that way. It was like standing outside of myself as I watched my flailing body fall into a pit. But at some point, I hit the bottom. And believe me when I say the impact hurt worse than the fall.

The thing of it though is that there's always a rope dangling from the top. It isn't easy, but I could climb back out. I might get rope burn along the way, I might fall down and have to start over, I might have blisters when I got to the top. But it could be done. I just had to climb.

As I cleaned, I thought about how I would feel if I were in his shoes. We were supposed to be partners and I bailed on him. He was right; I just disappeared. It wasn't fair.

He tried to give me a hug the other night after I passed out on the floor of the bathroom. He helped my drunken, distraught body to the bed as he had more times than I could count. All he wanted was a hug before he lay me down and I acted like I was too drunk to realize what he was doing. Then I dropped to the bed like a crash test dummy.

Jeremy made me happy. And in those past few weeks, I didn't want to be happy. I felt guilty for any shred of joy that crept up on me. It just wasn't fair. Why did I deserve to be happy after what I had done?

I killed people.

I killed dozens of humans while escaping the compound. I killed almost two dozen when I was trapped inside.

My son died because of me, so in a way I killed him too.

I killed the people in the compound I couldn't save because there was almost no hope in finding them again.

It was my fault all those people died at the party. If I would have never met Peterson, if I would have never saved them, those people would have gone on living. Maybe in hell, but they'd be alive.

I wanted to hurt myself so badly that I was willing to hurt him too.

But I'd lose him too if I weren't careful.

What I'd been through was awful, yes. But he didn't deserve to be punished for it.

So, I kept going. I kept cleaning because that was all that I could do. I couldn't bring myself to walk out of that door. But I could clean.

I cried as I pulled the vacuum back and forth against the shag rug I'd once gushed over. I cried as I wiped the dishes. I cried as I mopped the hardwood floors. I cried as I showered. I cried as I pulled on a pair of loose yoga pants and Jeremy's gray Pink Floyd T-shirt. I cried as I sat on the couch and rolled a blunt.

It wasn't a constant, obnoxious cry. My eyes just wouldn't stop watering. The hole in my chest felt just as big as it had a few minutes before.

But as I gazed around the dust less, flowery smelling, freshly cleaned apartment, I did feel a touch of relief. It wasn't happiness. It wasn't even contentment. Just a touch of accomplishment. It wasn't much.

But at least I showered that day without my fiancé doing it for me.

At least my bed side table had enough room for a glass of water again.

At least I could get a cup of coffee without having to wash a mug in the morning.

It really wasn't much. But even just the little touch of relief was better than how I'd been.

CHAPTER THIRTY-FIVE

JEREMY

When I first got to Olivia's, I'd gone to the cabinet in her kitchen. I knew where she kept them because of the last time I relapsed. I guess it would have made more sense to get drugs just about anywhere else.

But I was lonely.

No part of me had feelings for her. I wasn't even attracted to her. I wanted Laila but she didn't want me. And I just wanted to be around someone that wanted me around. I wanted to feel like I mattered.

More than anything, I wanted to be high.

I felt guilty for it before I even got there. The moment I pulled my phone from my pocket, I felt guilty. But I wasn't going to do anything. I didn't *want* to do anything. Except get high and talk to someone who wasn't going to tell me I was doing everything wrong.

I saw the seven fifties and started to grab them. Then I saw the OxyContin in the back. I wouldn't have even noticed them if it weren't for the familiar little green shape.

Honestly, I don't know why I did it. I hated myself for it later, but I just wanted to leave. I couldn't leave her. I didn't want to leave *her*. But I wanted to leave my shitty life behind for a few hours. So, I did.

I only needed three. The overdose risk was pretty high when

snorting or shooting an oxy eighty with no tolerance, and I didn't want to die. I just wanted life to feel worth living.

So, I went to her bathroom, crushed the pill on the counter, rolled up a dollar bill from my back pocket, and sniffed it up my nostril.

Then I heard her come in through the front door. I wiped up the powder, then my nose, and headed out into the hallway. She carried a few grocery bags in her arms, kicking the front door shut. Her gaze met mine and she smiled. "Hey, you. What's up?"

"Here." I grabbed the bags from her hands, carried them to the kitchen, and set them on the counter.

She tailed behind me. "Thanks."

"No problem," I said.

As she turned to put the milk in the fridge, she met my gaze. "So, how are you?"

"Pretty good. Laila's home, so that's good."

"That's what I've heard." She smiled. "How is she doing?"

I forced one back. "She's okay."

"Wow, really? After what happened to her, I figured she'd be a disaster," she said. "I know I would. Anyone would."

I raised my hand to my eyes. "Yeah, she's a little bit of a mess."

She crumbled up a plastic bag and put it inside the other. "And that's why you're here, huh?"

"We got into a fight. It wasn't even really a fight. I just... yelled at her."

"Well, this has been traumatic on you too, Jeremy. You're allowed to be hurt," she said.

I pulled myself onto the counter. "No. No, it was wrong. I shouldn't have said the things I said."

"What'd you say?" she asked.

"Something about throwing herself a pity party."

I decided to leave out the comment I made about her pushing me away. I didn't want Liv to think I was legitimately considering leaving her because I wasn't. No part of me didn't want to be with her. I was just mad.

"Yeah. Probably shouldn't have said that," she said.

"Yeah, definitely shouldn't have said that."

"Did you at least apologize?" she asked.

"No. I just stormed off," I said.

Olivia turned to face me. Then she pushed up her glasses and squinted a bit. She leaned in a bit closer to look at my eyes. "You're high, aren't you?"

"No. It hasn't kicked in yet."

She set the box of mac and cheese down and put her hand to her hip. With a shake of her head, she ran her tongue along her teeth. "What did you take, Jeremy?"

"Just some oxies."

I didn't mind telling Olivia when I used. I never had. We used to get high together. She wasn't going to judge me. She wasn't going to preach about how drugs were bad. We both knew that, we weren't stupid. But that didn't change how good they made me feel. And most importantly, she wasn't going to tell anyone else.

"Orally?" she asked. I shook my head. "So, you're about to be super fucked up."

I smiled. "That's the plan."

She frowned. "You have to have known how stupid that was."

"Can you not? Please?" I said. "I've been having a really hard time. And I know getting high isn't going to take it away, but I just want to stop hating my life for a minute."

"How many did you do?"

"Just three. I have no tolerance. I don't want to die. I'm not stupid."

"Did you snort or shoot it?"

"I don't want tracks so..." I shrugged.

Olivia sighed. "Are you hungry? I was going to order a pizza."

"Yeah, I could go for pizza."

"Not like I could let you go home any time soon. Laila would kill me if she knew you got drugs from me." She put the mac and cheese in the cupboard. "She scares me."

"Don't worry, I don't want to go home for a while. And I stole it. She can't blame you for that."

"She'd still kill me."

CHAPTER THIRTY-SIX

JEREMY

It'd been a few hours. I was just starting to come down. The air around me didn't feel warm anymore. I'd looked at the flowers in the center of the table an hour prior and thought they were the prettiest thing in the world. Now, I could see their wilting edges. The drips from my nose were starting to make my throat sore. The fluorescent lights that hung above me had looked peaceful and relaxing. Now, they felt cold and dark.

The euphoria was gone.

And that shitty, hating my life feeling was back.

"It just sucks, you know?" I rubbed my eyes. "She's devastated and I get it. Everyone deals with things differently, but it's just… It's been almost two months. And she's in the same place she's been since it happened."

"I hate to be that person, but it really hasn't been that long." Olivia poured some Pepsi into a glass. "What she went through in there… I mean, Jeremy, you guys were going to have a baby and she gave birth to him in a cell by herself. She didn't have so much as a pillow for comfort." Her voice softened. "And then he died. Then somehow, she manages to get all of these people out of this torture chamber only to have a quarter of them blown to pieces by the same person who held them all captive," she said. "Look, I know she and I aren't friends or anything. It'd be a little weird if we were, all things considered. But I feel for her."

"It's not like I don't."

"I know that. And I get you need someone to be there for you too." She reached across the table and set her hand on mine.

I yanked it back to my lap.

Nope. Nope, nope, nope.

That was not why I was here. I'd come to get high, not because I had feelings for Olivia. Holding her hand was a boundary I would not cross. No matter how much I missed physical touch, she wasn't who I wanted it from.

She retreated her hand back to her glass. "You have to be patient with her, Jeremy. You had to know this wasn't going to be easy after all the shit you felt her go through."

I gave a bare nod.

"You said she makes you happier than anything ever had. You want to make it work with her, don't you?" she asked softly, almost like she was hoping I'd say no. "You love her, right?"

"More than anything."

"Then you're going to have to work to make it work," she said.

"Yeah. Yeah, you're right."

She forced a smile. "Then go home. Tuck her in. Clean up your place. Go to bed. Make her coffee in the morning. And apologize."

"Yeah, I probably should get going. It's getting late. She's probably worried."

"I have a twelve-hour shift in six hours so that's probably a good idea."

I stood. "Thanks for having me over."

"Thanks for coming."

I scratched my head. "Sorry for stealing your drugs."

Olivia rolled her eyes. "Just don't do it again."

"I won't. But I'll keep in touch."

I definitely would, but obviously I wasn't going to say that.

"Please do. And give Laila my regards."

"That's probably not the best idea."

"Yeah, probably not, huh?" she asked. "Maybe I'll send a fruit basket or something."

I chuckled. "I'll see you later."

She smiled. And I disappeared.

I landed halfway up the steps to our apartment. I didn't want to just teleport into her space after we'd argued like that. I owed her an apology. I couldn't just jump in and intrude.

As I slowly trudged up each step, everything still looked a bit foggy. I felt a bit lighter than I had earlier. I was certainly more emotional. Whatever anger I had earlier had been replaced with guilt.

I fucked up.

I basically threatened to leave her. Then I hung out with my ex and did drugs.

There I was, being the most typical, least unique bad boyfriend around. Fiancé, actually. Bad fiancé.

I didn't actually do anything wrong by hanging out with Olivia. We didn't touch each other besides that awkward graze of our hands. But either way. If she went and hung out with her ex who still had a thing for her after a huge fight like that, without even telling me where she was going, I'd be hurt at the very least.

When I made it closer to the apartment, I heard *You Don't Know What Love Is* by The White Stripes playing over the Google Home. I would have appreciated the irony until I made it through the threshold and took a look around. My jaw nearly dropped.

She was up.

Not literally. Literally, she was lying on the couch with a little red throw blanket tucked beneath her sleeping arms, as most people were at two in the morning. Her eyes fluttered back and forth. Damp, clean hair rested against her soft white cheeks. She wasn't in that same yellow tank top and blue, fleece Eeyore pants she'd been wearing all week. Instead, my Pink Floyd T-shirt hung loosely on her shoulders.

The apartment around her was nearly spotless. It wasn't a complete disaster when I'd left earlier, I'd been keeping up on the light cleaning.

But the rugs had been vacuumed, the room smelled like soft cleaning agents, and the TV wasn't covered in dust.

The tax documents on the table were now coated in writing and laid in a neat pile. The small light fixture above the table sparkled like diamonds.

It made me feel worse. I didn't mean she had to get up right then and clean the house. But I guessed that was essentially what I'd said.

I headed to the couch. I crouched onto the edge of the coffee table and reached forward to shake her shoulder. "Laila," I whispered. Her eyes fluttered open and she met my gaze. "Do you want to head to bed?"

She looked at me for a moment. And my heart raced. Did I still look high?

She sat up and stifled a yawn. "No, I was trying to wait up for you. I guess I just passed out."

"Yeah, sorry I was gone for so long."

"No, don't be," she said. "You needed some time to yourself. It's okay."

My chest tightened because it wasn't time to myself. But I gave a nod anyway.

She pushed hair from her face, blinking away sleepiness in her eyes. "Can we talk?"

"We probably should, huh?"

"I said some really shitty things earlier."

"So, did I," I muttered. "I was a dick, I'm sorry."

"No, you weren't," she said. "You didn't say anything that wasn't true."

"I did. You're going through a lot, if time is what you need—"

"You're going through a lot too." She reached out and took my hand in hers. My stomach flipped. That hand shouldn't have felt so good, but it did. I looked up to her pretty green eyes. "And I shouldn't have acted like you weren't. You're going through the same things I'm going through. You lost people too."

"Not like you did," I said gently. "I wasn't there, I didn't live what you lived."

"That doesn't make it any easier." She twined her fingers through mine, staring at our hands on my knee. My stomach spun, though I wasn't sure if it was guilt or joy. "I... I haven't been blocking you out to hurt you. I've been blocking you out to hurt me."

My eyes turned up to hers, confused. "What do you mean?"

"I... I don't deserve to be happy. I know it sounds stupid, but I just... I don't feel like I've done anything to deserve all of this. I don't deserve this life. I don't deserve you. I fucked up everything, Jeremy. I..." Tears overwhelmed her eyes. "You didn't get to meet our son because of me. Our baby's dead and that's my fault. And I... I don't know if I'll ever stop hating myself for that."

My throat grew so tight, I had to swallow a few times to make words leave my lips. Fuck, I was the biggest piece of shit. She was already hurting so much, and I just had to make it worse.

"Baby." I reached forward with my other hand, carefully lifted her chin to meet my gaze, and thumbed the tear from her cheek. "No one deserves to be happy more than you."

She licked her trembling lips and struggled to unclench her jaw. She was trying so hard not to cry. I hadn't seen her cry a lot recently. Most of the time, I would try to speak to her and she would turn her head as far as she could to avoid my gaze. That, just saying those thoughts aloud, in addition to the shitty things I said earlier, brought her to tears she fought so hard to keep inside.

Her head shook. "I don't."

"Everyone deserves to be happy," I whispered.

"Murderers don't deserve to be happy," she said. "I'm a mass murderer, Jeremy. That's what I am, I'm a murderer. I killed so many people. Even people I didn't kill are dead because of me. I don't, I don't deserve to be happy."

"No." I squeezed her hand. "You didn't do anything you didn't have to."

"You don't know what I've done."

"I don't care what you've done. I felt what they were doing to you. I don't care who you had to kill. As far as I'm concerned, anything you did was justified. Whoever is dead at your hands deserved it."

Tears welled in her eyes. "Micah didn't."

"You didn't kill him."

"I could have prevented it." Tears silently spilled down her cheeks. "There's a million ways I could have prevented it. I could have prevented the bomb. I could have gotten Chris out. I could have killed Peterson. I could have done so many things differently and I hate myself for it. But I've been taking it out on you and that's not fair. You deserve better. You need me as much as I need you and I haven't been there for you. And I'm sorry."

"That's bullshit," I said.

Her brows furrowed.

"You shouldn't be apologizing." I tucked a damp lock of hair behind her ear. "You're struggling, and that's okay. I shouldn't have lashed out at you and made everything worse. You haven't done anything wrong. Don't blame yourself. "

"It's easier said than done."

"It takes time. Time I should be giving you instead of bitching about. You don't need to apologize for anything, I'm the one who's sorry. I started a fight with you for no reason and I'm sorry. No buts, I'm just sorry."

"No, I get it," she whispered. "I need to quit wasting the time I do have. You were right. I have to get up. I'm not ready to jump back into everything. I don't know how I feel about being in big crowds and stuff, but I at least need to stop lying in bed. I'm wasting my life. And life's too precious to waste being unhappy," she said. "That's what Chris said."

A soft, sad smile pulled at my lips. "That's something Chris would have said, huh? But I mean it, Lai. I was in the wrong tonight. I shouldn't have talked to you like that. I'm supposed to help you, not tear you down."

"I told you not to tiptoe around my feelings when I got back. You were right. You didn't do anything wrong."

There was my shot. I should have told her. I should have just said it. Yes, I did do something wrong. I went to Olivia's, and I got high. Nothing happened, we just ate pizza. But I did do something wrong.

But I didn't say it.

Because I was worried that if I said that, she'd have thought I meant what I said earlier. That I'd leave her. And I wouldn't. I'd never leave her. I'd never want to be with anyone but her. But I was worried that's what she would think and I'd hurt her even more.

"I didn't mean it. About you pushing me so far that I wouldn't come back, I mean. I didn't mean that."

"You did." She touched my cheek. "And you weren't wrong. You can't keep kicking someone while they're down and expect them to keep coming back for more."

"It's just a rough time. I know that. I'll never leave you, I didn't mean it, Lai. I'm here, I'll always be here."

"But it's hard for both of us. We need to be there for each other. You can't be here for me and get nothing in return. You deserve more than that." She pushed hair from my face, cupping my jaw with her free hand. That gentle touch gave me a burst of serotonin I hadn't experienced in weeks, and I didn't want it to leave. "I'm going to try harder. I'm going to do better."

God, I fucked up. I wanted her to do better, but not for me. I wanted *her* to feel better. I didn't want her to feel like she had to be perfect for me to love her. I just wanted her to let me be there for her while she struggled.

The fight was one thing, getting high was another. She was opening up, I should've been open too. I would have saved everyone so much pain if I had. But I didn't know how. Would my honesty make her shut back down?

Fuck, what am I supposed to do?

"I didn't want you to do all of this." I gestured around. "I don't expect you to be super woman. I was just mad. I didn't mean it."

"I have to quit wallowing. I have to move on. I have to make my life worth living. It's not going to happen overnight. I can't just spring back into things but I'm going to do better. I am, I'm going to do better. I—I have to. I have to do better. I have to." Her watery eyes met mine. "I don't want to lose you too."

Butterflies danced in my stomach, but it ached simultaneously. I was a piece of shit. I never wanted her to feel like I'd leave her because she was struggling. I was just upset. Maybe it was for the best, but I didn't mean to hurt her. I didn't want her to feel the way she did. I just wanted her to feel better and I made her feel worse.

And then I got high with my ex-girlfriend.

"I'm not going anywhere, Laila." I spoke through the lump forming in my throat. "I'm never going to leave you. I'm so sorry, baby, I wasn't trying to hurt you. I fucked up, I'm sorry."

I wasn't just apologizing for the argument. And I truly was sorry. But she didn't know the half of it.

She leaned across the distance between us and touched her lips to mine, hands finding my neck. She held my face close to hers. Her kiss was gentle, yet so passionate.

My stomach flipped, fingers sliding to her defined hips.

I should have pulled away and told her. I told myself to. I told myself to back off and tell her what happened before I made things worse.

But it just felt so good to hold her again.

It felt like home. It felt like where we were supposed to be.

After a moment or two, she leaned even closer. She put her arms around my neck and lifted her knees around my thighs, kissing me harder and rolling her torso close to mine.

The table creaked beneath our weight, and Laila giggled before teleporting us to the couch in the same position.

I smiled against her lips, letting the ease of her touch spread through me like a fire on a cold night.

This was where I'd wanted to be. I wanted her to lean on me, and find comfort in my embrace, but now...

Now it felt gross.

It was like I manipulated her into wanting me by threatening to leave her. I wasn't one of those douchebags. She was hurting and I was a huge dick.

I was never going to leave her, not unless she asked me to. She was hurting me but only because she was hurting. It wasn't out of spite. I knew that and I still did what I did. I didn't even give her the opportunity before I leaped off the wagon.

The relapse was bad but I shouldn't have hung out with Olivia. Relapse, Laila could accept and move past. But hanging out with an ex after a fight like that couldn't have been a good idea. I wouldn't have felt so shitty about it if I didn't do something wrong.

Again, I told myself to pull back and tell her. She would have understood in that moment. It might have hurt, but it would have been better than hiding it.

But I'd already hurt her so much that night. I didn't want to hurt her any more than I already had.

For the first time in my life, I felt like the biggest fuck boy in the world. I always took pride in being a good boyfriend and then a good fiancé. But nothing I did in the past eight hours gave me any brownie points. I was one of those shitty guys who talked to his girl like she was garbage and still came home to a clean house and got to act like nothing happened.

Fuck, I hated myself. But I just missed her so much. I missed moments like that *so* much.

Her hips glided gently along mine, grinding against the bulge growing at my pelvis. She pushed her chest closer into me, and I felt her nipples harden through the thin fabric of the T-shirt.

All I wanted to do was rip her pants off and pound her 'til she screamed. I wanted to feel her clench around my cock, I wanted to feel her nails scraping down my back, I wanted her to moan my name, and...

Fuck, I wanted her. I wanted her in a way I hadn't wanted anything in ages. I hadn't had sex in close to five months, and I wanted to fucking *rail* her.

Which was why I had to pull away.

I wouldn't take advantage of her. She was hurt and she was only kissing me like that because she was afraid that she'd lose me.

"What's wrong?" she asked between uneven breaths.

"I don't want you to want me because I was an asshole. I want you to want me because I'm good to you. And I wasn't. I wasn't good to you tonight."

She leaned forward and kissed me again. Her teeth gently bit my lower lip before sucking it ever so slightly, rolling her body into me again, like I was a beach, and she was a wave.

As her pussy rubbed against my cock growing harder in my jeans, my eyes rolled back, imagining how wet she was beneath those leggings, imagining how good it'd feel to bury my cock deep within her...

Breaths short and uneven, Laila leaned back and rested her forehead against mine. "I want you because I love you," she whispered.

"You want me because I threatened to leave you." I gently touched her waist. "A few hours ago, you didn't even want to hold my hand. You don't really want to do this. And it's okay. I'm okay, Lai. I didn't mean it, I was just mad."

"I do." She lifted hair behind my ear. "I don't want to have sex, but I want *this*."

I felt her hand trembling at my neck, and it made my stomach turn. She wasn't ready. And that was okay, it really was.

I took my hand from her waist and brought her trembling fingers to my lips. I kissed them. "Baby, it's okay."

Her gaze grew frustrated. "It's not okay. I want to, I really do."

"You want to want to," I said softly.

"No, I *do* want to. I don't know why I'm so nervous." She paused. "I love fucking you. This isn't fair."

"It's really okay, baby." I pushed hair from her face. "We can take things slow. I love kissing you, I'm cool with this. And it's kind of fun, right? Like how it was before we had sex for the first time."

An annoyed, pissed off laugh escaped her. "He took so much from me. And now I'm just letting him take this too."

"No." I lifted her chin to meet my gaze. "This is going to get better. Things always get better."

An ironic, annoyed laugh left her lips. She looked up to meet my gaze. Long, dark hair fell in her face. Her green eyes met mine. A sweet, almost sad smile lifted her lips. Her head was turned to the side slightly like she was posing for a picture.

Fuck, she was beautiful.

"Things don't usually just 'get better' for us, Jeremy," she said.

"They will." I touched the side of her neck until my fingers slid into her hair. "We're going to get a happy ending eventually."

She licked her smiling lips. "Probably not. But we should enjoy the happy moments when they pass through."

I smiled. "We should."

Then she leaned back down and carefully pushed her lips to mine. She kissed me softly at first, fingers resting on my cheek. Gradually, she slid it downward, grazing my neck, teasing a trail down my chest. Just that tingling touch was enough for me to let out a soft sigh.

I closed my arms around her waist, simply holding her body close to mine. I wasn't going to go past that, but damn, it felt good to hold her.

Then that hand on my chest drifted lower, all the way to my jeans. As she fiddled with the button, I laughed and pulled my face from hers. "What are you doing?"

She flashed a flirty smile. "What does it look like I'm doing?"

I chuckled as she undid the zipper. "You just said you weren't ready."

"I said I wasn't ready to have sex." She pulled my boxers down. "I didn't say that I didn't want to do *anything*."

I wanted to give her the same smile she gave me, but this wasn't what I'd wanted. I felt guilty, and wrong, and... "I don't feel right about this, Lai."

She dropped her hand back to her thigh. "You don't want to?"

I laughed. "Of course, I *want* to. Clearly, I want to." I gestured to my groin.

"Then what's the problem?"

I touched her cheek. "I thought you wanted to take things slow, baby."

"I do. And this is taking things slow. I fucked you after our first date, remember?"

"I remember." I laughed.

"We were taking things slow then too." She grinned.

"I just don't think this is right. I feel like I'm taking advantage of you."

Her eyes grew dopey, tilting downward.

Fuck, I felt so bad. If I could rewrite the last eight hours, that's what I would have done. I wanted to change the whole thing. I didn't want it to go like that. I wanted her to want me because she loved me, not because she was afraid she'd lose me. But then I told her no and she looked even more heartbroken.

I thumbed her chin, lifting her gaze to mine. "Is this really what you want?"

She smiled, and it looked genuine. "I really do.

"And you're sure?" I asked. "Because if you're not, I can wait. It isn't—"

"I'm the one who initiated this, so yeah. I'm pretty sure." She laughed.

"Pretty sure isn't the same as one hundred percent sure." I thumbed her jaw. "I don't want to take advantage of you. I was a dick to you earlier, I was meaner than I've ever been and I—"

She leaned in and pushed her lips to mine. She rolled her ass down against my cock, her boobs rubbed my chest, and my mouth fell open in a sigh. "Baby, I'm not drunk, I haven't smoked in hours. There's nothing clouding my judgment. We've had plenty of makeup sex in the past too. You aren't taking advantage of me." She kissed from my lips to my neck, hot breath teasing my ear. My eyes rolled back, and my hands tightened at her hips. "I want to make you feel good," she whispered, kissing softly. "Don't you want to make me feel good too?"

Fucking Christ, I'd never been so hard in my life.

"Lai," I whispered. "I just don't want you to regret this. It feels—"

"Don't you want me?" Her voice was a seductive whisper, fingertip tracing along my cock.

"You know I want you," I murmured. "I just—"

"Then how about I just let you know if I change my mind?" She took my hand from her hip and gently guided it between her thighs.

She was still wearing her pants, but the fabric was soaked, and my dick hardened just thinking about how turned on she was. "Okay?"

Deep breaths panting in and out of me, I gave a slow nod.

She smiled, grabbed the waistband of my boxers, and tugged them down. As her fingers closed around my dick, she ground down onto my hand, and I felt the slight bulge of her swollen clit through the thin fabric.

Fuck, it was so hot.

"Are you sure you're okay?" I whispered.

"Yeah," she whispered, breaths fast and uneven. "Fuck, I need these off."

I laughed, reached up for her waistband, and helped her yank them down her legs.

Once they fell to the floor behind her, and she got back into position over my thigh, I grazed the tip of my finger over her opening to get it wet. She let out a little whimper as I slid it to her clit, rubbing in a slow, rhythmic circle. Her lips parted, eyes widening, slight glow illuminating them. "That feels so good," she whispered.

I smiled as her hand returned to my dick. She closed her fingers around the base and rubbed up and down slowly.

Holy fuck, the relief that coursed through me was immeasurable. She was hardly touching me, but it felt so god damned good. Sure, five minutes ago, I'd been fantasizing about pounding the fuck out of her to ease this intense sensation of arousal, but this little bit was plenty.

This was all I needed. Her touch, those soft little sounds that left her lips, her cum dripping around my fingers, and the pleasure that warmed her face.

She breathed out a quiet moan against my lips and I almost came that quick. Not my proudest moment, I'll admit. But she was so fucking sexy, and it'd been *so* long.

"You're okay?" I whispered.

She nodded, another moan escaping her lips. Her hand kept moving up and down on my dick as her top teeth met her bottom lip, biting ever so gently. Those pretty green eyes shifted between mine, and I swore, it was like she was posing for a picture. "It's so good, baby."

My pointer finger slid between her lips to her opening. "Tell me if you want me to stop, okay?"

"I don't want you to stop." The words left her beautiful lips like a soft breath.

Fuck. Her voice. How hard her clit was beneath my thumb. The way she looked in the flickering light of the TV, and the light that shined in her eyes.

It was so perfect. It felt like nothing had changed. It felt like everything was okay again. I knew it wasn't. I knew everything was still a fucking disaster, and I knew that my actions today made it no better, but this moment of intimacy made everything just a little bit easier.

Slowly, I pushed my finger into her cunt, watching her expression carefully. Her eyes closed, her lips parted, and a moan fell from her mouth. My thumb slid to her clit and her head rolled back.

I'm not sure how I expected it to feel after birth but it wasn't much different than it'd ever been. Something didn't feel quite the same, but it was still hot as hell. Maybe a little wider toward the back but the opening was just as tight as it'd always been. And when I felt her muscles tighten around my finger, I wanted to put my dick in her so bad.

She kept moving her hand up and down, then got distracted as I moved my fingers against her G-spot.

God damn, I wanted her. I wanted her like I never wanted anything. I wanted to bury my cock so deep inside of her. But I knew she wasn't ready, and her hand felt a hell of a lot better than mine. Plus, she was this wet from hardly touching, and that filled me with an intense shock of pride.

Her eyes met mine, and she grinned. "What?"

I smiled back. Shaking my head, I said, "You're just beautiful."

She laughed. "Shut up."

I moved my thumb a bit, watching her mouth fall further open and her eyes glow brighter. "No, you're beautiful." My other hand slipped below her shirt, skin soft and smooth beneath my fingers. I squeezed her breast, pinched her nipple, and quaked with pleasure when she moaned again.

Her movements didn't slow, and neither did mine. We held one another's gazes with each stroke, and that only added to the intense state of intimacy. This was better than fucking her until she screamed. It was slow, and sensual, and it was getting better with each touch. Every moan she let out, every tremble of her cunt around my fingers, every time she dug her fingers into my shoulder to keep herself upright...

Fuck, I was gonna come. I didn't want to yet. I wanted to enjoy it for as long as she'd let it. But it'd been so long, and I didn't know how much longer I could hold back,

Her leg started to shake, and she moaned again, this time rolling her body forward and wrapping her arm around my neck. Her chest pushed into mine and my eyes closed into her hair, breathing in that familiar scent, basking in the little whimpers she released and the feel of her nipple hardening beneath my hand.

"Don't stop, baby, don't stop," she whispered.

And just like that, I busted all over her shirt. My hips arched forward, pleasure I hadn't felt in so long overtaking my body with each contraction. Stars shadowed my vision, pleasure taking hold of my entire body.

I wanted to stop for a second to breathe, but her moans got louder at my ear. Her arm tightened around my neck, fingers digging into my shoulder.

"It feels so good," she murmured. Her leg quaked harder against my thigh, hips curving down into my hand "Fuck, don't stop."

I kept my even pace, pinching her nipple harder. She exhaled a loud, heavy moan at my ear. I kissed her shoulder, then up her collar bone. I felt the texture of her scar beneath my lips, and I thought about jarring away, but she moaned louder, grasping ahold of my hair, holding my head closer. I wasn't sure why she liked me kissing there. Maybe it was cathartic, maybe it was a way for her to take her power back to receive pleasure from a place that'd brought her agony.

Maybe it was just because it felt good. I didn't know, but I rubbed her G-spot harder and massaged her clit faster.

A squeal of pleasure echoed at my ear, and mini contractions squeezed around my fingers.

I felt guilty for how the night had started, but then I looked at her. Not even just enjoying it, she was *loving* it. She didn't want to do anything else, but she didn't want me to stop either. Her eyes glowed the brightest green, and her head rolled back in pleasure. She ground her whole body toward me, practically dancing, lost in a tsunami of ecstasy, and I was giving that to her.

This wasn't how I'd pictured making her feel better, but I was happy to provide the service.

"Come for me, baby," I whispered.

Her brows curved at the center. She bit her lower lip, and fuck, she was the sexiest thing I'd ever seen. Her back arched.

Then her pussy tightened and loosened around my fingers. Over and over, at least for a good twenty seconds. I released her breast and grabbed her hip instead, holding her upright as each little quiver threatened to send her falling over. Her eyes stayed on mine, shining brighter with each tremble, twinkling like glowing emeralds, and she held me so tight for stability.

Smiling as the contractions slowed, she let out a faint laugh and collapsed into me.

The same joy shined through me as I held her close, breathing in the floral smell of her shampoo, basking in the warmth of her body. I kissed the side of her head and squeezed her as tight as she'd allow.

God damn, it felt so good to hold her.

"I love you," she murmured at my ear.

"I love you too," I whispered.

CHAPTER THIRTY-SEVEN

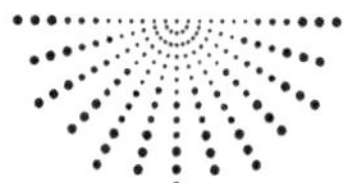

AUGUST 27, 2019 - LAILA

The past few weeks had been better than their predecessors. I wasn't back to myself, not really, anyway. But I was doing better. I still hadn't left the apartment, but I'd made a lot of strides.

I started cleaning throughout the day again. It was becoming habitual to run the vacuum and dust. I still had to push myself to stay on it, but I was doing it.

I'd managed to shower every evening since our fight. Maybe that seems like a small accomplishment, but it actually meant a great deal to me. I was forming a routine again.

I even took over most of the management duties at Moe's again. Still, I couldn't bring myself to talk to most of the staff in person. But I sent out the schedules to everyone, I spoke to a few servers on the phone. A simple feat to most. But a big step in the right direction.

My mom came over one morning before work and had coffee with me. She seemed so happy to see me. I'd pushed her away after the bombing too. I wasn't even sure what Jenna saw that day.

Leah and I had talked a bit here and there. She kept asking me to come over, or to let her come over, and I kept telling her I was tired. I wasn't. I just didn't want to see everyone. I didn't want to talk about the bomb, or the baby, or the guy who was locked up in her basement.

Whatever Amy did to his head, he was a zombie. Jeremy said he didn't have thoughts. I didn't completely understand what that meant, but apparently, he rarely spoke, except for the occasion when Peterson would talk through him. Even then, all he would say is that he wanted to talk to me. But I couldn't bring myself to do it. I was taking baby steps. Talking through some surrogate version of my captor was *not* a baby step.

Jeremy and I were doing good again though. He felt guilty for the things he'd said that night, but I wasn't mad. I knew I had been a bitch to him. Sure, he could have phrased things in a less asshole-like manner, but he deserved better than I had given him. I didn't want him to feel guilty. I was the one who completely neglected him.

I had a habit of forgetting that he had feelings too. When I was dealing with shit, I forgot how what I was going through affected him. As a woman, I'd go on and on about how I wanted men to talk about their feelings, but then I treated him like he didn't have any. I was so caught up in my own shit, I forgot he was going through shit too. And it wasn't fair. It wasn't partnership.

We hadn't fooled around again, but he didn't seem to mind. Spooning before bed and making out, every once in a while, seemed to be fine with him. It wasn't so fine with me, but he seemed perfectly content to wait as long as I didn't push him away entirely.

Honestly, that little high school version of sex we'd had left me feeling a lot better than I expected it would. At the time, I thought it would just make him feel better. I thought it might make me feel a bit more comfortable, and that it'd feel good obviously, but I didn't think it would make me feel better about life.

But it definitely did. The way he studied my face as he moved his hand around inside me made me want more. He was so gentle and caring while he did it, but also so aroused by seeing me turned on. It was like a loop that I didn't want to escape.

I *really* wanted to have sex. And yet, I was still incredibly nervous about it. I wasn't even sure why. Consciously, I knew Jeremy would never force me to do something I didn't want to. No part of me thought he was ever capable of hurting me. I knew he'd never force me into something I didn't want.

Every fiber of my being knew that he loved me. But for some reason, I was still scared. I didn't know if it was the scars and my self-esteem or just the idea of being penetrated that made my stomach twist. Either way, I was uncomfortable with the idea of doing one of my favorite things despite how badly I wanted it. Even with someone who I knew loved me and I wanted to spend the rest of my life with.

It didn't even make sense. It was like two parts of me were arguing inside of myself.

Jeremy was really understanding but it still sucked. I wanted to fuck. But I just couldn't get into it. That whole PTSD thing was really annoying.

"Shit, did you pay the water bill?" I asked Jeremy. I sat cross legged on the freshly made bed with a cup of coffee and a mound of paperwork spread out in front of me. "I don't think I did."

"You gave me the envelope and I took it up to the water authority on Wednesday." Jeremy pulled his shirt off and threw it in the hamper.

"Oh, that's right," I said. "I completely forgot."

He smiled, pulled a shirt from his drawer, and threw it over his head. "And you paid the sewage over the phone and the garbage bill went out in the mail today. The quarterlies are covered."

"And I finished payroll earlier. And I sent out the schedule for next week."

He smiled. "Everything is taken care of."

I knew how relieved he was that I was working again. That he didn't have to do it alone. He was still taking on a lot of the day-to-day issues. But he didn't have to do it all anymore.

"It is."

He sat on the bed beside me. "How are you feeling?"

A slight smile pulled at my lips. "I'm okay. I'm doing better, I think."

"You seem better." He smiled and took my hand in his.

"I think I am. I'm not where I want to be, but I'm better."

He held his smile. "It's a marathon, not a sprint."

"And how are you, Jeremy?" I placed my chin in my hand. "How are you *feeling*?"

He laughed and leaned backward against the pillows. "I've had a lot on my mind lately, actually."

"Oh yeah?" I gave a playful grin and leaned over him "Like what?"

"Why did Jack White and Meg pretend to be siblings when they were in *The White Stripes*?" He stroked his chin. Then he turned to me. "Do you think it was a publicity stunt or was it, like, some weird kink?"

I laughed. "Life's greatest questions."

"When I was a kid, I actually thought there were three people in *The White Stripes*. Because I knew his wife was in the band but I heard his sister was in it too. So, I was really confused when I found out that his wife was the sister."

I smiled, set my coffee down, and lifted my legs around his pelvis. "That'd be a pretty weird kink."

"Really weird kink."

"I don't think it was a kink though."

"No?" he asked.

"No. I read some interview that said they wanted it to be about the music. Not their relationship. And he's really private about his personal life so I think he just didn't want to be seen as a husband and wife duo. They both wanted to be seen as artists. Not just a couple. And I think that's kind of beautiful."

"That does seem more likely than publicizing an incest fetish."

I laughed. "A little bit."

He smiled and reached forward to touch my cheek. "You look pretty today."

Not to toot my own horn, but I kinda did. I'd done my makeup. I curled my hair. Granted, only to sit around my house and fill out papers, but I put in some effort.

"I don't look pretty every day?"

He laughed. "You always look pretty. But you look different today. Happy or something."

"I feel accomplished." I smiled. "I got a lot done today. I finally got around to organizing the hall closet. I've been saying I was going to do that since we moved in and I just threw all of our shit in there. But today, I did it. And I reorganized the kitchen cabinets."

"So basically, what you're saying is that neither of us are going to know where anything is for the next month."

"Basically."

He smiled and moved his hand from my cheek to my neck. The other slid to my back. He gently pulled me toward him. We kissed for a moment.

Then he murmured, "I'm glad you're back."

I just smiled and kissed him again. But only for a second because a voice behind me made me jump. "Well, I'm sorry to interrupt."

I spun my head around and rolled off of Jeremy's lap. "Jesus, Leah. Are you trying to give me a heart attack?"

She stood in the doorway wearing the cutest, black lace-up top I'd only seen her wear twice. Once when she and I went to a concert in 2017 and then again when we went to a gay bar in the city. She'd slept with the bouncer a few times, so she managed to get me in before I was old enough to enter legally. Even got me an over twenty-one stamp.

Her lilac hair hung around her perfect contour. She wore a dark plum lipstick. A gorgeous black and gray smoky eye rested above her green irises. Thick black wings lined them.

"You're young, you'll be fine. But come on. Go get dressed."

I tilted my head to the side. "What?"

She narrowed her gaze. "You made me a deal two years ago and you aren't breaking it to lay in bed all night and drink alone."

"A deal? What deal?"

She narrowed her gaze. "You little shit. You forgot, didn't you?"

"Uh-oh," Jeremy muttered. "I didn't remind you, did I?"

Leah licked her teeth below her smile. "Whatever, you forgot my birthday. But you aren't busy, and you promised me you'd go out and get shitfaced with me for my birthday when you turned twenty-one."

Oops. Yeah, definitely forgot about that. In my defense, I had a lot on my plate. But yeah, my bad.

My jaw dropped. "Oh my god, I'm so sorry, Leah."

"Whatever. You're going through shit, I'll let it slide. But I'm not going out to celebrate my birthday by myself." She put her hands on her hips. "You're getting your ass up and you're going out with me. It's been a hell of a year and I'm really not happy about the whole twenty-nine thing. So as my best friend, it is your duty to get your ass up and have fun with me."

"Why didn't you call me?" I asked.

"It's my birthday. You were supposed to call me, bitch."

Also, true.

But I wasn't feeling up to it. I did feel good that day, but I still didn't want to. I was in my comfort bubble. My apartment quite literally was my safe space. I didn't want to leave it.

"Leah, I really—"

"Uh-uh. No. You're not getting out of this. I'm sorry, Jeremy, but I'm stealing your fiancé for the night."

"That's between you guys." He gestured between us.

"But Leah—"

"Laila, you have not left the house in months. It's weird, it's not normal, and it's unhealthy. Going out and getting shitfaced with your soon-to-be sister in law will be good for you. And me. I need some adult, woman conversations that aren't centered around college or dumb, superficial bullshit."

I tried to pull down the unwilling grin that lifted my lips. "I don't think getting shitfaced is exactly healthy either, Leah."

"Maybe not for your body. But it's good for the soul. At least, it's good for my soul," she said. "Trust me, you need this. And bitch, I have had a rough year. Do not make me beg you to keep your promise. If you don't get your ass up, I'm pulling you up by the hair on your head. You're gonna have to kill me to get me out of this apartment alone. We need girl time. And you need to help me find a girl that will let me fuck her. Okay? Okay. Let's go."

Whether I liked it or not, I had made her a deal. And clearly, she wasn't going to leave. She was my best friend. And it *was* her birthday.

"You have to help me find something to wear."

"Chop-chop then." She clapped her hands. "I'll find you clothes, you pick out the shoes."

CHAPTER THIRTY-EIGHT

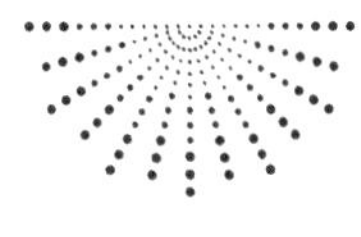

LAILA

Thick cigarette smoke wafted into my lungs, and fiery whiskey burned down my throat. Loud rock music thudded into my ears, and I was surprised at how much I was enjoying it. I glanced over the busy bar, noting the jukebox in the corner.

It wasn't a real bar. It was above a firehall in the middle of town, overflowing with old hicks sipping beer and playing darts. Definitely not the kind of place I predicted we'd find Leah's type.

I glanced her way. She insisted I come out with her, then stared down at her phone as we munched on onion rings. In fairness though, the change in scenery was better than I'd expected.

"Who are you mad typing over there?" I asked her.

Her cheeks flushed. She shuttered it. "Nobody."

"You're a big fat liar. Why are you blushing?"

"I don't blush, I have red undertones." She sipped her margarita.

I quickly reached across the table and snatched her phone with a childish grin. She reached for it in my hand. I laughed and yanked it back.

"Fine, read it if you want. But believe me when I say that you're about to see a part of me you never wanted to."

I set her phone back down. "Gross."

She rolled her eyes. "You're one to talk. You fucked my brother one room over for a good three years."

"Desperate times."

"You could have at least tried to be quiet," she muttered.

"Jeremy is great in bed, take that up with him," I said. "But seriously. Who is that?"

She met my gaze. "I'm not sure how you're going to feel about this."

"Oof," I muttered. "So, someone I know?"

"Indeed."

I sipped my drink, grin pulling at my lips. Leah hadn't dated in all the years I'd known her. That blush and bashful grin made me happy. She deserved a little romance. I couldn't think of any lesbians I knew off the top of my head though.

"Who is it?" I asked.

She raised her glass to her lips and chugged for a moment. Once it was finished, she said, "I'm trying to fuck Haley."

"Haley. My Haley?"

"Your celly."

"No shit," I muttered. "I knew she was gay, but wow."

"Bad wow?" She pulled a cigarette pack from her purse and lit one at her lips.

"No, I mean. Good for you, man. She's hot so that's cool. But are you guys just trying to fuck? Or like, something more?"

She took a drag off her cigarette and offered it to me. I accepted and she continued, "Me and relationships aren't really a good combination. I just have too much going on in my life to worry about someone's feelings. You know?"

I laughed and inhaled a few drags. "That's probably best. I can't see you two working out in a relationship."

"No?" She tilted her head, almost as if she was hoping I'd disagree.

"I love you, you're my best friend. But you're a cunt." She laughed. "And so is Haley. You need someone super meek. But maybe I'm wrong, maybe you guys would be a cool, bitchy power couple."

She chuckled. "She's actually pretty sweet, believe it or not."

"I do not, but maybe she is to you." I smiled. "So, you guys have been talking a lot?"

"We have. It's kind of a weird dynamic. The way we met, the fact that she knows a version of Chris than I don't..." Leah shrugged. "I don't know. It's nice that I don't have to hide anything, you know? And she lives far away so I can't read her mind all the time and that's really relieving."

"Yeah, I definitely wouldn't want to know every thought the person I'm fucking with is thinking twenty-four seven."

"It's just weird, you know? I haven't fucked with any one person in a really long time. Like, almost a decade. I've had hookups, plenty of hookups. But I think I'm starting to develop some feelings and it's really fucking bizarre."

"Feelings aren't a bad thing, you know." I lifted my glass. "Makes the sex better. Less pressure and all that."

"And how would you know?" She grinned. "You haven't had sex in, like, ever."

I rolled my eyes and took a sip from my glass. "So, Jeremy's been talking some shit."

"Nah," she said. "Okay, maybe a little. But not really shit. He was just asking for advice."

"Oh? And what advice did you give him?"

"To be patient. Sex after what you've been through is complicated. I told him to let you take the reins."

"Well. That is good advice," I muttered. "It used to be so simple. Things are just messy now."

"You should do molly."

Zero to sixty in no time. It'd been years since I'd done ecstasy. And granted, I loved that shit. But I was older now. I was also a little reluctant to use substances.

I laughed. "I'm good with my whiskey."

"No, I'm serious. There's been studies where they give people with PTSD MDMA and it dramatically reduces their anxiety and lessens or completely disintegrates flashbacks. And obviously it makes you horny."

"Getting turned on isn't the issue," I said. "It's more like... I don't know. Hard to explain, I guess."

"Well, I have an eight ball. So, if you want a line or two." She smirked, wiggling her brows.

"You do realize those studies were done in the presence of a licensed psychiatrist during guided therapy sessions, right?"

"Hey, I got it to have a good time. I don't think anything's going to fix what's going on up here." Leah tapped her head. "Look, all I'm saying is if you wanna have a good time, I got the supplies."

While I may not have been apt to get fucked up beyond belief, there was something I remembered clearly about Molly. I never felt cloudy on it. Everything was crisp and clear. It felt as though I had this divine understanding of the universe. I didn't actually, but that's how it felt.

What did I remember most of all though? The overwhelming abundance of happiness.

I laughed. "Why did you get so much?"

"'Cause I don't want to roll alone." She grinned. "Alright, I get it. I know we aren't kids anymore, but we aren't stupid. I'll take an ice bath if I start overheating, you literally can't overheat, so we're covered if we OD. And we've had a really shitty fucking year. Since October, our lives have been a disaster. It's August, Laila. We've had what—eight months of absolute hell?"

"I don't know."

"They don't call it the hug drug for nothing." Her smile widened. "I don't think either of us have been genuinely happy in a good minute. Let's just be happy tonight."

I bit back a smile. I hadn't done anything but smoked weed and drank since I was sixteen aside from whatever Peterson had given me. It felt a little childish to recreationally use party drugs the way I used to.

But in a lot of ways, she wasn't wrong. I couldn't feel joy without a side of guilt since I was taken in March. I had moments of accomplishment or contentment, but I wanted to feel joy again.

Maybe if I was that irrevocably happy again, I could fuck my fiancé.

"How are we going to get home then?" I asked. "We did drive here."

"Well, we're only about a mile or two away from your place. So, we could walk. But I'm sure Jeremy would be happy to come pick us up. Then he can teleport me to Haley's." She grinned. "She said to come over in a couple hours so…"

"This is true," I muttered. "Alright, under one condition."

"What's that?"

"You give me a little line right before we go home."

Her smile returned. "Deal."

CHAPTER THIRTY-NINE

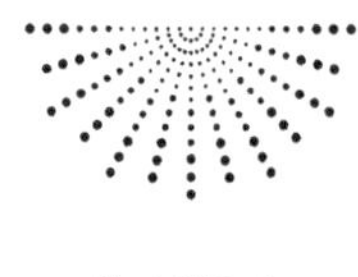

LAILA

"I forgot how much fun walking in the dark was." I spun in a circle and stretched my arms out in either direction. Warm humid air swirled around me, seeping into my nostrils. Stars twinkled in the cerulean sky. Crickets chirped in the bushes; cicadas hummed in the trees. And my lips were heightened in the biggest smile. "I don't think I've done this since I was like fifteen."

Leah laughed. "Back in the days when you had to ask your parents to drive you anywhere you wanted to go."

"Or walk." I smiled and closed my eyes. "I usually went with the latter."

She chuckled, gripped my arm, and pulled me off the pavement into the grass. "Your dumb ass is going to get run over."

"It's like midnight and we live in the boonies."

"Either way. Could you imagine that? All the shit you've lived through. Just to get taken out by some little Jetta walking home from the bar." She laughed as she spoke.

I laughed too, interlocking her elbow with mine. "The irony would almost be too poetic for reality."

She leaned her head on my shoulder, still laughing. Then she fell silent for a moment. "What do I do?"

276

I almost didn't hear her. My mind was too caught up in the sensa-tion of the dewy grass stuck to my toes around my pink flip flops. Usually, an unpleasant sensation. But just about all feelings are wonderful when you're rolling face.

"About what?" I asked

"Haley."

I laughed. I hadn't seen Leah interested in anyone for as long as I'd known her. And I loved Haley, but I wasn't her biggest fan. Still though, I wanted Leah to be happy.

Then again, at that moment, I wanted *everyone* to be happy.

"You really like her, huh?"

"Yeah, I think I do. I mean, I don't know. It's weird. She's like, super fucked up. No offense or anything."

"None taken," I said. "Captivity'll do that to you. I wasn't even there a fraction of the time that she was and I'm the living, breathing personification of fucked up."

"But it's like, that's why I relate to her. I don't know. She's blunt and honest and I love it. There's none of that confusing, beating around the bush shit." She laughed. "By the way, no bush."

"You're gross." I laughed. "I'm not really following, but go on."

"I don't know. It's just weird. I haven't liked anyone in a long time."

"True."

"And I think she likes me. Which is also pretty weird."

"Not really. You guys are practically the same person. I like you better but, you know. And you're both vainer than whoever Carly Simon was singing about in that one song. I can see why you'd be attracted to each other."

She laughed and pushed my shoulder. "Shut up."

"It's true though," I said. She chewed her lip. "Look, you should go for it. You've spent a good chunk of your life worrying about your siblings and putting yourself on the back burner. But now it's time to focus on you. You deserve a shot at happiness. Hannah's eighteen now, you don't have to keep putting your life on hold. And if shit comes up with Chris, Haley will understand. It's not like she's human. But for now, you should do something for yourself. You deserve it."

"It feels kinda wrong, you know? Not because of Haley or anything. Just, like... I don't know. When I start to feel happy, I feel guilty."

"Because of Chris?" I asked. She nodded. "I don't think I've told you this, but Chris didn't want you to hate your life. He said something once, to tell you in case he didn't make it out and... I can't remember it verbatim, Haley might. But he said he wanted you to be happy. Life's too short to waste being unhappy or something."

It grew quiet for a moment. Then she smiled. "I miss him."

I thought back to those conversations between the walls and smiled too. Usually, thinking about that would have brought me to tears. But it made me smile that night. "Yeah, me too. He'd be judging the shit out of us right now though."

"Always was a straight edge." She laughed. "But let's not think about that. Did you see the moon tonight?" Her finger raised toward the sky. "It's so pretty."

I smiled, turning up to look at it. It was only a crescent. It wasn't any spectacular shade of yellow or red. But it looked beautiful. Everything was beautiful.

I drew in a heavy breath, feeling the humid air coast into my lungs. "It smells like summer."

"Well, it's summer so." Leah smiled.

"Yeah, but it just smells so warm."

I took it all in for a moment. The hot, dewy air against my skin. The smell of the heat and honeysuckle breezing into my nose. The sound of the cicadas, the glow of the moon, the dampness against my feet.

Everything felt beautiful. It looked beautiful, it smelled beautiful. Life simply was *beautiful.*

I was grateful I'd done that molly with Leah. My mind felt light and airy. I was happy and I didn't feel guilty for it. It was the first time all year that I felt happiness without guilt, actually.

Not to say that drugs were a good thing. They can be unbelievably bad. But they can be fun, too.

Leah laid her head on my shoulder. "I'm tired of walking. Can you call Jeremy?"

That sounded good to me. As much as I was enjoying my walk, I was also craving some time with my fiancé. More specifically, his dick.

Then I slid my phone from my back pocket, went into my contacts, and clicked his face. I held it to my ear and kept on walking.

After two rings, he answered, "Hey, baby."

"Hey." I smiled. "Can you do me the *biggest* favor?"

"Probably." I heard him chuckle. "What is it?"

"Can you come pick us up?" I asked.

"Too drunk to drive?"

"Something like that."

He laughed. "Yeah, I'll come get you. Where are you?"

"We're like," I mumbled as I looked around. "I don't know actually. We started walking a while ago."

"How about you just send me your location?" he said.

"But you know what I don't get?" Leah bit into her McDouble while we left the drive through, talking through a mouthful.

"What don't you get?" I leaned across the center console and put my head on Jeremy's shoulder. One of my hands rested on his at the gear shift and the other played with a button on his shirt.

"We call it a *ham*burger. But there's no ham in it. It's beef. Ham is pork. So why do we call it a hamburger? We should call it a beef burger," Leah said.

Jeremy laughed. "How much did you guys drink?"

"Just enough." I held my thumb and fore finger out.

He chuckled and took my hand in his. "Seems like more than just a little bit."

"We're not puking, we're fine," Leah mumbled.

I nuzzled my face against his shirt. It was so soft. In all actuality, it was kind of scratchy. But it felt like velvet against my cheek in my current state of euphoria.

Jeremy laughed. "Am I taking you home, Leah?"

"No, sirry," Leah said.

"You have to take her to get laid," I said.

"Oh, alright. Who are you hooking up with?" He glanced in the rearview mirror.

I traced my fingertips up and down his arm, barely even hearing their conversation. I was more fucked up than I'd been in a long time. But in a good way. Not a sick, I need to sleep this off kind of way.

My body was warm and fuzzy. As corny as it may've sounded, my heart felt like it was overflowing with love. Everything just felt so *good*. They call it ecstasy for a reason.

I remember thinking that it was strange how I didn't feel emotional pain over what I was going through. But I felt so connected to everyone else's feelings. I felt connected to everyone and everything around me but in a blissful kind of way.

I was happy as ever while still remaining levelheaded. I wasn't foggy, everything was clear. And soft. Everything felt soft. The air rushing in from the car window and sliding into the bottom of my lungs. Jeremy's rough, yet still smooth, fingers laced between mine. The fuzzy material of my sweater against my skin. It wasn't like floating or spinning. I was as level as a perfectly laid vat of concrete. But I was happy. I felt *good* for the first time in a very long time.

"Baby," Jeremy said.

"Huh?" I looked up to meet his gaze with a smile.

He glanced down at me and grinned. "You didn't hear any of that, did you?"

My smile widened.

"I asked when you guys are going to start planning all this wedding stuff." Leah popped her head up between me and Jeremy in the front seats.

"Oh. I don't know." I lay on the center console and looked up at her. "I haven't really thought about it."

"Damn, girl. Do you even want to get married?"

"I mean, I want to *be* married. I don't really want to *get* married," I said.

She rested her head against my seat and passed me a lit cigarette. "What does that even mean?"

I lifted my feet onto the dashboard as I raised the cigarette to my lips. "Like, the whole party thing. A, it's a lot of work. B, it's kind of pretentious. And C, I don't have good luck with parties. I died at the first party you threw me, and a bunch of people died at the last one."

"I mean, you just stopped breathing. You didn't really die."

I did actually. She just didn't know that.

"Eh." I took another hit off the cigarette and handed it back to her. "Still not a good vibe though."

"True." She looked out the window. "But like, you guys should at least start planning."

"We could just go to the justice of the peace," Jeremy said.

"That'd be cool with me."

"That's some horse shit," Leah blurted. "You can't do that. We all have to be there."

"We'll see. We've only been engaged for a few months. There isn't any rush."

"Dude, it's been like half a year and you guys haven't even set a date."

"We're having a long engagement." Jeremy smiled, lifted my hand to his lips, and kissed my knuckles.

"Lame," she muttered, and munched on a French fry.

I smiled and moved my head closer to his chest.

It had been a long time since I felt that happy without an edge of guilt. The second I realized I was happy since I got out, I blocked it from my mind. It was shameful to be happy when I considered all of the shit I did wrong.

But it was like I couldn't feel guilt or sadness then. Just bliss. Like taking off a bra after working outside in ninety degree heat all day. Complete and utter relief.

CHAPTER FORTY

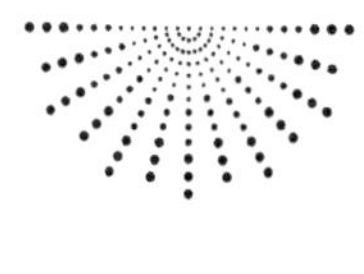

LAILA

Jeremy handed me a bottle of water and sat on the end of the coffee table, facing me. "So how was your night?"

I hadn't stopped smiling in more than an hour. I genuinely meant it when I said, "Really good."

He smiled, and his gaze met mine. He squinted a bit, still smiling, and leaned closer. "Are you tripping?"

"Rolling, actually." I struggled to hold my cheeks down. "There was probably something else in it, but I feel great right now."

"Your pupils are almost your entire iris. I didn't notice in the car, but holy shit. Are you alright?" He studied my eyes. "Maybe I should get you another water."

"No, I'm good actually. There is such a thing as too much water, you know. I'm not even that hot. But my body can withstand really high temperatures so. I don't know. That was nice. I should give Leah some money, I don't think it was cheap."

He smiled, shaking his head. "You're really fucked up, huh?"

I grinned. "But in a *really* good way."

He chuckled.

I sat up, took his hand, and looked between his vibrant blue eyes. "Can I tell you something?"

"Sure." He made a face, studying me. "What's up?"

"I really appreciate how supportive you've been since I've been home. And I'm sorry about the things I said when we got in that fight," I said. "I know this isn't easy for you either."

His gaze found mine and he smiled. "It's okay, Laila. Really. It was just a fight. We both said shitty things that we didn't mean."

"But that isn't us." I ran my thumb along the back of his. "We don't talk to each other like that. We don't say horrible things just to hurt each other."

He gazed down at our hands. "Yeah. Yeah, I know."

"We can't do that again," I murmured. "We have to talk. *I* have to talk."

He glanced up to meet my gaze. "It wasn't just you. I was letting that anger build up for a while and I shouldn't have done that. I shouldn't have waited until it exploded in a moment of pointless jealousy. I know there's nothing between you and Brody. I shouldn't have gotten so angry."

"But you were right. I was pushing you away." I gave a smile. "You keep pushing someone closer and closer to the edge, eventually they're going to fall."

"I still shouldn't have said what I said. It was manipulative. I don't want to be like that with you. I don't want you to think that any part of me meant that."

"I was an inconsiderate bitch," I said. "What I said about losing Micah and Chris... That wasn't fair. I know this isn't easy for any of us. You're just better at hiding it."

His gaze shifted down.

That always was a strong suit of Jeremy's. He knew how to hide shit better than anyone I'd ever met.

"All you needed was time," he said. "My reaction was childish. When I said it was all about you, there wasn't a reason for me to be so condescending about it. It'd only been a month or so. It's only been two now. Healing from what happened in there isn't going to happen overnight and I shouldn't have expected it to."

"Either way. We both could have handled it better."

"It was a really hard time. And it still is. But we just have to keep moving forward. It'll be alright."

I allowed my smile to come back to my lips. "I don't think there's anywhere left to go but up. I can't imagine things any worse than they've been this year."

He smiled back and touched my cheek. His gaze looked between mine for a moment. It was like words stuck to the end of his tongue. Like he wanted to say something, but it wouldn't come out. So, he kissed me instead.

Not that I minded though. I was floating on a cloud. I closed my eyes and leaned into it.

After a moment, he chuckled and pulled his hand away. "Do you want something to eat?"

"No, I'm good."

"Are you sure? There's coffee cake left from this morning."

My smile widened. "Babe, I'm fine. You don't have to take care of me."

"I've just never seen you this high."

"I did, like, four lines. I'm fine, baby. I'm great."

Jeremy laughed. "I bet you are."

I licked my smiling lips. Then I pressed them to a line. "So, I have a question. Or more of a proposal, I suppose."

"Oh yeah?" He gently locked the fingers on my other hand with his. "What's that?"

"I want to have sex."

He raised his brows. "She said enthusiastically."

I laughed. "I'm sorry. That wasn't very sexy, was it?"

He gave a smile. "Baby, you're really fucked up."

"Yeah, that was intentional."

He was quiet for a moment. "Ouch."

Oof. I should have phrased that differently. Nothing says sexy like 'I had to get shitfaced to want you.' But it wasn't that. I wanted him just as much when I was sober. I just couldn't get into it. Now though, he'd barely kissed me and my panties were drenched.

"No, I didn't mean—" I put my hand to my face. "It wasn't

supposed to come out like that. I just, it's been kind of hard to get into it and—"

"Baby, you don't have to do this. I'm fine with waiting." He pushed hair behind my ear. "You aren't ready. That's okay."

"It's not that I'm not ready. I... I want to. I've been wanting to."

"You haven't wanted to in a long time. And I'm okay with that. But I would feel like such a dick if you ended up—"

"Jeremy, it's not the first time I've had sex on molly. I didn't regret it then either." I touched his cheek. "Everything feels better on molly."

He grimaced. "See, considering this is the first time I've seen you on it, that's also not a pleasant thought."

I laughed, lifting my palm to my face. "God, I'm sorry. It's been a while, I think I kind of forgot how to do this."

He tugged my hand to my side. "I just don't want to do anything with you unless you really want to. If you don't enjoy it, I won't enjoy it and the whole thing would be kind of pointless."

How did I do this before? What did I do? How does one seduce?

Such a dumb question, really. But I'd genuinely forgotten. It used to be so simple. I just said, 'hey, fuck me,' and he'd say 'how hard?' Now though... Everything was different.

But I was still on a mission. I knew what I wanted. And damn it, if he wasn't gonna fuck me, then I'd fuck him.

I stood, put my hands on either side of his neck, and pushed my lips to his. They parted, bottom lip caressing against his. Tingles stretched from my mouth, to the pit of my stomach, and then a tad further south. I lowered my knees around his thighs.

It felt amazing. Everything felt amazing. Nothing bad was on my mind. His hands on my hips felt safe and strong. His lips against mine were like two pieces of a puzzle fitting together after spinning it around a million times to get it in place.

I pulled back a bit to catch my breath. His eyes met mine.

"Do you want to?" I asked softly.

His hands tightened on my hips. "Lai, come on. Of course I want to, but—"

"Then take off your pants." I smiled.

He laughed. "Baby—"

I stood back up, unbuttoned my jeans, and dropped them to the ground.

He bit his bottom lip. His gaze traveled up my legs. It was the same look he'd always given me. Like I was the most beautiful thing he'd ever seen. I'd been so worried about what he would think of my scars. But he looked at me just like he always had.

I smiled. "Take off your pants."

He licked his lips and swallowed hard, eyes still shifting over my legs. I watched the bulge in his jeans begin to grow. His gaze met mine. "Are you sure?"

I reached for his hand. "Come here."

He twined his fingers between mine. As he stood, he raised his hand to my face and gently pulled it up so our eyes met. His hand moved to the small of my back and lifted me slightly upward toward him.

I reached for the front of his pants. They were steady as I released the buttons and pulled down the zipper. Then I hooked my thumbs around the waist and pulled them down. All the while, my lips stayed against his.

As they fell past his knees, he moved both of his hands to my hips. He began to lift me into the air and I jumped into it. He let out a quiet laugh. I giggled at his neck. Then he kissed my cheek. His hands slid to the backs of my thighs to hold me up.

He leaned back a bit to meet my gaze. "You're really sure? Like, a hundred and ten percent?"

I smiled, nodding. "Let's go to the bedroom."

He smiled, leaned forward, and kissed me. Butterflies flapped in my belly. He carried me down the hallway, one hand squeezing my ass. I giggled as he fiddled with the handle. When he almost dropped me and mumbled, "Shit," I turned and swiveled it open.

He laughed, still kissing me, and carried me to the bed. He began to set me down first. I think he realized that would put him on top, so he carefully spun around and sat on the edge instead. I adjusted my knees and locked my hands together around his neck.

We kissed each other long and hard for a moment. With each brush of his lips, I felt my lacy panties grow even more damp. His hands slid over my torso and down the sides of my thighs. I felt the lump in his pants growing against me.

Fuck, I wanted him.

"Can I take off your shirt?" he whispered at my lips between fast breaths. His hands were practically trembling at my bare hips where my shirt rode up.

I nodded and gave a smile. Gently, he gripped the bottom and lifted it over my shoulders. My stomach turned when his gaze traveled over my torso.

But not because I didn't want to. I wanted to. I wanted to *so* bad. I just wanted to see his face when he saw the scars on my torso. I wanted to make sure there wasn't a look of disgust as he took in my stretch marks and cicatrices.

And there wasn't. His eyes moved over me just as they had on my legs. Like I was perfect.

And for a moment, I felt like I was.

He smiled, fingers sliding against my cheek. "Are you okay?"

"Are you?"

"I'm a little out of practice, but yeah, I'm good."

I pushed hair behind his ear. "Yeah, me too."

His eyes studied mine. "Tell me if you want me to stop, okay? You don't have to do anything you don't want to."

"I know."

His tone was so soft, as were his eyes. "Please, just... If I touch you somewhere you don't like, or if I'm pushing too hard, or... Please tell me. You don't have to let me keep going if you don't want me to."

My smile lifted higher. Damn, I loved that man. He really was the sweetest person I could share my life with.

I brushed hair from his face, leaning a bit closer. "I'm okay, baby."

I moved my hand down his chest and grasped the bottom of his shirt. His eyes stayed on mine as I raised it up over his head.

Then he gazed at me for a moment. A gentle smile pulled at his lips. His pupils nearly grew to the size of mine. Then he carefully pulled my body closer against him. "You're so beautiful."

Chills erupted over my arms and fluid slid between my legs. As I pushed my lips to his, he pulled my hips closer into him.

And from there, it was a dance. My mind vanished, and my instincts took hold. All of the physical sensations overwhelmed the processes in my mind that formed rationalized thoughts, replacing them with pleasure and excitement.

It was like I was lost. I lost myself in him. Our hands traveled over one another's bodies, exploring, embracing, relishing, and I dissolved into it. I got lost in his touch. I allowed myself to only focus on how it felt. The gentle graze of his fingers over my panties, the heat of his breath on my neck, the quiet groans he let vibrate between our kiss.

When his finger peeled away the fabric that covered my groin, and he touched the pad against my clit, elation was the only word I could use to describe how I felt. He'd hardly touched me, but I was mesmerized by the sensation.

Arms tight around his neck, moan breaking our kiss, my forehead rested against his, and our eyes met.

"You're okay?" he asked between deep breaths.

"I'm *great.*"

"Are you sure?" He clutched my cheek, holding it close, eyes flicking between mine. "Because—"

"Don't stop." I kissed him softly, rotating my hips closer into him. "Please don't stop."

Smile heightening his lips, he gently pushed two fingers inside. I gasped, then moaned as he massaged my G-spot.

But when I tried to pull his boxers down, he caught my hand. "I want you to come first."

"I want you to come too."

Jeremy smiled, calloused fingers holding my cheek passionately. "I will. Just not yet."

His thumb moved up and down against my clit. My leg began to tremble. Another moan escaped my lips. "But I want you to enjoy it too."

He licked his smiling lips. Then he flicked his thumb up and down again, forcing a surge or pleasure through me that left me rocking closer into him. My mouth dropped open, moan falling from it. His thumb at my cheek brushed against my lip, pulling it down a bit. "Trust me, I'm enjoying this. Watching you is always my favorite part."

While that may have been true, he could watch me bounce on his dick. I tugged at his waistband.

"Baby," he whispered, breath uneven at my neck.

"Hmm?" I murmured, rubbing against him. We both groaned at the pleasure that quivered between us as the head of his cock brushed my clit.

"I'm gonna come so quick." He laughed. "You won't even get to enjoy it."

"That's okay." I kissed his neck. "I just want you inside me."

He laughed. "You're killing me, woman."

I did another little shimmy with my hips, watching his eyes roll back when the head of his cock touched my clit. "If you come quick..." I rolled my body in a gentle wave, teasing the head of his cock with my cunt. "You can get down there and lick my clit." He laughed again, and my smile widened. "Deal?"

"Only if you stop teasing and let me get inside you."

I grinned, sliding a hand between us. I took his shaft in my hand, slid it to my opening, and watched his mouth drop open. Just barely lowering myself, taking the head of his cock into my opening, he let out a soft groan.

But I lifted my hips and slid his dick to my clit instead.

He grunted with disappointment, hands tightening on my hips. "You're evil, woman."

I grinned, rubbing it back and forth from my clit to my opening over and over again.

"You know what?" he asked.

My smile stretched. "What?"

His hand replaced mine on his cock, and he resumed what I was doing, but so much faster. He rubbed the tip in fast circles against my clit, then brought it back to my opening, arched his hips forward slightly, and pushed inside just a little bit. I gasped with bliss, lowering my hips, trying to take him all the way in.

Then he brought his dick back to my clit, rubbing it back and forth fast enough to make my leg quiver.

My knees buckled, and I collapsed into him, groaning with something between pleasure and disappointment.

He chuckled at my ear, rubbing from my upper back all the way to my ass as he kissed my shoulder. "Who's teasing who here?"

I giggled, tightening my arms around him. My knees molded into the blankets, and I brought myself as low as I could get, eyes closing with euphoria as my pussy stretched around him.

And then, that instinct took over again. Like a dance. My hands traveled over his body, exploring each inch, basking in each groan he let out at my ear. I was so lost in his embrace, in the pleasure he was giving me, that everything else vanished. Nothing else existed. It was only me, Jeremy, our pleasure, our passion, and everything disappeared.

"You're okay?" Jeremy whispered in my ear, almost too low for me to hear.

"I'm perfect." I smiled, nodding as my legs hooked tighter around him. "Are you okay?"

"I'm amazing," he whispered with a huff of a laugh. "Fuck, you feel so good, baby."

Smiling, enveloping myself in the sensation of completion that washed through me. Full, and euphoric, and joyous. The pressure of him inside me, his thumb against my clit, his breaths against mine, his wide blue eyes.

Jeremy chuckled. His hand at my hip slid to my face, tilting my chin so our eyes met. "I fucking love you."

Smiling, I grasped the side of his neck, eyes locking with his. "I love you so much."

And I did. Sex with Jeremy was always amazing, but this was exhilarating. I was connected to him on the most intimate, spiritual level, and I didn't want it to end. It was like every cell inside of me was bursting and rebuilding at once. I was overwhelmed with pleasure, and love, and elation.

That molly was a genius idea.

His hands slid to my back. I felt them run against my scars, but it didn't make my stomach hurt. It didn't make me cringe. Because I heard his fast breaths at my ear. I felt his heart racing against my chest.

They didn't change how he saw me. I aroused him as much as I always had. He was so fucking turned on, and that had everything to do with me, and nothing to do with my scars.

"You're so god damn wet, you know that?" His arms tightened around me.

My stomach flipped. I closed my eyes, sliding upward and rubbing my clit against his pelvic bone. "'Cause your dick feels so fucking good."

He panted out a heavy breath. His head shook, something of a laugh leaving his lips. "Keep talking to me like that and I'm gonna come in two seconds."

I grinned and lowered my lips to his neck. I rocked back and forth faster, closing my eyes in bliss, grinding my hips deeper into his. "I thought you liked when I told you how much I loved your dick."

"Oh, I do." He squeezed my ass harder, free hand sliding into my hair and grabbing it at the scalp. "But you better be ready for me to lift your ass up because I'm so fucking close to busting inside you." I laughed and rolled my hips upward and back down. He breathed out something between a grunt and a sigh at my ear. "Jesus fucking Christ."

"Fuck, I missed this." I moaned into his ear. "I missed your dick inside of me."

He arched his hips higher, breaths uneven at my ear. His hand traveled to my breast. He cupped it gently, thumb and forefinger pinching my nipple. "Yeah?"

"Mhmm," I murmured. "I dreamed about it, actually." My hips pushed further into his pelvis, and the euphoria took hold. His curls brushed my clit, and for some reason, that sensation heightened my pleasure by a thousand, flipping deep inside my belly, forcing little contractions through my cunt. "The taste of your lips." He exhaled deeply, thumb flicking against my nipple. "How good you eat my pussy—"

"Fuck." He grabbed my hips and hoisted me off of his dick. His hand slid to its place, thumb gliding against my clit. Breathing fast, his cum shot all over my stomach. His eyes met mine and I smiled.

I knew he wouldn't last long. Typically, we'd go for anywhere from twenty minutes to two hours. But it'd been almost six months. It was alright though. Kinda boosted my ego, actually. A million scars, a bunch of stretch marks, and a kid later, and he still thought I was hot.

His head clunked to my chest. "Shit. I'm sorry."

Laughing, I rolled onto the bed and spread my legs. "Make it up to me."

Jeremy laughed too. Grinning, he teleported to the hardwoods before me, grabbed my thighs, and pulled me to the foot of the bed. His fingers slid inside of my still dripping pussy. They weren't much next to his dick, but when he lowered his lips to my inner thigh, tingles spread all over my body.

Those bright blue eyes stared up at me, tongue sliding along the drips between my legs.

Fuck, I had no idea why that was so sexy, but my pussy clenched just at the sight.

As his tongue trailed to my vulva, brushing each lip, I expected him to tease me like he'd done a moment ago.

Instead, his lips brushed mine, and his tongue parted through. I have no idea how he managed it, but somehow, he sucked my clit and flicked his tongue up and down simultaneously, still curling his fingers back and forth in a 'come here' motion against my G-spot.

Unable to do much else, stars painting my vision, overwhelmed with pleasure and desire, my head rolled back, and a near scream left my lips. I buried my fingers into his messy black waves, and I screamed with pleasure. His free hand slid up my stomach to my breast, massaging it slow, thumb rubbing back and forth against my nipple.

Leg shaking, whole body arching toward him, I molded into the pile of linen, immersed in pleasure, only able to focus on the sensation itself.

It's so fucking hot when you do that, his voice said into my thoughts.

"When I do what?" I made out between gasps.

Roll your head back and arch your back, he thought. *You look fucking gorgeous.*

Responding was virtually out of the equation. The most I could manage was a moan of bliss, digging my fingers into his scalp, arching closer into him, lost in a wave of paradise as the contractions took hold, exploding with passion, painting the backs of my eyes with stars.

So fucking pretty, he whispered into my thoughts as the euphoria tapered.

CHAPTER FORTY-ONE

LAILA

I laid my head against Jeremy's bare chest. The musty smell of his sweat touched my nose. I listened to his quick breaths beneath my ear. He kissed my hair, trying to regain a normal breathing rhythm. I chuckled and snuggled closer against him. His arm at my back tightened around my waist to pull me closer against him.

I was coming down. And usually, the come down on MDMA was a fucking bitch. But I felt high off of him. It balanced out all of those negative affects.

It wasn't the first time I felt that. I knew it had something to do with the bond, but I was grateful for it either way. He made me feel better than anything else ever had.

He twirled a piece of my hair between his fingers. "Did that live up to your dreams?"

I smiled, eyes turning up to his. "Exceeded my dreams, actually."

He smiled too. Then he kissed my forehead. "Mine too."

Still smiling, I lay back down. My gaze caught the sparkling jewel on my left hand. And Leah's words vibrated through my mind. Our conversation walking along the road. Then what she'd said in the car.

I realized something in that moment.

Life's too short to live it unhappy. And no one made me happier than the man whose arms held me close to him.

"Baby," I whispered.

"Hmm?" he asked.

I turned so my chin rested on his chest and my gaze met his. "I have a question."

"What's that?" he asked.

"Before I ask, you have to promise to say yes." I smiled wider.

"That doesn't seem fair."

"That's the deal. Take it or leave it."

A long exhale. "Yes."

I propped myself on my elbow and met his gaze. "Marry me."

Jeremy laughed. His finger grazed my engagement ring. "That's kind of the plan, isn't it?"

"I mean, soon. Like tomorrow. Let's just run off to Vegas."

"Seriously?"

My smile widened. "Let's do it. Let's just take the leap. You and me, together forever."

He laughed. "What's the rush?"

"Honestly?"

"Well, I don't want you to lie."

"Leah said something earlier and it reminded me of something Chris said in there. He had messages for all of you guys, and I couldn't remember exactly what they were then, but I had this moment of clarity tonight."

"Oh, yeah?" His smile fell, but he kept twirling my hair. "What did he say?"

"It was something he asked me to tell Leah and Brody. He said to tell them to be happy. Not to waste their lives being miserable, whether he was there or not. And I still want to find them. I'm *going* to find them. I am. I wasn't ready to think about going up against Peterson again, but now I know that I can. That I have to." I paused. "That's not where I was going with that. Hang on, what was I saying?"

"That Chris wanted Leah and Brody to be happy," he said softly.

"Right. Chris said that there's too much to be grateful for in the world and that we shouldn't waste it being unhappy. 'Find something that makes you happy and never give up on it,' or 'do it every day' or something. I don't know. But I know what makes me happy. *You* make me happy."

"You want to do me every day?"

I laughed. "I mean, yeah. But that's not what I meant."

His hand cupped my cheek, smiling. "I know what you meant."

My smile widened. "So? What do you say?"

"Well, we have to get a marriage license first. Then we have to wait at least three days to get married, but no more than sixty."

"So, Thursday?" I grinned.

He chuckled and pushed hair from my face. "Baby, that doesn't give us any time to prepare. Your mom and your sister want to be there and so do all of my siblings and Max and Ray and Lydia. And you know they'll all hate us if we elope. Plus, I don't even have a tie, and you don't have a dress—"

"You said I could wear a burlap sack and you'd still want to marry me. You remember saying that, don't you?"

He smiled. "Three weeks. How about three weeks? We can go get our marriage certificate in the morning."

"Three weeks?"

"That'll give us enough time to throw something simple together." He gave a gentle grin. "Nothing fancy, just enough time to work the schedule out for everyone."

I smiled wider. "Three weeks."

"Three weeks," he said. "We're getting married in three weeks."

Butterflies. More butterflies danced in my stomach. I couldn't pull my lips down if I wanted to and my entire body lit up with anticipation.

"You're going to be my husband." My smile heightened.

"You're going to be my wife." Jeremy's eyes widened, and he carefully ran his thumb along my jaw.

I brought myself further up to him. The hand at my lower back squeezed a bit harder. He pulled me closer into him.

"I love you," he said against my lips.

"I love you more." I smiled. I wasn't even high anymore, and I couldn't stop smiling.

It was a pure and beautiful moment. I finally felt like I'd figured it all out. The past few months of my life had been filled with painful trials and what felt like eternal suffering. But it wasn't eternal. Things were better. Things had to get better. Things would be better.

They *had* to get better.

As those warm hands held my bare body, I thought back to my dream when I was in the hospital.

I was going to get the life I wanted. I was going to be happy if I had to breathe the joy into existence. It was *my* life. So much of 2019 had been wasted on my turmoil and torture. But it had to stop. This life was a gift that Micah gave me with his own and I had to make something of it.

First, I would be happy. I would find myself again. I was going to build back the life around me that fell to shambles. I was going to get married and reconnect with my friends and family.

Then, I was going to save the other two hundred or so people I hadn't managed to the first time around. I was going to bring Chris home.

Once everyone was safe, I was going to kill Peterson. I wasn't sure how. I wasn't sure when. But I would find him. Then I'd kill him.

CHAPTER FORTY-TWO

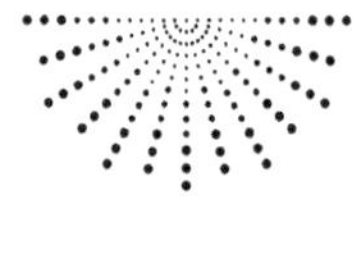

LAILA

"Three weeks." Leah put her hand to her face. "You're giving me three weeks."

"You don't have to do anything," I said. "This is our wedding, you're a guest, not our planner. It just makes sense. Hannah's going back to school soon. Celena and Wyatt will probably be going back to West Virginia at some point or another. Plus, Jenna's summer break is going to be over soon. Three weeks gives us enough time to get clothes and reserve a caterer. It's not going to be extravagant. Just quick and sweet."

"You have to pick out a dress, like, today," Hannah said. "It usually takes at least two weeks to be ordered. Then you need alterations. Oh my god, what about the cake?"

"I have an appointment to try on dresses tomorrow, but I might just get something off the rack. I don't need anything fancy. And Jeremy's just going to wear a button up and a tie."

"Off the rack." Hannah's hand lifted to cover her mouth. "You're not wearing a tux?"

"It's too damn hot for a tux."

She rolled her eyes. "Child."

"And I already talked to Beverly about a cake. I've been eating her food for years; we knew what we wanted so we put our deposit down this morning. And we got a free sample cake since we didn't do a tasting."

"Are you just going to do it here?" Leah asked.

"It's still a mess from the explosion," Jeremy said. "Plus, there's a lot of bad vibes around this place with our parties. Not to mention the fact that we still have some dude tied up in the basement."

"Yeah, it's too close to Peterson," I said. "I don't want Amy to be able to get in someone's head and fuck shit up. We're just going to do it at my Mom's by the creek. Her garden's gorgeous so we can get some cute pictures there. And there aren't going to be many of us. Just family and a couple friends. We don't need much space so Mom's house will be fine. And it's summer, so we can do it all outside. We can use the patio as a little dance area, rent some tables and cover them with some pretty cloths. I'm going to handle the flowers so that pretty much covers décor. I know a few caterers, so we don't have to worry about cooking or anything. And decorating will be a bit of a bitch, so we might need some help with that the day before. But everything else is basically covered."

Leah laughed. "You're crazy. Twelve hours ago, I mention you guys getting married and you're like, 'Eh, at some point.' And now you got a whole damn wedding planned."

"You forgot one major detail." Hannah put her hand on her hip.

"What?" I asked.

"Who's going to marry you?" Hannah said.

"Oh, shit," I muttered.

"Yeah, I guess we didn't think about that," Jeremy said.

"I could do it." Adam came down the maid-steps with a smile. "It only takes like five minutes to get ordained on the internet. Congrats, by the way."

"You did introduce us," I said.

That settled it then. Our wedding was planned. A month from that day, we'd be husband and wife.

Jeremy made a face. "Then that'll make Brody my best man."

Adam laughed. "Not awkward at all."

"We're going to be lopsided up there, huh?" I began. "You're going to have Brody and Kai. And I'm going to have Jenna, Hannah, Celena and Leah."

"And Wyatt," Jeremy said. "Everyone always forgets about Wyatt."

"Maybe I should be a groomsman," Leah said. "I'd rather not have to wear one of those ugly ass, frilly dresses."

"They're not going to be frilly and ugly."

Leah laughed. "Babe, the last time I wore a dress was to my first communion when I was eight. Love them on other girls, but not my thing."

I waved my hand in a shooing motion. "Alright, you stand with Jeremy. But black slacks and a plain shirt then."

"What color scheme are you going with?" Hannah asked. "Blue?"

Jeremy laughed. "Green, right?"

"Green. Most of the décor is going to be vines and flowers that I grow so green's just easiest."

"Green's pretty," Leah said.

Jeremy tucked his arm around my waist and pulled me close to him. He kissed my hair and placed his hand at the small of my back.

Hannah's eyes shifted over the two of us. She smiled. "You guys look happy."

I leaned closer into him, smiling. "Things aren't exactly how we pictured them. But nothing ever is, right?"

Leah smiled. "Well, we've got a lot of work to do. Word to spread and whatnot. Just family and close friends, right? Does that include Mémé and Papy?"

"I think so. That's okay, right, babe?"

"Yeah, of course. And you can bring Haley, Leah. We'll tell Max, and I gave my mom a call this morning. I'm meeting up with Jenna for lunch. Then, we just need to talk to Kai, Celena, Wyatt, and Brody. Oh, and Ray."

"Totally fine either way," Hannah said. "But I'm assuming Mary isn't a part of the guest list?"

Jeremy fell silent.

Leah chewed her cheek. Then she said, "She has been a big part of our family for a long time. Total cunt, but..."

Truthfully, I hadn't given it much thought. But now? Since our conversation the day after the bomb? I understood her a bit more. Still wasn't crazy about her. But had I gone to all of what she had to protect my kid and then not have been invited to her wedding... My heart would be broken.

"Yeah, I think Mary should be there."

"Really?" Jeremy pulled back.

"Yeah. I think so, don't you?"

He paused. "If you want her there. She is your mom."

I gave a quick nod, not thinking much of it. "We should probably start heading back to the diner though. I'm kind of tired."

Hannah gave an understanding smile. "So, what time tomorrow?"

"Twelve thirty. It's in town, so we should all just meet at the diner and walk," I said. Jeremy handed me my jacket and I lifted it over my arms. "So be there at twelve, twelve fifteenish."

Leah said, "Alright, cool. I'm invited, right?"

I smiled. "Obviously. Could you fill Celena in and see if she'll come?"

"I'm sure she'll be there," Hannah said.

Adam sat at a bar stool. "Dude, what kind of bachelor party are we going to have for a guy who doesn't drink?"

"Oh, shit. We have to do the bachelorette party, don't we?" Hannah said.

"I think that's Jenna's job with the bridesmaids help. But we don't need to do all that. We'll just hang out at one of our houses and eat food or something. Only one of my bridesmaids is above age anyway."

"Just no strippers," Jeremy said.

"Yeah, please no strippers," I said.

They looked between each other and grinned. "Oh, of course not," Leah said.

Hannah smiled. "We would never."

"I'll make sure she isn't hotter than you." Adam grinned.

Eh, whatever. I trusted Jeremy. He'd probably gotten pretty cozy with PornHub lately anyway. What was the difference if it was a naked girl in front of him rather than on a screen? I still had enough trust in him to know he wouldn't cheat.

"No hand stuff and no sweatpants," I said.

"Gross," Jeremy muttered, slipping his Converse on.

Adam smiled. "I feel like that's fair."

I turned to Leah and Hannah. "But I really don't want a stripper, guys. Please don't put me in that position."

The thought of some random guy thrusting his junk in my face was probably the worst thing I could imagine at that time. It had only been one night since I had sex with Jeremy after what had happened.

I loved Jeremy. I'd been naked with him a thousand times. And that even had its moments.

But anyone hovering over me for a lap dance would make me uneasy. Who knows, maybe if I was drunk enough, I would've been alright. But the thought made my stomach churn.

"What about a female stripper though?" Leah asked. "You're bi, right?"

"Yeah, but no thanks. Really. No strippers for me. I don't care if you guys have strippers at Jeremy's, but I'm serious. No strippers." I met Leah's gaze.

She frowned. "Alright, no strippers. But can we make sure your parties are on different nights so I can see the titties at Jeremy's?"

"Please don't."

I laughed. "It's really not a big deal, baby."

"But I don't want a stripper." Jeremy looked at Adam. "Remember you two tried to get me to go to a club when I turned eighteen? Remember me saying no then too?"

"You're so lame, dude," Leah muttered.

"No, there's going to be a stripper whether you like it or not." Adam said. "There is supposed to be a stripper at a bachelor party. You don't drink or gamble. The only thing that would even make it a bachelor party would be a stripper."

"You can take the lap dance then," Jeremy muttered.

"See, that's what I call a compromise." Adam grinned.

CHAPTER FORTY-THREE

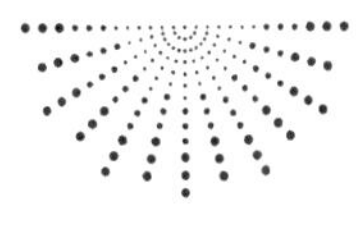

LAILA

It was more refreshing than I'd imagined to be outside again. I wished I'd have done it sooner. Then again, maybe it was just so nice because I had something to be happy about. The warm summer air made me feel alive as I sipped my iced coffee in front of the window while I watched the thick green foliage whoosh by me.

The wedding was gonna be fun. I was gonna marry my best friend in front of all the people that I loved. I was gonna dance, and sing, and smile, and take pictures, and I was going to be happy.

There was one concern though. It was summer—ninety-three degrees, to be exact—and I wanted a dress with sleeves and a high neck. That wasn't gonna be easy to find.

"Can I ask you something?" Jeremy squeezed my hand. He glanced from the road to me, then back to the road. "You don't have to answer if you don't want to."

"What is it?" I asked.

As we rolled to a stop at a red light, he met my gaze. "Why do you want Mary at the wedding?"

"You don't want her there?" I asked.

"I don't know, I have mixed feelings about it," he muttered. "She did try to kill me."

"That's not what she was trying to do." I looked out the window.

He paused. "I just, I'm confused. I thought you hated her."

"I don't know. It's complicated. I hate what she did. I hate that Moe is dead. I hate what happened to you."

"But?" he asked.

I rubbed my eye. "At the funeral last year, she said that one day it would make sense to me. Something about me not understanding yet."

"You know why she did all of that?" His thumb slid against my knuckle.

"I don't completely get it. Everything she did was awful and evil and wrong but... But she knew."

"She knew what?" Jeremy asked.

I should have picked up on his tone. But honestly, I was on cloud nine. We were about to have everything we wanted, and I wasn't paying as much attention to him as I should have.

"She knew I was going to lose Micah. She knew I was going to be taken. She knew I was going to be tortured. She knew what that place would turn me into, and she wanted to prevent it from happening."

"What do you mean? How do you know that?"

"Because she told me," I said. "She didn't explain much of the details on *how* she knew. But I figured it out when I was in there then she kind of just confirmed it."

"I don't understand." He turned to meet my gaze. "I talked to her while you were in there. She acted like she knew nothing."

"Because she doesn't know much. She knew it would happen while I was pregnant. She didn't know when or why or how or who. All she knew was the what," I said. "It's hard to explain."

"But Moe..."

Killing Moe was wrong. And I'd never be happy that she did it. But it was done. And I would do far worse to keep my children safe.

"I wish he were still here. And I hate what she did to him. But she was trying to protect me. She was trying to give me an opportunity to get away before this happened. Even if she didn't get to him before I got pregnant. If I would have packed up my shit and started over somewhere else, if I would have never looked into Lydia and Chris and

Amy... I could be starting over somewhere with my new baby right now. That's what she was hoping. I don't *like* what she did. But I get it. She killed to protect her child."

Jeremy stayed quiet.

I turned to meet his gaze. "Wouldn't you have killed for your son?"

He bit his lip.

"Because I did. I'd already killed over twenty people when Micah was born. Trying to protect the both of us when they tortured me."

That was the first time I told him a glimmer of what I'd done in there. It wasn't some heart to heart; it came out as simply as if I were telling him about a load of whites I washed a red towel with.

He turned to meet my gaze. I expected a look of fear or disgust. But it didn't come. He didn't look scared or shocked. It was almost like he was relieved. "That's why the pain would stop after a minute or two."

"I killed a lot of people trying to protect him. Trying to stay alive for him when I didn't even want to breathe." I paused. "Humans. I killed a lot of *humans* trying to protect him. My count is well over forty after our escape. Maybe even more. I stopped counting at twenty-one."

He held my gaze. "I know I hesitated a second ago. But I would have killed anyone to protect our son too."

"Then you can understand what Mary was trying to prevent last year."

He grew quiet for a moment. "I guess I can."

He stared out the front window. He anxiously tapped the wheel. There was almost a look of anger at the edge of his brows. I reached across the center console and gently put my fingers over his.

"What is it?" I asked.

He slid his fingers between mine. Then he let off the break and moved through the light. "It's alright, baby."

"No, you're upset. What's wrong?"

"It just seems like everyone knows more about my kid than I do. I understand that you're not ready to talk about him. Don't think I'm upset with you. It just..." He paused for a careful breath. "I don't know. I wish things were different."

I could see how much it hurt him. I knew how badly he wanted to know about Micah. But it just hurt so much.

"It's hard to talk to you about him."

Jeremy glanced my way. "Why is that?"

"It's hard to tell anyone something you know is going to hurt them," I murmured.

His gaze caught mine as we came to another stop sign. "Not knowing hurts too, Lai."

I felt my eyes beginning to sting and turned to the window. "I'm sorry, I'm not trying to block you out."

"It's okay." He reached over the center console. His fingers touched mine that rested on my thigh. "Please don't think I'm upset with you. I'm not, really. I just…"

"You want closure," I said. "I… I'm going to talk about it soon. I am, I promise. But right now, I just… I want to be happy."

He raised my hand to his lips and kissed my knuckles. I turned to meet his gaze. He gave a sweet smile. "Let's be happy then."

CHAPTER FORTY-FOUR

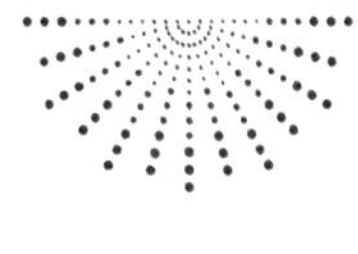

LAILA

I expected planning a wedding to be a lot more fun than it was. In the movies, the bride always looks so happy and radiant. Even during the planning, her smile stretches from ear to ear. At every angle, the light hits her jaw just right and her eyes twinkle in the luminance of the sun.

I was not one of those brides.

Truly, I was excited. Even the chaos was fun. But it was also very trying.

Since we were under limited time, Jeremy and I immediately called a caterer from a restaurant in town that we loved. It was the first place we'd gone on a real date to. They were happy to do it, they even offered us a fifteen percent discount for belonging to the local business association. But they were booked for the Saturday of our wedding and we *really* wanted their food. It was sentimental. We were early enough along that we could change the date so we did. Suddenly, we were getting married on Thursday, September 19th instead of Saturday September 21st. That was another thousand phone calls to adjust the date to the guests, then to the bakery and the dress place.

Then was the challenge of finding a dress. With my scars, it was never easy to find something to wear regardless of the occasion. But it's especially hard to find something that makes you feel like the most beautiful girl in the world when you hate every part of your body.

"At least try it on." Jenna held out a pretty, strapless ball gown with a deep V-neck and an open back.

It was beautiful. I would have loved it six months prior.

I used to love my back. Not something you hear a long of girls boast about, but it is one feature about my body that I genuinely love. I was of the lucky few that had no back fat and love handles, even before the weight loss of captivity. But I hated my back now. I hated it most of all. Backless was no longer an option.

"I can't wear that." I turned back to the long-sleeved rack.

"Baby, you'd look beautiful," Mom said. "Come on. If you're not going to let me pay for your wedding dress, at least try on the ball gown for me."

I thumbed one with lacy flowers streaming up the arms.

"I like that one." Celena gestured to the one I held out.

I pulled it a bit further and saw the open back once more. Chewing my lip, I let it fall back to the rack.

"I'm sure we'll find something," Hannah murmured from a rack behind me. "How do you feel about mermaid?"

"You're definitely skinny enough to pull off a mermaid right now." Jenna gave a supportive smile.

"Oh, the irony," Leah murmured.

I chuckled. "I'm open to a mermaid."

"Alright, cool," Hannah said. "No strapless, right?"

"Definitely no strapless. And I want sleeves," I said.

"The scars aren't that bad, baby." Mom frowned. "It's going to be hot. Get short sleeves."

"I like it warm." I continued leafing through the gowns.

And that wasn't a lie. I did like warmth. A gift of holding the ability to manipulate and create fire, I supposed. But still, it'd have been nice to feel comfortable in a strapless or open back. Something sexy. I just wasn't at that point yet.

I kept thumbing through the long-sleeved section. Then suddenly, I found it. The perfect dress. Exactly the dress I had been envisioning since I said yes. I audibly gasped.

It was a beautiful, vibrant shade of white. From neck to ankle, every inch was covered in flowery lace. It came all the way up to the collar bone, so I knew it'd cover the scar on my breastbone. The sleeves went down to the wrists, long enough that the flower shape of the lace would even cover parts of my hands. It was a form fitting, trumpet style. The fabric was thin, so I wouldn't be too hot. Every detail was perfect.

Until I turned it around.

Still, a beautiful dress. But on the other side, the back was almost completely see-through. Instead of lace, it was a thin layer of an almost tulle-like material. A more expensive version, I suppose. But a similar concept.

It swooped down in a large U just above where my ass crack would be. Thin lines of lace traveled throughout it like vines. A line of beautifully placed buttons climbed all the way to the collar.

It was perfect. For someone whose back didn't look like a scratching post.

I pushed it back to the rack.

"Hang on," Leah said. "That was gorgeous."

"It had an open back," I said.

"No." She pulled it out and gestured to the back. "There's vines of lace. It'll cover."

"I don't think so."

"At least try it," Leah said. "Worst case scenario, you hate it and put it back."

"It is really pretty."

"That's gorgeous." Mom smiled. "Please try it."

I did love it. I wanted Leah to be right, I wanted it to cover the scars. Maybe it would.

"Fine," I said.

As I stepped into it and gazed at myself in the mirror from the front, I was in love. Every detail was perfect. It was somewhere between a trumpet and fish tale shape, hugging the curve from my waist down into my small hip and thigh perfectly. It was tight in all the right places. Elegant, but sexy. Sexy without skin, so I'd feel beautiful in it.

Jenna was right, my body was just the right size to fill it out. Just a few pounds heavier, or even a few weeks closer to Micah's birth, it would have looked awful through the waist. But all of the swelling had just gone down and I'd only gained a few pounds since coming home. It literally looked flawless on my body. I was never skinny enough before to wear something so tight and actually feel comfortable before my post-captive size, but I loved it.

It came to the perfect place on my neck just above the scar. A thin choker would cover. You could still see the bite scar, but I could style my hair to cover that and pat some foundation overtop.

It was tight through the arms and shoulders but not too tight. Just the right size that made it look like it had been tailored especially for me. The train was short, but still obvious. Every inch was covered in beautiful lace flowers over a bright white under dress.

It fit like a glove. It was perfect.

But I hadn't seen the back.

As I opened the door and started out to the area where everyone sat, all of their jaws dropped. Mom and Hannah even started to cry.

"That's it." Celena set the cake she was munching on to the table. "That's it, dude. You look amazing."

"That's so pretty." Leah gazed over me in the mirror.

"Holy shit, my baby sister's getting married." Jenna grinned. Her eyes looked me up and down with excitement. Then I turned around to look at myself in the corner of mirrors.

When I first saw myself in the glass, I loved it. I had that moment where it hit me. *It's real, it's happening, I'm getting married. I'm a bride.* I felt as beautiful as I did before I was covered in those daily reminders of what happened to me.

But once I made a few more steps, the corner of mirrors reflected from the mirror on the other side of the room. And my stomach sank.

I had to bite my bottom lip to keep it from trembling. The knot in my throat grew so large I couldn't even swallow it. I managed to retain my composure, but it was ruined.

I couldn't wear it.

My back looked hideous.

I didn't look like a beautiful, blushing bride. I looked like some kind of undead zombie.

"That's so pretty," Mom murmured, eyes shifting over the back.

It was. It was gorgeous. But I wasn't pretty in it. "I can't wear this."

"What?" Hannah asked. "Laila, it's beautiful. You look amazing."

"Yeah, Jeremy's probably gonna jizz in his pants just looking at you in that, dude," Leah said.

"My back." I caught Jenna's gaze in the mirror. Her mouth hung open in terror. It was as though she'd just looked a beast of Hell dead in the eyes. Like I was a monster.

"You can wear a shawl or something," Leah said.

"No." My eyes welled with tears I struggled to blink away.

"It's not even that bad, Laila," Mom said. "It looks worse to you than it does to anyone else."

I watched Jenna's wide eyes.

My head shook. "I'm not wearing this. Somebody help me get it off."

"Laila—" Hannah began.

"Do you know what I see when I look at those?" I snapped my head around and looked between them. "You don't want to. I don't want to worry about how they look on my wedding day. I want to feel beautiful, and pretty, and strong. I'm not going to wear something that makes me feel helpless."

None of them were able to hold my gaze.

"Can someone please help me get out of this?" I asked.

Mom stood and managed a sweet smile. "Alright, baby."

CHAPTER FORTY-FIVE

LAILA

I looked up at the TV, not even really paying attention to what I was watching. The tranquil, eucalyptus scent from my wax melts settled in my nose. Sweet coconut cream flavored icing popped on my tongue. If nothing else, my wedding cake was going to be amazing.

"Hey, baby." Jeremy set some groceries down on the floor by the front door. "I didn't think you'd be home so soon. How'd shopping go?"

I stuck my fork back into the coconut cream cake. The white fluff was like a little cloud of heaven on my tongue. "I got the bridesmaids their dresses."

"Not yours?" He made his way beside me to the couch. As he sat, he stole my fork, took a bite, and passed it back to me.

I dug the fork back into the cake and pulled out a scoop. Plopping it into my mouth, I said, "Nope. Not mine."

"Why not?" He teleported a fork into his hand and took a bite from the cake.

"Because I looked disgusting in everything."

He smiled. "I'm sure you looked amazing."

I laughed. He'd say that no matter what. And it was sweet. But that didn't make it true. Nothing I tried on looked good. I'd stepped into a few ballgowns and felt like an idiotic ball of tulle. I'd tried a few flowy, A-lines that I'd have adored a few months before. The only one I did like was that first one. But the back ruined it for me.

"Remember how you said I could wear a burlap sack if I wanted to?" He smiled, shaking his head a bit. "Well, I hope you like burlap, baby."

He took another bite of cake. "You're beautiful in everything."

"I wasn't today." I raised the entire cake to my lap and dug in for a bigger bite.

"What didn't you like?" he asked.

"What do you think?" His gaze softened. I gestured to my scars. "They're terrifying if you aren't prepared to see them. You should have seen the look on Jenna's face. There's going to be pictures, you know? I don't want to see my scars in them. That's all I'm going to see if they aren't covered."

He lifted the cake from my lap back to the table. "I bet you looked gorgeous." His lips moved to mine and his hand found my neck.

"From the front, I really did," I said. "Do you think I could just cut all of the skin off my back and have Leah heal it?"

He gave a bare smile. "I don't think that would work, baby."

Honestly, I didn't see why it wouldn't. Although, I guessed I could bleed out. That wouldn't be ideal.

"I just hate them so bad."

He pushed hair from my face and gently kissed me again. "You're so much more than those scars."

"I know that." I pulled back a bit to meet his gaze. "But they're hideous. The ones on my arms, and my neck, and going down my body, I don't mind as much. I still don't want to see them in my wedding dress, but they don't look as brutal. They *weren't* as brutal. The ones on my back are just…"

Jeremy licked his lips and bit the lower one. He pushed hair behind my ear. "I'm sorry you have to go through this, Lai."

I leaned forward and rested my head on his chest. "I'll be alright. I just have to find a dress."

He kissed my head and circled his arms around my waist. "Do you want me to come with you?"

"No. You're just going to say I look good in everything and you know nothing." I made a shooing motion.

He chuckled. "Because you do look good in everything."

"Laila," I heard Leah call from the open stairway.

"Where you at, lady?" Jenna said behind her.

"In here." I leaned off of Jeremy into a sitting position.

They made it through the doorway. Jenna carried a long dress in a black bag. Leah stood beside her with a sewing machine in a giant sewing kit. They both wore wide smiles, eyes meeting mind.

"What's all this?"

Jenna gave an excited grin. "You loved this dress."

"The first one?" I stood. "But the back—"

"That's why we got the sewing machine," Leah said. "Most of it's going to be hand sewn, but we brought it just in case."

"What are you talking about?" I crossed my arms. "That dress was four thousand dollars, guys, who bought it? And what do you mean hand sewn?"

"Jeremy, you need to get out of this apartment. And don't come back until we give you the okay," Leah said.

"Alright, I can take a hint."

"We're serious," Jenna said. "Stay out of here until further notice."

"Alright, alright." He stood.

"You can thank us later," Jenna said.

Jeremy kissed my cheek. Then he started to the door.

As he went downstairs, I looked between them. "There's no way to cover the scars in that dress."

"We have a plan," Leah said.

"And if you hate it, you didn't pay for it. Just find a new one," Jenna said.

"What's your plan?" I asked as Leah hung the dress up on the curtain rod. "And why didn't you have to wait for it to come in?"

"They sold us the one you tried on because it was already your size. We explained the situation, that the wedding is soon and we don't have time to make the alterations we need to before the wedding if we have to wait for it to come, gave them a big sob story," Jenna said.

"All you have to do is put it on and let me make some marks on your back." Leah turned to meet my gaze. "This was your dress, Laila. And no one's going to take that from you. We're going to make it yours."

"How?" I asked.

"I teach the embroidery club at school." Jenna smiled.

"And I can draw." Leah gave a similar smile. "Just trust us, alright? Let us do the work, you judge the final product."

I had no faith that they could make that dress work. We'd all seen it. It was sheer. My scars stood out like Carrie on prom night beneath the fabric.

But Leah was a half decent artist. And I knew Jenna could sew. I thought I'd hate it. But if they thought they could make it work; I'd let them try.

I thought for a moment. "Fine, but I'm getting drunk."

"Just don't spill anything on the dress that costs more than my car," Leah said.

"Clear liquor. Got it."

CHAPTER FORTY-SIX

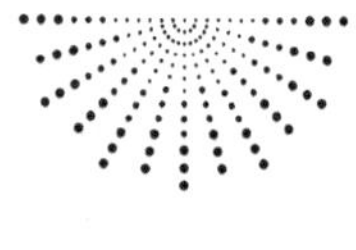

LAILA

While wearing the dress, I lay on my stomach. Leah spent about an hour drawing against my spine with an array of markers. It hadn't been exactly comfortable, but my bed was comfy enough.

Once Leah had finished, Jenna began stitching at the dining room table. And I sat with my cake. Such a damn good cake.

"Lai," Jenna said.

"Hmm?" I looked up and sipped my martini.

She turned up from my dress. "I'm sorry I looked at you like that."

Of course, I knew what she meant. But I didn't want to get into all of that. It was what it was. I knew how my back looked. I knew it was scary, I knew it wasn't pretty. Her reaction was what I expected from anyone seeing it for the first time without prior knowledge of what'd happened.

I bit into another piece of cake. "Huh?"

She frowned. "Earlier. At the bridal shop. You saw my expression when I saw your back. I saw it break your heart and I'm sorry."

"Oh," I muttered. I was too tipsy to really care either way. "Yeah, it's okay. They're creepy, I know."

"It isn't that." She set her needle down and took a sip of water from the glass on the table. "I just didn't realize how bad it was. I saw the other scars, but no one told me about that. I didn't know how much you went through."

"It's okay. I know they aren't exactly attractive."

She searched my gaze. "What happened to you, Lai?"

I looked away and stabbed another bite of cake onto my fork. Shaking my head, I shrugged a bit. "I don't want to talk about it."

Jenna licked her teeth. I felt her gaze on me, but I didn't return it. "You're my little sister. And I feel so far away from you."

I took another forkful into my mouth. "The details would keep you up at night, Jen. Believe me when I tell you that it's better for everyone if you don't know."

She narrowed her gaze a bit. "You want to tell me, I can see it."

She wasn't wrong. I'd wanted to tell her for years. But I wanted to keep her safe more. I didn't want her to know everything that I did. I didn't want her to know that we weren't technically related. I especially didn't want her to know that our father was not her dad.

I took another sip from my martini. "It's complicated."

"We were close once." Her soft blue eyes held mine. "Weren't we?"

I smiled. "We were."

"And I don't know you anymore, Lai," she murmured.

"It's been a rough couple of months. I'm going to try to do better keeping up with everyone. It's just been hard."

"It's been more than just the past couple months. Try the past couple of years," she said. "I thought it was Jeremy at first. I wondered if maybe he was controlling or something. Then I'd see the two of you together, the way you hang on each other like ornaments on a Christmas tree. The gentleness between you and I'd think that couldn't be it. Or maybe you were just so in love that you pushed your family out of the picture, but you were so involved with his family. Then I thought maybe it was just you growing apart. But then you went missing, and something changed."

I had no clue where she was heading. Had I not been drinking, I probably would have put two and two together sooner.

"I'm kind of lost here, Jen." I sipped my martini and met her gaze again.

She set the sewing needle down and straightened up. "It didn't make sense. Your abduction was so perfect. Calculated and precise." Jenna studied me. "You're a nobody. You own a little diner in the middle of nowhere. No one wanted ransom, but they were careful to abduct *you*. Not Hannah, the pretty little eighteen-year-old. So, sex trafficking seemed unlikely."

I started to see it then. The gears behind her eyes were shifting faster than a rollercoaster's. She knew something.

"Still not following," I murmured.

"Jeremy, Leah, even Adam. His whole family, really. Mom too. Everyone gave me this look when I said something about holding onto hope for you. They said that you were alive. Like they *knew*." Her unwavering gaze stayed locked with mine. "No one could have known you were alive. I'm your sister, I held onto hope obviously. But I was starting to get scared when the cops gave up. Then I'd see Jeremy and he was just so... I don't know. He looked awful, Laila. Almost remorseful. And I wondered if he had something to do with it for a while. I tried not to, but you should have seen him."

That stung. Jeremy was many things, but never abusive. "He would never hurt me, Jen."

"I know that now. But at the time, it made sense. But it didn't make sense, too." She chewed her jaw. "Mom would meet up with him from time to time. They'd have coffee or lunch. And when I told her my suspicions, she was almost appalled. She insisted that Jeremy was in love with you and that he'd never hurt you. And I knew Mom couldn't be a part of it, you're her baby. But she wouldn't explain their meetings. She had no reason to meet him and it was weird. Sometimes she'd come back seeming uplifted, and other times, she came back distraught. Almost like she was getting updates."

I furrowed my brows. Then I began to realize what she was getting at. She figured it out. "What do you mean?"

"It was strange, Laila. It *is* strange." She squinted at me. "Should I go on?"

"I don't understand."

Obviously, I knew exactly what she was getting at. But I wasn't going to tell her a word before I knew what she knew.

A smile pulled at her lips. "Alright, you're going to play dumb. I get it. I'll keep going then." She cleared her throat and leaned forward in her chair. "It got *really* weird when you were gone. Ray, that's his name, right? That Mexican cop?"

"Ray Ramirez."

"He had been working on your case already, conferring with Jeremy's family, which I also found weird. He didn't reach out to me so I reached out to him. Actually, I didn't just reach out, I went to his office. And when I introduced myself, he referred to me as 'one of your sisters.'" Her gaze narrowed a bit. "To my knowledge, I'm your only sister. Aside from your soon to be in-laws, anyway. And I would have just chocked it up to a misuse of words but I knew you were friends. He knew you, he knew you only had one sister. But not even just that, he started to stammer when I corrected him. He was nervous, Laila. He realized he used the wrong word and it made him worried. It clearly wasn't just a misuse of word. Then I met Celena and I couldn't help but notice some resemblances between the two of you. The little heart shaped face, the plump lips you definitely didn't get from Mom. And then that kid, Kai, I think? Really fucking bizarre how he looks so much like Dad."

She held my gaze, carefully watching my expression. I should have known she'd figure it out eventually, but I hoped that she wouldn't. I didn't want her to have to live with the burdens that I did.

"For a while, I was sure you were dead. So, when Mom woke me up at four a.m. to tell me you were alive, I just about shit myself. I cracked up all of my paranoia to just that. But then we saw you in the hospital and I...

"I heard people talking. The other ones that got out. And they were talking about you. Like you were some God or something. They were talking about all the people you saved and I... I knew something wasn't right. There was a bigger picture here. Way bigger than I could see. Like, why did the news barely report on you? Why was it so vague when they talked about all the people being held? And I brought it up to Mom, but she seemed to brush it off. It was like she was lying to me without really lying. Like she was keeping something from me. Something *big*."

My heart was racing and I'm sure she saw it. She was my big sister; we'd been lying to our parents together our whole lives. I knew I couldn't lie to her without her knowing that I was, but I had to try.

"Jenna, you're thinking about all of this too hard. It was just a wrong place and wrong time sort of thing," I said.

"You've always been a shit liar, Lai."

"I'm not lying—"

"Just let me finish, then tell me I'm wrong." Jenna's gaze grew more serious and less playful. "I tried to keep pushing the thought from my mind. I was still toying with Jeremy having something to do with your disappearance honestly. I still wasn't sure how and I guess I'm still not. But after visiting you in the hospital, seeing the way you laid against him, the way you held his hand... If he did play any part in it, you had some serious battered woman syndrome.

"There were just so many things that didn't add up. You told me this guy fucked someone else a few months before and then you were suddenly engaged to him. And that's not my sister, my sister doesn't let guys treat her like shit. And Mom, she was so supportive of the two of you, even after that, and I didn't understand, Laila. It didn't make sense. But then you told me you were pregnant, so I tried to excuse it. He made a mistake, you were having his baby, you wanted to have a family. I could justify it."

"That's complicated, Jen."

"But then, we got back from our trip to visit you. And you were already settled in. Okay, maybe you just got an earlier flight than us. You have money, Jeremy's family has money, maybe you could pull some strings. But almost all the flights had been cancelled or delayed because of a storm. Still, I tried to push it away.

"We were on our flight when Leah invited us to the party, and I thought it was bizarre how she was able to organize something like that so quick. To get all those people there. Some of them weren't even

Americans. But again, I pushed it away. I know you guys have money; money can buy just about anything."

"Jen—"

"But I went anyway. If for nothing else, to do some digging. I wanted to know what happened to my little sister. Everyone was keeping it from me, but I was damned and determined. I knew there was more to the story." She narrowed her gaze a bit. "Do you know where I was standing when the bomb went off?"

A lump thickened in my esophagus. "Adam said you were inside."

"I was." Her lips pulled up in a half smirk. "I was in the kitchen. Looking out the back door. More specifically, I was watching you."

My stomach sunk as the memories flashed behind my eyes.

"I saw you. Crying as you hugged all of those people, all of those strangers. I still hadn't figured out why they looked at you the way they did, but it seemed innocent enough. Then, I saw you talking to that cop and his kid. Then, happily chatting with Jeremy.

"Then that guy came over and I saw you getting angry. You lunged at him, and Jeremy broke his hand. I was so confused. I mean, I still am. But then, I saw that remote in his hand." She held my gaze. "And Jeremy was so quick to jump in front of you. But then, you were just... Gone."

Shit.

That right there was why we didn't invite humans to Christmas dinner.

"Jen—"

"Mom dropped a bottle of wine and ran over to me, but I just stood there in disbelief. I couldn't believe what I just saw, until I saw it again. All of them, all of these people, doing unexplainable things. People were disappearing and reappearing, and... Then I saw you. And Leah. Then Celena, and Kai." She chewed her cheek. "That light coming out of your hands. Holding them over those people's wounds until they were normal again."

My heart raced.

"Then I saw Jeremy chasing that guy. I didn't tell the cops I saw it because it was obvious that he was protecting you. And honestly, I don't give a damn what happens to him. Make it slow and painful for all I care.

"That's when it occurred to me that whatever role Jeremy played clearly wasn't to hurt you." Her gaze was unwavering. "Mom pulled me out of there so quick. She asked if I saw anything and insisted we go to the hospital, even though we weren't even close to the bomb. She was just trying to get me out after she saw that you were okay. At that point, it was obvious that she knew. She knows what you are and what you can do, and she doesn't want me to know. I didn't even bother asking her because I knew she would lie."

At that point, I had nothing to say. She always was the smart one. I had to have known she'd figure it out eventually. I should have had a plan, but I was completely blindsided.

She rubbed her chin, watching my reaction to every word she spoke. "I tried to talk to you. I called, and texted, and called, and you just wouldn't answer. I came to see you and Jeremy told me you didn't want to talk to anyone. I knew you were traumatized, even more than the people who were injured, so I figured I'd give you time. Then you called out of the blue and said you were getting married yesterday and I knew you were ready. I could talk to you."

"Jenna…" I began. "What you saw…"

"Don't tell me I'm crazy, Laila. I saw it." Her eyes stiffened. "I saw you. I saw you save those people."

"This is dangerous, Jen," I said. "You don't understand."

"I'm not going to tell anyone." She held my gaze. "You're my sister, I would never do anything to hurt you."

I believed that, but my chest was tight. "This is all really complicated."

"I know that. But I want you to explain it."

Leah came up the steps with a bottle of Grey Goose. I glanced her way.

"You should just tell her. She isn't gonna let it go."

I looked between the two of them. Then, I turned to Jenna. "Are you sure you want to know?"

"I want to know everything."

It was a strange feeling. Fear, obviously. I was afraid of what could happen to her. I was afraid of what she would think of me. I was, I was scared.

But I was relieved too. I'd felt so torn from my sister since 2016 when I learned what I was. And I always wanted her to know, but it made sense to keep it from her.

Yet, she'd figured it out on her own. And she wasn't scared. She looked happy. She finally understood that the wedge that had grown between us wasn't because of anything either of us had done. It was just a part of a grander scheme.

I lifted my martini and chugged until it was finished. "I'm going to need another drink for this."

"I'm on it." Leah sat at the table beside me and popped the cork out of the bottle.

"I guess we should start with Dad."

CHAPTER FORTY-SEVEN

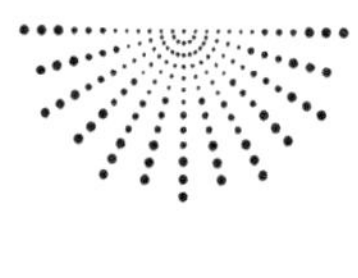

LAILA

"So, what you're saying is that Mom and Dad lied to us our entire lives," Jenna said as she buttoned the back of my gown. "About basically everything."

"Essentially," I said. "But for good reason. They were trying to keep us safe."

"And you're some fairy hybrid?" she asked.

"Not exactly," Leah said. "She isn't a fairy. She's a quarter Fae. Although, those are her most dominant abilities."

"And Fae can control the elements." Jenna waited for reassurance.

"Yes. There are six primary branches of Fae based on bloodline." I met her gaze in the mirror. "The ones who control fire, the ones who control water, the ones who control air, the ones who control earth, and the ones who control spirit."

"But that's five."

"The sixth is the Elite." Leah hopped down from her perch on the kitchen counter. "The Elites are the hybrids of the Fae. They can control all five. That's what your dad was."

"Which are you?" Jenna looked at Leah in the mirror.

"I'm from the Sprite bloodline. I control spirit," Leah said.

"So that's how you healed those people," Jenna murmured. "But I don't understand what spirit has to do with healing."

"Spirit is complicated," Leah said. "Every living creature on this planet is connected to spirit. Spirit is more like the life force that vibrates through the universe. Or at least, that vibrates through our universe. It's energy, it's connection, it's alive. It's our thoughts, our memories. It's what allows us to exist."

"And your family, what are they again?"

"Guardians," I said.

"And they teleport," Jenna said.

"Jeremy and Chris can also manipulate and create electricity," Leah said.

"Chris..." Jenna began. "Who's Chris again?"

"Our oldest brother. He was kidnapped almost a decade ago. The people who took him are the same people who took Laila," Leah said.

"And that's how they found you?" Jenna asked.

"Kind of. That's how we found each other, I guess."

Leah said, "Everyone knows Laila in our world."

"What do you mean?" Jenna looked at me in the mirror, making her way up the meticulous buttons.

"She's really powerful." Leah gestured toward me. "And after she saved all those people, her name *blew* up."

I searched for a way to phrase it and settled on, "I'm kind of a big deal."

"I knew you had to be important for someone to go through all that work to kidnap you. I knew it. What else are you?"

"My biological mother, Mary, she's an Angel. She was at Moe's funeral, you probably saw her. That's who Mom was yelling at when we got to the burial," I said. "Dad was part Fae, part Guardian. So, I'm one quarter Fae, one quarter Guardian, and half Angel."

"What else can you do then?"

I let out an ironic chuckle.

"A better question is what she can't do," Leah asked. "Can't turn coal to gold, can you?"

"Not that I'm aware of," I said. "I don't really know what else I can do yet, Jen. There's a lot I haven't quite figured out. I can teleport though, so that's cool."

"How did you figure all of this out?"

Leah laughed and grinned at me in the mirror. "Yeah, you can explain that one."

"Oh, boy." I awkwardly scratched my head.

"What does that mean?"

"Hmm, well. This is kind of hard to explain," I muttered.

"So how do you feel about soulmates?" Leah met Jenna's gaze in the mirror and sipped her vodka.

"I don't know. Never really gave it much thought."

"That's about to change." Leah chuckled.

Jenna turned back to me in the mirror. "Care to elaborate?"

"I didn't know any of this when Jeremy and I first got together. And he heard the stories, but he didn't think they were real either."

"Like I said earlier," she said. "The weirdness started after you guys got together."

"Yeah, so..." I cleared my throat. "It sounds really weird when I say it out loud."

"Pretty weird inside our heads too." Leah poured herself another glass.

"It's all pretty weird." Jenna muttered.

"Okay, so humans can't have soulmates. It has something to do with the size or the energy of the souls or something? I don't know, all of the stories were passed down word of mouth, so no one knows the real story. But even in our world, no one thought it was legit. The whole soulmate thing and all that."

"We all thought it was a myth," Leah said. "The stories of the par animarum."

"Is that Latin?" Jenna asked.

"It translates to paired souls."

"Kind of broken English, but you get the picture," Leah said.

Jenna blinked a few times. She moved her hands from my back and held my gaze. "What does that have to do with anything?"

"Legend has it when you fuck your soulmate for the first time, your powers double," Leah said from behind her glass.

Jenna creased her brows in confusion.

"It activated the powers Dad and Mary bound when I was a baby to keep me safe from all of this," I said.

She continued watching my gaze. "Jeremy. He's your... How do you say it?"

"Par animo," Leah said.

"But we usually just say soulmate."

"What does that mean?"

"A lot of things," I said.

"Remember what you were saying about how Jeremy looked when you saw him while Laila was being held?" Leah asked. Jenna gave a nod and Leah continued, "It wasn't because he had anything to do with what happened. He loves Laila more than anything, he couldn't hurt her if he wanted to. It was because he felt every awful thing they did to her as if it were happening to himself. And there was nothing he could do. There was nothing any of us could do."

Jenna's gaze softened. "Seriously?"

"Yeah. He didn't see what I saw. He didn't know where I was. But he felt it."

She was quiet for a moment, processing. "My god."

I watched her expression in the mirror. Her eyes shifted back and forth quickly, she nibbled on her lower lip. She looked confused and enthralled at the same time. The confusion definitely outweighed the fascination though, at least in that moment.

"It's a lot to take in at once," I murmured. "But I'm glad you know now."

"I'm sure I'm going to have a hundred more questions. But I need to process all of this first," Jenna said slowly.

"A lot of it comes with time."

She shook her head, as if shaking off the conversation. Then she brought a smile to her lips. "Alright, well. For now, we have a wedding to plan."

"That looks amazing," Leah said as she gazed over my back.

Jenna said, "It'll be gorgeous when it's done."

"How about you let the person who's going to be wearing it be the judge of that?"

Jenna grinned. "Let me get you a mirror. Turn around and close your eyes."

I smiled, spun around, and cupped my hands over my face. "Just tell me when."

Although I wasn't sure they could pull it off, I prayed that they would. I wanted that damn dress. It was so pretty. I felt like a beautiful, blushing bride in it. And I wanted to feel beautiful on my wedding day.

"Okay, so you're doing a flower crown, right?" Jenna asked, voice growing distant.

"Yeah, veils aren't really my thing. That whole metaphorically flipping over my purity shit isn't for me.

"Well, Leah had a great idea," Jenna said.

"Why not do a flower belt too?" Leah said. "You can grow it to the size of your waist so it won't look tacky. It'd cover a good portion of the scars. But then again, it might take away from the elegance of the gown."

"And that gave me the idea. The dress is gorgeous, but you didn't want anyone to see your scars. So how could we cover them without taking away from the dress?" Jenna placed a mirror in my hand. "Keep in mind that it isn't finished. I still need to stitch the whole right side and part of the bottom, but I think this will give you a good idea of what we're going for. If you hate it, we'll find something else."

"But I don't think you're going to hate it," Leah murmured.

"Open your eyes, sissy. What do you think?" Jenna said.

I opened them. Then I looked in the handheld mirror.

And I instantly began to cry.

It was perfect.

Leah had drawn a beautiful tree over the scars with a gray marker. The branches and leaves were placed carefully to perfectly camouflage the scars. Each line and slit was now a branch or a leaf. The ones that didn't fit into the branches were covered by vines and flowers.

Not a single scar was visible. And the image was gorgeous. It was it. It was the dress. It was *my* dress.

"Happy tears?" Jenna smiled, searching my gaze.

I smiled back, tears streaming down my cheeks. "Definitely happy tears."

"Well, get it off before your mascara ruins it," Leah blurted.

CHAPTER FORTY-EIGHT

JEREMY

Warm. I felt so warm. Like I was cuddled up in a blanket with a cup of coffee, sitting beside a fire, watching snow dance outside the window.

I wasn't though. There was no snow. No fire, no warm blanket, no toasty cup of coffee. And I certainly wasn't looking out a window. My eyes weren't even open.

A hand shook my shoulder. My heavy eyes lifted open.

"Huh?" I said.

"Three weeks, you said?" Olivia set a bottle of water in front of me.

I struggled to focus my disoriented gaze. "What?"

Olivia's eyes shifted between mine. "You're getting married in three weeks. Right?"

"Oh, yeah. Three weeks," I murmured.

She managed a soft smile. "That's exciting."

"Yeah, we're really happy about it," I mumbled.

I propped my cheek against my palm. My eyes began to close again

A warm fire. A cozy blanket. Snow dancing out the window. That's where I was. I wasn't sitting in Olivia's kitchen, not really. I was floating in another dimension. One that was peaceful. Not happy, just peaceful. Tranquil. Content.

That was a good word for it.

In my stoned reality, I was in a place of pure contentment.

"Jeremy." She shook my elbow.

"Huh?" My eyes shot open, blinking to meet her gaze.

"How much did you take?" Her eyes jerked between mine. "Are you alright?"

"No. No, I'm good." I cleared my throat. "Sorry."

Olivia's eyes moved over me in pity and her head shook. "You need to talk to her, Jeremy."

"We are," I said. "We're talking a lot more. We're good."

"I mean about you."

I still struggled to hold my eyes open. "No, I'm alright. Everything's good right now."

Olivia frowned. "You're not good, Jeremy."

"I am. I am, really," I said. "I'm not getting high every day. I'm good."

In that moment, I was *great*. I was higher than I'd been in years. And in hindsight, I hate myself for it. But in that moment, I didn't care about anything but how *good* I felt.

"Does she know you're here?"

"Leah and her sister came over to work on her dress, they told me to leave. I didn't really have time to talk about where I was going," I said.

"But does she know you've been seeing me?"

"No, but it's not like that. We aren't doing anything. She's not my parent, I'm allowed to go out with my friends."

I knew I shouldn't have been there. I knew how much it'd hurt Laila. I knew how pissed I'd be in her shoes. I knew it was wrong. But I just wanted to get high.

And Olivia's was the only place I could. She had medical training. I didn't want to die, and I knew she wouldn't let me. I was using but I wanted to do it safely and Olivia was how.

Really, I was using the shit out of her. It was fucked up and I regretted it on the deepest level. But when I was using, I was a selfish little prick.

"We aren't really friends anymore, Jeremy," she said "We're exes. And I'm still in love with you, and you know that. I can't see how she would be okay with this, even if you don't feel the same way. That's the only reason this has gone on for as long as it has. But you know that too."

"You don't think we're friends?"

She gave a bare smile. "I'm not stupid, Jeremy. I'm a place where you get high and sober up before you go back to your fiancé."

"That's not true."

It was definitely true.

"You can't keep this from her, Jeremy. She has the right to know if you're about to marry her."

"Yeah. Yeah, I know." I rubbed my tired eyes. "She's just... She's doing better, and I don't want to ruin that. I can't tear her down right now."

She gazed at me for a long moment. When the silence settled back in, my eyes fell shut again. Then she reached forward and lifted my chin. That forced my eyes open quick. She touched my face. And that was a no-go. Even as fucked up as I was, I knew that couldn't happen.

"Your pupils are pin pricks, and your lips are turning blue. I'm getting the naloxone."

"Olivia, I'm fine," I said again. "I'm not even that high."

"You can barely keep your eyes open, dude. You're falling out every other second. Stay here."

I definitely didn't want that. Naloxone plus drug addict equals instant sobriety. And why would I want to be sober? I was wrapped in a warm blanket, drinking a hot cup of coffee by the fire, watching the snow fall out the window.

"I'm okay," I murmured. My eyelids felt like sandpaper against my eyes. They were heavier than lead. Every second that ticked by, they were becoming harder and harder to keep open. But I genuinely did think that I was fine. Everything felt fine enough. It always does when you're that fucked up. "Everything's okay."

"No, you're not," I heard Olivia say. She gripped my shoulders. My vision was blurry and becoming distorted. I wasn't sure my eyes were even open.

"Jeremy." She tapped the side of my face. When I didn't respond, she moved her fingers to my neck.

I was there but not really. I could hear her, I could even see her a little bit. But it was mostly a daze. More like a dream than anything. Like one of those dreams where you can see it all so vividly as it's playing on the back of your eyelids, but you can't even remember a bit of it when you wake up.

"Damn it, Jeremy," Olivia muttered. I began to fall out of my chair and she helped me to the floor. "Fuck. Fuck, dude. Don't you die on me, alright? I'm going to get the naloxone."

"I'm fine," I grumbled again.

"No, you're fucking overdosing," Olivia said. "You aren't fine, Jeremy."

I couldn't even really see her. It was like a shadowy, blob of a human standing over me with Olivia's voice. But I grabbed her arm. "Don't tell Laila."

"Damn it, dude." She ripped her hand back. "Fuck. Fuck. Stay with me, alright? Stay with me."

I knew what I was doing was wrong and I wanted to stop. But I just couldn't bring myself to.

I didn't want to be clean. I had no interest in being sober. It hurt too much.

Even though Laila seemed better, my son was still dead. Maybe that sounds like a dumb thing to be hurt over to most guys since I never met him, but for me it was devastating. I'm sure there were thousands of guys who prayed their girlfriend would abort their unplanned child and hated the mother for ruining their partying days.

But that wasn't me. Family was everything to me. It always had been. I loved my big, chaotic exciting family. Adding to it could never be a bad thing. More life to love and protect was a blessing.

But I didn't get the opportunity to love or protect him.

If she would have miscarried, or even if she would have had an abortion, it would have been easier than that. All those months I sat there staring at that little ultrasound and praying for the day when I'd get to really see him.

Being a dad meant so much to me. And I knew I could still be a dad, but not to Micah. Not to the little boy I felt kick through Laila's belly. Not to the little boy who I'd assembled a forever empty nursery for.

It was killing me inside. I just wanted to see him. I wanted to hold him. I just wanted my fucking son.

But he was dead.

My son was dead.

I had Laila. But we couldn't even talk about our baby. She wouldn't talk to me about him at all and it fucking hurt.

Everything fucking hurt.

I just wanted to press rewind. I wanted a redo.

Sure, the oxies weren't going to turn back time. But they kind of dulled it for a while.

In that moment, curled up by the fire, sipping that warm coffee, wrapped in that blanket, I looked down. Coffee in one hand. And a little ball of warmth wrapped in blue cloth suckling on a binky in the other.

That was the moment I realized Olivia was right. I was dying.

But I wasn't just content in that moment. I had my son. He wasn't dead, he was right there. He was in my arms. And I was happy.

CHAPTER FORTY-NINE

JEREMY

A smack stung across my cheek. "Get the fuck up, you little shit."

I blinked, trying to level out my vision. The recessed lighting on the ceiling was as bright as the sun on a snowy day. I blinked again, struggling to focus on the people standing in front of me. But it was all a blur. Just forms. Bodies. Not people, just forms.

"I'm alright." I cleared my throat and slowly sat forward.

"The fuck you mean you're alright?" Adam barked.

I began to see his face through the black haze. His brows were furrowed over his blue eyes. Messy, dark hair fluttered in front of them.

"What are you doing here?" I mumbled.

"You told me not to tell Laila," Olivia said from the table a few feet away. "But I had to tell somebody."

Once the initial shock of waking up settled in, I was stone cold sober. That's what naloxone does. It instantly turns off all the opioid receptors in the brain and reverses the effects.

And with that sobriety came anger. It shouldn't have, Olivia did what she had to. She saved my life. But she told my brother. One of my fiancé's best friends.

I narrowed my gaze at her. "Cool. Thanks."

Adam handed me my jacket. "Get your coat on. We're talking."

My head shook. I raised it outward and pulled my hands through the sleeves.

"I'm sorry I woke you up," Olivia said to Adam. "I just... I didn't know what to do."

"No, it's alright. Thank you for calling. I'm glad you did," Adam said.

I struggled onto my feet. I knew she called Adam out of concern but it was still a bitch move. And then she stood there and talked about me like I wasn't in the room. At the time, I didn't see a reason to throw me under the bus like that. I took one too many, it wasn't like I was in full blown addiction.

Now, I know that I was. But I couldn't see that then. I thought I was fine. I thought I had it together. But I was far from fine.

"I'm sorry, Jeremy." Olivia said.

I laughed. "Whatever, Liv."

"You can't get high like this and not tell anyone," she said. "You can't just sweep it under the rug, Jeremy. You're an addict, you—"

"I'm fine. I just took too much; it won't happen again. You didn't need to call anyone," I said.

"You would have died if I wouldn't have been watching you." Olivia made a face. "You would have fucking died."

"I was fine—"

"Thanks again, Olivia. I'm going to take him home." Adam placed his hand on my shoulder.

"Thanks."

We spun through the air and landed in his bedroom. I started to the door. "Thanks for the lift, but I'm going to—"

"You aren't going anywhere, shit head. Sit your ass down." Adam pointed to the bed with a darting gaze.

"I'm really not in the mood for a lecture right now, Adam."

"Tough shit. Sit down," he said behind gritted teeth. I hadn't seen Adam that angry in a long time, if ever.

And it didn't feel justified. I was a grown man. I wasn't a teenager anymore. Everyone else was allowed to get fucked up as much as they wanted so why did it matter if I did too?

But he knew. Meaning that if I didn't have this conversation, he was gonna tell Laila. And she didn't deserve this right now. She was finally doing good again. I couldn't bring her back down.

I plopped onto his unmade bed and rubbed my eyes.

"I swear to God, I'd punch you right in your fucking face if it weren't for the fact that you're getting married in three weeks and Laila will kill me if I fuck your face up." Adam's lips curled down, nose twitching up in disgust. "And if it weren't for the fact that she'd feel it."

I rolled my eyes and leaned back onto my hands.

When I didn't say anything, he licked his teeth. "How long have you been fucking her?"

"Who?"

"Olivia, who else?"

I narrowed my gaze. "I'm not fucking her."

He tightened his jaw. "If that's the first place my mind went, you know damn well that'll be the first place Laila's goes too."

"Laila doesn't need to know about this," I blurted. "All it's going to do is hurt her, she doesn't need anything else on her plate right now."

"I can't just not tell her," Adam said. "You overdosed, Jeremy. You almost died."

"I didn't almost die."

I totally did. And I knew that. But admitting it would mean admitting that it was out of control. And I couldn't do that. That'd mean I had to quit, and I didn't want to.

"You needed Narcan. You did, dude, you almost died," he said. I looked away and chewed the inside of my lower lip. "You back on heroin?"

"No."

"So, pills?" he asked. "Vics? Percs?"

"Oxies." I chewed my lip until I tasted blood on my tongue.

He frowned, pulled the chair from his desk toward the bed, and sat in front of me. "How long has this been going on? Since you relapsed while she was gone?"

"No. No, that was a onetime thing."

He fell quiet for a moment. Then a slow breath left his nostrils. He rubbed the back of his neck. "So, when did you pick it back up?"

"A few weeks ago. Me and Laila got in a big fight." I licked my lips. "It wasn't even really a fight. I don't know. There was yelling, and I was screaming. Just a lot of screaming."

"Yeah, she told me about it. She said she needed that. She's been doing a lot better since then."

"I threatened to leave her. I don't know why I said that. I didn't mean it." I paused and rubbed my tired eyes. "It's like she got better because she was scared to lose me. And I would never leave her, I was just mad. I manipulated the shit out of her, and that's fucked up."

"She's tougher than you give her credit for," Adam said. "I know you want to shelter her from everything because you don't want her to get hurt, but she can handle it, Jeremy. She has to know about this."

I looked down at my cold hands. My nail-beds were still a little blue. Lack of oxygen and all that.

"She needs to know, Jeremy. You need to talk to her."

"I can't. She didn't leave the bed for a month. She's finally doing better."

"She's going to find out at some point. You know she will. It's better she hears it from you than someone else."

"No, I'm careful. I don't get high when she's around. I make sure I'm sober before I go home. The only way she'd know is if someone told her."

He got quiet for a moment. "When you guys started dating, do you remember what I told you?"

I rolled my eyes. "I don't know, you told me a lot of shit."

"I told you not to put me in a position that would jeopardize our friendship," Adam said. "Now you're putting me in a place that does just that."

"Yeah. Yeah, I know. That's why Olivia shouldn't have called you."

It got quiet again. After a long moment, Adam said, "Why are you using again?"

"I don't know."

He studied me, eyes washing over me. "This is about the baby, isn't it?"

I looked away. "In a way. It's just... I don't know. It's about all of it."

"What do you mean?" he asked.

I huffed. "Our lives are one disaster after the next after the next. I... I don't know. It's just everything. That shit that happened last year with Mary, Laila would have never had to go through if we weren't together. But she was okay, we were moving on. She was pregnant and we were working on our apartment and making a living. We built the nursery, and we bought a family car, and we were getting ready to get married. We had a normal, ordinary life for a minute. It wasn't about what we are or the wars between the races, let alone some maniac who's obsessed with my fiancé and cut out my brother's eyes." I chewed on my bottom lip. "It was just about us. Then everything happened and things just aren't the same."

"You said they were getting better," Adam murmured.

"They were. They are. I mean, Laila's doing better. Things are good between us. It feels like it used to. But I just..." I paused. "It's just not the same. I love her. I love her more than anything, you know that."

"I do."

"I'm just... I don't know. I'm happy she's better. I really am. She's smiling again and she's laughing. And she's taking care of things with the business, and she's cleaning the apartment, and she's growing some flowers in all the windowsills, and she's..." I trailed off, searching for the words. "She's more herself, and I'm so glad she's back. It felt like she was gone for so long, but she's back now, or at least mostly. And it makes me happy, but I'm also really torn up about it because it's almost like she's doing all of this stuff for me."

"But how is that a bad thing?" Adam asked. "Regardless of why she's doing better, she is. That's all that matters."

"It's not bad necessarily," I said. "I don't know, it's hard to explain. It's just not like her. She didn't even want to get married and now she wants to elope. And after that fight, she like, I don't know. I said a lot of really shitty things that I shouldn't have. I was just... I was mean. And then I went to Olivia's and I stole some of her pills and we ate pizza and we talked. It was nice because she actually cared about what I had to say. It wasn't all about Laila for once. And I was mad still, but I regretted the shit I said, and then I regretted going there, and I had to go home.

"So I did, and I get there, and it was like she did a complete one eighty. She cleaned the house, and she took a shower, and she was on the couch. And she hadn't been out of the bedroom except to go to the kitchen and the bathroom in a month. She started opening up, and she listened to me, and she said she was going to do better. And I should have told her. I should have, but I didn't. Then she kissed me. And I should have stopped her, but I didn't. And one thing led to another and before I knew it, neither of us had our pants on and I just didn't want to ruin it. She didn't want to stop, and I just... It was great, but it was like she just wanted to make me happy. She made some comment about how she didn't want to lose me too, and now I just... I don't know. It's just not her. And I feel like shit."

"So Laila," he murmured. "That's why you've been using."

"Not really. It's just... I don't know. So many things. Everything's just a mess. None of this should have ever happened. Chris should have never disappeared. Laila should have never lost the baby." I looked up and met his gaze. "I should be a new dad right now. I should be staying up all night helping her feed him, and change him, and... This just wasn't how it was supposed to go. I'm just... I'm..."

"Depressed?" Adam asked.

I rubbed my mouth. "Yeah. I'm depressed."

"2019 hasn't been your year, man."

"An understatement, but yeah."

"This year has been hell on all of us. Especially for you and Laila," Adam murmured. "But you know how bad it hurts to not know what's going on in her world. The longer you wait to tell her about your shit, the more it's going to hurt when she finally figures it out. At least you know what's happened to her. We all know what's happened to her. She just hasn't given you all the details. But this, these are choices you're making, Jeremy. You can't completely block her out of your addiction. You're an addict, you're always going to be and addict, and she knows that. She's chosen to be with you anyway. You can't marry her if you don't tell her that you're using. That isn't fair to her. One way or another, she's going to find out. When she does, if you aren't the one to tell her, it isn't going to go over well for you."

I looked down at my hands.

"You want her to talk to you about her problems, right?" Adam asked. I gave a nod. "Alright, well, you've got to give some to get some, you know? How can you expect her to open up if you won't?" When I didn't respond, he said, "Okay, let me ask you something."

I turned to meet his gaze.

"Do you want to continue to use? Or do you want that happy, normal life you were talking about?" He creased his eyes a bit.

"It isn't that black and white."

"It is though. You can't have them both. So, if you had to choose." His eyes shifted between mine. "Would it be Laila? Or would it be the drugs?"

"Obviously, it's Laila," I said.

"So, doesn't that mean you should quit using?" he asked.

I looked away. "Yeah, I guess."

"Because you can't marry her when you're in this state of mind," Adam said. "Look, Jeremy. You're my brother. I'm not going to throw you under the bus. But if you don't get clean, you're leaping in front of it."

I heard him. And I knew he was right. There was no denying that. But it's so much easier to *say* 'get clean' than it is to *actually* get clean.

"I'll make you a deal," Adam said. "I won't tell Laila about all this. She's happy and I don't want to put her through any more shit right now. I won't tell anyone else either. But only under the condition that you quit using. Because if you guys get married, and you continue to use drugs, it's going to end in one of three ways. The least likely is that she forgives you. Possible, but highly unlikely. The second, more likely than the last, is that she hates you for lying to her and divorces you. And the third, probably the most likely, is that you die. And none of those are ideal. The only way there's a happy ending is if you get clean."

Again, he wasn't wrong. That was the type of addict I was. It wasn't enough until I was at death's door. This was my fourth overdose. I wanted it to be my last.

"Yeah, I guess so."

"I can find you suboxone if you don't want her to see that you're going through withdrawals."

"I don't know if I'll need any. I haven't been using that much, the withdrawals should be pretty mild."

"You're going to get clean then?" he asked.

"Yeah," I said. "Yeah, I'm gonna get clean."

The second I said it, I did believe that. I didn't want to lose her. I loved her, I always did and always will. That never changed.

And I knew he was right. She wouldn't stay with me if I kept using and hiding it from her. Eventually, she'd figure it out. She learned everything else at some point or another, and I knew she'd find that out too.

I had to get clean.

But the instant I was out of Adam's sight, I just wanted to get high again.

CHAPTER FIFTY

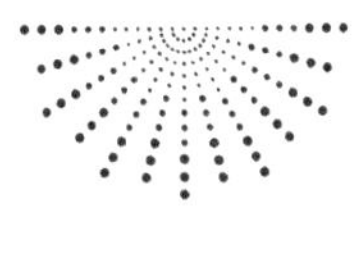

JEREMY

After Leah came home, Laila texted me and said I could come back whenever. Adam said I looked close enough to normal that she wouldn't notice, but Leah definitely would.

That being said, I high tailed it out of there before she could see me. The last thing I wanted was Leah finding out I relapsed again. She'd been pretty easy on me when Laila was captured, but I knew she'd chew my ass out for it then. Plus, there was no way she wouldn't tell Laila. Certain things she might keep from her, but me overdosing wasn't one of them.

When I made it to the living room, I heard the shower running and Laila's tone-deaf voice adorably singing along to *Helena* by My Chemical Romance. Recently, she'd been on a bit of a preteen, emo kid music kick. She didn't have a very good voice, but it sounded happy. She really was doing better. She was starting to be happy again.

It made me smile.

I lowered myself to the couch and pulled off my shoes. Adam was right, I had to choose. It was Laila or the drugs. I couldn't continue to repeatedly fall off the wagon if I wanted to keep the life we had. Losing her would kill me in a way nothing else could. She'd broken up with me before, she wouldn't be afraid to do it again.

A moment or so later, the shower turned off. I gazed at the bag of weed on the table. Aside from nicotine and caffeine, weed was the only drug I knew I could do without sending me down the rabbit's hole. Still, I pushed away the urge to smoke. Not because it would make me want to take the pills that sat at the bottom of my pocket, but because I wanted to prove to myself that I could.

Of course, weed wasn't addicting. I didn't see it and *have* to smoke it. It was more of a habitual thing. I'd sit down on the couch, smoke a bowl, maybe a joint if we weren't running low, and play a few chords on the guitar. It was my nightly routine.

But the more that I thought about not picking up that bowl, the more I thought about those pills that were burning a hole in my pocket. I wouldn't have enough time to snort them, but I could swallow them before she made it out of the bathroom. One more time before I quit forever. Just one more.

The mind of an addict was a tricky thing. I could say it was complicated, but it wasn't. It's actually pretty simple.

A lot of people seem to think that an addict chooses the drug over the people they love because they love the drug more than them, but that's not it. We love the way we feel when we're high. We love the fact that the pain kind of numbs for a while. Regardless of what the pain is from, whether it be some childhood trauma or a self-esteem issue. It's not that it takes the pain away. You still feel it, it just kind of camouflages it for a little bit. It's like for that hour or two, you can bear it. You can breathe.

It's not that we don't love our friends and family when we're using. I think about mine more when I'm high. Of course, I thought about how it would impact them if they knew I was using. That's why I hid it. I didn't want my good time to hurt anyone else in any way. I just wanted that breath. That moment where the weight lifts.

It's not that my loved ones didn't make me happy too. They did. I love them, I may've loved them even more when I was high. But in a way, those I loved contribute to that weight on my shoulders. I wanted them there, but sometimes I wanted to take the backpack off and breathe.

I wanted that feeling.

Deciding to choose the better of the two evils, I grabbed the joint laying there and held it to my lips. I found a lighter and struck it. I sparked the end and breathed in a deep drag.

A moment after I lit it, Laila came out from the hallway and plopped onto the couch beside me. She spun her legs over my lap and wrapped her arms around my neck. As she sat on top of me with the sweetest smile, a wave of guilt flooded over me.

What the fuck was I doing? I loved her more than I loved anything, why wasn't I putting her first? She'd been through the worst shit imaginable and she still managed to hold that big, happy smirk. She was climbing out of her dark place, why was I sliding further into mine?

"I was saving that, you know." She gave a playful grin.

I handed it to her. "I'm sorry."

"I'm kidding." She took it, eyes still gleaming. "Long day?"

I looked up and met her bubbly gaze. I wanted to tell her. I should have told her. But I couldn't make the words come out of my lips. I couldn't take that smile away. She'd be devastated if I told her I'd just overdosed.

"No, it was pretty uneventful." I smiled. "Why do you ask?"

She took a hit. "You just look tired."

"I'm okay. But how was your night?"

"Really good." She smiled wider.

"So you resolved the dress issue?" I asked.

"We sure did. Well, actually, *we* didn't. Jenna and Leah did. I just stood there."

"Oh, yeah?" I asked.

With a big grin, she said, "It's perfect."

"I bet it is." I smiled back. "You always look perfect."

"Shut up." She laughed.

My hand rested on her outer thigh, and my eyes shifted over hers. I kept telling myself to tell her. I had to tell her. But she looked so happy. She'd been in such a bad place and suddenly, she looked so happy. The edges of her upturned lips nearly touched her widened, glee filled eyes.

How could I tell her something I knew was going to ruin that smile?

"What is it, baby?"

"What do you mean?" I asked.

"You sighed. Why'd you sigh?" She took another hit off the joint and passed it back to me.

I could have told her. I should have just fucking told her. But I didn't.

Instead, I changed the subject to something else that was bothering me.

"Is this what you really want?"

"What do you mean?"

"Marriage," I said. "Do you really want to get married?"

She gave an awkward smile. "Of course I do. What—Do *you* not want to get married?"

"No, I do." I smiled. "I really do. I just don't want you to if you don't really want to."

"Why wouldn't I want to?"

"You didn't really want to when I first asked. And I just... I don't know. I've felt like you're doing a lot of things to make me happy lately, and I feel pretty guilty about it. I don't want you to rush into something you don't really want just because it'll make me happy."

She turned her head to the side a bit. "Baby, I've been doing these things to make *me* happy. If they make you happy too, that's a plus, but the changes I've made weren't exclusively for you. I needed to get up and turn things around. You were right when we—"

"I wasn't right." I frowned. "I was mean to you."

She gave a soft smile. "You could have been a bit more gentle, but you were still right. I was wasting my life away. I had to at least try to be happy. I started actually making an attempt and day by day, I got a little bit happier. I mean, I know I'm not in the greatest place still, but I'm doing better. I'm trying to be happy. And the wedding has helped too. It's giving me something to look forward to. I want the life we were planning before all of this. I want to marry my best friend."

A smile pulled at my lips.

She gave a playful grin. "You do still want to marry me, don't you?"

My smile became more legitimate. "Of course I do."

"But?" She took another hit off the joint and passed it back to me.

"But I just really don't want you to regret it."

And I knew that she would. As soon as she found out I'd been lying to her to go get high, she'd wish she never said yes. And I could have resolved that guilt then and there. I could have told her. But I didn't.

Laila licked her smiling lips. She looked down at her hands. She pushed hair from her face. "Can I tell you something?"

I turned my head to the side and waited.

"When I was in there, I fantasized about a lot of things I wanted to do when I got out. Eating a taco, smoking a joint, drinking a margarita." I laughed quietly. She smiled and looked up to meet my gaze. "But mostly, I fantasized about you."

My smile widened. "Oh yeah?"

"Not like that, you perv." She smacked my chest. I chuckled. "Well, okay, yeah, sometimes like that. As you know." Her grin heightened. I gave one back. "But mostly, just about moments like this. Spending time together, cuddling, watching TV. There were other things too. Like family portraits and matching family Halloween costumes," she said. "But the wedding was something I thought about a lot. This ring." She smiled and twirled it around her finger. "I thought about it a lot too. I just... I don't know. Marriage was never important to me before. But then you were so excited, and it made me excited."

My lips turned up in a true, genuine smile. I made her happy. My love for her made her happy.

Fuck, I couldn't take that away. No matter how miserable I was, I couldn't take that happiness from her. She needed it so much more than I did. She *deserved* to be happy.

"Really?" I asked.

"I knew that I wanted to spend the rest of my life with you, but the wedding part was kind of stupid to me at first. But honestly, I think it's playing a part in getting me out of this bout of depression. It's something that I *have* to do, that I'm enjoying doing. It's keeping me busy and making me happy at the same time. And just something to look forward to, ya know?"

I took her hand from her lap and twisted her fingers through mine. "I'm glad you feel that way."

Grinning, Laila settled into my lap, getting comfier. "You know what else I did today?"

"No, what else did you do today?" I asked.

"I ordered lingerie." She grinned.

I laughed. "Don't you have an entire drawer of lingerie?"

"I do, but I needed something for our wedding night. You've already seen everything I have. And none of those fit me anymore."

I smiled, hands moving from her thighs to her hips. "Yeah, and I always take them off you anyway."

"Yeah, 'cause you're lame." She rolled her eyes, but her smile stayed.

"How am I lame? I love your body, why would I want you to cover it up?"

"Because it makes me feel sexy." She leaned forward and touched her lips to mine.

"You should always feel sexy." I kissed her jaw.

She rolled her eyes. "You have to say that."

I laughed, met her gaze, and pushed hair from her face. "I say it because it's true. You're the prettiest girl in the world."

"Oh my god, Rihanna died?" She dramatically put her hand to her chest.

I laughed. "What?"

"If I'm the prettiest girl in the world, Rihanna must have died."

"Ha ha, you're so funny." I gave a mocking grin.

Fuck, I couldn't lose her. I had my girl back. She was herself again, or at least as close to it as she would ever be. I had to keep it together. I couldn't fuck things up.

I had to stay clean. I had to. I had to get it together, and I had to stay clean. If I wanted her, I had to stay clean for her. And I did, I wanted her.

But that was far easier said than done.

I'd been using on a semi-regular basis. Being high wasn't a distant memory from my adolescence anymore. It was recent and it felt so damn peaceful.

Laila made me feel *good*. But drugs made me content. Numb. They brought me back to that fire, bundled up in a blanket, with my son in my arms.

CHAPTER FIFTY-ONE

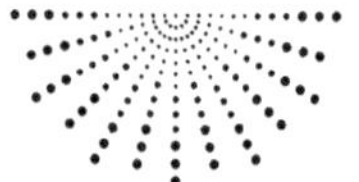

SEPTEMBER 16, 2019 - LAILA

Blaring alarms vibrated in my ears. Sweat puddled against my clammy skin. Flashing red lights burned against my eyes. It didn't smell like cleaning agents though. It smelled like dust and debris.

I was there again.

But I wasn't staring up at a stainless-steel ceiling. Instead, I was staring up at a dark blue sky with white and gold twinkling stars.

My heart pounded against my chest. I shot forward. Waves clapped against the shore ahead. The room itself was gone, only the floor and that wall with the fucking steel door remained.

Humid summer air filled my nostrils. The salt in the water coasted up from the shore. My fingers gripped the cool metal table.

I *felt* that table beneath my fingertips. I could feel the wind in my face. I heard that ringing from the alarm in my ears just as I had that day. I tasted iron on my tongue. I smelled the familiar scent of burnt flesh.

I was there. I was *fucking* there.

I even felt the burn in my legs as I pulled myself to my feet.

I tried to teleport, but it wasn't working. It was as though that ability was numb. The way my tongue and jaw felt after a trip to the dentist for a filling.

I walked to the edge of the building and tried to spin the air toward me to create a vortex to catch me. It failed just as teleportation had. Then I tried to bring a flame to my hand, and it wouldn't ignite either.

My stomach churned. My heart slammed against my ribs. I gazed off the edge.

How was I here? What was this? What was happening?

Beep.

Click.

My heart sunk and my breathing grew short.

I spun back to the wall with the door.

A white light brighter than the sun shined in from the small window. I raised my hand as a makeshift visor. The door slowly inched open.

Standing no more than three foot off the ground was a small, glowing person.

"Why did this happen, Mommy?" a little voice said from the glowing orb.

"Micah?"

"Why did this happen, Mommy? Why is he doing this?"

I darted across the room.

But once I was close enough to touch him, a light blue shield of electricity formed at the door frame just before his glowing form. As I made contact with it, I fell backward to the cold floor I remembered all too well.

The door was open, but I was still locked in that room.

"You love me, right, Mommy?" His quiet little voice rang through my ears.

Tears dribbled from my eyes. I brought myself to my knees as close to him as I could get. I reached outward and touched the forcefield, hot pain shooting up my arms.

"I do, baby," I said. "I do, I love you so much."

"Then why did you let this happen?" he said. "Where are you, Mommy? Why aren't you here?"

"I'm right here, Micah. I'm right here, baby." I pushed my hands as far as I could into the force field.

Smoke rose where they met. My hands hurt so bad. But I had to get through it. I had to get as close to him as I could. I had to hold him. I had to see his face beneath that white light. I just had to get to my baby.

"We can't let this happen." He reached his small, glowing hand out toward the force field. But his glowing white hand stopped against it too. "I need you, Mommy."

"I'm so sorry." Tears overwhelmed my eyes. "I'm so sorry, Micah. Please forgive me. Please, please forgive me. I'm so sorry."

"What are you doing there, buddy?" Peterson's sickening voice said. Out of the corner of my eye, I saw his neat black slacks dangle around his legs. His thin white lab coat flowing in the wind.

But I kept my gaze on my son. That piece of shit didn't matter, only my baby mattered.

"Just talking to Mommy, Daddy," Micah said.

My stomach spun. My head shook. I pushed harder into the wall of sparkling energy.

"That's not your daddy." I furiously shook my head. I frantically searched for his gaze through the bright white light. "He's the reason this happened, Micah. He's the reason. He hurt us. Don't believe anything he tells you—"

"That's enough, Laila." Peterson put his arm around what must have been Micah's shoulders. Then he pulled him into his hip, leaned down, and kissed his head.

"Don't touch him!" I thrusted my fists into the force field, ignoring the pain. "Don't fucking touch my son!"

Peterson pushed his glasses up. He looked down at me like an angry gorilla at the zoo. My hands stung like I'd just submerged them in a vat of battery acid but I kept punching. I had to get through it, I had to get to my baby.

"Your son?" Peterson smiled. He tucked his arms around the bright white form and lifted him to his hip. The white light wrapped around Peterson's neck. Peterson grinned. "This is *my* son."

"No, he isn't!" I slammed my fists into the force field again and again. "Just give him back! Just give me my baby!"

He laughed. And I sobbed.

"You made the wrong choice, Laila. You could have had it all." His hand stroked what must have been Micah's head beneath the light. "I'm sorry your Mommy is the way she is, buddy. But I promise she'll come back one day."

"Just give me my son back," I bawled, hands and forearms now charred from hitting the force field. "Please just give me my baby. Please. Please give me my son."

"You don't deserve him. You won't allow him to be who he has to be." Peterson frowned. "You still have so much to learn, Laila."

"Please." Tears poured down my cheeks. "Please give me my son back. Please, I'll do anything, Peterson. Just give me my baby. I just need my baby."

"Laila," Jeremy said. "Laila, it's a dream. Wake up, baby. It's okay, you're okay."

My eyes fluttered open. No more flashing lights, only dull blue moonlight through the curtains. No more iron on my tongue or salty water in the air. No cold cement floor, only soft sheets.

But the smell of burned flesh lingered.

His concerned blue eyes searched mine. He held my flaming palms to the sheets.

That must've been the pain I was feeling in my hands. I wasn't smacking a forcefield, I was burning my fiancé.

I gasped and pulled away. My tears turned to hyperventilating sobs. He released my hands "I—I'm sorry, you were hitting me."

"No, no. I'm sorry." Struggling to catch my breath, I grasped his hands and sent white light into them. "I'm so sorry."

Once the blisters healed, he reached forward and wiped my cheek with his thumb. His gentle gaze shifted from my left eye to my right. He pushed messy brown locks behind my ear.

"Do you want to talk about it?" He gently thumbed away my tears. I bit my trembling lip. The tears started to pour. His eyes softened. He soothed his thumb against my cheek. "Hey. Hey, it's okay. It's okay, baby. You don't have to talk about it. It's okay." Knotted black hair fell in his eyes. "It's okay, baby."

I clamped my chattering teeth together. "Can you just hold me?"

His eyes grew even more dove-like. "Yeah, baby. I'll hold you." He lowered himself beside me, wrapped his arms around my shoulders, and pulled me close to his bare chest.

Teeth chattering, I placed an arm around his back. I hadn't quite caught my breath but I wasn't hyperventilating.

I breathed slowly. *In and out. In and out, Laila.*

He didn't say anything, he just held me tight.

After a few quiet moments, I quietly broke the silence. "It felt so real."

He gently kissed my hair. "I know, baby."

I nuzzled my face into his neck. "I didn't mean to hurt you."

"I'm okay." He ran his fingers against my back. "We're okay."

I bit my trembling lip and closed my eyes. "I thought I was doing better."

"You are, baby." He kissed my hair again. "It was just a nightmare. We all get them sometimes. That doesn't mean you aren't doing better. You're doing great."

I held my breath to keep a sob from escaping.

"It's okay, Laila." He pushed hair behind my ear and kissed my forehead.

I turned up to meet his gaze. His hand found my cheek. The other held the small of my back. "I wish none of it ever happened."

He frowned. "Me too, baby."

I laid my head back against his chest. "You have an alarm set, right?"

He kissed my hair again. "I do."

"Thank you for being so understanding."

"Always," he whispered. He kissed my forehead one more time and laid his head back to the pillow. "I love you."

"I love you too."

CHAPTER FIFTY-TWO

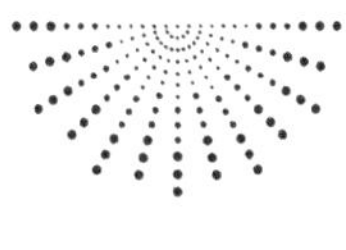

LAILA

The sweet scent of yeast and bacon filled my nose. Warm, inviting sunlight shined against the grayish white granite countertops. Java lingered on my tongue. Bird chirped outside the open window. A hot breeze coasted in from the screen.

Footsteps peddled in the hall. I turned from the window. Jeremy stifled a yawn, knots of black waves falling in his face. He stretched his arms above his head, T-shirt riding up to show his pale chest.

I supposed I shouldn't have felt so bad about being so skinny. It's not like my man had much meat on him either. Not sure what it was about skinny white boys with long hair, but they always did something to me. That isn't to say I'd mind some muscles, he used to have those. But he was pretty cute like this too.

"Good morning." I smiled.

He touched his lips to mine and slid his hand around my waist. "Morning, baby."

"There's coffee." I gestured toward the pot by the sink.

He glanced around the kitchen. I raised the plate of waffles from the counter and held it out in front of him. "And waffles too?" He grinned.

I smiled. "And bacon and eggs."

"Are we having company?" He picked up a waffle and took a bite.

"No, I'm just really bad with portions."

He smiled and grabbed a couple plates from the cupboard. "What's all this for then?"

This was because I lay in bed for three hours unable to fall back to sleep after that dream. At some point, I had to stop staring at the ceiling. So I got up, washed two loads of laundry, dusted the living room, mopped the floors, and made breakfast. But he didn't need to know all of that. Then he'd worry about me. And he didn't need to. I was okay. I just couldn't sleep.

"I don't know, I was just in the mood to cook. And I figured I should eat a big breakfast since my bachelorette party's tonight. I need something in my gut to throw up later."

He tossed another waffle to his plate and poured some syrup over them. "That's probably a good move."

I swiped one and bit into it. "I thought so."

He walked to the dining area and sat. "So, what are you guys doing tonight?"

I lifted the scrambled eggs off the heat and pulled the bacon from the microwave where I'd set it a few minutes before to stay warm. I started toward the dining table and sat beside him. "I don't really know. I didn't plan it. Do you know what you guys are doing at yours?"

"No, they won't tell me anything." He sipped his coffee. "Honestly, the whole thing is kind of weird. Just because I'm not married doesn't mean I'm not in a relationship. Why do we start out marriages with a party that could potentially destroy the marriage?"

I laughed. "I'm not worried about that."

"No?"

"Nah."

A boyish grin crept up his cheeks. "Well, that's mature of you."

Shrugging, a half-smile lifted my lips. "I mean, Brody's going to be there. So, I'll definitely find out if you do some shady shit."

He laughed. "I'm not going to do any shady shit."

"I know, baby." I leaned in and kissed him. "I trust you."

His smiled warmed my heart. "So, what are your plans today?"

"I'm meeting Ray at my Mom's and Lydia is going to help decorate." I raised my cup to my lips. "Cutting flowers to make bouquets and growing them back and what not."

"That's probably good for her." Jeremy's phone buzzed on the table. He reached for it and scrolled for a second.

"I don't know, I guess we'll see. Ray asked me if she could help so here we are. What about you? What are you doing today?"

"Apparently, I'm going shopping." He shuttered his phone. "Leah said my slacks have a hole in them and there's a rip on the sole of my nice shoes. I guess I'm also supposed to buy you a gift?"

"That's a thing?"

"I don't know, according to Leah it is."

"Shit, does that mean I have to get you a gift?" I asked.

He kept his brows raised as he laughed. "I don't know."

"Well, ask Leah." I gestured toward his phone.

He picked it up, typed for a moment, then set it back on the table. "Maybe we should have just eloped."

"I told you so." I lifted my coffee to my lips and sipped.

"Why do weddings seem like so much fun?" Jeremy muttered. "This is like a second job."

"Again, I told you so."

"Yeah, yeah. I know. You're always right."

"Not always. But often."

He chuckled and his phone vibrated on the table. "So, yeah, I guess you're supposed to get me one too. And I'm supposed to get a gift for all the groomsmen, and you're supposed to get a gift for all your bridesmaids."

My eyes widened. "What?"

"That's what she said." Jeremy rubbed his mouth.

"The wedding is in three days," I said. "Why didn't she tell me this?"

"In all fairness, you specifically told her that she was a guest and not a planner."

"I did, huh?"

"You did."

I laid my head to the table. "Well, fuck me."

"I mean, let me drink my coffee first but I'm down." He grinned and took a sip. I flipped him off. He laughed. Then he put his hand on my back. "We have Prime so, you know. Two-day shipping."

"This is true."

I hadn't just cooked the big breakfast because I needed to stay busy. It played a large part. But the other part was because I woke up and couldn't stop reliving that dream. I kept seeing that glowing white body and hearing Micah say, *"Why did you let this happen, Mommy?"*

Then I thought about the look on Jeremy's face as he held my burning hands to the bed. I thought about that pain soaring up his arms into mine. I thought about how it wasn't fair to him either. And I wanted to do something to make it up to him.

After a moment, I said, "I'm sorry I burned you."

He shrugged, munching on a waffle. "Better me than the thousand-dollar bed. At least you can heal me."

"Still. I don't know why that happened. I haven't done that in so long."

He reached out for my hand and reassuringly twined our fingers together. "Your body responds to fear. And in your dreams, your body doesn't realize there isn't a threat. It's normal after what you've been through. It's okay, Lai. I'm fine."

"It just felt so real. I... I felt like I was really there."

"Night terrors do that." He ran his thumb over my knuckles.

"It was just different somehow."

He met my gaze. "What was it about?"

"It was weird. I don't know, I was back in my cell. Or *a* cell, I guess because the ceiling was gone from where I'd blown the roof off, so it wasn't *my* cell because I destroyed that one." I paused. "Then the door opened, and Micah was there. I just... I don't know. I know it wasn't. But it felt real."

He tightened his hand around mine. "He would be a little small to stand."

"He was older. Maybe three or four?"

Jeremy smiled softly. "What did he look like?"

I gave a similar smile. "I don't know. I never really saw him."

"Not even when he was born?"

I looked down. "When he came out..." I cleared my throat. "He was like, glowing. Like this little ball of light."

He licked his lips, almost smiling. "That's what you meant when you said he saved you."

My eyes burned with tears I struggled to keep inside. "He healed my leg. Then I was able to get out." I smiled for a moment. Then tears burned across my eyes. "I never got to see his face. Just that bright light."

He didn't say anything, just daintily ran his thumb along the back of my hand.

I wiped the edge of my eye. "I guess it's a good way to remember him, right? Just this beautiful, angelic, white light."

Jeremy smiled, eyes glistening with tears. "I wish I could have seen it."

I pulled my hand from his and turned it up to face him. "Do you want to?"

A slight, sad smile touched his mouth. "If that's okay."

Expression gentle, I extended my hands out to his. He squeezed them tight, gave a smile, and shut his eyes. I closed mine and thought back to the moment that bright light filled the room. My light in the darkness.

My hands lifted his slippery little body to my chest. I held him as close to me as space allowed. The feeling of that little body against my skin would always remain the most intimate, beautiful moment of my life.

I tried not to think about how scared I was when he didn't breathe. I tried not to remember the terror when I laid him against my thigh. Jeremy's hands tightened a bit, both of us staring down at the orb on my lap.

When I saw the blood pouring beneath my legs, I pulled my hands from Jeremy's. I opened my watering eyes and forced a sad smile. He blinked hard, tears seeping to his beard. He raised his hands to wipe the salty water from his skin. A sad smile pulled at his lips too.

"Thank you," he whispered. He reached out and put his arms around me.

"I'm sorry it took me so long."

His voice was nearly a whisper. "I'm sorry I wasn't there."

That wasn't his fault. It was mine. It would always be mine. He wanted to be. He did everything in his power to keep me safe. I'd never resent him for not being there. I'd always hate myself for it, but I'd never hold it against him.

I closed my eyes and squeezed him tighter. It wasn't much, but it was opening up. In a way, it felt like growth. Like moving forward.

CHAPTER FIFTY-THREE

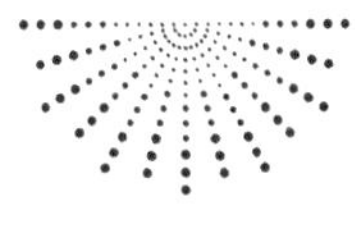

LAILA

"Baby." Jeremy squeezed my hand as we drove to my Mom's.

I looked up from my phone. "Yes, my love?"

"Did you ever get ahold of Mary?" I nodded. "And she is going to be there?"

"At the wedding?" I asked. "Yeah, I think so. Why?"

He bit his lip and breathed out a slow sigh. "I don't think I want her to be."

"You don't?"

"I was hoping she just didn't want to. And then I was just gonna suck it up but... I don't know, I just don't think I want her there."

I didn't have to ask why. And I got it. I wish I would have checked sooner, but I this was his wedding too. If he wasn't okay with it, that was okay with me.

"Oh. I guess I could call her. I'm sorry, baby. I just thought that since she was such a big part of your childhood and everything that you'd want her there."

"Yeah. Yeah, I know. There's no reason to apologize. I kind of did, I still kind of do. I'm really torn about it but I just... Mary was the closest thing I had to a mom in my teenage years after Annie died and I... I don't know. A big part of me does want her there. I love Mary, she's my family. But I just…"

"She tried to kill you, Jeremy. You don't need to explain." I twisted my fingers into his.

"It's not even that. Maybe she *was* just trying to slow me down. The only thing about that day that still pisses me off is that it's going to cost another four grand to finish fixing all the damage, even if I do the work myself." He paused. "It's the whole thing with Ally."

I realized for the first time how selfish it had been to invite Mary in the first place. What happened last October wasn't something Jeremy liked to talk about. I didn't like to talk about what happened to me either, so I understood. But somehow, it seemed to have gone right over my head. Maybe because I had grasped some understanding in why Mary did what she did. Jeremy seemed to as well, but it didn't wipe the slate clean.

"Oh, god. I'm sorry, I don't know why I thought that would be appropriate. That would be like you inviting Peterson."

"It's not really the same. Mary didn't actually do it, she just orchestrated it. I guess it's similar but…" He paused. "It's not really the same. She's practically been family since I was a kid, so it makes sense. I just… I just don't think I want her there."

"It was inconsiderate," I muttered. "Either way, I'm really sorry."

"It's okay. She's your mom. I get it, but…"

"I'll get ahold of her tonight before the party."

He stared back at the road ahead. "You know she was the first person to show up when I found my dad?"

In all the years we'd been together, that may have only been the third time I ever heard him so much as mention his father. He wasn't even the one who told me that he found his dad's body, Adam had been. I never pushed him to talk about it. It was the most sensitive subject imaginable. But I'd always been a little curious.

I held his hand a bit tighter. "No. No, I didn't know that."

"Yeah. She was our Angel then too. Actually, she was my mom and dad's. They worked a lot more cases than we do. She didn't babysit or anything, but she was around a lot.

"When I found him, he was still hanging. Dangling, more like." His face changed, brows pulling together and jaw clenching a bit. "He must have been there for a while. He was, like... Purple. And swollen. And... I don't know, he gave us breakfast before school that morning. But usually, Dad picked Chris up because the middle school didn't have a bus that reached us. Elementary school had a few kids off the main road by the house, so they took us on one of those tiny buses. Me, Adam, Brody, and like four others.

"And that day, when we were loading up onto our bus, Chris was jogging toward us because Dad didn't show up at the middle school like usual. So, he rode home with us. And when we got there, Hannah was just chilling in her play pen thing with a sippy cup. We figured Dad was in the shower and forgot or something. Chris picked up Hannah, and Adam and Brody went to the kitchen to get something to eat, and I went upstairs to look for him.

"And um." He paused as he squinted a bit before clearing his throat. "I opened his door, and I just saw him, ya know? Just hanging up there. That's Leah's room now, you know. So, I teleported up to him and then put him down on the ground, and I started crying, and screaming for help..." He grew quiet for a moment. "And then Mary was there. She had to physically pry my hands off of him. Then she teleported me out into the hallway. I kept trying to teleport back in, but she just grabbed me, and she hugged me. She wouldn't let me see him like that. It's kind of funny though, isn't it? How she gave birth to you, but you only met her a couple years ago. And that she was a motherly figure to me for my entire life up until last year."

He wiped the corner of his eye and laughed ironically. "And then she basically paid someone to rape me. Just so you would break up with me. So that our son wouldn't exist."

It was because she abandoned him. She did just what his dad had done. She chose someone else—in that case, me—over him.

That hurt him. It would've hurt me too. Granted, I probably would have said so from the start. But Jeremy was never good about coming forward with something he knew would hurt someone else.

"Jeremy." I tightened my fingers between his. "I'm so sorry you had to go through all of that."

"It sucks because I love Mary. She's family to me. You're right, she did play a huge part in my life. She made sure we didn't end up in foster care, she helped Annie get the deed to the house. She saved my life more times than I could count. She helped me with so much. And I do, I really do love her." An audible sigh left his lips. "And I think that she loves me too. But her kind of love is vastly different than mine and yours. She sees everything in black and white. She doesn't... She's just... I just don't want her at our wedding."

"I completely understand, baby."

My mom wasn't exactly ecstatic about her being there either. I only invited her because I knew *she* wanted to be there.

But I understood Jeremy's perspective too. She hurt him. It was his wedding too. He didn't have a say in most things, but he deserved a say on that.

CHAPTER FIFTY-FOUR

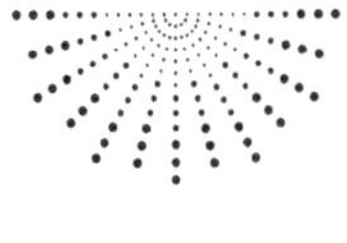

LAILA

The smell of daisies and roses wisped up my nose. Hot summer air brushed my cheeks. My gaze shifted over the soft petals in my hand. The peaceful sound of water falling along the rocks in the creek drifted to my ears.

Lydia and I sat on the back patio of Mom's old cottage styled home. It had been mostly quiet so far. She said hello when she first arrived, she politely said thank you when I set her lemonade and cookies onto the iron patio table.

But she seemed disinterested. She would trim the flower, gently set it down, sigh, grow its blossom to its peak of beauty, cut it again, carefully lay it on the ground, and sigh again. It was a sad, tiring loop.

As she laid the white rose down on top of the last, I said, "Lydia."

Her soft blue eyes turned up to mine. "Yeah?"

"Are you having fun?" I asked.

She nodded and turned back to her flowers. When she laid another down, she sighed once more. I cleared my throat and gently put my hand on her shoulder. "You don't have to do this with me, kiddo. If you don't want to be here, I can take you home. Or I can have your dad come pick you up."

"No, it's okay. We have a little apartment, so I don't get to use my powers very much. I have my plants in the house but it's small and... I like to use my powers. It just makes me sad sometimes."

I sighed with her as I grew the flower's bud again. I knew exactly what she meant. Sure, it was lovely to use my abilities. I loved it most of the time. But then I'd remember how I learned to use them and...

"Yeah, it makes me sad sometimes too."

"I bet it makes you sadder than me," she muttered. "I remember the first time you made something grow."

"So do I."

I did remember. But I didn't even know what I'd done. I felt him whipping me, I heard his voice, then I screamed and felt the earth shake. I heard a loud boom. Then a scream. Then silence. And then, Peterson's voice telling me how beautiful what I'd done was.

"I never liked that guard," Lydia said. "He yelled a lot."

A strange thing to say about murder. But hey, those were our lives.

She was such an odd little girl. I wasn't sure how to communicate with her yet. She saw me at the most vulnerable point in my life. She'd always have those images of me in her mind, and she didn't hate me for it. That's was the strangest part. She almost respected me for all those lives I'd taken.

I cleared my throat as I trimmed the rose blossom. "So how are you adjusting to living with your dad?"

"Pretty good," she said. "I like my dad. I didn't remember him that much, but he's nice to me. He was when I was little too. I was really sad when Mom told me he was dead. I think he was too. He really loves me," she said. "More than Mom did."

Deciding to weigh on the positive rather than the negative, I said, "He really does, kiddo."

"I always thought Mom really loved me too." She shook her little head. "But I guess she didn't."

I closed my eyes. Clearly, one of us couldn't focus on the positive. We had to address the elephant dancing through the garden.

My gaze turned to Lydia's. "Do you want me to talk to you like you're a kid? Or like you're my friend?"

She turned and set the scissors down. "Like you're my friend."

I shifted from my kneeling position onto my butt lotus style. She did the same, facing my direction, little arms holding her knees.

"I never got to be a mom, Lydia," I murmured. "But even when I was in that prison, when I was being tormented every single day, I still wouldn't hurt my baby. No mother would. Your baby means everything to you when you're a mother."

She looked down. "Not to my mom."

"The only way it doesn't is if you're very sick in the head," I murmured. "Something goes wrong in your brain to be able to do what your mom did. All of those horrible things you saw that you never should have. Those scars you're going to have to live with every day for the rest of your life," I said. Her eyes came to mine. "That bullet that you still feel inside of your chest. To do something like that to your baby, you have to be sick, Lydia."

"Will she get better if she takes medicine? Because maybe if she could get better, she could come back home. Maybe we could all be better together."

No. She wouldn't. But I wasn't going to take away the hope of a child. "I don't know. Maybe one day."

Her gaze turned to the ground. "Do you still feel it sometimes? The way I still feel that bullet?"

"Sometimes."

She turned back to the rose bush. She tilted her wrist to me. "Do you know why he put mine in?"

"No, I don't."

"When I was six, before we had that window in our room," she said carefully, as if trying to remember every detail, "I walked into the room Mommy went into and saw them..."

"The stress tests?" I asked quietly.

"I tried to run away. I didn't know what they were doing before, but when I did, I got really scared. I didn't get really far, but the guards shot me with one of those little darts. I woke up and he... He said that they were for my own good. So that he could always find me."

"Well, they're gone now. He can never find you again."

"I know. And I know I shouldn't, but I miss them."

My lips turned downward in a frown. "You miss your Mom?"

"Even the doctor sometimes. He wasn't always mean."

It sent a chill down my spine. But she wasn't wrong. Peterson did have a certain degree of kindness to him. In another life, he may have been a good man. In mine, he was the villain. He always would be. Still though, he had played a big part in Lydia's upbringing. He helped raise that little girl. I understood how she could miss him.

"It's okay to miss them. We all love someone whose hurt us."

Lydia lifted a rose to her hands. She carefully pulled off each petal and let them flutter to the ground. "I wish I didn't. I wish none of it ever happened."

"Yeah. Me too, kiddo." I chewed my cheek. "But since you've been through so much, you're going to be so strong when you grow up." I gave a smile. "I didn't even know how to use my powers at your age, let alone do what you do with them."

"It's just a part of me."

"A great part of you."

CHAPTER FIFTY-FIVE

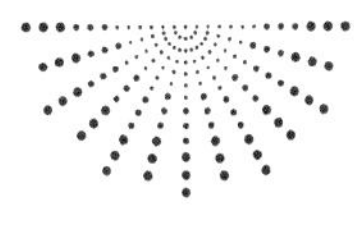

LAILA

My gaze shifted around my overcrowded bedroom and a smile eased up my cheeks. All my sisters sat around sipping wine with smiles and letting out billowing laughs. Halsey played over the Google Home speaker on the dresser. And I was just so happy. Life felt normal.

It'd been a hell of a year. But I made it out on the other end. I was gonna get my happy ending with my favorite people by my sides. Before the week was over, I was going to be married. I was going to be lying in this bed with my husband. And I was going to be able to call every woman in the room my sister.

I lifted my glass of wine and finished it off, tasting Moscato on my tongue. Hannah grabbed the bottle from the nightstand and filled it back up. "Thank you."

She smiled back. "How excited are you?"

I grinned and raised my glass to my lips. "It'll be a good time."

Jenna laughed, plopping onto the bed beside me. "I think we're more excited than you are."

"It's just kind of arbitrary," I said. "Jeremy's already my partner. I mean, yeah, it'll be nice that we'll be recognized as a married couple instead of just two people that are together. But the party's more for you guys than us. I just wanted to go up to the courthouse, sign the paper, and call it a day."

"For such a hopeless romantic, I'd expect you to be more enthused by all of this." Celena dropped to the bed beside me.

I laughed. "I'm not really a hopeless romantic."

"Bullshit," Leah said. "You're the happiest person I know."

"No, I'm really not." I laughed again.

I genuinely wasn't. Prior to Jeremy, my interest in love was pretty slim. I'd always thought of relationships as time consuming and a tad bit silly. Now, I'm incredibly grateful to have a partner that would fight, kill, and die for me. Then though? It freaked me the fuck out.

Not that I thought falling in love was bad. It was just strange. Why were people conditioned to believe that falling in love and legally binding themselves to another person was the ultimate goal in life? Having kids, that always seemed fun. But changing my name to fit into someone else's family? No, that was weird. Wasn't a fan.

Still though. I was grateful for the tax break I'd get next year.

"Yeah, she really isn't," Jenna said. "Laila was never into love stories and fairytale endings before Jeremy."

I gave a smile and looked down at my engagement ring. "Just ask Adam how I felt about love before Jeremy came into the picture."

"I believe that," Hannah said. "But I'm glad my brother found you."

I smiled and sipped my wine. "Yeah, me too."

Jenna gave a quiet laugh. She laid her head onto my lap, holding her wine on her chest between her fingertips. "Hey, do you remember when we were kids and we made a pact that we were never going to get married?"

"Sorry to break my covenant." I grinned. "In a lot of ways, I still don't like the concept. But I don't know, it feels right with Jeremy."

"Speaking of which, I wonder what the guys are doing right now," Celena said.

"Probably stuffing ones into some stripper's G-string," Leah said.

I laughed, envisioning Jeremy's face turning red as he awkwardly looked away from the naked girl dancing in the middle of a room. We may have both gotten around when we were younger. But in all the time we'd been together, I couldn't think of one time I'd witnessed him check out another girl. I did, I definitely did. But I never caught him doing it. Not that I really cared one way or the other, but it was still a sweet sentiment.

Hannah tilted her head. "I wonder how Kai feels about strippers."

"Probably pretty grossed out," Leah said. "Modesty is pretty important in the Fae Realm."

"Yeah, he's probably as uncomfortable as Jeremy." I shifted to the edge of my bed. "I mean, Kai's a very gentle person. I can't see him being enthralled by a naked girl gyrating around."

"Yeah, he's a prude," Hannah said under her breath.

Celena laughed. "He seems like a missionary only kind of guy."

"I wouldn't know," Hannah muttered.

They'd been together for almost a year now. And call me a whore, but there's no way I'd have gone that long without fucking the guy I shared a bed with. "What do you mean?"

"They haven't had sex," Leah said.

"Shit, really?" Celena asked. "Me and Wyatt fucked before we even had a title."

"Not everyone is a hoe like me and you, Celena." I grinned.

Laughing, she smacked my leg. "Shut up, I'm not a hoe."

"I've been in your head, you kind of are," Leah said. "But no shame, hoes for life."

"Hoe pride." Jenna pumped a fist in the air.

I met Hannah's blue eyes and grinned. "Are you saving your flower for your wedding day?"

"My flower," she mocked. Her head shook and she laughed. "I don't know. If so, not by my choosing. Kai is just really... I don't know. Gentlemanly. He didn't really know what the age of consent was when he got here, but I explained and he was kind of disgusted. Not with the law, I mean. But like, with the idea of having sex so soon, especially when he realized I was young enough in this world to be seen as a child. I don't know, he said that isn't how people do it back home. And I think he's kind of scared of my brothers."

"Nah, I think he's just a typical Fae," Leah said. "Society's different there. Men are different. I mean, in a lot of ways, it's more sexist. In most areas, men work while women cook and take care of the kids. But it isn't like our version of women being housewives. It's not like women's only purpose is to be a wife and mother. They do adorn mothers though—one of the primary deities in their religion is known as the 'great mother.' But she wasn't just a mom, she was a warrior too." Leah leaned back against the pillows and sipped her wine. "Sex is just something that is taken very seriously. It's about bonding. They wait. Not necessarily until marriage, but they court for years. And when they do finally mate, they genuinely mate for life. Most Fae only sleep with one person in their lives."

"Speaking of sex." Jenna tapped my upper arm. "How's your sex life going?"

I laughed and sipped my wine. "It's going."

"Is it?" Celena asked.

"We've had sex a couple times since I've been back."

"Why couldn't you have had this libido when you lived with me?" Hannah muttered.

"It's just different." I managed a smile. "We aren't doing it every day like we used to. But I don't know. I'm just not as horny as I used to be."

"So, I take it you aren't going to make me any nieces or nephews any time soon?" Jenna sat forward from my mound of pillows at the head of the bed. She took a sip from her glass of wine.

A sensitive question, but one I understood. She'd been planning a baby shower prior to my disappearance. And truthfully, I wanted a baby too. I wanted what I'd missed out on with my son.

But I wanted to mourn the one I lost first. I didn't want to replace him with a new baby. I wasn't ready. Had it have happened, I'd have been ecstatic. I'd be terrified of what happened to Micah happening again, but I'd still jump for joy. The whole truth though?

Getting pregnant again couldn't happen for a long time. Because I had to kill Peterson first. I didn't want to be pregnant when I had my opportunity. Without a second's thought, I'd swing into action to get revenge and save the people we'd lost at the first compound. And I didn't want to risk my baby's life again. I had to be ready to fight. If I were pregnant, I wouldn't be.

"Not any time soon."

"I figured. Mom wanted to ask but she wasn't sure how."

"I just don't think I'm going to be ready for that for a while."

"Well, are you on birth control?" Leah asked.

"Nah, we can use condoms," I said. Leah laughed. "What's wrong with condoms?"

"Nothing's wrong with condoms. If you use them. But I know you and Jeremy. You get all caught up in the moment. You're not going to waste time dicking around with a condom. You're going to get pregnant again."

I waved my hand in a shooing motion. "We'll be fine."

"You should know from personal experience that your man's pull-out game is weak," Celena said.

CHAPTER FIFTY-SIX

JEREMY

The scent of cheap perfume, Axe body spray, and weed filled my nose. A nauseating combination. The weed tasted pretty good though. I leaned against the banister and drew in another hit.

Adam sat at a chair in the middle of the living room with a blond, nearly naked woman on his lap, bouncing along to the pop music vibrating through the space. He practically drooled as she turned around and shook her mostly bare ass in his face.

Granted, it was a nice ass. But it was just stupid to me. I didn't see the point in a naked woman putting her tits in my face if I couldn't touch them. Not to say that I wanted to sleep with anyone but Laila anyway, but the point remained. Strippers weren't my thing.

"This whole thing is weird." I took another hit off my joint and passed it to Kai.

"Very strange." Kai took a hit. "Why are human women like this?"

I lowered myself to the arm of the chair beside the stairs. "It's a way to make a decent living here. But some women just like doing it too."

He curled his lip in disgust. His head shook. "And men here actually like this."

"Clearly, some do." I gestured to Adam. "Not my cup of tea. I don't want to see someone naked that I can't touch. I mean, besides porn. But that just makes busting quicker."

He furrowed his brows as he handed me the joint. "What's porn?"

He was dead serious. He almost looked offended when I laughed and hit the joint. "You know, suddenly I feel a lot better about you dating my baby sister."

"I love her. But I don't ken that I'd even want to see her do that."

I laughed and took another hit. I couldn't relate. The thought of a random girl dancing naked on top of me in exchange for money made me uncomfortable. But Laila stripped for me a few times and it was pretty hot. Obviously, I wasn't gonna tell him that.

It definitely made me feel better about Hannah though. Kai really was a good guy. He always had been. If I had to pick someone for Hannah to end up with, it'd be Kai ten times over.

"You know what I never realized before?" I asked.

"Hmm?" He took a drag off the joint.

"We're in the exact same situation with each other. You're dating my little sister, I'm dating your little sister." I paused. "I'm *marrying* your little sister."

"I guess we kind of are, huh? Same age difference too."

"Really ironic," I muttered. "So, if you guys ever have kids, our kids will be double cousins. Maybe even closer than that genetically since you guys are twins. That might be kind of difficult to explain without sounding incestuous."

Kai laughed. "It may. Can't say me and Hannah are ready for all that just yet though."

"Yeah, obviously. She's got to graduate college. At least one of us has to be successful."

If any of us were gonna make something of our lives, I was sure it'd be Hannah. She was the one who got good grades and got into a good college. She smoked weed and had a drink here and there, but she never got out of control. She knew how to handle her emotions without drowning them away. She had big plans. I was proud of her for that.

Kai watched me for a moment. Then a faint smile edged up his cheeks. "Are you alright, Jeremy?"

"Yeah, I'm good."

I was really fucking far from good. I don't think I even remembered what it meant to feel good.

It's not that I was unhappy with where my life was. I was happier to marry Laila than I'd been in my entire life. But I hated what happened to my life in the past eleven months and I hated myself because I knew that I was only making it worse.

I wasn't clean. Even at that very moment, I had a few Vicodin coursing through me. They were wearing off by then, but they were there.

I was trying to be, I was trying really fucking hard. But I couldn't remove the temptation. I could teleport anywhere I wanted at any given time. To a hospital, to a pharmacy, to an evidence locker. I could get drugs in a million places and it only took me a handful of seconds.

And I did. Day after day, I stole a pill here, a fist full there. However much I wanted on that given day.

I hadn't seen Olivia since the day I overdosed because I knew Adam was right. Laila could accept a relapse. Putting pills up my nose at my ex-girlfriend's house every night wasn't the same as relapsing. It was nearly cheating.

The crazy thing was that no one seemed to know when I was high. Even Adam didn't realize I was still using. Maybe it was because I was careful not to go over when I was too fucked up or maybe it was just that everyone was too caught up in their own shit to put two and two together. Either way, they hadn't noticed, and I wasn't going to point it out.

I was enjoying having my cake and selfishly gorging myself on it. At least, the part of me that wasn't overwhelmed with guilt did.

I knew that what I was doing was wrong. I knew that I was the only one who could stop. I knew that I was hurting myself every time I got high. But it didn't make me want to get high any less. If anything, it made me want that euphoria even more.

Even when I was with her, I was thinking about getting high. It was like I was having an affair with my old friend Opium.

Brody grabbed my shoulder, drunkenly laughing. "Aren't you going to get a dance?"

"Yeah, I'm gonna pass on that. But I'll give you some money to put in her bra."

He handed me a lit blunt. "You're so boring."

I took a long hit and handed it back to him. "You wouldn't either if you were in my shoes."

He plopped onto the couch I leaned against. "I mean, if I were you, I'd probably want to see *someone's* tits."

I narrowed my gaze. "You're just jealous 'cause you've never seen Laila's tits."

His round cheeks turned red. A smile pulled up his lips.

"What was that look for?"

"Nothing," Brody said.

"What the fuck is that supposed to mean?" I asked.

Adam approached, took the blunt from his hand, and plopped down beside Brody "I think the only people in this room who haven't seen Laila's tits are Kai and Wyatt."

"When did *you* see Laila's tits?"

"She flashed someone at a party, like, five years ago," Adam said. "I mean, I didn't *try* to look, but they were there and..." He grinned. "I mean, I've never had a thing for her. She's always been my friend. But she's got pretty titties."

I scrunched up my nose. "I'm definitely going to have Leah wipe that memory from your head when she gets home."

"At least I don't jerk off to them." He gestured to our brother.

I turned my gaze to Brody who awkwardly scratched his head. "When did you see my fiancé's tits?"

He bit his upturned lips. "Remember when you got a new phone and sold me your old one?"

Oh no. No, no, no. If he'd gone through my phone, he'd seen a lot more than just Laila's tits. There were at least a good two hundred videos and nudes on that thing.

My eyes widened. "No, I reset it."

"Yeah, but you forgot the SD card," Brody muttered.

"You deleted it, right?"

"Obviously I deleted them," Brody said. "But you can't delete a memory."

I leaned across the couch and smacked him in the head. He laughed and covered himself with a throw pillow. I hit him a few more times for good measure though. Adam and Kai laughed.

"You're really going to have to get over your obsession with her, bro," Adam said. "She's going to be our sister the day after tomorrow."

"Seriously." I took a hit off the blunt. "It's creepy, dude."

"Look," Brody said, "tonight, is not about my feelings. Tonight, is about getting fucked up and enjoying Jeremy's last night as a bachelor."

It really was stupid. I hadn't seen myself as a bachelor for a long time. But if I didn't get my shit together, I was about to be one again.

As the music stopped playing, Wyatt stood from the chair everyone had been using for their lap dance and came to join us on the couch. I passed him the blunt and stood. Then I pulled my wallet from my back pocket.

"Nah, I got it, dude." Adam stood and handed me three hundred-dollar bills. "Only fair since you didn't even get a lap dance."

Fair enough. The stripper was more for them than me anyway. Then I made my way across the room to the woman who was pulling a pair of jeans up over her thong. "Thanks for coming. This should be enough, right?"

"Yup, that'll do. You're the groom, right?"

"That's me."

"And you really don't want a dance?" She put her hand on her round hips.

"Yeah, I'm good. But here." I reached into my back pocket and pulled out a twenty, adding it to the three hundreds. "Thanks for coming."

"Thanks." She grabbed the cash and pushed it into her bra. "Your fiancé one of those girls that would be a bitch about getting a lap dance at your bachelor party?"

"No, not really. Just not my thing. Respect and all for what you do, I'm just a monogamy kind of guy."

"A dance doesn't make you polygamist." She laughed. "But hey, I get paid either way. So whatever works for you, bro." She pulled her blouse on over her bra. "You guys have a good night."

"Yeah, you too."

She headed toward the front door and I made my way back to the couch. As I sat, I heard a dull yell somewhere nearby. I squinted and looked around. "Do you guys hear that?"

Wyatt rolled his eyes and said, "Oh, yeah. We hear it."

"We hear it all the damn time," Adam grumbled.

"What is it?" I asked.

"That guard tied up in the basement," Brody said.

I creased my brows. "What's he saying?"

"Probably calling out for Laila again." Adam sighed.

"It's like this all the time?" I asked.

Brody said, "Since you guys set a date for the wedding."

I stood.

"Don't," Adam said. "Don't let that fucker ruin your night."

"He won't." I started toward the basement.

"C'mon, bro," Adam called. "It's not worth it."

Oh, but it was.

CHAPTER FIFTY-SEVEN

JEREMY

My gaze stayed on the stairs. I walked slow, hearing each step creak beneath my feet. I wasn't even sure what I was gonna say to the guy. But god damn it, he was the reason I'd been in hell since March. He was the reason I lost Laila, he was the reason I never got to meet my son, he was the reason I was back on drugs.

I hated that fucker. And I needed to say something.

"Laila." His voice sent a chill up my arms. "I knew you were going to come visit me eventually."

"Sorry, Laila's not available at the moment." I made it to the landing. Then I turned his way and gave a cocky grin. "Can I take a message?"

Dried blood clung to his cheeks and through his hair, courtesy of yours truly. His thin lip was busted open. I'd expected that to have healed by now, but perhaps someone else had gotten a few swings in. His skin had a light, ghastly shade of gray to it.

The front of his jeans was wet with piss. We'd given him a bucket, but I supposed he'd chosen the latter. Maybe he'd hoped we'd unchain him to let him clean up. That wasn't gonna happen. He could chill in his own filth for the rest of his life for all I cared. When Dad had designed the basement, he'd done just about everything imaginable to seal it off from the rest of the house. Though muffled, noises still crept through. But smells didn't. That piss and shit, that's what I cracked the odor up to.

He narrowed his gaze. "Oh. It's you."

I pulled a chair from the corner of the room and set it in front of him. I sat down with my legs on either side and laid my arms against the back of the chair on top of each other. "Sorry to disappoint you."

He met my gaze with cold, grayish blue eyes. "What do you want, Jeremy?"

I tilted my head to the side. "What do you want from my fiancé, Peterson?"

He gave an annoyed smile.

Hadn't known what I was gonna say until that moment. But seeing that face. The disappointment that I was there and she wasn't, it came to me.

I breathed out a soft laugh. "You know what's funny?"

"Hmm?"

"You actually believe that you love her." I squinted a bit as I gazed over him. "I saw the look on your face that day. Well, not your face. The face you're wearing. But still, I saw the expression. You meant it when you said you loved her, didn't you?"

He gave a smile. "With everything I am."

"Bet it hurts to know that I'm marrying her in two days."

Maybe a petty thing to say. But I couldn't actually hurt the guy. He didn't feel anything I did to that body. There was no use in wasting my energy. The only way that I could get to him was through my words.

He narrowed his gaze. "Bet it hurts to know that I fucked her."

My jaw tightened. "You didn't fuck her. You raped her."

"We've both been inside regardless. And let me just say, I completely understand your pathetic obsession with her. I didn't always, but after that night." He licked his smiling lip. "Boy, do I understand now."

I wanted to punch that smug smile off his stupid fucking face. I wanted to smash it into the fucking cement until it was nothing but mush. But I knew how those spells worked. He was channeling through the guard. He couldn't feel it.

I laughed. "*My* pathetic obsession with her? I'm marrying her, dude. She's about to be my wife. Find your own and quit being neurotic over everyone else's."

"Laila's the only one I have eyes for, Jeremy. She always has been. Can you say the same?"

I didn't know what he meant. Was he referring to the fact that I'd been with other girls before her? That was the only thing I could think. Powerful Witch and telepath or not, he couldn't have known that I was using. That couldn't be what he was referencing.

I squinted a bit. "You know what the funny thing is? You think some part of her will forgive you. You actually believe that at some point, she's going to leave me. And maybe she will. Maybe our paths will go different ways at some point. But you're delusional if you think that she'd ever want you."

His smile fell. He gritted his teeth together. His nostrils even flared a bit. He was fuming but trying to remain composed.

"You tied her down to a table with metal shackles and cuffs that left her aching for weeks. She had bruises that didn't heal until after my son was born. After what you did, she could barely piss for a month. She still has nightmares about it, did you know that? Did you know she wakes me up catching things on fire and screaming about killing you?" His angry expression shifted then. His eyes softened and his lip even quivered a bit. "I guess you wouldn't. But I do. And do you know why?" I narrowed my gaze.

His brows were turned down, his eyes were nearly watering, and his jaw was tight. It hurt him. He didn't see himself as a monster. For whatever reason, he felt justified. Maybe I crossed a line by saying those things, maybe it'd have hurt Laila to know that I let him know how much he hurt her. But I could see the pit my words were forming in his stomach and it was the closest to beating the shit out of him that I could get.

"Because I felt it. I might not have been there, but I was with her. I couldn't stop you but damn it if she didn't know that I was there," I said. "You thought you were breaking her, Peterson. But you weren't. You were creating your own worst nightmare."

His hurt expression softened to something I couldn't quite place. Maybe it was pride. Then his lips lifted slightly. "Maybe so. But I helped her become who she needs to be and that's all that matters."

His words went right over my head. I just wanted to hurt him again. I did a moment before; I could do it again. I just had to say the right thing.

"You made her hate you," I said. "She's never going to love you. She's never going to want you. You are her enemy. And that hurts, doesn't it? Knowing that she loves me more than anything else alive, but she hates you even more than that?"

He laughed. "You're about half right."

I thought he was saying she didn't hate him, but he knew she did. He knew she hated him unlike she hated anything.

"She hates you," I said. "She hates you more than she hates anything. She's never going love you if that's what you're hoping for."

"I said I'd have her back," he said. "I know what I am to her. I'm well aware of how what I've done has affected her. But I will have her again one day, Jeremy. That isn't a threat, it's a promise."

I gritted my teeth. "You'll have to kill me first."

He smiled. "See, you actually have that backwards."

Another line I should have thought on harder. But I just wanted to fucking hurt him. I wanted to hurt him, but more than anything, I wanted answers.

"What do you even want from her, Peterson?" My eye twitched. "Why do you keep begging for her to come talk to you?"

"There are some things I need her to know."

I licked my teeth. "I can give her the message."

"That's alright. I'll wait."

I felt my nostrils flare and I clenched my hands tighter. With a shake of my head, I said, "Why would you put her through all of the shit you did if you gave a flying fuck about her anyway?"

He smiled. "Because it had to happen."

"What do you mean?"

"One day, you'll understand."

"Quit with the cryptic bullshit and just answer the damn question." My voice dropped to an octave I didn't even realize it could hit.

He bit his grinning lip. "I had Laila for three months. And for the last one, we weren't even doing stress tests. You've had Laila for almost four *years*. And she managed to gain partial control on only two of her abilities in that time. But while with me, she unlocked every element. Not only did she unlock them, but she *harnessed* them. Unlike any other I've ever seen."

"Because you were fucking killing her," I barked.

"I would never." His tone was annoyed. As if I'd just insulted his favorite celebrity. "I was training her. She needs to be strong. She wouldn't have been ready if I hadn't done what I did."

"If you cared for her even a little teeny tiny bit, you wouldn't have tortured her. You wouldn't have raped her. You wouldn't have let her baby die."

He narrowed his gaze. A smile pulled at his lips. "Even if she won't admit it, there's some part of her that wanted me."

I gritted my angry, trembling teeth to a line. I knew that wasn't true. Didn't make my crave to bash his head in any lighter, but I wasn't angry because I believed that. I was angry that *he* believed that.

"And the torture, that wasn't just for fun. As much as I like to hear her scream." His smile slid further up. "It wasn't about that. It was about helping her grow. And I did, I helped her become the most powerful creature to ever walk the earth. And as far as the baby goes, if she would have listened to me, if she would have called for help, she would have never lost him."

I clenched my fists so tight that my short finger nails drew blood from my palms. "If you wouldn't have fucking taken her, he would still be here. It's not her fault that you did what you did."

He smiled. He fucking *smiled*. "Sometimes to build an empire, you have to burn the village that once stood in its place."

Those words would play over my mind a thousand times for the rest of my life. *To build an empire, you have to burn the village that once stood in its place.*

I thought he meant Laila. Creating her, turning her into a warrior. But that was only half of it.

"What kind of empire are you trying to build?" I narrowed my gaze.

"One day—"

"No, fuck that. What the fuck are you trying to build?" I snapped. "What is your goal in all of this, Peterson? Obviously, you're experimenting on us. But what I don't understand is *why*. You aren't afraid of us, and you seem to think you love my hybrid fiancé, so it's not racism. And you aren't trying to eliminate us, or you would just kill the people you've caught."

His smile widened. "You'll thank me one day."

I narrowed my gaze. "I'll never have a shred of respect for your existence to thank you for a damn thing."

"You will."

"Who did you have following her? How did you get to know her so well before you met her? How did you know we would take Daniel in?"

He smiled again. "Everyone knows Laila Callidy and Jeremy Skoulda where I'm from."

CHAPTER FIFTY-EIGHT

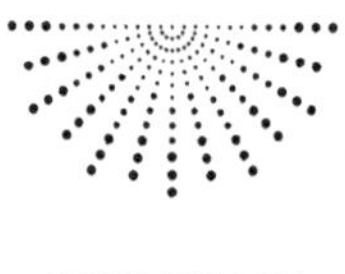

JEREMY

When I got home, Laila was curled up in bed with an empty green bottle of wine wrapped against her chest. Jenna lay beside her on my side of the bed with her arm gently draped around her sister. Hannah's head laid against Jenna's feet as a pillow. Celena slept on the floor with a mini throw pillow beneath her head and Leah's head rested on her lap.

I couldn't help but laugh. There wasn't even a way to get onto the bed without stepping on someone.

But her small little body drunkenly clutching that bottle of wine was easily the most adorable thing I'd ever seen. Although, every time I looked at her, I thought she was the most adorable thing I'd ever seen. Still, something about it made me smile. Maybe it was her still bright red lipstick, or the thin black lines that were pasted against her eyelids. Maybe it was her cute little heart shaped face resting on the pillow, leaving a layer of cream-colored makeup on the white sheets.

Or maybe it was because she was a part of my family. She'd befriended my sisters like they were her own years before marriage was even in the realm of possibility. My family tree was full of nuts and she willingly chose to hang herself on a branch among them. Just the thought made me fall even farther in love with her.

I'm still not sure why that wasn't enough to make me want to get clean. But the fact of the matter is that the old saying about the water and the horse is true.

I was sitting right there, watching the beautiful stream coast down the mountain side in front of me. My mouth was drier than the sand of the Sahara. Yet, I wouldn't lean down to take a sip. I knew that I should, that I was killing myself with dehydration. I had every opportunity to gulp it down and replenish my strength. But I just wouldn't. I just wouldn't take a fucking drink.

I teleported across the room and lowered myself to Laila's eye level. Leaning forward, I kissed her forehead. Her eyes fluttered open, and she smiled.

"Hey, you," she murmured.

"Hey." I pushed a stray hair from her face behind her ear. "I just wanted to kiss you goodnight, I'll sleep on the couch tonight."

She smiled and reached out to touch my cheek. "I'll come out with you. I need a drink anyway."

She carefully maneuvered Jenna's hand until she rolled over and fell back to sleep. Laila started to her feet, drunkenly wobbling a bit.

My arms went around her waist.

"Sorry, there was a lot of wine," she said.

I tucked my hands at the small of her back and teleported to the couch in the living room. "That's okay, I figured you'd be pretty drunk."

She rested her head on my chest. "I'm not that drunk, really. Just wine drunk, it's not the same."

I chuckled and kissed her hair. Then I squeezed her a bit tighter. "But you had fun tonight?"

Laila met my gaze. "There wasn't a penis cake, so that was disappointing." I laughed and she smiled. "What about you, babe? Did you get that lap dance?"

"No. No, lap dance. But there was a stripper," I said. "Kai's the only other one besides me who didn't get one. I like that guy, you know."

She laughed. A smile tugged at the edges of her lips. "Was she hot?"

"She was alright. Not as pretty as you."

She gave a playful grin. "Duh."

I smiled, leaned down, and kissed her. She reached onto her tip toes and lifted her arms around my neck.

A moment or so later, she pulled away and started to the kitchen. "So, did you do anything fun?"

Telling her about my little chat with her kidnapper seemed like a bad move. She was happy. And I didn't think it'd make her mad, but it'd definitely lower her vibe.

"Not really. The whole thing was pretty weird, honestly. By the way, did you know that both Adam and Brody have seen your boobs?"

She walked back into the living room. An embarrassed grin lifted her lips. "I know Adam has. We hung out in my partying days, I took my top off a lot back then." She grabbed a bottle of water from the fridge and turned to meet my gaze. "But I don't know how Brody did."

"That's kind of my fault actually." I lowered myself to the couch.

She sat beside me, pulled her legs upward into a lotus position, and opened her bottle of water. "What do you mean?"

"Well, uh..." I laughed. "Okay, so remember last year when I sold Brody my old phone?"

She creased her brows for a moment. Then her eyes widened. "No."

"Yeah."

"You have, like, an entire PornHub of me on your phone." Her eyes were as wide as the ocean. "You didn't reset it to factory settings before you gave him the fucking phone?"

"No, I did. But I guess I forgot to clear the SD card." I gave an awkward laugh.

"Lovely," she muttered. "Oh my god, I wonder if he watched the videos."

Since my dick was in her for most of them, it'd be fucking weird if he had. "I really hope not."

"That's a big oof." She grimaced. "I can't believe you didn't clear the SD card."

I laughed. "I'm sorry."

She took a sip from her water, looked up to meet my gaze, and gave an awkward grin. "So, is that what you did all night? Talked about my tits?"

Laughing again, I said, "Not *all* night."

With a roll of her eyes, she said, "I'm never going to be able to look Brody in the eye again. Jesus, there was that one video on there. The one you wouldn't delete. That day at the park on our second anniversary? You remember that?"

Ah, yes. Back in the days when we were young and into public sex. Now, we prefer to do that in the office of our restaurant. Couldn't say I didn't miss fucking in the grass though, there's something fun about that.

I smirked. "Oh yeah. I remember."

Her cheeks turned red and she put her head to her hand. "I knew that would come back to haunt me. You should have deleted it."

"I will *never* delete that."

Her blushing cheeks got even brighter. It was cute watching her try to conceal her embarrassment. Then I laughed. "Ya know, it's funny how you're more ashamed of us fucking in the woods than showing countless people your boobs at parties."

"They were strangers, not my brother-in-law."

"Well, one of them was your brother-in-law," I said.

"Yeah, but Adam's different," she said. "Adam's my friend, all my friends have seen my boobs."

"Does that mean Max has also seen your boobs?"

Another awkward grin pulled at her lips. "Couple times. We made out once, you know."

My brows furrowed. "No, I did not know."

"Really?" She cocked her head to the side. "I swore I told you that."

"You definitely never told me that."

She smiled and reached for my hand. "Oh, c'mon, babe. Don't be like that. It's a small town, everyone's made out with their friends a couple times."

It didn't *actually* bother me. Max was way below Laila's league and not close to how attractive I was. Not to be cocky, just the fact. And now that he knew I had magical powers, the chances of him trying anything were pretty slim. The chances of Laila doing anything with him were even shorter.

"When did that happen?" I asked.

"Freshman year, I think? Maybe sophomore, I don't know. We were at a party. He was drunk, I was drunk." She shrugged. "One of those awkward, one time make out sessions. I don't even think I'd lost my virginity yet then."

"Why would *you* make out with *Max*? I mean, I like Max, he's a cool dude. But you aren't just out of his league, you're like playing a totally different sport."

She laughed. "I don't know. I was an awkward looking kid, I just started getting pretty. That teenage angst was setting in. He was there, we were both horny kids."

I grimaced. "Gross."

She smiled, set her bottle down and lifted her leg around me until she was sitting on my lap. Her gaze met mine, still grinning ear to ear. "Don't worry, you're a better kisser."

I smiled and moved my hands to her hips. "That so?"

Still smiling, she leaned forward and gently touched her lips to mine. "*Much* better."

I smiled and pushed my lips into hers. She pulled back a bit and met my gaze. "So, you really didn't get a lap dance?"

"I really didn't." I smiled and pushed hair behind her ear.

"What did you do all night then?" she asked.

I breathed out a sigh as her fingers fiddled with a lock of my hair. "Mostly, everyone was just getting drunk. Then, I..." I rubbed my mouth. "I don't know if you want to hear this."

"What is it, baby?"

"I... I talked to Peterson."

Laila leaned back so she sat closer to my knees. "Oh. Why?" she asked. "It was your bachelor party; you were supposed to have fun."

"Yeah. Yeah, I know. I did. I just, uh... After the stripper left, when the music stopped, I heard him screaming in the basement. So, I just— I don't know."

She got quiet for a moment. Then she looked down. "What did he say?"

"Mostly just that he wanted to talk to you."

Silence stayed. Then she looked up to meet my gaze. Tears didn't well in her eyes, but it looked like she was struggling to keep that from happening. Her brows pulled together, her lips curved down. "I don't want to do that."

Knew I shouldn't have told her. Fuck, I didn't want to ruin her night. She'd been so happy a few moments prior.

I tucked dark hair behind her ear. "Yeah, I know, baby. That's what I told him. Aside from that, it was mostly just competitive. My horse is bigger than your horse, kind of thing."

She looked down again. Biting her lip, she looked back up. Then she managed a smile. It was forced. But it was also Laila to make a joke about something that definitely was not funny. "For the record, your horse is definitely bigger."

But I let out a quiet laugh anyway. At least she smiled.

I threaded my fingers through hers and raised her knuckles to my lips.

CHAPTER FIFTY-NINE

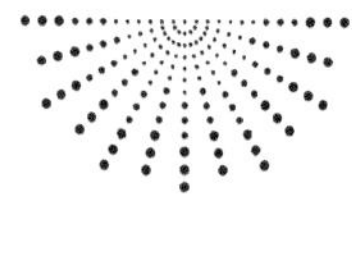

LAILA

The day after the bachelor and bachelorette party was hectic. But a boring kind of hectic. Primarily, I spent it running around from one place to another, fighting like hell to get everything done before the day's end.

In the morning, I went to the hair salon. I hadn't had my hair done in close to a year, so my brown roots had long pulled their way into the jet-black locks that reached the middle of my back. They threw some color on and practiced styling it for the wedding.

Then I went to the nail salon. They wiped off my chipped black nail polish and painted them with some soft, neutral beige over the acrylics. I didn't really like them, but Mom said they'd look pretty in the pictures, so I went with it.

Afterward, I went back to Mom's. Almost everyone was there decorating, delicately placing flowers in vases and hanging fairy lights from trees. We worked as a team, setting up tables and draping cloths over them. Our powers made the use of a ladder needless. We were there until about six thirty getting everything but the final touches ready.

Then, we did a quick run through of the ceremony. It mostly consisted of Jeremy and I making weird faces at each other as we stood at the archway. Adam would laugh, then Leah and Jenna would yell.

It was fun. Those were moments I would remember most when I thought of our wedding. His silly little smiles as I crossed my eyes and stuck out my tongue. The turn up of his lips that crinkled the edges of his big blue eyes. His snicker as he held my hands in his.

When we were done with the rehearsal, Jenna and Leah told Jeremy to leave so I could try on my dress one more time before the wedding. To put it lightly, I was floored. It was elegant, yet still free spirited enough to represent my personality. The tree over the spine covered each cicatrix perfectly. I felt as beautiful as I did before the scars. Maybe even more so.

Once I tried on the dress one last time, there was nothing left to do. All that remained was the ceremony.

I plopped onto the bed. My head hit the pillow, and I exhaled deeply. Jeremy collapsed beside me and did the same.

"At least it's almost over," I said.

He rolled onto his side and smiled. "Then the fun part starts."

I smiled and swiveled to face him. Then I took his hand in mine. I pulled it close to my face and squeezed. "At this time tomorrow, we're going to be married."

His smile widened. His hand cupped my cheek and pushed hair behind my ear. "You're going to be my wife."

"You're going to be my husband." My smile stretched higher.

"I can't wait." His thumb grazed down my cheek and stopped at my bottom lip. "Baby?"

"Yeah?" I asked.

"What comes after this?"

I cocked my head to the side a bit. "Marriage?"

"Yeah, I know that. I mean, everything else." He paused, as if unsure how to go on. "With Peterson and all of the prisoners."

"Oh." I turned my gaze to our hands.

The golden question. One I'd pushed to the back of my mind a lot lately. I wanted to find them, but the only lead we had sent an ache to the pit of my stomach.

"I know that you're still healing, but I also know that you're still hell-bent on saving them. So am I, obviously," he muttered. "But we're going to have to do something with that guy tied up in the basement soon. We can't keep him there forever."

"Yeah. Yeah, I know."

"I get it if you aren't ready to work it all out—"

"No, you're right. I have to face this shit eventually. And I will," I said. "I will, but I want to get married first. I want to stay as happy as I've been for a little while. Just a little while."

He gave a bare smile. "Alright, ma chérie."

My stomach swirled. I leaned forward and nuzzled my head against his chest. "We deserve to be happy. Even if it's just for a little while."

That it was. Just a little while.

CHAPTER SIXTY

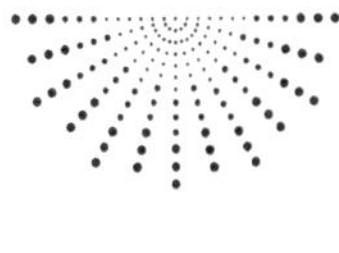

LAILA

The soft, flowery scent of my perfume mixing with hairspray wafted to my nose. I chewed on a piece of spearmint gum. The sounds of my sisters bustling around in the bathroom bounced into my ear.

My body felt a little squeezed in the gown, but I loved it. I loved every inch of it. In that mirror, in that moment, I didn't feel an ounce of insecurity. I was beautiful. My long black curls billowing around my face. The brilliant red lipstick. My sparkly brown eye shadow beneath dark black wings. The lace that lined from my shoulders down my arms and torso.

"Oh my god," Mom murmured. "My baby's getting married."

Jenna clasped the last button of my gown. I laughed, fiddling with a curl at my face and pushing it under my crown of flowers.

"You look so pretty." Leah's eyes washed over me in the mirror.

"You're a bride." Hannah grinned.

My eyes traced over myself in the mirror. For the first time in a long time, I didn't hate the girl staring back at me.

Her body was different than it used to be. The ratio between her hips to her waist was narrower than it had once been. Her shoulders tapered more than they used to and her breasts were much smaller. But still, beautiful all the same.

She was beautiful.

I was beautiful.

The scars on my wrists were covered. My dress was floor length, so I didn't have to worry about the giant bullet shaped white flesh on my thigh. The lines on my back were camouflaged by the tree. It was perfect.

Except for one very small detail.

When I tilted my head upward, the scar at the base of my neck was visible.

It was too late then; I didn't have a choker that would look okay with my dress. So, I accepted it. It was what it was. I looked how I looked. And as much as I hated that scar, even still with it, I was still beautiful.

"What is it?" Jenna met my gaze in the mirror.

"Nothing." I smiled between her and Leah. "It's perfect. Really, I love it. You did amazing on the embroidery. Thank you both so much."

She smiled and gave a nod. "I'm glad you like it."

"Oh, shit." Leah walked to her purse that laid on Mom's bed. "I forgot to give you your gift from Jeremy. You gave Brody yours, right?"

I nodded. "Yeah, as soon as it came in the mail."

She nodded. Then she lifted a tiny white box and a folded piece of notebook paper from her bag. "I helped pick it out so if you hate it, you can blame me."

I laughed and flipped the piece of paper open.

Hey beautiful,
You don't have to wear it if you don't like it, but Leah said it'd match your dress. It's new, and it has a little blue, so then you just need something old and borrowed. Anyway, I hope you like it but if you don't, I saved the receipt. I think you will though.
Either way, you're gonna look gorgeous.
I love you more than anything
See you up there

<3

I laughed, knowing he'd saved the receipt because I'd made a comment about how shitty his taste in jewelry was the day he proposed. With a grin, I flipped the little white box open. As I did, my jaw dropped and my eyes began to water.

He literally couldn't have picked a better piece. There I was, just thinking about how I wished I had a choker that matched my dress and covered the scar on my neck.

Staring up at me was a small pendant, no more than the size of a dime with a painted oak tree almost identical to the one on my back beneath a layer of epoxy. It was planted on a dark green field with a light blue sky behind it. The pendant was looped onto a centimeter-thick line of bright white ribbon with a clasp on either end.

My eyes began to leak more water. I raised my hand to wipe them but Jenna grasped it. "Don't wipe, dab." She handed me a tissue.

I laughed and gently held the paper to the corner of my eye.

"So, you like it?" Hannah asked.

"Help me put it on."

She walked around me, careful to avoid my train. I pulled the necklace from the box and handed it to her over my shoulder. As she clasped it and let my long hair fall back down, my jaw began to tremble.

It was the last piece to the puzzle that I hadn't realized was missing.

"God, you look beautiful." Mom's eyes washed over me in the reflection.

I didn't say anything, just smiled. My fingers ran along the intricate stitches that descended the bodice. But I agreed. I felt absolutely perfect.

"Guys." Celena peeped around the doorway. "Everyone's asking if you're ready."

"Yeah, I think we are."

"Hang on a second," Leah said. "What's your something old? The dress is new, the earrings are borrowed, the necklace is blue."

"I'm glad you asked." Mom smiled. She bent down and lifted her blue floor length gown from the ground. She fiddled with something at her ankle for a moment. Then, she stood back up with a silver anklet in her palm.

"That's an heirloom, isn't it?"

"It is. Luka gave it to me on our wedding day. Apparently, it's been in the family for hundreds of years. I have your dad's somewhere too, he always said to make sure to give them both to you." Mom glanced at Jen. "Sorry, hon. You're not a Fae."

"I have cankles anyway," Jenna said.

I laughed and wiped my eye once more. It would've been wonderful if my dad could have walked me down the aisle. But his anklet would have to do.

Then I turned to Leah. "Do you know anything about the history of these things?"

"They're the Fae equivalent of passing on a wedding ring to the next generation. You give the pair to the first child of every generation that marries. It's supposed to carry the love of your ancestors. They use anklets instead of rings because it's meant to keep you grounded."

Mom's smile looked sad, but it made me happy. I vaguely remembered seeing that anklet growing up. I'd never thought much of it, but I'd always thought that it was pretty. Getting to wear it on my wedding day made me a little giddy. "Your dad can't be here today. But you wearing this would mean everything to him."

I smiled back. "Do I get to keep it?"

Mom chuckled. "It's yours, baby girl. Maybe you'll get to give it to your baby one day. I have your dad's too, remind me to give it to Jeremy."

I continued to smile as Mom lowered herself to the ground. She lifted the base of my dress, fastened the clasp, and stood back to her feet.

"Something old, new, borrowed and blue," Hannah grinned.

"I think you're ready, Lai," Jenna said.

Smiling, I turned to Celena and gave a nod. "Time to marry my best friend."

More than anything else, that's what Jeremy was to me. He'd be my husband. He'd be the father of my children. He'd be my business partner, even my partner in crime. But more than anything else, he was my best friend.

I wouldn't understand why until memories from our first life began to surface. Because that's how it all began. It was never meant to be anything more than that. But Earth would be a far different place had we remained only friends.

CHAPTER SIXTY-ONE

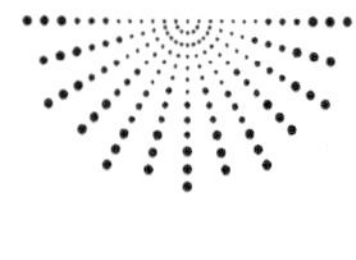

JEREMY

"Damn." Adam adjusted his tie in the mirror. "I can't believe this is really happening."

"Me and Laila getting married?" I looked up from the buttons on my shirt.

"Yeah, man. It's wild. Do you have any idea how crazy she used to be before you guys met?" He laughed. "Just so weird to think about who she was then and who she is now. And you, too. I mean, I always knew you'd get married. But just the growth in who you are now compared to who you used to be."

We'd definitely come a long way. The whole thing had been tough. And this past year had been the hardest road we'd travelled. But by its end, I'd be married to my best friend. So, it wasn't all bad.

I fastened the last button at my neck. "Do you think I went too short on my beard?"

"I don't know, but it's too late now, bro. You can't un-cut it."

I ran my fingers through the scuffle. "I just didn't want to look homeless."

"You look fine, chill. No one's gonna be looking at you anyway, everyone looks at the bride." He sat on Laila's old bed, pulled a joint from his pocket, and sparked it against his lips. He tried to pass it to me.

"No, thanks. Laila said not to get high until after the pictures," I muttered.

It was ironic because I hadn't been truly sober in weeks. Hell, I wasn't even sober as the hypocritical words left my mouth. Not to say that I was completely inebriated, I hadn't done anything in about four hours. I was at the tail end of my high. By then, I was using them mostly to keep from getting sick. But the fact remained. I wasn't sober.

"Hey, are you guys almost ready?" Brody poked his head around the corner. "Celena said we're starting in five minutes."

"Yeah, I just have to get my tie on."

He took a step into the room and reached into his pants pocket. "Alright, cool. I'll let her know. But I'm supposed to give you this first." He passed me a small black box. "Laila said she's sorry she didn't have time to wrap it."

I laughed and took it in my hands. After fidgeting with the plastic tape for a moment, I tore it open. Inside sat a small styrofoam packaging with a copper guitar pick laying on top.

I lifted it to my hand, squinting a bit to read the engraving.

I Will

Always

Pick You

I chuckled. Of course, it was a pun.

Brody smiled. "She said to tell you to flip it over."

I did, reading the inscription on the back.

J.S. & L.C.

Nov. 4,

The day we met.

I smiled and ran my finger along the engraved metal. Such a simple gift. Yet even now, all these years later, I still carry it in my wallet.

"Can I talk to you for a minute, Jeremy?" Brody asked.

I looked up and slid the pick into my back pocket. "Sure, what's up?"

He turned to Adam.

"Alright, guess that's my cue. I'll see you guys up there."

I looked to Brody as Adam brushed past him. "What's up, dude?"

He gave a bare smile and shut the door. "I just want you to know that I'm happy for you."

I smiled back. "Oh, yeah?"

Not exactly the reaction I'd been expecting. He'd been in love with my about-to-be wife for at least the last year. It wasn't that I blamed him. She was easy to love. But I hadn't received a congratulations since she'd said yes. It was a little surprising for him to say it now. I was grateful for it though.

He held my gaze. "Look, I owe you an apology."

"For what?" I asked.

Brody ran his fingers through the short hair at the top of his head. "I don't think I ever apologized for what happened last year."

"Oh." I turned back to the mirror to tighten my tie. "You didn't do it to be malicious, Brody. I don't... I don't hold it against you."

"That doesn't make it right. Some secrets aren't yours to share and I should have respected that. I should have given you the opportunity to handle it and I didn't."

"It wasn't just me and Laila being manipulated." I pulled the tie up to my throat. "Mary took advantage of your feelings. She knew you loved her, and she used it."

"Yeah, but..." He rubbed his eyes, down his cheeks, and to his mouth. "You're my brother, Jeremy. I... I should have had your back." His sincere blue eyes were steady on mine in the mirror. "I tried to ruin your relationship. That's fucked up, family doesn't do that to each other. Especially our family."

"Yeah, kind of fucked up."

He looked down. "I don't even know what I was thinking. I was just so mad. It wasn't like I thought I had a chance; I knew that I'd never compare to what you guys have. I just... I was so mad at you. I didn't understand how you ever landed Laila in the first place."

A shitty thing to say. But hell, neither did I.

"Then I saw you with the siren. And I tried to keep it inside, I really did. But the day you got back... You were holding her and I knew you guys had just fucked, and it just made me so mad because you were acting like nothing was wrong. She was sitting on your lap and laughing and I... I was just so jealous. I didn't understand how you could do that and go back and act like nothing happened."

"I really don't blame you, Brody. You were in a really shitty situation. I knew you had a thing for her, I shouldn't have been flaunting around the way I was."

"You weren't flaunting. You were being normal. The two of you hadn't seen each other in weeks, obviously you were going to be all over each other."

"It is what it is. We can't change it."

"Yeah, but I did you dirty. And I... I want to be a good brother, Jeremy." His eyes were earnest and kind. "The way you and Adam are. The way Hannah and Leah are. The shit I pulled... That's not how you treat your brother. Regardless of the outcome, I'm sorry for the way my actions affected you."

I gave a smile and turned to face him. "It's alright, man. Let's just leave all that shit in the past where it belongs."

His gaze turned to his shoes.

"Is there something else?" I asked.

His eyes grew dreary. "I'm sorry that I love her."

I leaned against the dresser and gave a sad smile. "She's easy to love. I can't blame you for that. She's everything. She's soft but powerful. She's kind, and smart, and generous and beautiful. Sweet as pie but she can still be a crazy, raging bitch." He chuckled and I smiled. "She's everything. The perfect combination of every good and bad human characteristic there is."

He laughed. "I'm going to try to not love her. She's yours and I know that. I'm going to stop. I can't keep doing this to myself."

I held his gaze. "It doesn't bother me that you love her, man. I've told you this. It just makes me sad because I know that it hurts you. You're my baby brother, I don't want you to hurt. I want you to be happy. I want you to love someone the way that you love her. But I want them to love you back. I'm sure she's out there somewhere. But you're gonna walk right past her if you're thinking about Laila."

"Yeah, probably less heart ache that way. Loving someone that loves me back, I mean."

"But she isn't *mine*. I just get to love her. Even this whole thing, it's just to celebrate that. She'll never be mine. She'll never be anyone's. Laila will always belong to Laila."

He smiled for a moment. "I know that I can't ever be with her. But if I had to choose someone for her to marry, it'd be you. No one's going to treat her as good as you do."

Those words cut like a knife. Of course, I pretended it was a sweet and gentle moment. But he was wrong. Plenty of people would treat her better than I was treating her at that time. Part of me wished it were him that had the bond with her because he would love her the way she deserved to be loved. He'd be honest with her. He wouldn't hang out with his ex-girlfriend and put pill after pill up his nose then proceed to lie to her about it. He would never knowingly hurt her the way that I had.

But I was too selfish to do the best thing for her. I loved her. I would never stop loving her. I knew I was bad for her, at least the person I was at that time was. But I loved her, and I couldn't risk telling the truth and losing her.

The music began to play, and I licked my smiling lips. "I think that's for us."

He smiled. "You ready to go marry your best friend?"

Smiling still, I adjusted my tie one last time. "Let's do it."

CHAPTER SIXTY-TWO

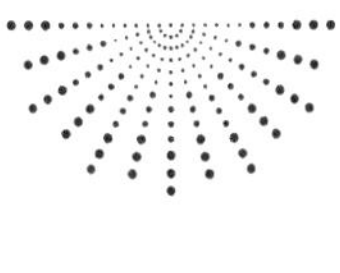

JEREMY

Adam and I stood at the archway patiently waiting for the groomsmen and bridesmaids to start down the aisle. I gazed out over the small crowd. Then again, calling it a crowd would suggest there was actually a group of people, which was entirely inaccurate.

The chairs, all thirteen to be exact, were arranged in a half moon around the altar. We were having the ceremony in the back corner of the yard on the slightly terraced hillside behind the creek. I think Laila's dad used it as a quad trail at one point, but aside from the pathway itself, Rachel had completely transformed it.

The parts of the hill that would typically be a rock filled muddy mess were overflowing with tiny flowers of a thousand different hues of pink, white and yellow. They slid down the mountainside like a waterfall from a cliff. They fell off of the modest wooden retaining wall a few feet above the beaten path that was recently coated in moss.

Over the past few weeks, Laila had been coming over daily to take care of the plants in anticipation of today. Most of the work was already done, but she was very concerned about the walkway. It was usually an uneven, mushy mud-pit, as most of the outdoors were in Pennsylvania.

She said that since she was walking the aisle barefoot, she had to figure out some way to make it more comfortable and more beautiful at the same time. I suggested she plant some moss and use it as a runner for the aisle of sorts. Her eyes widened with excitement. She ran to the local nursery, grabbed a few bags of moss seed, and threw it over the entire walkway, from the edge of the retaining wall to the hillside that led to the stream.

"Why didn't I think of moss?" she'd asked as we sat on the retaining wall smoking a joint after she'd sprouted the seeds. "It's nature's carpet."

Each day when she came back from caring for her moss, she seemed a bit happier. That moss may have done more for her mental health than I had.

There wouldn't have been enough room to separate the bride's side from the groom's if we wanted to, but we didn't want nor need to. It was a tight squeeze for the six guests we had, but everyone who mattered managed to fit.

Mémé and Papy sat in the second row on the far left with big smiles. At least, Mémé smiled. Papy never really smiled. His however-many-thousand-dollar suit looked so misplaced on that fold-up chair.

I said hello to them before I got dressed, but aside from that, I hadn't seen them in at least six years. They looked about the same as they always had. Prim and proper. Papy's short gray hair was combed neatly against his scalp. His clean shaved jaw looked just as tight as it always had.

Mémé did look happy though. She always looked happy. Her thin lips stretched up into her crystal, mascara lined eyes. That was the only makeup she'd ever worn. Just a perfect gray bun and mascara. I distinctly remembered her making a comment about my mom's red lipstick at the last holiday we'd spent at their house prior to Mom's death. She called her a whore. Dad yelled, Papy screamed, it was a great big thing.

Nevertheless, our relationship with them had always been strained. Dad's lack of interest in them surely played a part in that. We would call on holidays, they'd send us a small gift on our birthdays. On

Mother and Father's Day, we would all chip in and send them something fancy. But we were never really close.

They were the only elder relatives we had left, and yet, Leah had been more of a parent to us than they had. They helped financially a time or two, but when push came to shove, they weren't there. When Dad died and we had no one left, they were willing to let us go into foster care. Granted, taking on five kids was a lot, especially since three of us were under ten. But Annie did it.

Damn, I wished she could have been there. Annie was the only mother I ever remembered. I had glimpses with Mom, my real mom, but I was six when she died. It was a flash here and there; a smell that reminded me of her, a distorted image in a dream, but never anything that was significant. I vaguely remembered Dad, but mostly just his lifeless body hanging from the ceiling fan. It was kind of hard to remember any of the good times after that.

With Annie gone too, the only parental figure I had left was the same woman who tried to destroy my relationship.

Now that I thought of it, some part of me wished Mary were here after all.

Max sat beside Papy scrolling on his phone until the music started. He was typically in a stained white T-shirt and pair of basketball shorts or filthy jeans. It was almost surreal to see his hair freshly washed with a collared button-up and clean pants. His hair was a few shades lighter than I'd realized. Maybe I could see why Laila made out with him once. He was a husky dude, so it was still kind of hard to picture. But I guess he wasn't too bad looking when he wasn't filthy.

Lydia sat beside him in a little pink dress. She had a white bow nearly the size of her head atop her head. She gazed down at a cluster of flowers in her hand. She pulled the pedals, dropped them to the ground, and watched them fall.

Ray sat beside her scrolling on his phone. He wore a black button up over black slacks with a pink tie. My guess would be that Lydia picked it out. He looked so content to finally sit beside her. He'd glance at her from time to time and smile when she looked back up at him. It brought a smile to my lips. Then it reminded me of my son who should have been there that day too. But I forced that thought to the back of my mind and looked beside him.

Haley sat to his right wearing a strapless yellow gown leafing through a book on her lap. The light scars on her neck and arms stood out like a sore thumb on her ebony skin but she wore them like armor. Still, it was heart wrenching to really think about a Werewolf with scars.

The only way to slow down a wolf's healing is to poison them with wolfsbane as they heal. Healing scars like that took weeks, a month at the very least. That meant that she was being drugged with it daily for weeks or even months. The type of agony a wolf goes through after being poisoned with wolf's bane is almost indescribable.

Before that moment, I'd thought that the purpose of the scars was solely to track their location and ground the Guardian abilities. But to put a wolf through that kind of treachery would be useless besides the sadist's way of reminding his victims of his torture for the rest of their lives.

Unless there was some other reason for them.

Five people. It almost made me chuckle. Five people were guests at our wedding. They looked misplaced sitting beside the eight chairs for the wedding party and Laila's mom. Maybe she was right. It had been a lot of work for five guests.

Although, it was all of the people that mattered most. Well, besides Mémé and Papy. I could've done without them. But they'd probably given us a few hundred bucks, so at least there was that.

The music got a bit louder. Adam lifted himself to his tip toes to look past me over the hill side. "Oh, okay we're starting. Here, turn around."

I shifted until I was looking behind him. "Aren't I supposed to see her walk down the aisle?"

"Yeah, but not until they're like, right here. You'll just see a blob from this distance," Adam muttered. "Alright, alright. Here comes Celena and Wyatt."

I looked over the flowers on the hillside. Slow piano music played off of a mobile speaker somewhere near the chairs and bounced into my ears.

Wyatt moved beside me. He patted my back. Celena smiled my way before moving to the other side of the altar. That moment was when it sunk in. It didn't feel like I was getting married until they joined me beneath the flower covered archway.

Kai and Hannah trailed closely behind. They joined us at the altar with grins that stretched across their happy faces. Hannah brushed past me with a kiss on my cheek and I smiled back. Leah wasn't far behind either, smiling as she stood beside Kai. Finally, Brody and Jenna came beside us, offering warm grins and sweet, murmured remarks.

As the song changed to something a bit softer, my stomach sunk.

I shouldn't have gone through with it. There was a nauseating, swirling sensation in my gut. It was wrong and I knew it.

I'd been lying for over a month already. Much longer if you count that kiss Olivia forced on me while Laila was in captivity.

I wanted to marry her. I wanted to spend my life with her. Every part of me *wanted* what I was about to get. But I didn't deserve it.

I knew it wasn't fair to get married without telling my fiancé about the biggest battle I was facing within myself. But I just didn't want to run the risk of losing her.

A large grin pulled at the lips of everyone in the wedding party. Adam met my gaze. "Alright, man. Look at your wife."

As I turned and met her nearly glowing green eyes, every notion of skepticism immediately left my mind. Every thought of negativity dissipated from my consciousness.

Whatever guilt I'd felt a moment before must have been misplaced. It couldn't be wrong. Nothing about the two of us together could be wrong, not when just looking at her made me feel like this.

As our gazes met, I felt my jaw drop a bit. She was the most beautiful thing I ever saw.

Although, she wasn't exactly as I had expected her to be. I knew the dress was going to be pretty, but I assumed it would be a different kind of pretty.

Laila had always had a thing for sex appeal in her taste in clothes. I wouldn't say she dressed slutty, but provocative wouldn't be a stretch. She rarely wore modest necklines before the scars, he was often in crop tops or very tiny yoga shorts in the summer. For that reason, I expected her wedding dress to be less elegant than it was. Maybe a big foofy ball gown, or something low cut.

But it was the most womanly, sexy-without-being-slutty dress I'd ever seen.

It hugged her tiny waist and narrow hips as if it were a second skin. Despite the heat, the sleeves were long, tightly fitting the length of her arms to the point where her wrists met her hands, just barely resting on the back of her palms. The neckline came up to her collar bone. It touched the white choker I'd sent with Leah to give to her. She'd made some remark about how it would match her dress, which I didn't really see yet.

I knew that dress wouldn't have been her first choice six months prior and that she only wore it because it covered those scars she hated so badly. But it was beautiful. *She* was beautiful.

Laila didn't look like the girl I fell in love with as a young man in that dress. She looked like the woman I was going to love until the day I died. Then again, maybe it wasn't the dress. Maybe it was just her.

She had changed so much over the past few years; she was almost unrecognizable in comparison to who she once was. I supposed I was too. We were kids when we met. She was seventeen, I was twenty. We were practically babies. But then, we were two grown adults, beginning yet another chapter in the book of our lives.

Her plump red lips turned up in a smile. She stuck out her tongue and crossed her eyes in a typical, goofy Laila fashion. I laughed. And she grinned.

As they made their way to us, Rachel smiled at me. I smiled back. Then she turned to her daughter, touched her lips to her cheek, and started toward her seat.

Laila drew closer. I reached out my hand to take hers. She handed her bouquet off to Jenna before looking up at me. Her big green eyes grazed over me the same way mine danced over her.

"Now, would the wedding party please take their seats with the audience," Adam said.

Everyone besides Brody, Jenna, Adam, Laila and I made their way to their seats. The rest of the guests sat too.

"Jeremy and Laila would both like to thank you all for coming together to celebrate their love and commitment to one another." Adam looked down at some white note cards in his hand. "We have all gathered here today to celebrate the love between two people we all care for deeply." Adam licked his lip, shaking his head. Then he looked up from his notecards, huffed, and slid them into his back pocket. "I found some ceremony script online for today, but honestly it's really boring, so I'm going to go off book here."

"Oh, great," Laila murmured, squeezing my hands.

Adam chuckled, glancing between the two of us. Then he looked back to the crowd. "When I first met Laila, close to six years ago now, I never thought we would be standing here today. No part of me realized how much these two would eventually mean to each other. But the moment they met, it was like the rest of their worlds disappeared. Their entire universes started to revolve around one another's. Jeremy is the sun that controls the orbit of every planet in Laila's solar system, and Laila is the sun at the center of Jeremy's. The two of them dedicate their entire lives to each other. Let's face it, guys, they're pretty pathetic."

There were a few murmured chuckles from the audience as Laila and I looked at one another with smiles.

Damn, she looked amazing. I couldn't stop staring. Besides our children, nothing came close to touching how beautiful she looked that day. The pictures don't do the memory of that moment any justice. She'd been so unhappy for so long. But that grin she couldn't pull down; it was like being lost at sea and seeing the light of a rescue boat in the distance.

"These two are almost never apart. They mean everything to each other. Time and time again, we've seen them go through worst things than anyone could imagine. But no matter how bad things have gotten, no matter how much easier it would have been to give up, they always come back to each other. And each time that they do, they come back loving each other harder and stronger than they did before. It's like the love between them grows larger and stronger with every tragedy they live through," Adam continued softly, looking between us and back to the crowd.

"Jeremy and Laila are the epitome of what true love really means." Adam smiled. "Neither of them are perfect. They're both a fucking mess,"

"Thanks," Laila muttered.

Adam laughed. "They're both a mess, but that's what love really is. It isn't expecting a fairytale. It isn't about perfection. Love is about accepting someone for every awful thing that they are and loving them unconditionally regardless. Love is about moving past the boundary of expectations and caring for someone regardless of the things they've done. Love is about loving *every* part of someone. Not just the parts that look pretty on paper. Love is just as much about loving your partner's flaws as it is about loving the best things about them. And that's what these two do. Neither of them are perfect, and they love one another with everything they have regardless." He smiled as he looked between us. "Anyone alive would be lucky to have what these two have.

"This ceremony won't manifest a bond of love and care that Laila and Jeremy don't already have. The purpose of this wedding is for one reason." His smile widened. He looked at Laila and then to me. "To celebrate the power of unity this couple shares. To be joyous in their love beside them. To show the world what real love looks like. They are kind, they are affectionate, they are best friends. They may be two incredibly imperfect people, but to one another, there is no one more perfect. These two love with their whole hearts, something we all strive for from the time that we are children."

He looked back to the crowd. "This marriage, as with any marriage, will require daily dedication. It is a duty as much as it is a blessing. To have the marriage you want, you will have to work for it every single day. You will need to love with everything you have and be patient through every difficult situation. You'll have to swallow your pride at times. You will have to talk and listen. You will have to forgive and move forward with love and compassion. Every day, you will have to make the important things matter and let go of the things that don't. So far, you guys have done a pretty good job at that so I think you can handle it."

He smiled as he turned his gaze to Brody. "Can I please have the rings?"

Brody reached into his pocket and passed them to Adam. He turned to me and placed the wedding ring in the palm of my hand. "These rings are simple pieces of metal. But they symbolize much more than that. You wrap them around each other's finger today to be worn until you take your final breaths. These little circles of gold are meant to symbolize the never-ending cycle of love that marriage represents.

"Now, Jeremy. Repeat after me." I smiled at Laila. "I, Jeremy Skoulda, take you, Laila Callidy."

I took the tips of her fingers between mine. "I, Jeremy Skoulda, take you, Laila Callidy."

"To be my lawfully wedded wife."

"To be my lawfully wedded wife," I repeated, smiling as her cheeks turned pink and her lips pulled upward in a grin.

"To be my best friend, my partner, and my shelter."

"To be my best friend, my partner and my shelter," I repeated quietly, looking between her eyes as the words left my lips.

"I vow to respect and honor you through the best of times, and hardest times."

"I vow to respect and honor you through the best of times and hardest times," I continued.

"I vow to be your strength when you're weak and your biggest supporter when you succeed," Adam continued.

"I vow to be your strength when you're weak your biggest supporter when you succeed," I muttered, watching joyful tears well in her eyes.

"I vow to be whatever you need me to be," Adam said.

"I vow to be whatever you need me to be," I said.

"Your friend, your family, your partner," Adam continued.

"Your friend, your family, your partner."

"I vow these things from the bottom of my heart, for as long as we both will live."

"I vow these things from the bottom of my heart for as long as we both will live," I repeated, smiling. My fingers gently slid the ring up her finger until it clanged against the engagement band at the base of her hand. And my stomach flipped with joy.

"Now, Laila, please repeat after me." Adam set my ring in the palm of her hand. She smiled, holding my gaze. "I, Laila Callidy, take you, Jeremy Skoulda…"

"I, Laila Callidy, take you, Jeremy Skoulda."

"To be my lawfully wedded husband."

Her smile widened. "To be my lawfully wedded husband."

"To be my best friend, my partner, and my shelter," he said.

"To be my best friend, my partner, and my shelter." Her voice shook, fighting the urge to cry.

"I vow to be your strength when you're weak your biggest supporter when you succeed," Adam continued.

"I vow to be your strength when you're weak your biggest supporter when you succeed."

"I vow to respect and honor you through the best of times, and hardest times."

"I vow to respect and honor you through the best of times and hardest times," she said.

"I vow to be whatever you need me to be," Adam said.

"I vow to be whatever you need me to be." Laila slipped the ring in her fingertips over the nail of my ring finger.

"Your friend, your family, your partner," Adam said softly.

"Your friend, your family, or your partner." Laila inched the ring closer over my finger.

"I vow these things from the bottom of my heart, for as long as we both will live."

Her eyes sparkled with tears as she smiled, repeating Adam's words as she slid the ring the rest of the way down my finger until it was secured nicely at the bottom. "I vow these things from the bottom of my heart, for as long as we both will live."

Adam cleared his throat. "Jeremy, do you take this woman to be your wife, to have and to hold, to love and care for and protect, through sickness and in health for the rest of your days?"

I smiled down at her. "I do."

"And Laila. Do you take this man to be your husband, to have and to hold, to care for and protect, through sickness and in health for the rest of your days?"

She smiled, eyes locked with mine. "I do."

Adam laughed. "By the power vested in me by the internet church I joined two weeks ago, I now pronounce you husband and wife. You may now share your first kiss as husband and wife."

I lowered my hands to her hips and pulled her close. She reached onto her tip toes and twisted her arms around the back of my neck. Our lips met and applause erupted from the audience.

Her lips smiled against mine, and I couldn't help but smile back. Then I lifted her into the air. She giggled and I grinned.

We may not have always kept those vows, but we never lost the love behind them.

CHAPTER SIXTY-THREE

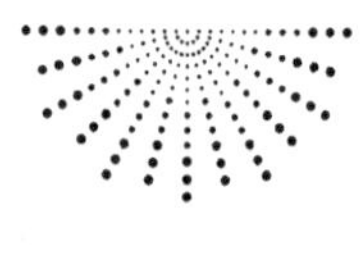

LAILA

I laughed as Jeremy lifted me into the air with his lips on mine. My legs extended outward. The train of my dress created something of a drape behind me. I heard everyone laugh from the audience. Cell phone cameras flashed like we were on the red carpet.

He smiled as he sat me down. "You look amazing."

"Wait, you have to see the back. Look, look." I excitedly dropped his hands and spun around. "Isn't it pretty?"

"Wow." Jeremy ran his fingertip along the embroidery before his thumbs caught on the back of my hips. "It's beautiful." His lips lowered to my cheek. "*You're* beautiful."

"Isn't it?" I spun back toward him.

"You're supposed to walk back down the aisle together, dumbasses," Leah called.

He laughed, leaned in, and kissed my forehead. Then we did so, hands twined together as we headed down the mossy hillside, smiling at first, then making stupid faces at the cameras as we drew closer to the thick wooden log used as a bridge between the yard and the trail. When we got a few feet from it, Jeremy abruptly teleported behind me, put one hand beneath my knees, and the other behind my back.

"""

Hoisting me into the air, I let out a little squeal, and Jeremy grinned down at me.

Tucking my arms behind his neck, I said, "You better not drop me."

His smile widened, and he shook his head. "Never."

Joy lifting the edges of my lips, I craned forward took his face in my hands, and kissed him long and slow.

I was floating in the clouds. That's how it felt. Like floating. My stomach was spinning with happy butterflies, and my heart fluttered with excitement.

Happy. We were *so* happy.

A thousand flashes still blinded my gaze as Jeremy pulled back to see the path over the bridge.

When we got to the grass, he carefully lowered my feet to the soil, steadying me by my hip.

"I guess this was better than eloping."

He laughed. "Oh yeah?"

"I think so, don't you?"

"Not really. There were only five guests. It was kind of a waste of money, but it was beautiful."

I narrowed my gaze but held my smile. "*You're* the one who insisted we do a whole big wedding."

"Yeah, yeah. I know." He smiled. "It's gorgeous, really. Everything's perfect. *You're* perfect."

"Maybe not perfect, but you're stuck with me now, Jeremy Skoulda."

"There's no one else I'd rather be stuck with, Laila Callidy." He grinned, reached forward, and placed his hands at my hips.

I didn't even remember until years later. He pointed it out a few years down the line. Apparently, I'd said that exact same quote in the cabin the first night he brought me there. That little banter became something of a catchphrase between the two of us.

I smiled, lifted my arms behind his head, and he leaned in for a kiss. "I love you so much."

"I love you so much more," I murmured, touching his cheek. "After we take some pictures, do you want to go find somewhere to consummate our marriage?"

He gave a playful grin. "Don't you think that's a little cliché?"

"Clichés aren't always a bad thing. And we're super cliché anyway."

"We could go do it first. Then we'll look *really* happy in our pictures."

"But you'll mess up my hair," I said.

Jeremy lowered his lips to my cheek, then trailed down my jaw and onto my neck. "I can be careful," he whispered at my ear, breath teasing a layer of chills to my skin.

I closed my eyes as goosebumps bubbled over my skin. He kissed my neck, tugging me even closer, bodies so tight together that I could feel the soft thud of his heart against mine.

He leaned back, still holding my hips. "But we can wait."

After that sweet, panty soaking kiss? "No, I think now's better." I turned to the crowd, having almost forgotten they were snapping photos until I turned their way. "We'll be back, we just have a quick errand to run."

"Errand my ass." Adam gave a boyish grin.

"Don't you fuck up her hair!" Hannah yelled.

I laughed, and Jeremy smiled. He yanked me in close, and we disappeared.

We landed in his old bedroom at the main house. Smart move, we knew no one else was home. The apartment wasn't a good move either. A business was being run downstairs, and I had a habit of struggling to keep my voice down.

Jeremy's hands tightened around my back. I lifted myself further onto the tips of my toes. He fiddled with the buttons on the back of my dress. Focusing, his lips against mine slowed. I laughed and pulled away.

"It takes an army to get in and out of this thing."

Jeremy laughed, hands trailing up my bodice. "Does that mean I get to fuck you while you're wearing it?

I grinned, rolled back to my tip toes, and touched my lips to his.

Smiling against my lips, he leaned down to the floor of my skirt, lifted it up my legs, and grabbed my hips. Carefully holding the dress up, he walked me backward to the bed. He kept it lifted, an incredibly considerate move. I didn't want to dance around in a cum drenched dress all night.

I grasped his tie and tugged him down to me. Once he was kneeling between my legs, I leaned away and rested my forehead to his. Breaths hard an uneven, surreal sensation washing through me, I met his bright blue eyes. "You're my husband."

His grin turned to a genuine smile, hands gently skimming up and down my thighs "You're my wife."

There was no better word for the emotion that bubbled through me than delight.

I was married. I was bound to my best friend for life. Of course, I'd been bound to him for years, but now, I got to say *my husband* instead of *my boyfriend*. It was only a word, but its meaning carried an insurmountable weight.

We always knew how much we meant to each other, but the title was like proof of it to the rest of the world.

"You look really hot in a tie," I murmured at Jeremy's lips. "You should do that more often. Not just for weddings and funerals."

"Hate to break it to you, baby, but you fell for a band Ts and bleach-stained sweatpants kind of guy."

"I guess I did, didn't I?" I grinned.

His hands slid to the bottom of my dress and lifted it to my lap. "But like you said. You're stuck with me now."

I grinned. "Looks like it."

His palms slid up my inner thighs. My stomach flipped. Pleasant chills erupted over my skin. He smiled, fingers grazing my panties. "You're okay, right?"

I held my smile and gave a gentle nod.

And I really was. He was on top of me, and I was better than okay. With his hands on my skin, with his gentle eyes on mine, I was safe. I was comfortable, and I was excited.

Everything was... perfect.

Jeremy smiled back, thumbing my cheek. "Just tell me if that changes, alright?"

"Just kiss me," I whispered.

He gave a faint laugh as he leaned down and touched his lips to mine. It was just that—a touch. Not a heavy kiss, but a soft caress. Just enough for my nerve endings to burst with temptation.

As I traced the buttons on his chest down to the zipper on his slacks, his fingertips feathered my panties. I took in a quiet gasp, pressure building deep in my core from that tiny touch.

When he peeled back the fabric though, brushing my clit, my gasp morphed into a soft moan, pleasure heightening when he rotated his fingers in a gentle circle.

His slacks dropped to his knees with his boxers, and I grabbed his tie, yanking him in closer. He let out a soft groan, body curling toward me, cock brushing against my cunt.

I found the knot of the tie close to his neck and pulled it free.

He sighed with relief. "You know I'm gonna need help getting that back on."

I laughed, undoing each button down his chest. "I'll do my best."

He smiled, kissing me softly again. Those gentle strokes against my clit dipped lower, pushing gently into my opening, thumb taking over on my clit. A soft moan broke through our kiss.

"Fuck, I love when you do that," Jeremy murmured.

I glided a hand down his chest, wrapping my fingers around his cock. "When I do what?"

He kissed me again. Then he curled his finger inside of me, thumb massaging my clit. My head rolled back, hands tightening around his shoulders, another moan of bliss escaping my lips.

"That." His voice was a gravelly whisper, bringing a pleasant quiver of chills through me. "When I try to kiss you while I'm touching you but you can't focus and moan in my mouth."

I giggled and felt my cheeks get hot. "I'll keep that in mind."

Jeremy grinned, kissing down my neck toward my collar bone. He massaged slow and hard against my G-spot, thumb moving in careful circles against my clit.

A slow, quiet gasp left my lips, and I wrapped my leg along his outer thigh, bringing him closer into me. He chuckled, eyes meeting mine. That expression always made moments like these so much better. He touched me with precision, but his eyes were so kind, so soothing.

That expression was like a portal to another dimension where only the two of us existed. Nothing else was real, and nothing else mattered.

Smiling, his thumb brushed my lower lip. "You're gorgeous."

"You caught me on a good day." I grinned, teleported him to the bed, and jumped on top of him.

He laughed as I struggled my gown around us. I used my knees to maneuver up the bed, lifting the under skirt with me until I was kneeling over his pelvis. He gently pulled the skirt outward until it coasted around both of us like a blanket.

I lowered myself to him and gently kissed him. His hard dick slid between my lips, sliding against my clit. The little tease made that pressure within me build higher, and I wanted more. I wanted all of him.

Angling myself closer, still kissing, the crinkle of plastic rattled.

I opened my eyes and looked down. A foil wrapper. One I hadn't seen in a long time.

"Adam gave it to me," Jeremy said. My eyes went back to his. He smiled, shrugging slightly. "It'd make this a little less messy. I mean, unless, you know... You don't want to use it."

That expression in his gaze told me what he was asking.

Micah hadn't exactly been planned. I wanted the next one to be as much as he did. But not yet.

"It's probably a good idea," I said.

Something flashed in his eyes. Maybe a hint of grief, or a small wave of disappointment.

That stung, and I felt guilty for it. I knew how badly he wanted to be a dad, and I wanted to be a mom just as much. But now wasn't the time. I was doing better, but I wasn't ready yet. I wasn't sure when I would be, but I wasn't yet.

Jeremy forced a smile, touched my cheek, and gently tugged my lips back to his. With his free hand, he grabbed the condom, laughed as he fought through my skirt, and moved to his dick. He slid it on, pulled the head back, and gently pushed it into my opening.

When I lowered myself onto him, I watched that pulse of euphoria overwhelm him, and that pressure in my stomach built higher.

This was perfect. It was everything I wanted our wedding to be. Simple, romantic, ending in the perfect place.

Here, in his arms, lost in a sea of sensuality, and intimacy, and pleasure. With each gentle wave of my body, every little grind of my clit against his pelvis, that journey to ecstasy intensified.

His hand at my hip made its way to mine. He coasted his fingertips along my palm, up my fingers, then collapsed them between the gaps. He grasped tight, yet still so soft.

Still rocking up and down against him, my eyes opened, and our eyes locked. He pulled my knuckles to his lips and kissed them.

In that single moment, everything else ceased to exist. The rest of the world simply melted away. He was inside of me, his eyes were on mine, and nothing else mattered.

It was just me and the most amazing man I'd ever met, basking in the bliss of one another's touch.

"Thank you," he whispered.

My smile widened. I slowed down and chuckled. "What for?"

"Saying yes." He smiled.

My cheeks warmed. "Thank you for asking."

"Well, I knew you wouldn't."

I laughed. "Shut up and kiss me."

Jeremy grinned, released his hand in mine, touched the side of my neck, and pulled me down to him. Simultaneously touching our lips together, he arched his hips higher. I gasped, his dick having hit something inside me that felt like pure heaven.

"Fuck," I whispered.

His lips curled into mine. "Does that feel good?"

I bared down, rubbing my clit further into the curls of his pelvis, body quaking with pleasure, barely managing out, "Yes."

"Keep grinding, baby," he whispered in my ear. "I want to feel you come."

Holy shit, I didn't know why that was so hot but warmth gushed between us. A smile pulled at his lips. His hand slid to my waist, pulling me closer to him.

That pressure building within strengthened until my leg was trembling, and I locked my arms around his shoulders.

"Fuck, I love when you moan like that," he murmured. "You're gonna come for me, aren't you?"

As if in answer, another heavy groan dropped from my lips. The heat of his breath tickled my cheeks as his chest shook with a chuckle. "Good, then I won't feel so bad when I do because holy fuck, this is amazing."

He kept his hips exactly where they were and tugged my face back to his. His bottom lip brushed against mine, then his tongue slipped through. It grazed my lower lip. That sensation got heavier, trailing from my mouth down to the pit of my stomach and into my cunt.

His breaths grew heavy against mine. "Right there," he murmured. "Right there, baby."

The ecstasy ruptured, fluid gushing between my thighs, near scream leaving my lips. Those waves of pleasure and bliss rolled over every pore, body electrifying, blacking out my vision. He was all that I could see, the rest of the room faded to blackness. Those beautiful blue eyes stayed on mine, watching me moan and tremble for him, holding me firmly, passionately.

"Fuck," he murmured, arms yanking me in tighter, holding me as close to him as we could get. He stiffened, rolling his hips upward, deeper, filling me completely. "Jesus Christ, Lai."

As the burst of euphoria slowed, light returned to the room, still lost in the aftereffects, but basking in every second.

Practically heaving, he dropped his head to my chest, and I collapsed into his shoulder.

"Well," he said between deep breaths, "I think our marriage is consummated."

CHAPTER SIXTY-FOUR

LAILA

We cuddled for a few minutes in the bed before deciding it was time to get back to our wedding. We'd taken all week off at the diner; we had plenty of time to get lost in one another's embrace all week. But this was our only wedding, and we needed to enjoy it.

There were at least a thousand photos taken that day. Since I hadn't hired a photographer, I was glad everyone was snapping their phones at us. There were a lot of genuine, candid shots that turned out beautifully. I'm pretty sure I took a picture with every single person at least twice.

Obviously, none of them came out perfectly since they were all taken on smartphone cameras. Still, I wouldn't have had it any other way. It was easily the best day of my life. Up to that point, anyway. My kid's births were tied.

The decorations were perfect, everyone looked amazing, and I felt like I was floating. It was everything I wanted out of my wedding day. Besides Jeremy's grandparents who I hadn't met yet, everyone there was someone important to me. Every single person was someone I loved with my whole heart. I didn't have to worry about impressing anyone because they were all people who'd seen me at my worst.

Those people, even the ones who weren't my blood, were my family. In fact, there were only two people there who shared my DNA: Kai and Celena. I supposed that was one of the most beautiful things about my family. Almost all of them were people I *chose* to consider family until my children came into the picture.

"This is beautiful," Max smiled.

I picked at the cookies on the dessert table and turned his way. His eyes shifted over the patio made into a dance floor. Mine followed. A smile edged up my cheeks. "It is, huh?"

Everyone looked so happy. Celena and Wyatt danced awkwardly with laughs and smiles, haphazardly swaying around the patio. Hannah and Kai danced elegantly a few feet away, as if there was nowhere else they'd rather be. Even Haley and Leah looked happy, which brought me more joy than almost anything.

The two of them had seen some shit, they deserved to find some shred of bliss after what they'd been through. It'd make Chris happy to see them like that. Two of his best friends, being as joyous as he wanted everyone he cared about to be. It was funny how I only knew him for a few short months but thought about him so often.

Adam and Jenna seemed to be making conversation as well, laughing and brushing their hands against each other's upper arms. They weren't exactly a pair I would have matched, but after a moment or two of thought, I could see the two of them making a good couple. Adam was one of the best men I knew, and Jenna had a bigger heart than almost anyone I'd ever met.

It was a little odd how my family had begun to intertwine with Jeremy's. Kai and Hannah, Celena and Wyatt—who may not have been blood but was just as much family as the rest of us—then Adam and Jenna. But it made sense. We were all caught up in a world that most people couldn't understand, but everyone there was already engulfed in it. We clung to each other, almost instinctively, because no one else could possibly grasp what our lives were like.

Jeremy stood with Brody, neat wavy black hair resting just above his white collar. He looked happy too. It seemed to be a dream come true for him. He'd lived a thousand nightmares before that day, and he would live a thousand more, but we would both always have that moment.

Mom sat at a table with Jeremy's grandparents, chuckling and telling stories about my husband and I as children. It was sweet to see them smiling as if old friends.

"Definitely the best wedding I've been to." Max smiled. "Except for the lack of single girls. Me and Brody are dying over here."

I laughed and turned to meet his gaze. "Sorry, man. I don't have that many girlfriends."

"Yeah, I've noticed. The ones you do have are taken."

"Or gay."

He chuckled. "Either way. It was really nice. I wasn't supposed to bring a gift, was I?"

"No, we don't need anything. I just wanted to elope, but our families would have been pissed so here we are."

"I'm glad you didn't." He smiled. "I wanted to see this. And Adam's little speech was really cool."

I smiled. "Yeah, he did great. Everything turned out amazing."

"I'm happy for you guys. You and Jeremy are the cheesiest, lamest couple ever and it's adorable. You guys deserve this. Especially after everything that's happened this year."

"It has been a hell of a year. 2019 has been pretty fucking shitty, and today doesn't cancel all of that out. When we look back on it later though, at least we'll remember it as the year we got married and started our lives as husband and wife."

He glanced over my shoulder and smiled. Suddenly, two hands gripped my hips and lifted me into the air. I laughed, breathing in the smell of Jeremy's cologne. I relaxed into his hard chest. His lips touched my neck as he sat me down, fingers lacing around my stomach.

"Hey you." I spun around.

"Hey." He smiled. His hands moved around to my hips. His gaze shifted to Max. "Mind if I steal her for a second?"

Max said, "She's all yours, man."

"Are you busy?" Jeremy asked. "Because I wanted to introduce you to my grandparents."

My stomach flipped. Obviously, I knew that moment was coming. It wasn't that I'd been dreading it, but I wasn't exactly looking forward to it. No one in the family ever uttered kind words in reference to Raphael and Adele Skoulda.

"No, I'm not busy."

"Are you nervous?"

"Yeah. Yeah, a little bit. But it's alright. Let's just do it."

CHAPTER SIXTY-FIVE

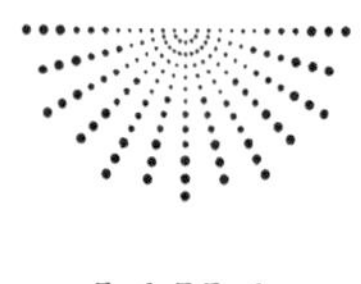

LAILA

"Mémé, Papy." Jeremy tapped his grandma's shoulder. She turned, gave a gleeful grin, and stood. "J'aimerais que tu recontres ma femme, Laila. And Laila, this is my grandma, Adele, and my grandpa, Raphael."

"Non, non." Adele reached out and placed her arms around me in a ginger hug. "Mémé, mon chérie."

"Elle ne parle pas Francais?" Raphael asked as Mémé and I pulled apart.

Well, no. I did not speak French. But I did know a thing or two.

"Elle en parle, mais elle est américaine, Papy," Jeremy said.

He shook his head and he rolled his eyes. But I smiled and extended my hand to him. He shook it quickly and pulled it back to his side. "Pas même in gardien non plus."

From there, all I could make out was context clues. Judging by Jeremy's furrowed brows, the tightness in his jaw, how his shoulders broadened, then by the sharp tone in Raphael's voice and the glare he shot my way, my grandfather in law was not fond of me.

Raphael said, "Voulez-vous des enfants mixtes, Jeremy ? Avec cette pute?"

Up until that point, I only understood a word here and there. But I knew what pute meant, as did any middle schooler who googled how to call people names in other languages.

My eyes widened, and Jeremy's mouth fell open. He scrunched down his brows. Before he could say another word, Mémé smacked him in the chest.

She said something, and Raphael began to respond, and then Jeremy abruptly interjected, speaking so fast that I didn't catch a word. But I certainly read his posture. His shoulders stiffened, his hand at my waist tightened, and his big eyes were wide in rage. He raised his finger and wagged it in his grandfather's face.

Raphael's tongue ran along his teeth. He opened his mouth to speak, but Jeremy kept going.

"Hey, are you guys ready to do the bouquet toss?" Hannah called from the buffet table. "We should get it done before the sun goes down."

"Jeremy," Mémé began. He turned to her, smiled, and shook his head.

He spoke slower to her than he had to Raphael but still too fast for me to catch a word. Then he smiled at her and sent his grandpa a glare.

Mémé smiled. Raphael rolled his eyes again.

"C'mon, babe. Let's go."

Clearly, they were not fans of mine. His grandfather in particular. But still, they were my in-laws so I would remain polite. Clearly, Jeremy had my back regardless.

"Au revoir." I smiled. Mémé returned it. And Raphael looked to his wine.

"Au revoir," she said.

As we shifted around, I looked up to meet Jeremy's gaze. "Your grandpa just called me a whore."

He glanced down at me. "You caught that, huh?"

"And something about blasphemy?" I asked.

"Yeah, he's racist. He doesn't think we should" —he held up quotes — "mix our blood."

"Racist?" I asked. "But I'm white."

"Oh." He laughed. "No, that's not what I meant. He wouldn't care if

I were with an Asian, or an African, or an Indian. As long as she was a Guardian. I don't know, some shit about keeping blood lines pure. It's gross. But he's my grandpa. Even if he is a bigot."

"Wow, that's weird," I muttered. "I guess I'm a minority now, huh?"

"I think your black friends would probably disagree. But he's an asshole. He wouldn't even say it to your face. He just thought you didn't understand."

"But he just did."

"Baby, he owns a multi-million-dollar company that makes almost all of its profits in the states. He speaks fluent English. Mémé's isn't quite as good but so does she. He did that to be a dick. As he often is."

"Oh," I muttered. If he could understand what I was saying, then I was gonna march my happy ass back there and tell him off. I started to turn. "Then what the fuck else did he say?"

Jeremy laughed and caught my elbow. "Let's just enjoy our wedding, okay?"

Eh, fair enough. I didn't want to look back on my wedding day and remember it as the time that I punched my grandfather in-law in the face.

I huffed. "Fine."

The reception was just as beautiful as the rest of the day had been. It was fun and exhilarating.

Jeremy and I shared our first dance as husband and wife. We swayed around the patio to *Always* by Panic! At the Disco. I'll admit, he did most of the dancing. It's not that I couldn't dance. I could dance. Well, *sometimes*, I could dance.

Okay, I really couldn't dance.

Unless I had a sword in my hand. Then I could dance around like no one's business. However, I didn't quite remember how yet.

But that's another story for another time. I'll get there.

Anyway, the night went on. He pulled my garter off with his teeth and threw it into the crowd of bachelors. Awkwardly enough, Brody caught it. I'm fairly certain I saw Wyatt run the opposite direction and push Brody toward it.

I threw my bouquet over my shoulder with a smile as Mom snapped a picture. Celena caught it, curled her nose in disgust, turned to Wyatt, and shook her head vigorously. Then we all laughed as he wrapped his arms around her and pulled her into him for a kiss.

Jeremy and I cut the cake with our fingers laced together. It was amazing, just as I knew it would be. At least, the parts of it that Jeremy didn't smear into my face.

Around nine thirty, Jeremy and I drove off into the moonlight in his obnoxiously decorated Charger. When we made it home, we kissed all the way up the steps. He hoisted me into his arms and carried me through the threshold with his lips still on mine.

As we stepped into our apartment, I was overwhelmed with the scent of roses. They were sprinkled in a delicate trail from the front door to our bedroom at the end of the hall onto the freshly made bed I knew we wouldn't be leaving for a while. On the dresser sat a few pre rolled joints, a sweet note signed by our families, and a bucket of ice with a bottle of wine inside.

I decided not to drink because I wanted to remember every detail. Much of it is kind of a blur now either way.

But I'll never forget how incredibly *happy* I felt from the moment I woke until the moment I fell asleep that day. I hadn't been that happy in such a long time, I'd almost forgotten what that kind of bliss felt like.

The last time I was that happy was before any of it all started, before I knew what I was, but after I'd met Jeremy. When I was even more naïve than I was then. Just submerged in total, childlike joy as the two of us drove too fast down pot hole covered back roads, smoking joint after joint as we talked about the world and our lives.

After what happened to me, I thought that moments of happiness were meant to appear and fade as quickly as they came. But my wedding day changed that. I'm not sure why, but after that was when I began to find what normal felt like again. I'd become a better version of myself.

The worst of the trauma had lifted. I would never be the girl I was when I was taken, but why would I want to be?

She was dumb. She had a practically boundless abundance of abilities and chose to only master a few of them. She was soft. She was afraid to kill. She cared far too much for far too many. She was weak. She wasn't the warrior who wore a white gown that night.

But ultimately, she had to make the mistakes she did to turn her into the legend she was becoming.

She wasn't always the wisest. She let her heart rule her mind. She let the worst of her get the best of her too many times.

She was young.

But now, even after all of the mistakes she made and had yet to make, I forgive her.

CHAPTER SIXTY-SIX

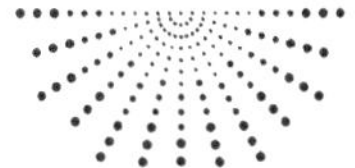

SEPTEMBER 27, 2019 - LAILA

Jeremy's hands slid along my bare side and grazed my breast, lips teasing my neck. My eyes flickered open. Warm light shined in from the bedroom window. The smell of several day-old cologne and perfume mixed with sweat against the soft sheets.

I smiled, rolling around to meet his gaze. "Well, good morning."

"Morning, beautiful," he whispered at my ear. He nibbled the lobe, hand sliding along my bare torso.

"What time is it?" I asked.

His open palm trailed down my stomach, past my belly button all the way to my pelvis. "Does it matter?"

"I guess not." I stifled a yawn.

It really didn't. Max was handling the diner, and Jeremy and I were handling each other. The only time we'd left the apartment since the wedding was to grab food from downstairs. When we weren't gorging ourselves on one another, anyway.

Eight days had passed since our wedding. In that time, Jeremy and I spent almost every waking moment in our bed. We spent some time on the couch too. And the shower. And the dining room table. Even the coffee table once.

To put it simply, we were *really* enjoying married life so far.

"I just woke up," he murmured. The palm of his hand slid against my inner thigh, pulling it over his as he suckled at my neck.

I chuckled, eyes turning up to his. A grin pulled at my lips. "Looks like you woke up on the right side of the bed."

He smiled, bit his lower lip, and moved his hand to my hip. He squeezed a bit, pulling my body tighter to his.

I giggled, running my fingers through his hair. He kissed down my jaw, then either side of my neck. His lips traveled to my collar bone, onto my chest, and down my stomach.

"Baby, I literally haven't showered in two days," I murmured.

He kissed my hip. His eyes met mine. He smirked, hand sliding between my legs. "I literally don't care."

Well, hell, then neither did I.

His eyes met mine as he lowered his mouth to my inner thigh. The tip of his tongue glided against my skin. My stomach flipped, liquid gushing between my thighs. He grinned. Then his tongue drifted against my cunt.

I sighed, and his smile widened. His fingers slid to my opening and my head tilted back with a moan. He chuckled. His tongue made a slow, teasing circle around my clit. I bit my lip, letting a moan fall from my mouth. I arched my hips closer to his face. His finger curved up, massaging against my G-spot.

My stomach swirled with excitement. I ran my fingers through his soft black locks.

The pressure of his tongue got heavier. Then he flicked it up and down. I gasped, head rolling back against the pillow.

Then his phone rang on the bedside table.

"Don't answer that," I murmured.

I wasn't going to, he said into my mind.

The phone continued to ring, but he just flicked his tongue faster. His other hand ran up my chest. He grasped my breast and brushed his fingertip against my nipple. He made slow, little circles around my clit before his lips opened.

Then, my phone rang too. Still pulsing his fingers inside of me and brushing his tongue against my clit, he spoke into my mind. *Don't answer that.*

I laughed. "I wasn't going to."

Then he flicked faster. A moan escaped my mouth. His hand at my boob moved to my stomach, then around my back to pull me toward him. My eyes closed in bliss.

A loud, cop-like knock thudded against our bedroom door. "Guys," Adam called.

I jumped and my hand flew to my chest. "Jesus Christ."

"Go away." Jeremy buried his fingers deeper inside of me. His thumb rubbed against my clit. I bit my lip to fight the moan that wanted to leave my mouth.

"It's important, you guys can fuck later," Adam said.

"Fuck off, Adam." Jeremy lowered his lips back to my clit. It took everything in me not to scream.

"Some crazy shit is going down, and you guys need to see it," Adam insisted. "Seriously, put your pants on for, like, five minutes."

A slow sigh left my lips. This one, not in pleasure. Clearly, Adam wasn't leaving until we got out of bed. And as much as I was enjoying this, we'd fucked plenty in the last week. If something was going down, we may need to know about it.

I tugged Jeremy's chin upward. "We have the rest of our lives."

"But we were having fun." Jeremy smiled, sitting up to meet my gaze.

"Rain check?"

He brought himself to his knees, sighing "I guess."

I sat up and pulled my robe from the frame of the bed. "You really should have knocked at the front door." I stood and pulled the fabric through my arms. "We could have been fucking in the living room."

"I assumed you wouldn't be having sex in the hallway," Adam called.

Jeremy stood and pulled on a pair of boxers. "Well, you assumed wrong."

I walked to the door, pulled it open, and tightened my robe. "What's up, Adam?"

His blue eyes were wide in some type of shock, maybe even fear. "You guys need to get dressed and come to the house. Like asap."

"Is everything okay?"

"No one's hurt, if that's what you're asking."

I cocked my head to the side slightly. "Care to elaborate?"

"You... You have to see it for yourself," Adam said. "Just come to the house, alright?"

"Okay. Sure, we just need to get dressed."

"Just make it quick. Like, super speed." Then he disappeared.

CHAPTER SIXTY-SEVEN

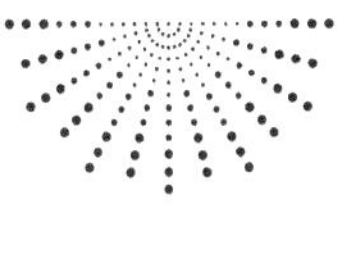

JEREMY

We landed in the kitchen. The scent of apples and cinnamon filled my nose. Warm air brushed around me. And strange, mumbled gibberish echoed from the open basement door.

"Good, you're here," Leah said. In her hands, she held an old recording machine. "Did Adam fill you in?"

Laila shook her head.

"No, he said we had to see it for ourselves," I said.

"Well, he isn't entirely wrong." Leah set the old video camera on the counter. "Alright, Lai, you aren't going to like this. But you have to see it. We all do."

"See what?"

"The guard, in the basement. He's... I don't know. Something is happening. He's... I can't, you just have to see it."

I felt her palm begin to sweat. It tightened around mine. "No. No, I don't want to see him. That's what he wants, he wants to—"

"It isn't Peterson." Leah collected the recorder back into her hands. "He hasn't been in there for a while. It's... It's something else. I really don't have time to explain, we need to go down there now."

"Leah, I can't," Laila said, firmer that time. I saw her chest beginning to pulse with fast anxious breaths. "I don't want to. I won't, I won't see him."

"Trust me, you *need* to," Leah said with wide, uneasy eyes. "I'm going to record it for future reference, but you need to see it with your own eyes. This is... I don't know, I just have a feeling that this whole thing is *big*. Bigger than we thought it was. But I think somehow, you're at the center of it all." Her eyes were still wide as she walked to the open basement door. "I'm going down. Come down when you're ready. My guess is that the show really starts when you're ready to see it."

Laila clenched her trembling jaw to a line. Leah disappeared down the steps. I turned to Laila and reached out for her cheek

"Are you okay?" I asked.

Her eyes avoided mine. She placed her palms against my biceps. "Yeah. Yeah, I just..." Her head shook. She closed her eyes. "After everything, you wouldn't think such an unimportant, tiny man would make me feel like this."

Regardless of what Leah thought, I wasn't going to tell her she had to do anything she didn't want to. If she didn't want to walk down those steps, I wasn't going to try and persuade her too. But I planned to go down there. Because if she weren't ready to deal with it, I'd do it for her.

I lifted her chin to meet my gaze. "And how do you feel?"

Her big green eyes met mine. Aside from her shaking breaths, you'd have thought she was handing an order note over the serving hatch in the diner. "I think I'm scared."

"If you don't want to go down there, I can handle it. But if you do, I'll be right beside you. No one's going to hurt you."

"Yeah. Yeah, I know. Let's get it over with. I'm alright. I might not be later, but I'm okay."

I kissed her forehead and ran my hand along her arm. "I'll be there, then, too."

A soft, sad smile pulled at her lips. Then she moved her hand to mine and led the way downstairs.

As soon as the basement door opened, hysteric yells poured into my ears. It wasn't cries, or pleas. It was more like manic, disoriented rambles. There were tinges of anger, even laughter.

"The seven lamp stands," his voice said frantically. "The seven lamp stands, and the seven stars. Eyes blazing like fire, and hair as white as wool. And I—I will give him the morning star. White as wool, and the seven lamp stands. The seven stars, the seven stars in his hand, and the morning star. Give him the morning star."

Laila met my gaze. I wasn't sure if she knew what that meant, or where it was from, but I did. Anyone who went to Sunday school as a kid would have. It was the scary story Christians told around a campfire.

We hurried down the steps and rounded the stairwell to the area where he was chained to the wall.

My mouth dropped open when my eyes fell on him. Our prisoners never got five-star service or anything, but that guy looked sickeningly ill. If he weren't talking, I would have thought he was dead.

His already white skin was paler than cotton. The whites of his eyes, I would have expected to be bloodshot. But instead, the once pinkish red veins were a slightly grayish shade of blue. His lips had faded into the nastiness of his skin, it was almost impossible to tell what was his mouth and what was his face.

As he looked up, his gaze locked with Laila. He collapsed to his knees, extending his arms upward. "Do not be afraid for I am the first and the last. I was dead and now I live. I am alive forever! I hold the keys to death and Hades!"

Adam met my gaze. "You know what that's from, right?"

Everyone who did any extensive reading on Christianity did. "Revelation."

Laila gazed at the man, forehead scrunching down. She didn't look afraid now. Puzzled, maybe, but not scared. She took a step forward, still holding my hand in hers.

"They shall hunger no more, neither thirst. Neither shall the sun light on them, nor any heat." His gaze shifted back and forth between Laila's. "And there, appeared a great wonder in heaven." A deranged smile stretched up his pasty cheeks. "A woman clothed with the sun and the moon at her feet. And upon her head, a crown of twelve stars. And she, being with child, travailing birth and panting to deliver he unto the world."

You've gotta be shitting me.

This motherfucker was seriously comparing my wife to the bitch in Revelation who birthed the child that would bring on the end of the world.

As if what she'd been through hadn't been hard enough, now he was gonna make my dead kid out to be Satan too.

Laila watched him carefully. Her head tilted a bit. She dropped my hand and drew closer. I almost reached to pull her back, but it was about her. If she were ready to face it, I wouldn't stop her. I *couldn't* stop her.

The man smile grew soft, staring up at Laila as if she were a god. The chains rattled, pulling against their brackets in the wall. He trying to get close enough to touch her. And I would've stepped in, but those chains were strong enough to hold Wyatt. They weren't gonna fall for that puny man.

He humbly kneeled at her feet as close as she would allow. "He that leadeth into captivity shall go into captivity. He that killeth with thy sword must be killed with thy sword."

I turned to Leah. She stood far back in the corner with the small tripod. "How long has this been going on?"

"Since early this morning," Leah said. "But it was broken fragments. Now that Laila's here, he's speaking in full sentences."

"He's speaking in verses, not sentences," I muttered. "This is a verbatim remix of Revelations. Has he said anything else?"

"He kept saying, 'Laila has to know.' Then he'd go back to the broken, psycho rambling."

The man's hands reached out for Laila's. When she stood there unmoved, he lifted them to the sky. It was as though he was at the fore-front of a church on Easter Sunday, raising his hands in praise an imaginary man in the sky.

"And to the woman were given two wings of a great eagle. That she might fly into the wilderness, into her place, where she is nourished for a time and times, and half a time, from the face of a serpent. And the serpent cast out of his mouth water as a flood after the woman, that he might cause her to be carried away by the flood. And the earth helps the woman. She opens her lips and swallows up the flood which the dragon cast out of its mouth."

Laila lowered herself to her knees in front of the man. She'd been scared upstairs, but now she looked... Almost amused. "Who is 'he?' The dragon? Satan?"

I, however, was not amused. That whole book was a crock of shit. There was a god, I knew he was real. He was Mary's dad. Hell, he was my wife's grandfather. But he wasn't all loving. I didn't ask and receive. He fucked us and fucked us time and time again.

Nothing pertaining to that man applied to me. Or to her. We were nothing to him, and I had no interest in hearing the rambles pouring from that man's mouth.

But she did. And I wasn't gonna leave her.

The man's closed eyes opened and he met Laila's gaze. His hands outstretched, reaching just a few inches from the sides of her face. They didn't touch her skin, but he acted as though they had. "The dragon is yet to come. The seventh seal must be broken by He who shines brighter than the sun to release her unto the earth."

"I don't understand," Laila said.

"Blessed is he that readeth and they that hear the words of this prophecy. He that hath an ear, let him hear what the Spirit saith unto the churches. To him that overcometh will I give to eat of the tree of life in the midst of the paradise of god," the man continued. "Worthy is the lamb that was slain to receive power, and riches and wisdom, and strength, and honor, and glory and blessing."

Laila stayed crouched in front of him just as humble as he kneeled. Everyone else seemed frightened, or uneasy at the least, but not Lai. She seemed unshaken by the man's words as he went on. Confused, but not scared like she had been a moment before in the kitchen. She always had a soft spot for the crazies.

And so did I. But that line? The lamb that was slain? I saw where he was going with this.

He was referring to my dead son. And playing on that pain sent an angry churn to the pit of my stomach. My jaw tightened. My hand clenched in fury. I don't think Laila saw the connections I was drawing, and I didn't expect her to. She wasn't raised in the church. She didn't know what that shit meant. But I did and it infuriated me. If she understood it, she'd be just as angry.

"And lo, there will be an earthquake. The sun will become black as sackcloth of hair and the moon become as blood. The stars of heaven will fall unto earth, and the heaven depart as a scroll when it is rolled together. Every mountain and every island will be moved from its place.

"The kings of the earth, and the great men, and the rich men, and the chief captains, and the mighty men, and every bondman, and every free man will hide themselves in the dens and in the rocks of the mountains. And said onto the rocks, fall unto us and hide us from the face of him that sitteth on the throne. And from the wrath of the lamb.

"Hurt not the earth, neither the sea, nor the trees until we have sealed the servants of our God in their forehead." Tears began to pour down the man's face. He shook his head slowly, arms still outstretched. He smiled. "These are they which came out of great tribulation and have washed their robes and made them white in the blood of the lamb. They shall hunger nor thirst no more. And in those days shall men seek death and shall not find it. They shall desire to die and death shall flee from them." His hands shook as he struggled against the chains, desperately trying to touch her. She sat unmoved. Then his gaze shifted to me and repeated the last line. "Death shall flee from them." Then he turned to Laila and said it again, eyes nearly begging. *"Death shall flee from them."*

Laila leaned back and took in a deep breath. Her gaze wasn't fearful as she and I had both expected. Instead it was… It was curious? Concerned? As if in some way, she was communicating with him.

I'd read the bible a handful of times, and although it was complicated because of its awful grammar, it was more structured than the words leaving this man's mouth. He was speaking in riddles.

The man struggled further against the chains. "For the Lamb which is in the midst of the throne shall feed them and shall lead them unto living fountains of waters: and God shall wipe away all tears from their eyes." His smiling lips trembled. "The third angel sounded and there fell a great star from heaven, burning as it were a lamp and it fell upon the third part of the rivers and upon the fountains of waters. The name of the star is called Wormwood: and the third part of the waters became wormwood. And the fourth angel sounded and the third part of the sun was smitten and the third part of the moon and the third part of the stars; so as the third part of them was darkened, and the day shone not for a third part of it, and the night likewise."

Tears tinged with blood began to stream down the man's eerily white face. "And the fifth angel sounded, and I saw a star fall from heaven unto the earth: and to him was given the key of the bottomless pit. And he opened the bottomless pit; and there arose a smoke like that of a great furnace. And there came out of the smoke locusts upon the earth: and unto them was given power, as the scorpions of the earth have power. And it was commanded that they should not hurt the grass of the earth, neither any green thing, neither any tree; but only those men which have not the seal of God in their foreheads. And to them it was given that they should not kill them, but that they should be tormented five months: and their torment was as the torment of a scorpion, when he striketh a man.

"The head of a man, their teeth, like that of lions and hair of a woman, and breastplates of iron, and tales unto scorpions. Their wings as loud as chariots in battle behold their king, the angel of the bottom-less pit, Apollyon."

"Apollyon," Brody said from the corner. "That's a Demon, isn't it?"

"Yeah," I said. "We call him the Hebrew name. Abaddon."

"A really fucking old Demon," Adam muttered.

"I went unto the angel and said unto him give me the little book. And he said unto me, take it, and eat it up. And it shall make thy belly bitter, but it shall be in thy mouth sweet as honey. And I ate, and it was sweet as honey but made thy belly bitter," the man continued to ramble with a psychotic smile. His gaze which had been steady with Laila's turned to meet mine. "And there appeared another wonder in heaven;

and behold a great red dragon, having seven heads and ten horns, and seven crowns upon his heads. And his tail drew the third part of the stars of heaven, and did cast them to the earth: and the dragon stood before the woman which was ready to be delivered to devour her child as soon as it was born."

I gritted my teeth. I saw the metaphor he was making. Again, calling Micah the poetic version of the slain lamb.

"This is ridiculous."

"Shh," Leah urged, watching him carefully.

"And when the dragon saw that he was cast unto the earth, he persecuted the woman which brought forth the child." The man looked from me to Laila and then back to me.

I clenched my hand to a fist. I didn't want to hear this shit. My son was not evil. He was innocent. None of this was his fault. I had no desire to hear my dead child spoken of as a villain.

"Fuck this. He's out of his mind, this is pointless." I started to turn to the steps.

Then Laila spoke.

"No," she said. "Stay. Please."

I turned back. Damn it. Whether I wanted to hear it or not, she wanted me there. So I fucking stayed.

I crossed my arms against my chest. She smiled lightly and turned back to the man.

"For they are the spirits of devils, working miracles, which go forth unto the kings of the earth and of the whole world, to gather them to the battle of that great day of God Almighty." He looked between us. "Fear God and give glory to him; for the hour of his judgment is come: and worship him that made heaven, and earth, and the sea, and the fountains of waters."

I couldn't hold back the chuckle that came from my lips. Laila glared at me.

"A woman sit upon a scarlet colored beast, full of names of blasphemy, having seven heads and ten horns. The woman was arrayed in purple and scarlet color, and decked with gold and precious stones and pearls, having a golden cup in her hand full of abominations and filthiness of her fornication. Upon her forehead was a name written, *Mystery, Babylon the Great, Mother of Harlots and Abominations of the Earth.*"

"Must've been one big ass forehead," I muttered.

Adam stifled a laugh.

An unwilling chuckle left my lips again. I ran my fingers past my nose and down my chin. Laila huffed but didn't turn to look at me that time.

I was just dumbfounded by the way they were enthused by that insanity. The book of Revelation was written like a dream journal. Reading its choppy, misplaced contents was like trying to follow the rant of someone on a bad acid trip.

It was a bit eerie, but it looked like some Christian lunatic with a bad case of cabin fever to me. I couldn't take it seriously. Not only did it hardly make sense, but I had no reason to trust that he was even capable of speaking the truth.

"And he laid hold on the dragon, that old serpent, the Devil, Satan, and bound him a thousand years. But the rest of the dead lived not again until the thousand years were finished. This is the first resurrection. And the devil that deceived them was cast into the lake of fire and brimstone, where the beast and the false prophet are, and shall be tormented day and night for ever and ever," the man dragged on like a psychotic broken record. "And I saw coming down from God out of heaven prepared as a bride adorned for her husband. And God shall wipe away all tears from their eyes; and there shall be no more death, neither sorrow, nor crying, neither shall there be any more pain: for the former things are passed crystal.

"And the lord spoke, saying he that overcometh shall inherit all things; and I will be his God, and he shall be my son. And there came unto me one of the seven angels which had the seven vials full of the seven last plagues. The angel said 'Come hither, I will show thee the bride, the Lamb's wife. Having the glory of God: and her light was like unto a stone most precious, even like a jasper stone, clear as crystal."

I rolled my eyes as the quotes began to mix into each other once again. It was nonsense. You couldn't possibly follow it all if you tried. It was like some twisted form of poetry.

"And the city had no need of the sun, neither of the moon, to shine in it: for the glory of God did lighten it, and the Lamb is the light thereof. And the nations of them which are saved shall walk in the light of it. And the kings of the earth do bring their glory and honor into it. And the gates of it shall not be shut at all by day: for there shall be no night there."

He reached against the chains, ripping even harder.

And one came loose.

My heart immediately picked up in my chest.

He fell into Laila and grasped her face. She stumbled back and began to crab crawl away.

I leaped forward and grasped ahold of his shoulder. But he was way stronger than I anticipated. Definitely not like a malnourished person who hadn't seen sunlight in months.

He elbowed me hard in the gut. With a pained grimace, I took hold of his arm and pulled him back. But instead of pulling *him* back, I found myself holding a chunk of rotting flesh in my hand. Nearly all of the skin on his bicep laid in my palm.

I dropped it and jumped backward.

Laila sat on the ground, only inches from him. He was far more passionate then, nearly yelling as he leaned over her.

"They need no candle, neither light of the sun. For the lord God giveth them light and they shall reign forever and ever."

I yanked his chain back until he stumbled onto his ass.

"He that is unjust, let him be unjust still." The man continued pulling himself back to his knees. His gaze stayed steady with hers. "And he which is filthy, let him be filthy still. And he that is righteous, let him be righteous still. And he that is holy, let him be holy still."

"What the actual fuck," Leah whispered, looking at the flesh on the ground.

"The bright and the morning star," the man continued. His gaze was steady with Laila's. She breathed heavily on the cement with her palm against her chest. "The bright and morning star. Find the bright and morning star."

Laila stared at him with wide eyes. At that point, all that held him was a single chain connected to the wall and my hand around the other. I was strong and all, but it felt as though a bear were ripping against that cuff.

As I gazed at Laila, searching her gaze to see if she was okay, I suddenly felt a pain in my leg. I looked down. The man gripped it. He abruptly turned his face to my calf and dug his teeth into it.

"Motherfucker." I kicked him in the face with my opposite foot. But his teeth just dug deeper into my flesh.

"Jesus Christ," Leah murmured.

Laila stood, teleported to the armoire, and grabbed out a sword.

I continued kicking him harder, but the fucker wouldn't budge. Laila teleported to us and slammed it through his chest. He released his teeth and turned up to meet her gaze, seemingly unbothered by the three-foot piece of metal that stuck out of his heart.

"Remember every word I've given you today, Laila," he said. The crazed look in his eyes dissipated. Seriousness replaced it. The same smug gaze that'd stared into mine the night of the bachelor party. "You brought light into this world, Laila."

Her nostrils flared and her eyes widened. Her teeth gritted, eyes glowing like emeralds in their sockets. "This might not kill you but think of it as a premonition."

She lifted the sword and thrusted it into his chest again.

He laughed.

She lifted it and slammed it down again and again. It clanged off the cement below, but he just kept smiling. "Until we meet again, love."

"Fuck," She made out before she slammed it into him again. Then she pulled it out. "You," she screamed. She slammed it into his chest once more.

And he just smiled up at her.

"You looked beautiful on your wedding day," he said casually. She kept stabbing though. As he spoke, she only grew more and more angry. Blood splattered upward, landing like raindrops over our bodies, slapping our faces and necks. "Too bad that joy won't last."

My eyes widened but not enough for her to notice.

He turned his blood covered face to mine. Crimson liquid gurgling from his lips. "Just a matter of time, isn't it, Jeremy?"

I didn't know how he knew, but he knew. And he needed to shut the fuck up.

I teleported a sword to my hand.

"Someone once said that there are no secrets that time does not reveal."

I raised the sword and thrust it into his throat, severing his skull from his neck.

It rolled away like a golf ball that bounced next to a hole.

Silence followed.

For a short second, I made sure he was dead. When the dead mouth stayed silent, I turned my gaze to Laila. She stood above him with shaky, blood splattered fingers. Her lips trembled, followed by her jaw, until her entire body began to quiver.

I took a few steps toward her, placed an arm at her waist to steady her and another at her blood speckled cheek. "Are you alright?"

She nodded, unable to look away from the body at our feet.

"Let's get some air," I said.

CHAPTER SIXTY-EIGHT

JEREMY

As we landed on the grass outside, Laila pulled away. She bent over to grip her knees. She took in slow, calculated breaths. Her blood splattered hands quivered. She closed her eyes and tried to regain her composure.

"Are you okay?" I asked softly.

Laila took in a long, soothing breath in a desperate attempt to steady her trembling body.

"Yeah. Yeah, I'm okay." She was still bent over. Her hands coasted up and down her thighs. "I don't know..." Her voice shook. "I don't know how he does this to me."

"He tortured you." I rested my hand on her shoulder. "He... He hurt you more than anything could. It's okay to feel like this."

She pulled away and lowered herself to the ground. Her knees lifted to her chest as she panted out and heaved in deep breaths. "Can you give me a minute?" she asked. "I just—I need a minute."

"Yeah. Of course, baby. Do you want me to go inside?"

"I'll be in, just one minute. Then I'll move the body out here to burn it. Just... just give me a minute."

"Alright, let me know if you need anything."

I teleported back inside where Adam stood with Hannah. They gazed out the patio door at Laila rocking in the grass.

I said, "She isn't a zoo animal."

Hannah turned to me. "Is she okay?"

"Yeah, she just needs a minute. Quit staring."

"Right." She headed toward the bar where I stood.

Adam turned and met my gaze. "She looked really scared."

"I think we're all a little freaked out," I said. "Is Kai home, Han? Could he heal my ankle?"

She started toward the maid stairs. "Probably. I'll go get him."

"Thanks," I muttered.

Adam drew closer to me. Then he grabbed my face in his palm and looked into my eyes. His voice was nearly a whisper. "Are you high?"

I pawed his hand away. "No, Adam. I'm not high."

"I saw your face when he said something about the happiness you guys have right now not lasting. You were scared. That's why you cut his head off."

"I cut his head off because he was a zombie," I said. "And he bit my damn leg. You'd cut his head off too."

"So, you aren't using then?"

"No. No, I'm clean."

He studied me for a moment. "Alright."

He didn't believe me. Most people couldn't tell when I was lying but Adam could. He'd practically taught me how. But he didn't want to be right.

I wanted to be clean. I was trying. But yet again, my addiction got the best of me. Despite the fact that I knew it was wrong and it could ruin my marriage, I continued to get high.

Each morning, I'd get up. I'd go to the bathroom. I'd crush a few on the counter. Then I'd inhale it. I'd sit on the toilet for a while. And once the most intense portion of the high wore off, I'd go back to the bedroom and climb between the sheets with my wife.

Every time I snorted a pill, I told myself it'd be the last time. It never was, but I kept telling myself it would be. At first, I told myself that I just needed a little bump to keep the withdrawals at bay. But then I'd snort my little line and the rest of the pill just sat there. I couldn't just wipe it away, that'd be a waste.

We spent most of the past week locked in our apartment. Most of the time, we were joined at the hip. Or more like joined at the crotch. I don't even know how many times we'd fucked in the past week, but it was well over twenty. It was amazing. *We* were amazing. We were back, and we were good, and we were happy.

And I wanted to quit using, but then I'd go through withdrawals during our honeymoon and neither of us would enjoy our new married life.

Mid-day, I'd swallow a couple. They didn't really get me high, they just kept me from getting sick. Then when she fell asleep, I'd snort another. Maybe two or three. Sometimes four.

It was stupid. It was selfish. It was wrong.

I hated myself for it.

When I was younger, I thought that I just needed a reason to be sober. But that was hardly the case. I knew what my using would mean for my marriage, but I just couldn't stop. I wanted to, but I just couldn't. Or I guess I just wouldn't. Not until I was ready. And I wasn't.

Laila meant *everything* to me. Everything. She was the best reason I could think of to get clean, but at that time... She wasn't enough. I'd kill for her. Shit, I'd die for her. But I just wouldn't get clean for her.

But that's part of what makes addiction so trivial. I knew what I was doing. I didn't want to hurt her or my family. But I still wanted to get high. It made me sick with myself but not as sick as I would be if I tried to get sober.

The basement door slammed shut. I jumped, thoughts coming back to the moment.

"What the fuck was that?" Leah said.

"Beats the hell out of me," Adam muttered. He walked to the fridge and grabbed a water.

"Throw me one of those." I sat at the kitchen island. He pulled another one from the shelf and tossed it to me.

As I twisted off the lid, Leah sat beside me. "Have you ever heard of anything like this?" Leah pulled her lavender colored hair into a pony tail.

"I've heard of telepaths being able to possess people. Hell, I mean, you've done that," I said. "But not a corpse. There has to be brain activity. It's done with spirit and a dead person has no spirit. Spirit connects to all things that live but he was dead. A Witch had to have been involved for her to tether a human to someone from any distance like that. Even if they were a hundred feet away, that'd still be too far for a psychic alone."

"He said something about the first resurrection. You don't think he meant himself, do you?" Leah asked.

"No. No, I don't think so. That wasn't resurrection, that was possession."

"If dude was alive when Amy first made the connection," Adam began, "the Witch working with them could have cast some type of binding spell to them. Amy could be permanently linked to his body, even if he died."

"Yeah, that's probably how they did it."

Brody walked in from the hallway. "What I don't understand is how sincere he was when he was reciting. That wasn't Peterson, that was something else."

"It was prophecy," Leah murmured.

I scoffed and sipped my water.

"What?" Leah said.

"It was bullshit," I said. "It was bible verses, that doesn't make it prophecy. That same book has been memorized and recited countless times. There's no merit in it just because he was undead. It's that fucking piece of shit trying to get in our heads."

"I don't think so." Leah chewed her cheek. "Some of the things he said... There's too many creepy similarities to be anything less than at least slightly true."

"What—How he described my son as the antichrist?" I asked.

"Actually, he said the opposite," Brody muttered. "He was implying that he was the returned Christ."

"Laila did say he was the reason she was able to save all those people." Adam chimed in quietly.

"Well, he's dead. So that's obviously bullshit."

The room fell silent. I sipped my water again. I sat there for a moment. "I don't know. None of it made sense."

"It was a jumbled cluster-fuck," Leah said. "But I have the recordings. I'm going to study them. I'm going to try to get an Angel to take a look, maybe they'll see something we didn't."

"I know we've already put out word to the Witches about the whole situation," Adam said. "But maybe we should do some more digging. Only a really powerful one could pull off the spells that this bitch has. Someone's got to be missing them, or at least have some clue as to who they are."

"Maybe," Brody said. "But he had people from all around the world. The Witch could be anyone or from anywhere."

"Still worth a shot," Leah said.

"But you know what the weirdest part is?" Brody asked. We all looked at him. His face screwed up in confusion. "He knew what Laila looked like on her wedding day. How could he know that?"

"I don't know," Leah said.

He knew I was using too. And I had no clue how.

"We thought he was only bound to the guard," Adam said quietly. "But what if he's bound to Laila too?"

CHAPTER SIXTY-NINE

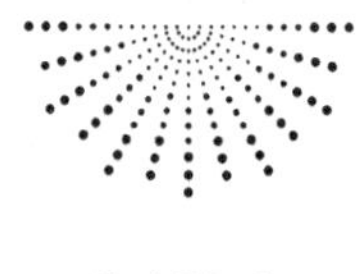

LAILA

My hair dripped onto the pillow beside my face, leaving it cool beneath my cheek. I'd taken a shower an hour ago, Jeremy had changed the sheets, but somehow, the scent of hospital and death still invaded my nostrils.

I knew that made no sense. I hadn't been to a hospital. I'd had almost no physical contact with that man in the basement.

But the smell wouldn't leave me.

I was sure that was some side effect of PTSD. Usually, all the senses that came along with the flashback dwindled shortly after the memory receded. This one had been different though. This one had been too close for comfort.

This wasn't a flashback at all, really.

I'd stared the man who tortured me in the eyes as I decapitated him. Yet, he was alive.

That was what made it so difficult. That was what made this so hard.

I killed him, but he was still alive.

Fuck, all I wanted to do was kill him.

A warm, ginger hand slid around my waist from behind. I knew it was Jeremy, but I still jolted.

He tugged away, voice soft. "I'm sorry. I was just..."

"It's okay." I hardly glanced his way as I took his hand and brought it back to my waist. The tenseness in his fingers softened as they opened over my belly. "I'm alright. Just a little jumpy."

Jeremy didn't say anything. Instead, he lowered his lips to my cheek.

As his scruffy beard brushed my skin, warmth filled my chest, settled through my belly, and soothed my tight muscles. Finally exhaling, forcing in one of those calming breaths I knew was supposed to help my anxiety, the scent of musky citrus filled my nose.

For the first time since this afternoon, that awful scent of hospital mixed with death drizzled into nothingness.

The chill that'd taken hold of me finally warmed.

My falling heart felt stable behind my ribs.

I didn't understand how my husband was capable of making my heartache dwindle, but he was the only thing in the world that never seemed to fail in that department.

"Thank you," I whispered.

He kissed my cheek again, tucking a dark tendril behind my ear. "What for, baby?"

I kept my gaze on the starry sky outside the window and raised a shoulder. "Being here when I need you."

A breath that almost resembled a chuckle fell from his lips. He nuzzled his head in closer, bringing my back tight against his chest, holding my waist tighter. "I'm here for as long as you'll have me."

CHAPTER SEVENTY

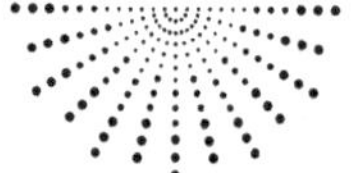

JANUARY 3, 2020 - LAILA

The hot meal in my palm smelled like heaven, scent of grease and burgers touching my nose. My sneakers squeaked against the black and white tiles, brushing past Celena. With a smile, I set the plates on the Formica tabletop. "Here we go." I looked between the couple. "Is there anything else I can get you guys?"

The man squeezed some ketchup onto his plate. "No, thank you."

"Alrighty then." I gave a friendly smile. "You give a holler if you need me."

"Sure." He smiled back, dipped a fry in his ketchup, then munched down on it.

As I made it to the counter, Jeremy came through the swinging door. "Hey, baby, I'm running to the store. Do you need anything?"

I tossed my arms around the back of his neck. "I do, can you grab me some tampons?"

"Sure." He kissed my cheek. "I'm just running down the street then, I don't feel like going all the way to Walmart."

I touched my lips to his. "Okay. Thanks, baby."

He smiled, pulled away, and started toward the front door.

I leaned against the counter and took a sip of my coffee. The taste settled on my tongue. A smile edged up my lips.

Life was good.

The past few months had been peaceful. There were no zombie possessions, no murders, no kidnappings. Things had been docile.

We hadn't gotten any new leads on Peterson either. Leah was running some facial recognition software in an attempt to find him, but we hadn't had any luck yet. It was starting to feel like we never would. I wouldn't be surprised if his crazy ass wore some human like mask when he went out in public.

No Witches had come forward with any info that might lead us to them either. Witches tended to stick to themselves. Their primary concerns were their covens. If they had an issue, they took care of it on their own. Our kinds, although allies, weren't exactly friends. We didn't fight alongside each other, we just referred to each other for advice and an occasional helping hand. In all actuality, we needed their help more often than they needed ours.

Lydia seemed to be adjusting to normal life pretty well. She was still an incredibly odd child, but all things considered, she was pretty stable. Ray was doing fairly well too. It was beautiful to watch him go from depressed widower to happy single father.

Leah and Haley were basically a couple then, although neither of them dare refer to the other as girlfriend. It was good for Leah. Haley too I suppose, but particularly for Leah. I'd never seen her so happy. She wasted so much of her life being bitter. For the first time since I met her, she was smiling on a regular basis. She was still digging into Peterson, but she didn't let it consume her the way it had before. She was allowing herself to live.

Jenna and Adam were casually dating then, but still keeping it below the radar. I think they were worried about what Jeremy and I would think. Although we were both indifferent to the whole thing. They sat beside each other at Christmas dinner and smiled as they brushed elbows or grazed hands, as if we didn't all see what was going on. It was kind of cute though. The last time I saw Adam flirting with anyone so heavily was with Adrian almost four years prior. After he killed her, he found himself in something of a dry spell. But with Jenna, he seemed happy. She did too.

Brody was beginning to see things from a different perspective as well. Over time, he gazed at me differently. It wasn't that same longing, wishful expression I'd seen for the past year or so. He looked content now. I knew he still loved me, but he wasn't as in love with me as he once was. He had just started his last year of community college and he seemed happy to be so close to graduation. I was happy for him.

Hannah had just started her first semester of college. It was adorable watching her grow from the fourteen-year-old I met when Jeremy and I first got together into a college girl. She busted her little ass pouring drinks at the shows in my basement while saving up for her first car too.

Now that she spent so much time on school and work, Kai had been pretty bored. He asked if I had any work he could do at the diner so I gave him some odd jobs. We didn't need any more servers, cooks, or bar tenders, so I just had him do miscellaneous things. Fixing broken floor tiles, repairing jammed windows, maintaining plants outside. Nothing particularly notable, busy work really. But it brought in a paycheck and seemed to give him a sense of purpose.

Celena and Wyatt had both grasped a good handle on their abilities. Celena had mastered her four Fae powers while in human as well as wolf form. Wyatt had gotten a good grasp on his Guardian abilities as well. He wasn't great at handling them in wolf form but he was improving.

Jeremy and I had been in a spectacularly good place. Things between us felt normal again. We had found some peace in the aftershocks the first half of 2019 brought us. Everything felt the way it had before. We were getting back to us.

As for me, I was like a new and improved version of myself. I was trying to train myself to reveal my other abilities although I hadn't made much progress. I learned that I was telekinetic two months before, but I often found myself using my ability to control air as a means of telekinesis. The two overlapped a bit which made it hard to distinguish between them.

I also discovered that I had the ability of astral projection. It made sense since that's how Angels were able to check on those they watched over without physically being there. It hadn't served me much good so far. It was kind of difficult to do because when I tried, I often found myself teleporting my body instead of my consciousness. Nonetheless, it would be unbelievably valuable in the future.

As far as my mental state went, I was the best I had been since my capture. I was happy with where my life was. I still had issues with everything when I thought about it hard enough, but I had decided not to let myself fall back into the pit of self-sorrow. As horrible as what had happened may have been, I couldn't change it.

I had to find solace in the fact that I did everything I could have with the cards dealt to me. I used to say, "Chris is still in there because of me... Micah is dead because of me... All of those people are still trapped because I failed."

But now, I said, "Hannah is still alive because of me. Micah died so that I could live. All of the people I helped get out are living happy lives now because I was able to set them free."

I hated that Chris was still in captivity. I wasn't going to stop looking for him and I'd be ready to fight the moment we found anything. But he wouldn't have wanted me to be so miserable. He wouldn't have wanted me to make Jeremy miserable.

Micah's death still took a toll on me no matter how desperately I tried to forget it. But I couldn't bring him back, no matter how badly I wanted to. That was the inevitable conclusion I had to accept.

He was dead.

But I had to go on living.

And I had to avenge him.

I would. One day, I would. Even Peterson knew that. But until that day came, I'd do everything in my power to stay on the bright side of things. That was all that I could do.

At least for now, everything was okay.

EPILOGUE

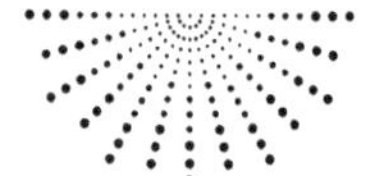

APRIL 2020 - CHRIS

The soft scent of baby powder touched my nose. A sweet, bubbly giggle filled my ears. Micah's smooth little fingers wrapped around my thumbs. My bony ass was a little sore against the vinyl floor, but I was determined.

"C'mon, buddy, you can do it." I smiled.

He giggled again, bouncing up and down. "No," his sweet little voice said.

"Yes." I laughed.

"No." He fell into my chest and fastened his arms around my neck.

I laughed again. My arms wrapped around him, hand coasting along the soft hair on the back of his head. Smiling, I kissed the side of his.

He was so close. I think he'd taken a step or two already, but I couldn't see it to know for sure. He'd been able to stand against the cot or holding my hands for a few weeks, maybe a month now though. He was coming along; he'd be walking soon.

Micah had been the light of my life for... Well, I wasn't sure exactly how long. He wasn't a year yet; I didn't think anyway. But there wasn't exactly a way for me to keep time. Haley used to help with that before.

She at least had a rough idea; she'd been scratching tallies with her claws on the cement since day one.

Now though, it was just me and Micah. And it made life feel worth living again.

I had family again.

His laughs were contagious. He did that a lot. Since before he could even sit on his own, he laughed constantly.

He was the happiest baby I'd ever met.

Fuck, I wished my brother could see this. I wished he knew how amazing his son was. I wished he would've gotten to know this little personification of love and joy. Even in this place, he was happier than any person I'd ever met.

Jeremy would never get to though. Damn, that hurt. I wished he would've known that his son was still alive. He wouldn't have killed himself if he had.

The rest of my siblings would though. They'd get to know their nephew too. Because I knew we'd get out of this place. I fucking *knew* it. They'd find it, and then they'd find us.

Jeremy may never get to know his son. But his son would know about him. If it were the last thing I did, I would make sure he knew who his father was when we got out of here.

And I'd make sure he knew his mommy was a hero to our people.

But we would. We'd get out. Even Peterson said it.

One day, we'd get out of here.

Although, had I realized that bastard had lied and that Jeremy and Laila were still alive, maybe we would've gotten out sooner.

The story continues in *The Precipice*. Turn the page for a sneak peek, or click the link below to download now:

https://www.amazon.com/dp/B091YSK6X9/

Sign up for Charlie's newsletter and receive a free copy of the Eluding Destiny prequel, *Blood Bar*:

https://liquidmind.media/eluding-destiny-prequel/

If you enjoyed this story, please consider leaving a rating or review on
Amazon:
https://www.amazon.com/dp/B08WJXR8RX/

Join Charlie's private reader group on Facebook and discuss all things
Eluding Destiny and Charlie Nottingham:
https://www.facebook.com/groups/661440911724435/

THE PRECIPICE CHAPTER 1

DECEMBER 22, 2022

"Oh, would you stop?" the man murmured to the crying child in his arms. His eyes met those big, glowing blue irises. Such a beautiful thing, how their eyes lit up that way. One of the few things he enjoyed about the Fae. "You liked me once. Don't you remember, Micah?"

He tickled his armpit. Micah giggled, pulling back and rubbing his fist against his big eyes. The man smiled. "There we are, esiasch. Will you please hush for just a few minutes now?"

Micah pointed to his uncle unconscious on the ground. "Cis."

"Chris, I know." He fought an eyeroll. "He'll be back soon, it's alright."

He pointed still. "Huwt."

"He's not hurt, he's sleeping. We have to be quiet." The man lifted his finger over his lips. "Let Uncle Chris sleep, esiasch."

Micah rubbed his eye again. The glow in them receded.

The man smiled. "Good job." He lowered him back into the crib. "I'm glad you can talk a bit now. You can tell me what you want to bring the most."

Still, for a child of his age, he could verbalize remarkably well. Not full sentences just yet, but he was sure he'd get there soon. All the time he and his uncle had together, surely they had nothing to do but talk.

If Micah were anything like the first version of him had been, he'd never shut up once he did. The man smiled at the memory. That child. Sweeter than a bee's nectar, that's what he'd always said. With a soul like his, he supposed he'd have to be. All that power in there.

But always so chatty. His mother had been too. Never knew how to keep her damn mouth shut. Not then, not now. In any life, that bitch didn't know a damn thing about being quiet.

He doubted he would get his father's silence. If there was anything to say about that child's father, it was that he knew how to keep a secret.

The man clenched his jaw at the memory. He dropped the bag onto the changing table. Diapers, they'd surely need those. The next place wouldn't have a toilet; they might need some for Chris over there too.

He tossed some into the bag and pulled open the drawer below, tossing the bathing necessities into the sack. Didn't want to have to make any stops at grocery stores. He supposed he could—they didn't have his face set up on any facial recognition algorithms—but he had no desire. It was time he got back to the few years he had left to enjoy in this place.

His mission here was simple. Pack the child's bag, take him to the next location, watch over him until Peterson was done with Chris, and then get back to his life. Let his three miniscule cohorts handle the rest.

He picked up a yellow onesie and held it out in front of the child. "Do you like this one?"

Micah smiled, nodding fast.

The man gave a smile back. He dropped it to the bag. Most of this wouldn't fit the boy for much longer. But—now that he thought about it—he'd better take it all. Perhaps if they had enough of the child's possessions, they'd finally get one of those locator spells to work.

He dumped them all inside.

Couldn't have that.

Micah pointed to a photo on the wall. "Mama?"

The man glanced up.

His jaw tightened again. "We'll get some more."

The child clutched the bar of the crib. He bounced, lips pouting down. He pointed with his other hand. "Mama!"

He huffed. Then he leaned over the bag and took the photo off the wall. He stared down at it for a moment.

Those bright green eyes. So similar to what they'd been all those years ago. Her face was prettier now too. Those plump lips perfectly proportioned beneath her small nose, the dainty roundness of her cheeks, the dark locks against her fair skin. So pretty.

His hand tightened on the frame.

But then he looked down at her neck. That scar. That big, ugly scar.

The man passed Micah the photo. The child smiled big.

He pointed to the picture and looked up. "Mama."

The man sighed. "Yes, esiasch. Your fucking mother."

But the child just smiled and looked down at the photo.

THE PRECIPICE CHAPTER 2

I glanced up at the ticking clock. Half past ten. I needed to get to bed soon. I was opening tomorrow.

I was almost done though. I just needed to check the note Sophie had left me. She said she couldn't work Tuesday. Or maybe it was Wednesday. Damn it, I couldn't remember. I reached for my notebook on the edge of the desk.

But just as my hands touched it, the strangest sensation I'd ever felt dropped in my chest. A sudden, collapsing gape. Like the air was siphoning from my lungs. It stretched from my heart down into the pit of my stomach. I heaved in an audible gasp. The book fell from my palm, hand raising to my heart.

A loud bang vibrated the light fixtures from our apartment upstairs, and I reached into Jeremy's mind. But I found nothing.

There were no thoughts. There was no vision through his eyes. It was just... Empty.

My heart raced as my stomach sunk. I teleported upstairs.

"Jeremy?" I stood in the living room and looked around. "Baby, where are you?" I hurried down the hall to our bedroom. My gaze traveled over the recently cleaned empty room and I furrowed my brows in confusion.

"Jeremy." I walked to the guest room and pulled the door open. The empty nursery stared back at me. I yanked the door shut.

"Baby, are you okay?" I yelled.

That's when I saw the bathroom light peeking from beneath the door. I grasped the handle, swung it in, and nearly hit him in the head.

Jeremy lay on his side against the tile. His lips were purple on his pale white skin. His eyes were closed. His leg was crooked in an odd contortion, foot caught against the edge of the toilet beneath the other. One of his arms laid lifelessly next to his body while the other was awkwardly tucked beneath his side.

My heart hammered against my ribs.

I dropped to the ground beside him and began struggling him onto his back.

"Baby, wake up." My hand flew to his neck, fingers searching for a pulse. I moved it around but couldn't find one. I had to be wrong. He had to have a pulse. He had to.

But he didn't.

His skin was warm to the touch but there was no pulse.

Tears poured from my eyes, head shaking. I grasped his shoulders and shook him again. "Jeremy." I climbed on top of him and pushed my fists into his chest. "Jeremy, wake up. Wake up, baby, wake up."

There was nothing lying around to explain it. There was no blood, no weapons, no other person. There was nothing for me to heal. He had no wounds. He was seemingly dead without a cause.

I didn't even think to look at the granite counter where grayish white powder laid loosely next to his driver's license.

I held onto him tightly and teleported to the house.

"Hannah!" I pumped my fists into Jeremy's chest. "Help! Hannah!"

"Laila?" Adam called from the kitchen.

I kept pushing into his chest, tears pouring down my cheeks. "Help! Somebody help me!"

It couldn't be happening. Not after everything we'd been through. That wasn't a death fit for him. If he was going to go, it had to be because a Demon or Werewolf or Vampire took him out. Not just sitting in the bathroom.

"Shit." Adam teleported beside me. "What the hell happened?"

"I don't know!" I pumped my fists into his chest without missing a beat. "He was upstairs and I was in the diner and I heard a thump and I went upstairs and he—He was on the floor."

Adam gritted his teeth. "God damn it, Jeremy." He disappeared.

Leah ran in from the kitchen. "What's going on?!"

"He's not breathing." I stared down at his pale face and blue lips. His chest wheezed a loud sound as I pumped, like a balloon that hadn't been tied and air escaped from. I heard his ribs crunching like a bag of chips beneath my tight fists. "He's not breathing. He's—He's not breathing."

"What happened?"

I continued thrusting my fists into his chest. "Get Hannah."

"Hannah doesn't need to see this—" she began.

I looked up at her with glowing green eyes, still pumping his heart with my fists. "Fucking get Hannah! *Now!*"

She gave me a look like I was crazy, but scurried to her feet and started up the steps.

Adam appeared beside me. He dropped to the ground and fiddled with a small white bottle. His shaking hands ripped off the seal and pushed it up Jeremy's nose.

"What the fuck is that?" I said.

"Just keep doing CPR." He squeezed the bottle up his nostril.

Then I saw the label.

Naloxone.

I glanced at it in confusion, still pumping my fists against his dead heart. Everyone in western Pennsylvania knew what naloxone was, even those who don't use drugs. We were in the midst of a heroin epidemic. And naloxone was the only thing that could save someone from an overdose.

He'd used.

And he hadn't told me.

But that didn't matter. I didn't even have the chance to think about how much that hurt, I just had to keep him alive. I couldn't lose him too. Everything was finally okay again. If I didn't have him, I didn't have a reason to keep living.

"C'mon, dude." Adam smacked Jeremy's face. "Wake up, Jeremy. Fucking wake up."

I continued pumping, but nothing changed. Adam was saying something I couldn't hear over the thumping of my heart in my ears and the horrible wheeze coming from Jeremy's lips.

Brody came down the steps, yelling something, but I couldn't hear him either. I couldn't hear anything.

I don't know how long I sat on top of him, furiously slamming my fists into his chest. It could have been only a minute, but it felt like a year. A year of watching his beautiful lips turned blue. A year of hearing the wheeze in his chest as I broke his ribs in a desperate attempt to keep oxygen to his brain until Hannah arrived.

"Laila." Leah gripped my shoulder. I could hear the sadness in her voice. Her eyes overflowed with tears. "Sweetie, he's gone."

"No." I pushed her hand away. "Get Hannah."

Adam gripped my face and turned it to meet his. Tears rushed down his cheeks like mine and landed on Jeremy's face. "Hannah can't help, Lai—"

"Yes, she can!" I screamed. "Get Hannah."

Adam bit his curling lip. I turned to Brody with a trembling jaw, continuing to pump my fists into Jeremy's chest. Even if he were dead, I had to keep as much oxygen going to his brain as possible until Hannah could heal him. I had to keep his body worth returning to. "Brody, please. Please get Hannah."

He had tears pouring down his cheeks too. "He's dead, Laila."

"You don't think I know that?!" I screamed. "I need Hannah. Please. Please, just bring her here."

"I don't see what good that's going to do—" he began.

"*Just fucking get Hannah!*" I screamed again.

He stared at me for a moment. Then he disappeared.

My arms grew so tired. I grasped his cheeks, lip quivering. I just wanted those eyes to open. "Baby," I whispered. "I need you, please wake up."

But his face remained still.

A loud sob left my lips.

I collapsed to his cold, dead chest. It was still beneath my ear. For the first time, there was no rise and fall inside those ribs. And as that realization dawned on me, my weeps turned to loud, painful sobs.

"Please come back to me, baby. Don't leave me," I murmured through trembling lips. "Not like this. Not yet."

It felt so different to lie on his chest without hearing his heart beating away against my ear. It hurt more than anything to think about never hearing that sound again.

It hurt like nothing else. There was this sudden emptiness lined with agony inside of me, like half of me was gone. Like I was literally half of myself. And the half that remained ached in a slow, dull throb.

He had to wake up. He couldn't leave me like this. He had to wake up. He had to explain it to me. He had to live.

We had so much more to do. We had to find Chris. We had to start a family. We had to *live*. We were only twenty-one and twenty-four. We had our whole lives ahead of us. We were too young to die.

"Baby." I returned my hands to his chest and began pushing again. "Baby, please wake up. Don't leave me here. I need you, Jeremy. I fucking need you. Wake up. Please. Please, just open your eyes."

"Oh my god," I heard Hannah say from a few feet away.

I abruptly sat forward and wiped my cheeks. "Bring him back," I said between sobs. "Please bring him back, Han."

She dropped to the ground beside us. Her eyes closed and her fingers found his.

I sat there anxiously for what felt like a decade. Every second that ticked by felt like months. It had to work. He couldn't die. He had to wake up.

"What's happening?" Leah said beside me.

"Shh," Hannah hushed, brows creased in focus.

My hands shook as I took Jeremy's in mine. As I unclenched his fingers, a rolled-up dollar bill fell to the wood floor.

It immediately brought me back to tears.

But I couldn't think about that right now.

I pulled his cool hand to my lips and kissed his knuckles. I had to push every other thought from my mind.

All I could think about was him waking up. He had to wake up.

After a few moments, Jeremy's eyes flung open. A deep grasp heaved into his lips.

My heart jumped with excitement for a fraction of a second.

Then his eyes rolled back, and his body began to convulse.

"Get him to the hospital." Hannah fell backward. "His soul's back but he's going to code again."

I gripped his shaking body and teleported to our closest facility. We landed on the ground. I called for help, trying to prevent his writhing head from hitting the wall.

In seconds, three nurses came trudging toward us. "What happened?"

My lips quivered. "I—I think he overdosed."

"Did you give him narcan?" another asked.

The last one wheeled a gurney toward us.

"He—He died and I kept giving CPR." As the bed drew closer, I teleported Jeremy's writhing body onto it.

"Good," the nurse said. "That's good. We'll take care of him, alright?"

I bit my trembling lip. "Please don't let him die."

Enjoying *The Precipice*? Click the link below to download now!
https://www.amazon.com/dp/B091YSK6X9/

New Normal: Celena's Story Part 1

Reprisal: Celena's Story Part 2

Origins of the Gods

(Completed Trilogy—fantasy romance, more information on the origins of the Fae and Angels, how life began on earth, where Guardians came from, and—most importantly—a badass forbidden romance)

Origins

The Thrones of Ore and Ice

Creation

Stand Alone Novels

Curse of the Gods: The Bridge Between Origins of the Gods and the Eluding Destiny Series

Sign up for Charlie's newsletter and receive a free copy of the Eluding Destiny prequel, Blood Bar:

https://liquidmind.media/eluding-destiny-prequel/

ABOUT THE AUTHOR

Charlie is a... Okay, talking about myself in third person is weird.

Nice to meet you! My name's Charlie Nottingham, and my whole world revolves around fantasy. When I'm not writing a new book, I'm either hanging out with my dogs, talking with my fans online, or reading some amazing urban fantasy, paranormal romance, or fantasy romance series (always a series, never a stand-alone, because I hate to fall for a character and never see them again). Or re-watching some Buffy or Supernatural. (They never get old!)